Once Upon A Term

Michael C. Cox

Mimast Inc

Mimast Inc

* * * * *

This book is a work of fiction. Names, characters, businesses, organizations, places, events, and incidents either are the product of the author's imagination or are used fictitiously. Any resemblance to actual persons, living or dead, events or locales is entirely coincidental.

* * * * *

This paperback edition published in 2015 by **Mimast Inc**

Copyright © Mimast Inc 2015,

Canadian ISBN 978-0-9866549-8-5

All enquiries regarding this electronic edition to:

Mimast Inc
Edmonton
Alberta T6R 2H9
Canada
email: mimast@telus.net

Acknowledgements

* * * * *

I could not have written *Once Upon A Term* without a computer, without access to the World Wide Web and without the experiences shared over the years with so many people whose names I may have forgotten or may never even have known. So I wish here to express my gratitude to information technologists everywhere, to contributors to the internet wherever they may be and to everyone who has enriched my life.

At the risk of upsetting anyone I have not named but simply thanked by the preceding paragraph, I must name and thank the following three people. First, there is my dear friend, Leif G. Stolee. It was Leif's enthusiastic response to my first short story that encouraged me to write fiction. Thank you Leif. Next, there is my good friend and colleague, Philip J. Barratt, whose many anecdotes provided more than enough stranger than fiction material for this book. Thank you Phil.

Last but certainly not least, there is my dearest wife and closest friend, Maureen. Without her love and support, I could *never* have written this book. She has watched over my grammar, corrected my spelling and provided me with the title. Thank you Maureen.

* * * * *

Needless to say, any mistakes in grammar and spelling, and any errors in facts used fictitiously, are my fault entirely. Nobody else is to blame.

* * * * *

"The writing of solid, instructive stuff fortified by facts and figures is easy enough. There is no trouble in writing a scientific treatise on the folk-lore of Central China, or a statistical enquiry into the declining population of Prince Edward Island. But to write something out of one's own mind, worth reading for its own sake, is an arduous contrivance only to be achieved in fortunate moments, few and far in between. Personally, I would sooner have written Alice in Wonderland than the whole Encyclopaedia Britannica."

Stephen Leacock (Sunshine Sketches of a Little Town)

INTRODUCTION

"Truth is stranger than fiction, but it is because Fiction is obliged to stick to possibilities; Truth isn't." Mark Twain

* * * * *

This story is fiction but not pure and simple. Beaumont Abbey School does not exist. The activities of its staff and pupils are products of my imagination but not entirely so. In my experience of teaching in the independent, private sector, in England, facts have proved stranger than fictions. However, all the companies, events, organisations and places in this book are either the product of my imagination or used fictitiously.

The names and characters are figments of my imagination and any resemblance to actual persons, living or dead, is entirely coincidental. Now, should any former colleagues think I have included them in my story and, heaven forbid, portrayed them unfavourably, may I point out that more often than not the law seems to benefit the lawyers rather than the litigants.

* * * * *

Beaumont Abbey I imagine to have been founded by Sir Athelstan de Beaumont in 1587, during the reign of Elizabeth I, as a Public School, meaning, of course, a private school. I apologise to my friends in North America for the confusion. Some four hundred years or so later, I imagine the school is still private and independent of the state school system.

In my imagination, the school would be located on the border of the northern counties of Cumbria, Durham and Northumberland. Its ancient stone buildings would be listed to protect them from man but not the elements. Its modern buildings would contrast sharply.

The academic staff would be highly qualified, all men, individualistic and bordering upon the eccentric. Many, but not all, would themselves have been educated at an all-boys private boarding school. Their pupils would be sent to Beaumont, from the British Isles and other parts of the globe, to be similarly educated and become steeped in tradition.

The headmaster or principal - I call him the High Master – would be responsible to the board of governors and, in theory, overall in charge of the school. The deputy head or vice-principal – I call him the Second Master – would be responsible to the headmaster and, in practice, overall in charge of the school. The Housemasters would be members of the academic staff and responsible for the boys in their boarding houses.

The Bursar – often an ex-serviceman - would be responsible to the board of governors and in charge of the financial management of the school and the non-academic staff with, of course, the exception of the headmaster's secretary who is often a law unto herself.

This story concerns the third and final term in the academic year, the summer term - I call it the Trinity Term – in which the school is on the brink of becoming co-educational.

CHAPTER 1

"Childhood has no forebodings, but then, it is soothed by no memories of outlived sorrow." George Eliot - The Mill On The Floss

* * * * *

Dr Llywelyn Pugh-Jones gently tapped the shell of his soft-boiled egg in time with the music emanating from his radio, precisely and almost permanently tuned to the BBC Radio 3 Breakfast Hour programme. He sat alone in the kitchen. Louise, his wife, had taken her breakfast tray and Daily Telegraph newspaper into the relative peace and quiet of the sunroom. If she had broken her routine and stayed in the kitchen, perhaps the High Master of Beaumont Abbey might have paid attention more to his wife than to the music Sergei Prokofiev composed for the film *Lieutenant Kijé*. If she had eaten her breakfast at the kitchen table he might not have had two ideas, one of which nearly led to tragedy.

Reginald Thomas De Vere, MA (Cantab) covered the hot porridge with cold milk, added a sprinkling of granulated brown sugar, glanced at his wrist watch and began the Times crossword. Eighteen minutes and 23 seconds later he had finished the crossword but not the porridge. He poured himself a second cup of coffee from his *cafetière à piston* before selecting a croissant from the woven silver basket on the breakfast table. Reg, as he was fondly known to his colleagues, had been a widower for almost four years. His wife, Madeleine, whom he had met in Paris and who had been three years his junior when they wed, had died of a brain tumour when she had just turned fifty. She had given him the silver cafetière on their 25th wedding anniversary. He had given her the silver basket. They owned a small holiday cottage on the Dorset coast. All being well, Reggie, as his wife fondly called him, planned to retire there after four more years as Second Master at Beaumont Abbey.

Anthony Parker-Smythe, purportedly a former major in the Royal Army Pay Corps, had finished his

1

porridge, his kipper, his cooked breakfast of two eggs, bacon, sausage and mushrooms and was halfway through his second slice of toast and marmalade when Elsie, his housekeeper came to clear the dining room table. His mouth was so full he could only nod in the direction of his china cup and saucer. She poured him some more coffee then disappeared before he could attempt a smile of gratitude, not that he ever smiled or was grateful. At the kitchen sink, Elsie began washing the dishes and resolving to hand in her notice at the end of the week. She had had enough of her employer, the Bursar of Beaumont Abbey, real name Tony Smith who, according to her late husband, had only risen to corporal in the Army Catering Corps.

Gregory Watson had, as usual, been for a 5k run, showered, shaved and changed into his gym kit and track suit before joining his wife, Kathy, and their two young children, Mark and Tracy, at the table for his bowl of cereal and glass of orange juice. He came to Beaumont Abbey straight from Loughborough University after gaining a joint honours degree in Geography and Sports Science and completing his teacher training. He was in his third year at Beaumont and expected to become Head of Physical Education when Walter Barnes retired at the end of the year. Greg looked forward to modernising the PE curriculum and Kathy looked forward to receiving more house-keeping money. Neither gave thought to the possibility of unforeseen difficulties.

Colin Harper overslept. It had been another disturbed night of bad dreams he might, with professional help, have erased from his mind. His colleagues in the Mathematics Department at Beaumont seemed not to notice or care about the dark rings around his puffy eyes and the bags underneath them. Had Dr Klaus Heilbronn, the Head of Maths, ever noticed or cared, he might have assumed his assistant, whom he had placed in charge of the computer room, was spending too much time staring too closely at too many

2

screens. One strikingly good-looking boy not only noticed but also really cared.

Rupert Jardine had inherited his angelic good looks from his English mother, an actress of good repute, and his devilish ways from his American father, an entrepreneur of ill repute and head of a corporation specialising in computers and software engineering. He was flying business class from JFK airport to London, Heathrow where a chauffeured car would be waiting. He had mixed feelings about returning to Beaumont. Only two members of staff really liked him; the rest tolerated him. He knew he had overstepped the mark with his last prank; he was only being allowed back because the member of staff involved had not been seriously injured and because Randolph Jardine was a very wealthy man.

It was Saturday morning. The summer term was about to begin. At 10 o'clock sharp the staff of Beaumont Abbey would assemble in the Long Room for the High Master's words of welcome, for the Second Master's notice of any changes affecting staff and for the Housemasters' lists of pupils flying in late from far flung regions of the globe or arriving on time but with a leg broken whilst skiing in the Alps. After the Chaplain's reminder that evensong in the chapel would begin at 7 p.m. on Sunday, the meeting would finish. The High Master would retreat to his study. The Second Master and staff would retreat to the Common Room for coffee or tea, biscuits and gossip. School would begin in earnest immediately after chapel on Monday morning. For most, the coming weeks would be hectic but normal. For a few, the summer term would be very hectic and not normal at all.

* * * * *

CHAPTER 2

"Meetings are indispensable when you don't want to do anything." John Kenneth Galbraith – American Economist

* * * * *

He was deep in thought and chewing thoroughly the last fragment of his second piece of toast when his wife returned to the kitchen from the sun room.

'Good morning, Llew,' she said. 'How was your breakfast?'

'Fine, thank you Louise,' replied Dr Llywelyn Pugh-Jones, the High Master of Beaumont Abbey. 'Lacking in taste but healthy and nutritious. Just what my doctor ordered.'

'Not that bad, surely?' said Louise.

'Let me think for a moment. One half of a fresh grapefruit - *no sugar*. One soft-boiled egg - *no salt*. Two thin slices of *whole grain* toast - *no butter*. One small glass of orange juice – *unsweetened*. Oh, yes! *No coffee. No tea.*'

'Sounds delicious,' said Louise. 'In fact it was delicious. I had exactly the same.'

'Really? *Exactly* the same? No sugar on your grapefruit?'

'No! I did *not* sprinkle any sugar on my grapefruit,' Louise said haughtily, knowing her husband would not notice the pot of honey on her tray. 'Anyway, I'm not the one with a heart condition.'

There was a history of heart problems in the Pugh-Jones family. Llywelyn's grandfather was forty-six when he died. Llywelyn's father was forty-nine when he died. Both men had heart attacks. Both deaths were blamed on the men being overweight, heavy smokers and Welsh coal miners. Llywelyn believed he had already outlived his father by two years because he had never worked down a coal mine, he had never smoked and he was not overweight. At his last medical examination, the High Master of Beaumont weighed 174 pounds, stood 6ft 3in tall in his cotton socks and measured 35 inches around his waist. His body mass index (BMI) of 21.7 was exactly in the middle of the normal range. He felt he was in good physical shape for a man of his age but Louise made him go for a medical when he returned from a staff meeting complaining of a pain in his chest.

'Before you ask,' said Llywelyn, 'yes, I did take my blood pressure tablet. Thank you for putting it on my tray.'

'Will you be back here for lunch?'

'Hopefully but I must have a word with the Bursar after the staff meeting,'

'What's Nosey Parker been up to now?' said Louise. 'Nothing illegal, I trust.'

'You're not very fond of our Major Anthony Parker-Smythe, are you?'

'No, to be honest. Something not quite right about him. Too smarmy for words if you ask me,' said Louise.

'I think you're being a trifle harsh, my dear,' Llywelyn said, knowing full well his wife was a pretty good judge of character. 'The major knows how to handle Beaumont's finances.'

'Now *that* I don't doubt for one moment,' Louise said, with a wry look on her face.

* * * * *

The chapel, the walled garden and parts of the main building date back to 1587 when the school was founded by Sir Athelstan de Beaumont. Some of the trees in the extensive grounds are even older. The Long Room is actually more square than oblong. A little daylight filters through the narrow windows high above the tall oak panelling covering the walls but even when all the lights are switched on, the room remains gloomy. Ronald Beech, the head caretaker, was in the Long Room when the Second Master arrived.

'Good morning Mr De Vere.'

'Good morning Ron. Everything ready for the meeting?'

5

'Yes, sir,' said Ron. 'Tom and Dolly were in here first thing this morning. I just popped in to check they had finished. Tom buffed the floor while Dolly did the dusting.'

'How long have the Browns been with us now?' asked the Second Master.

'Must be going on for ten years now,' said Ron. 'Worth their weight in gold.'

'Yes indeed.'

'Tom will keep watch as usual,' said Ron. 'When he sees you leave the Long Room, he'll let Dolly know the meeting is over so she'll have the coffee in the Common Room for when the staff arrive. Now, if you'll excuse me, sir. I must be getting along.'

The door into the room was in the far corner of the shorter wall. Near the door and just inside the room, were two rectangular tables placed end to end and parallel to the shorter wall. Six more tables, in two sets of three, were placed end to end and parallel to the longer wall. The names of past pupils were carved on these eight heavy oak tables and bore witness to the age of the school.

On the two tables by the door was a green baize cloth, creating the illusion of one large table, and a silver tray bearing a jug of iced water and two glasses. Behind each half of the table, and close to the oak-panelled wall, was a chair with a carved high back and a padded seat. On the table in front of the chair furthest from the door, Reg placed the walnut gavel and block that had belonged to his great-grandfather. Dr Pugh-Jones mistakenly believed the Second Master's great-grandfather had been a judge. The Second Master was never afraid to correct the High Master when he was wrong but on this point he kept his own counsel. His great-grandfather had simply been an auctioneer. Reg glanced at his watch then strolled outside to await the arrival of the staff.

'Good morning, Second Master. Nice morning,' said Gregory Watson.

'Good morning, Greg. Been for our morning run, have we?

'Oh Yes. Too nice a day to stay in bed,' said Greg. 'Am I the first?'

'Only if you exclude me as a member of staff,' said Reg, with a smile.

'I stand corrected. I'm the second,' said Greg. 'If you'll excuse me, I'll go on in.'

Heavy oak chairs, with low backs and no padding, had been placed on either side of the long tables (two sets of three) running parallel to the longer walls of the room. These hard chairs were for the staff. There were, however, four high-backed, padded chairs, one either side and at the head of the long tables and nearest to the baize-covered table. These padded chairs were for the housemasters. Greg sat on the hard chair next to the padded chair nearest to the door because he wanted to be seen by the High Master and the Second Master. He also wanted to be first out of the door when the meeting ended.

It was three minutes to ten when Colin Harper came scurrying up the path.

'S-S-Sorry S-Second M-M-Master. Am I late?'

'No, Colin. You cut it fine. I see the High Master heading our way. Get inside before he sees you.'

'Yes. R-right. Th-Thank you, s-sir.'

'Good morning High Master,' said the Second Master. 'How are you this morning?'

'Fine! Never felt better,' said Dr Pugh-Jones. 'All present and correct?'

'Yes. Everyone is here.'

'Good. Let's get started. Lead the way.'

* * * * *

When the Second Master entered the room, the staff stood up. Then the High Master entered the room and took his seat behind the baize-covered table. When the Second Master had taken his seat alongside the High Master, the staff sat down. The Second Master poured two glasses of iced water and placed one in front of the High Master. Even though the only sound in the room was the ice tinkling against the sides of the High Master's glass as he sipped his water, the Second Master struck the walnut block three times with his walnut gavel. It was exactly ten o'clock. The High Master cleared his throat.

'Good morning, gentlemen. Welcome back to Beaumont Abbey. I hope you all enjoyed your Easter break and are ready for the Trinity term. I am sure I need not remind you that the first half is a crucial time for the Upper Fives and Upper Sixes. Good examination results are not of course the be-all and end-all - *pause for a sip of water* – but at this time in a boy's life they will decide what options he may have for his future. It is up to us to see that every boy gives of his best. Beaumont has built up a reputation for academic excellence that should be reflected in the examination results. The future of the school may depend on them. I, as do the boys, put my trust in all of you. Thank you.'

As the High Master turned to leave, all the staff (except Geoffrey Rusbridge who was engrossed in the Financial Times) stood up and stayed standing until he had left the room and closed the door behind him. The Second Master sat down, drank some iced water and used his gavel again. David Peters stood up and said the delay of a flight from Singapore would mean five boys from Armstrong house might not be back in time for Sunday evensong. Some younger members of staff seated at the back of the Long Room sniggered when they heard the Housemaster read out the names in rapid succession: Chin, Chin, Kung, Fu and Woo.

The Second Master managed to keep a straight face and called upon the Housemaster of Burdett. Ralph Abrahams leaned forward out of his seat, said he had nothing to report and sat back down. Alan Radford reported for Gower that Morris Minor might be late. Before he could explain, someone at the back of the room whispered audibly *engine trouble* and caused more sniggering. The Second Master used his gavel. The Housemaster of Gower then explained the boy was recovering from influenza.

'Wedgewood,' said the Second Master, looking at E. Gordon Hamilton.

'Thank you, Second Master,' said Hamilton rising slowly to his feet, blithely unaware of the restless shuffling of some feet at the back of the room. 'I have six boys delayed on the same flight to which Mr Peters referred.'

'The flight from Singapore?' said the Second Master.

'Yes!' said Hamilton, a modern linguist.

'Your Chinese contingent?'

'Yes!' said Hamilton.

'How's their English coming along?'

'They speak English almost as well as they speak Cantonese and Mandarin,' Hamilton said somewhat tetchily. 'May I read out their names?'

'Yes, of course,' said the Second Master.

'Chén, Chéng, Liú, Wáng, Yáng and Zháng.'

'Thank you Mr Hamilton,' said the Second Master. 'Since some of us do not have your ear for the four tones of Chinese - the first two sounded the same to me - would you spell those names.'

'If you wish,' said Hamilton, again ignoring more restless shuffling of feet. After he had spelled each name carefully, including the accents over the vowels, he remained standing.

'Do you have anything else, Housemaster?' asked the Second Master.

'Just one question, if I may,' said Hamilton. 'What has the High Master decided to do about Jardine?' No more shuffling of feet or nervous coughing. The room was silent.

'He is being allowed back to complete his year in the Lower Sixth. No decision has yet been made about his continuing into the Upper Sixth.' The murmurs

9

around the room masked Colin Harper's sigh of relief at the news.

'When, may I ask, were we to be informed of this decision?'

'Today. Mary Cranborne sent a note to you, and the Heads of Maths and Physics, for a meeting with the High Master and myself this afternoon at 2 p.m.'

'Will Jardine still be denied privileges, Second Master?' asked Gregory Watson.

'That's something we shall be discussing this afternoon. We'll try not to deny the First Eleven its opening fast bowler.'

The Second Master looked around the room, glanced at his watch, picked up his walnut gavel and said, 'Coffee awaits us in the Common Room. Is there any other business, gentlemen?' No hand was raised and heads were shaking, so he struck the walnut block a resounding blow and declared the meeting closed.

* * * * *

Dr Llywelyn Pugh-Jones closed the Long Room door quietly and walked slowly from the portico out into the sunshine, unbroken by the few wispy clouds in a pale blue sky. Directly ahead of him was a concrete path leading straight to the main building and the Bursar's office. To his right was a gravel path, bordered on both sides by well-tended beds of assorted evergreen flowering shrubs – azaleas, japonica, rhododendrons, skimmia and viburnum – that would lead him first to the walled garden. He hesitated just for a moment then turned right onto the gravel path.

His doctor advised a brisk walk every morning. Llywelyn was a good patient and usually took his doctor's advice but not this morning. He was in no hurry to see Nosey Parker, as his wife Louise called the Bursar, Anthony Parker-Smyth. Llywelyn pretended he was just out for a stroll. It was after all a beautiful morning. He savoured the fragrant scent from the tiny white flowers of the skimmia and viburnum and feasted his eyes upon the purples and reds of the azaleas and rhododendrons. A thrush, hiding in the shrubbery, suddenly stopped its flutelike song when it heard Llywelyn's footsteps on the gravel path.

Perhaps the birdsong reminded him of the music on the radio that morning. Llywelyn began to hum Prokovief's sleigh ride tune, Troika, and to recall that in a short story by Vladimir Dal and published in 1870, Kijé was an imaginary officer brought into being by a bureaucratic blunder. Emperor Paul I of Russia promotes Kijé to lieutenant, captain and eventually to colonel. When the Emperor asks to see the colonel and the bureaucrats realise their original blunder will be discovered, they inform the Emperor that Colonel Kijé has died. The whimsical thought, of bureaucracy creating an imaginary person that the authorities treat as a real person, was going through his head when he arrived at the Bursar's office. Dr Pugh-Jones smoothed his thinning ginger hair, tousled during his stroll, drew himself up to his full height, knocked once and strode briskly into the room.

'Ah, High Master! Good morning, sir,' said Nosey, putting down his coffee cup and rising to his feet. 'Beautiful morning! You're looking extremely well this morning, if I may say so. How is Mrs Pugh-Jones these days?'

'She is very well. Thank you for asking, Anthony.'

'May I offer you some coffee?' said Nosey, reaching for the jug on the tray on his desk.

'I should refuse, doctor's orders and all that, but on this occasion I *will* say yes to a small cup,' said Llywelyn. 'Milk but no sugar if you please.' Having committed this minor transgression, he sat down and, while his coffee was being poured and he was attempting to prepare his opening remarks, he noticed Nosey also poured himself a whole cup of coffee and added two spoonfuls of brown sugar and a generous helping of full cream.

'Here you are, High Master,' said Nosey, reaching across his large mahogany desk to hand Llywelyn his half cup of coffee. 'I hope you like it. It's made from the *arabica* bean. They're a bit more expensive than the *robusta* bean but the coffee is more aromatic, has more flavour but only half the caffeine of coffee made from robusta beans.

'Only half the caffeine, you say? Very interesting.'

'May I offer you a chocolate biscuit?' said Nosey.

'Thank you, no,' said Llywelyn. 'Not good for the cholesterol and lipids in the blood, so I'm told.'

'Actually,' said Nosey, 'these are Belgian biscuits. Thin wafer coated in dark chocolate which, I am told, is good for you. Please try one.'

'Oh, very well. Just one. Thank you.'

The two men sat facing one another in silence, a silence broken only in their heads by the crunching of a chocolate biscuit and the swallowing of arabica coffee. His secretary, Mrs Susan Taylor, had reminded the Bursar that the High Master would be dropping in but had been unable to tell him the reason for his visit. Nothing in his visitor's manner so far led Nosey to believe he had anything to be nervous about. He kept calm and tried not to think about accounts and financial records. The High Master had instructed his secretary, Mary Cranborne, to tell the Bursar he would come to see him on Saturday morning straight from the Long Room. When Mary wanted to know the purpose of his visit in case Susan asked, Llywelyn told her to say it was just to say hello. 'No, Sue,' said Mary, 'Dr Pugh-Jones didn't say why he'll be dropping in. Probably just wants to chat. Nothing serious. Nothing specific.' But of course Mary Cranborne, BA. had worked for the High Master long enough to know that he would never chat, that he was always serious and that he would have something quite specific in mind.

'You wanted to see me, High Master?' said Nosey, breaking the silence.

'Yes, Anthony,' said Llywelyn. 'It's about money, I'm afraid.

* * * * *

12

CHAPTER 3

"I am always ready to learn. I do not always like being taught." Winston Churchill

* * * * *

'Mr de Vere just came out of the Long Room, Dolly,' said Tom, poking his head round the door of the small kitchen on the other side of the corridor from the staff Common Room. 'Better get cracking. Need any help?'

'No thank you, Mister Brown,' she said to her husband. 'You just make sure you've cleared that great big toy of yours out of the corridor before the gentlemen arrive.'

'My Fluomatic is the best scrubber and polisher on the market,' retorted Tom. 'Did you know it puts down the clean water, scrubs the floor and vacuums it dry, all in one. It's a champion machine, is that. It's a better scrubber than you ever were or ever will be.'

'Don't you go calling me a scrubber, my lad,' snapped Dolly with a glint in her eye. 'Get on about your business and clear the corridor *now*.'

The Second Master carefully returned his ancestral heirloom, the walnut gavel and block, to the velvet-lined ebony case. Unlike the rest of the staff, Reg was in no rush to leave the Long Room for a cup of Dolly Brown's coffee; it was not entirely to his taste. He would make himself a cup of tea if and when he went to the Common Room. Out of the corner of his eye, he saw E. Gordon Hamilton leave in a huff. 'Ernie's going to be trouble this afternoon,' Reg thought to himself as he turned off the lights and closed the Long Room but not before he made sure Geoffrey Rusbridge, their share-dealing Head of Economics, had realised the meeting was over and had departed with his Financial Times newspaper.

Gregory Watson was hovering to catch him when he stepped outside into the bright sunshine. 'Can I have a quick word with you, Second Master?'

'Is it about Jardine?' said Reg.

13

'No.' said Greg.

'Then you *may* have a word if you *can*,' replied Reg, despairing of any graduate, not just Gregory Watson, failing to distinguish between ability and permissibility.

'It's about my salary,' said Greg.

'What about your salary?' said Reg. 'Not enough, is that it? You know we pay you more than you'd get from Prescott Manor down the road? And that state-maintained school wouldn't give you accommodation and a telephone and entertainment allowance.'

'Oh, yes. I know that, Second Master. Kathy and I are very grateful. No, I just wanted to ask if any decision had been made about a salary increase in September.'

'I honestly couldn't say, Greg,' said Reg. 'That's a matter for the High Master, the Bursar and the Governors to discuss when they meet.'

'I understand,' said Greg.

They followed the other masters along the concrete path leading directly from the Long Room to a side entrance into the main building, an edifice constructed in the perpendicular gothic style. The weathered oak door was set in a heavy stone doorway enclosed within a square head over arch mouldings. The spandrels of the arch were filled with quatrefoils. From the Senior Common Room, voices of the staff and the aroma of coffee drifted down the corridor which ran the length of the building. As Reg and Greg strolled down the corridor they passed on their left in succession the Chief Caretaker's store room, the reprographics room, the stationery and book shop, Susan Taylor's room, the Bursar's office and the staff quiet room. On their right, they passed a number of small classrooms.

Halfway along the corridor on their left was a wider corridor leading to the imposing front entrance to Beaumont. On either side of this corridor was a stone staircase ascending to the Great Hall above. Halfway along the corridor on the stone wall to their right was a plaque stating that the building was formally opened in

1871 by the Rt. Hon. William Edward Forster. 'Do you know who Forster was?' the Second Master asked Greg. When Greg confessed he did not, the Second Master said, 'Time you did. Ask Quentin Waite.'

On their left, just beyond the corridor to the main entrance was Mary Cranborne's office followed by the High Master's study and the Second Master's office. On their right and across the corridor from those three rooms were some long oak benches with padded leather seats and backs; seating for parents of would-be pupils and anyone else waiting to be interviewed. On the stone wall above the benches there were photographs of the most distinguished Old Beaumontians. Next to the Second Master's office was a small kitchen. Immediately opposite was the Senior Common Room.

Just as Reg and Greg reached the door, they heard a sudden loud cheer. The Common Room fell silent when Reg opened the door and stepped inside. The silence had nothing to do with the arrival of the Second Master. All eyes were upon Arthur Matthews.

'I take it our mountaineer has reached the trickiest bit,' said Reg.

'Six feet to go,' someone shouted, breaking the tense silence. 'He's got 40 seconds to break his record.'

Arthur was edging on the dado rail with the toes of his shoes and hanging from the picture rail by his fingertips. Sometime in the past, a colleague had flippantly remarked that any mountaineer worth his salt should be able to traverse the Common Room without touching the floor. Arthur had taken the bait. Now, at the beginning of each Trinity term, when he returns from his Easter holiday climbing some mountain or other in Europe, Arthur edges his way around the four walls. Another loud cheer went up and a colleague shouted that Arthur had knocked fifteen seconds off his record and no pictures off the wall. The fun was over. Greg made Reg a cup of tea, poured himself a coffee and took the Second Master's advice.

* * * * *

'Excuse me for disturbing you, Mr Waite. May I ask you a question?' Quentin Waite MA (Oxon) LLM took off his reading glasses and fixed Greg with the look he often used when he was a barrister about to cross-question a hostile witness. 'Sorry to interrupt,' said Greg. 'I'm Gregory Watson. Geography, PE and Games.'

'How unfortunate,' said the Head of History.

'I beg your pardon,' said Greg.

'Geography and Physical Education. Not the ideal pairing.'

'Why would you say that?'

'I can think of only one occasion when P.E. as you term it played an important part in the History of the world,' said Quentin, putting down the Times Crossword. 'I don't suppose you have read *Mein Kampf.*'

'No, sir, I have not,' said Greg, aware that Dr Heilbronn was now glaring at them.

'Hitler believed strongly in the importance of physical education for the German youth. He increased the time for physical training from two hours per week to two hours per day. We may translate what Hitler wrote in *Mein Kampf* as follows: *A man of little scientific education but physically healthy, with a good, firm character, imbued with the joy of determination and will-power, is more valuable for the national community than a clever weakling.*'

'I didn't know that,' said Greg. And before Quentin could take another breath, he asked, 'Who was William Edward Forster?'

'Ah, a good question young man,' said Quentin, putting his pen down upon his Times newspaper. 'You read the plaque on the wall opposite our main entrance?'

'Yes, I did,' replied Greg, deciding not to mention that the Second Master had steered him in the direction of the Head of History.

'The Right Honourable William Edward Forster was one of Gladstone's Liberals. He was appointed Vice-

President of the Committee of Council on Education to introduce the Elementary Education Act of 1870. It became known as the Forster Act. It gave School Boards power to build and maintain schools out of the rates. Unless they were very poor, parents still had to pay fees. Some of Gladstone's own Liberals opposed the Act on the grounds that education should be compulsory and free. It was ten years before elementary education was made compulsory for children between the ages of five and twelve.'

'Forster trained and practised as a lawyer before he became a partner in a Bradford woollen business and later entered politics when he was elected member of Parliament for Bradford in 1861. He came from a Quaker family and was an active member of the Anti-Slavery Society. He married Jane Arnold, eldest daughter of Thomas Arnold, the reforming Headmaster of Rugby who was described by Thomas Hughes, a former pupil, in his novel *Tom Brown's Schooldays*. Have you read it?'

'No. I'm sorry, sir,' said Greg, feeling like a guilty pupil who didn't complete his prep. 'I did enjoy the film. It was released in 1951 and actually shot at Rugby School in Warwick. Robert Newton played Dr Arnold. He was terrific in the part. Tom was played by twelve year old John Howard Davies. He became a successful producer of television programmes like *Monty Python's Flying Circus*.' When he saw the puzzled look on Quentin's face, Greg returned to the film and said, 'John Forrest was terrific in the part of Flashman.' Then after a short pause, he said, 'Thankfully there are no cowardly bullies at Beaumont.'

'I shouldn't be too sure about that,' said Quentin, picking up his pen and his crossword. 'Hughes describes the 17-year old antagonist as a *dirty little snivelling, sneaking fellow* who was quite strong and who *played well at all games where pluck wasn't much wanted.* Might that description fit anyone you know here? Now if you will excuse me, I should like to finish this crossword.'

* * * * *

17

CHAPTER 4

"You may either win your peace or buy it: win it, by resistance to evil; buy it, by compromise with evil" John Ruskin

* * * * *

Miss Mary T. Cranborne BA held her post at Beaumont long before her hair turned grey and became restrained in a bun at the back of her head. When she heard Dr Pugh-Jones on one occasion refer to her as his PA, she took him to task. 'I am not your personal assistant, High Master,' she said, removing her half-moon glasses and fixing him with her piercing blue eyes. 'I am your secretary just as I have been secretary to two other High Masters before you.'

When Mary was a student at university she had had friends who were boys but they never became boy friends. After gaining a joint honours degree in English and Latin, she spent a year hitch-hiking around Europe visiting the museums and art galleries. During a week in Rome, she considered becoming a Catholic sister, or even a nun, but she dropped the idea on her first day in France. Throughout that year abroad, she never failed to describe her experiences in long letters to her parents but, during her two weeks in Paris, she only found time to send them a picture postcard of the Eiffel Tower with the words *Having a lovely time. Mary.* When she returned home to England, she successfully interviewed for the post advertised as *Secretary to the High Master of Beaumont Abbey.* She fell in love with the school and became wedded to her work.

At 1:55 p.m. precisely, Mary knocked and entered the High Master's study to announce the arrival of the Second Master with four other members of staff and to make sure she would not be needed to take notes; she had arranged to play tennis at 2:30 p.m.

'Would you ask the Second Master to come in and tell the others to wait a moment.'

'Certainly, High Master,' said Mary. 'Will that be all?'

'Yes, thank you. You run along and enjoy your tennis. It's a beautiful day.'

'Thank you, High Master. Let's hope it stays that way.'

'Indeed,' said Llywelyn, 'I do hope so, for my sake as well as yours.'

'Good afternoon, High Master,' said Reginald Thomas De Vere, MA (Cantab)

'Good afternoon, Reg. Please, take a seat. I'd like a quick word before we start.'

'Anything wrong?' asked the Second Master.

'No, no! I'd just like to be sure you're on my side and happy with my decision.'

'To let Jardine back, you mean?'

'Yes!' said Llywelyn.

'I doubt if you yourself are happy about it,' said Reg. 'Jardine is a nasty piece of goods. Fortunately, or unfortunately, depending upon your point of view, he's a very bright boy and an outstanding games player.'

'*And*,' said Llywelyn, gesturing with his right forefinger as though he were ticking a box on a questionnaire, his father as good as gave us our computer room.'

'Dad probably knew his son would be trouble and we'd want to kick him out,' said Reg.

'Let's have the others in now,' said Llywelyn. 'Mary said there were four staff waiting. I thought I invited three: Heilbronn, Newbold and Hamilton. Who's the fourth?'

'Colin Harper,' said Reg. He's Jardine's tutor. Teaches him Computing Science and, so rumour has it, other things.'

When the Second Master opened the study door, Dr Klaus Heilbronn was first to stride into the room. The diminutive Colin Harper crept in behind his Head of Department, a tall, heavily built man whose dark grey beard and moustache failed to hide the five inch scar on

19

his left cheek. Dr Herbert Newbold, Head of Physics, slipped in next obliging E. Gordon Hamilton, Jardine's Housemaster, to close the study door.

'Ah, there you are, Harper,' said the High Master, unable to conceal his look of surprise when Colin appeared from behind Dr Heilbronn like a startled rabbit popping out of a conjuror's top hat. 'Please sit down gentlemen.'

'With all due respect, High Master, may I ask what possessed you to permit Jardine to return to Beaumont?' Hamilton said barely before everyone was seated.

'First and foremost,' began Llywelyn, 'we must bear in mind that the wellbeing of each individual pupil is our prime concern. We have a duty…'

'With all due respect,' said Hamilton, interrupting the High Master, 'Gemeinnutz geht vor Eigennutz.'

'What is he on about?' whispered Dr Newbold into Dr Heilbronn's ear

'He quotes the words of the 1938 Reichsmark coins,' hissed the Head of Maths and Computing Science. 'I should translate them as *public interest before the individual*. It was the basis of Hitler's economic policy.'

'I prefer the translation *the common interest before self interest*,' said Hamilton.

'Spock!' muttered Colin Harper.

'What did you say, Colin?' said the Second Master. 'I missed that'

'Spock! I said Spock. In the film Star Trek II – The Wrath of Khan. When Science Officer Spock sacrificed himself, he quoted the Vulcan philosophy: *the needs of the many outweigh the needs of the few*.'

'My point is, High Master,' said Hamilton, scowling his disapproval at the digression, 'that Jardine is a bad influence on the rest of the pupils and a thorn in the side of the staff's flesh. I should like to know why he is being allowed back?'

'There are mitigating circumstances,' said Llywelyn, thinking of the computer room and language laboratory, 'which I'm not at liberty to discuss. Suffice it to say, we owe it to the boy's parents as well as the boy to give him a chance to redeem himself.'

'With all due respect, High Master,' said Hamilton, in a tone lacking any respect, 'I think you are making a grave mistake.'

'May I ask why you have called this meeting, High Master,' said Dr Newbold, breaking the uncomfortable silence.

'Yes. Yes of course, Herbert,' said Llywelyn. 'I wanted an up-to-date assessment of Jardine's academic abilities and suggestions on what might be done to ensure he fulfils his potential.'

'He is in the top set for physics,' said Dr Newbold, 'and I happen to be his teacher. Jardine is exceedingly bright. The subject comes easily to him. I am bound to say he has never been disruptive in my lessons.'

'No, I imagine not,' said Llywelyn, aware perhaps for the first time that it was Herbert's craggy features - a combination of black bushy eyebrows, piercing dark brown eyes, a square jaw and broken nose acquired when he boxed for Oxford – he, and no doubt the pupils, found unnerving. 'What about you, Klaus? What do you think of Jardine?' Everyone in the room waited patiently for the bulky Dr Heilbronn to stop stroking his beard and open his eyes.

'He should have little difficulty with the Mathematical Tripos. He has the brain to be a senior wrangler but...' Dr Heilbronn paused and ran a stubby finger down his left cheek along the scar which colleagues supposed he had acquired in a duel when he was a student at Heidelberg. In fact, he cut his cheek at a previous school when he was coaching a rowing team and cycled off the canal towpath into a blackthorn hedge.

'But?' the Second Master interjected to prevent Dr Heilbronn from closing his eyes.

'But he is not... He is not *leidenschaftlich. Er hat keine Heftigkeit.*'

'He is not passionate about mathematics. He has no vehemence,' interpreted Hamilton, nodding his head. 'In other words, you're saying Jardine couldn't care less about your subject, is that it?'

'No, no. He cares but he is not yet passionate enough to be a first class mathematician.'

'So how do we get the boy to take his studies seriously?' asked the Second Master. 'Colin! You're his tutor. What do you have to say?'

Colin Harper's BA was actually a first class honours degree in mathematics from Oxford. He had no other formal qualifications. His knowledge of Computing Science was profound but entirely self-taught. In his own unique way, Colin was a capable teacher but truth be told, he would probably not have completed a PGCE (post-graduate certificate in education) course and therefore would not have been allowed to teach in a state school. As a pupil he was a boarder at Canfield Preparatory and subsequently Canfield College. In modern parlance, Colin was, and always would be a bookworm and a nerd. The nearest he came to involvement in a sporting activity at Canfield was the one occasion when he was given a trial as coxswain for a rowing eight. He was the right size and weight. He had studied the river and knew exactly what course to steer. He was rejected because he was a not assertive enough.

The slim young tutor was half-hidden from the Second Master by Dr Heilbronn and intimidated not only by his vivid scar but also by the sheer size of the man. Holding onto the arms of his chair, Colin leant forward to peer at the Second Master over Dr Heilbronn's corpulence. 'What would you like me to say, sir?'

'Start with Computing Science,' said the Second Master. 'Is he any good at it?'

'He's b-brilliant!' gushed Colin. 'He's absolutely b-brilliant.'

'Is he any trouble in class?'

'N-no, not really,' stuttered Colin unconvincingly. 'B-bit high s-spirited at t-times…'

'When you say high spirited, what do you mean exactly?' asked the Second Master.

'W-well,' said Colin, 'he once loaded one of his programs into our network to replace the screen savers with some pictures of...'

'I have seen these pictures,' boomed Dr Heilbronn. 'Naked pin-ups! Disgusting! Fortunately, Colin made him remove them and gave him a job. What was that exactly?'

'I s-sent him to the Head G-Groundsman. Mr P-Parks made him w-weed the flower b-beds for w-w-one hour,' said Colin.

'How do you, as his tutor, get on with the boy?' said the High Master.

'V-very well, High Master,' said Colin. 'He's alright when he's away from the other b-boys, you know. I d-don't think he has m-many f-friends. He n-needs a f-friend. We all n-need a f-friend.'

'Yes. Yes we do, Colin,' said the Second Master, remembering his late wife and knowing he would be spending the evening alone, 'but take care not to become too friendly with Jardine. In term time the boarders are in our care twenty-four hours a day, seven days a week but we must remember we are *in loco parentis*; nothing more and nothing less. If we forget that, we could find ourselves in all sorts of trouble.'

'Thank you for your time, gentlemen,' said the High Master. 'I trust we shall be able to motivate Rupert Jardine with a nice balance of the carrot and the stick. I bid you good afternoon.' As the Second Master turned to go, the High Master said, 'Reg, may I have a quick word with you?'

'Of course, High Master' said Reg, shutting the study door after Colin Harper left in Dr Heilbronn's wake.

'Please!' said Llywelyn, 'Take a seat.'

'Something on your mind?' asked Reg, somewhat concerned about the young tutor and his tutee, Rupert Jardine.

'Yes,' said Llywelyn. 'After I left the meeting this morning I had words with the Bursar.'

'Oh!'

'So this is about Beaumont's finances, is it?' said Reg.

'I'm afraid it is,' said Llywelyn, ' and I should like your advice.'

* * * * *

CHAPTER 5

"Lack of money is the root of all evil." George Bernard Shaw

* * * * *

'The Second Master and the Bursar are here to see you, High Master.'

'Thank you, Mary. Please show them in.'

'Would you like me to bring the tea now or wait until Mr York arrives?'

'What time is he coming?'

'Three o'clock. Mr York said he will be here at three,' said Mary.

'Then let's have tea when he arrives, shall we.'

Dr Llywelyn Pugh-Jones had been High Master at Beaumont Abbey for almost eight years. When he first came to the school, from Broughton Grange where he had been the Deputy Headmaster, he had a thicker head of ginger hair and certainly more colour in his cheeks. He had become myopic within his first month of studying classics in the Sixth Form at Warminster and ever since his school days he had glasses for distance vision. In recent years he became increasingly presbyopic and now also needs glasses for close work.

When Reginald Thomas De Vere, MA (Cantab) and Anthony Parker-Smythe entered his study, Llywelyn looked at them through the upper part of his gold-rimmed bifocals and was struck, not for the first time, by their dissimilarities. Reg was about six feet tall - three inches shorter than the High Master but three inches taller than the Bursar. Reg had regained the weight he had lost during those months when a brain tumour was killing his beloved wife, Madeleine; nowadays he kept himself in good shape by swimming and playing tennis. Anthony by contrast had gained weight that he should have lost; he kept himself in bad shape by indolence and overindulgence.

Reg had a healthy suntan and was clean shaven. Anthony had a pallid face and sported a trim, black moustache. Both men were smartly attired. Reg was casually dressed in a dark brown open-necked shirt with a speckled bronze cravat, limestone coloured trousers, dark brown socks and suede shoes. Anthony was formally dressed in a white shirt with regimental tie, a three-piece, grey pin-striped suit, black socks and shiny leather shoes. Anthony's coat buttons were under strain; something even Llywelyn could not fail to notice.

Reg had taken the precaution of taking his Sunday walk around the grounds prior to this annual two o'clock meeting with the High Master and the Bursar. He would much rather have been on the tennis court partnering Mary Cranborne in a game of mixed doubles. It was another beautiful day, far too nice to be indoors with the High Master and Nosey Parker, a nickname he had overheard some boys use in reference to the Bursar. With luck the meeting would be fairly short but he was not counting on it. He was still recovering from yesterday's two o'clock meeting with the High Master, Dr Newbold, Dr Heilbronn, the insufferable E. Gordon Hamilton and that mouse of a fellow Colin Harper. 'No rest for the wicked, not even on Sunday,' Reg thought to himself.

Anthony had taken the risk of having a decent bottle of red wine with his slap-up lunch. He would rather have been stretched out, with his feet up, watching a soccer match on the television than be cooped up in the High Master's study but unfortunately there was no way he could duck this meeting. They held it every year at the same time, two o'clock sharp, on the first Sunday of the summer term. Anthony was never really nervous about attending because he always came prepared but he never really looked forward to it. Pulling the wool over the eyes of two academics was one thing. Dealing with Stanley Garnet of Banwell, Garnet & York, Chartered Accountants, was another thing altogether. Fortunately, Garnet always kept his visits to Beaumont to a minimum and left the donkey work to his junior partner, Robert York; and Anthony had an understanding with Bob.

'Perhaps you would begin, Anthony,' said Llywelyn. 'I see you have come prepared.'

'Yes, of course, sir.' said the Bursar. 'May I assume for the purposes of this meeting you just want the broad picture.'

'The broad picture, yes,' said Llywelyn, 'the broad to start with, I think. Yes.'

'Perhaps I should remind you both that although the figures for the Michaelmas and Lent terms are accurate, the figures for the Trinity term are estimates only. We can only guess at our income from renting out our facilities... like the swimming pool, for example.'

'Can't you assume the rental income will be the same as the last two terms?' said Reg.

'Well, yes,' said Anthony, 'but an indoor pool is not so popular in summertime.'

'What about the tennis courts and cricket pitches,' said Reg. 'Don't you rent those out?'

'Yes, we have managed to on occasion,' said Anthony, being careful to say *we* rather than *I*. 'We usually let the Old Boys use our facilities for free.'

'Quite true,' said Llywelyn, 'but the Old Boys Association regularly makes generous donations to the school and Beaumontians have occasionally left us substantial bequests. Let's not forget that.'

'Point taken, sir,' said Anthony.

'So! What is your assessment of our current financial position, Anthony?'

'We are in credit as of last Monday,' said Anthony, putting on his horn-rimmed glasses and glancing at the sheet of paper he had removed from a manila folder, 'but not by a great deal. It wouldn't take much to run us into debt I'm afraid.'

'So what do you propose, Anthony?' said Llywelyn, fairly sure the Bursar's proposals would be much the same as previous years.

'We must find ways to decrease our expenditure and to increase our income.'

Apart from schools like Eton, Harrow and Winchester, most independent schools were in the same boat as Beaumont and were presently discussing how they should balance the books and stay out of the red.

According to Anthony (actually according to the Independent Schools' Bursars Association), their problem of increasing expenditure was caused by (1) increases in teachers salaries to match pay awards for teachers in state schools, (2) increases in utility bills and (3) increases in National Insurance Contributions Beaumont, as an employer, was obliged to pay.

'Coincidentally, High Master' said Reg, 'Watson tackled me after yesterday's meeting. Asked if you had made any decision about next year's salary.'

'What did you say?' asked Llywelyn, fairly sure of the Second Master's discretion.

'I told him I didn't know and that it was a matter for you, the Governors and the Bursar to discuss when you meet on Wednesday.'

'Quite right!' said Llywelyn.

'Mr Watson was the new teacher who complained about being paid only at the beginning and end of term,' said Anthony.

'He's in his third year,' said Reg. 'He's hardly *new*. And he did have a point.'

'He stirred things up,' said Anthony, 'no doubt about that. Thanks to him we now have to pay the teachers one twelfth of their annual salary less deductions *each month*.'

'What's wrong with that?' asked Reg. 'Better surely than 16% in September, 17% in December, 16% in January, 20% in March, 19% in April and 12% in July.'

'Better for them, perhaps,' said Anthony, 'but Beaumont had to give up the ten weeks of interest it was making on the money it now pays out.'

'How much loss of interest would that be?' asked Reg.

'When we discussed this two years ago and the investment interest rate was 9.5%, I estimated the loss of interest would be more than £41,000. That's why I opposed the change,' said Anthony, polishing his glasses. 'It was bad enough we had to pay the ancillary staff monthly.'

'I thought they wanted to have a weekly pay packet,' said Reg.

'One or two trouble makers tried for that but I wasn't having any of it,' said Anthony.

'Who were they?' asked Reg.

'I don't remember their names,' said Anthony. 'I sacked them.'

'We digress, I fear,' said Llywelyn. 'I'd like to focus on salaries. Anthony, what award will the State School teachers receive in September?'

'The teachers' unions asked for twelve percent. They're getting ten and a half percent,' said Anthony.

'So we must raise our fees again,' said Reg.

'Yes, I'm afraid we must,' said Anthony.

'By how much?' asked Llywelyn.

'At least eleven and a half percent,' said Anthony.

'Oh dear. Most regrettable,' said Llywelyn with a sigh.

'The fee-paying parents won't like it,' said Reg. 'They...'

'Enter!' said Llywelyn, hearing a knock on the study door.

'Mr Garnet has arrived, High Master.'

'Thank you, Mary. Please show him in and bring us some refreshments.'

* * * * *

Most independent schools, including Eton, Harrow and Winchester, derive their income from (1) the fees they charge, (2) endowments and interest on investments and (3) gifts they receive. They also receive highly significant tax benefits from their charitable status. Beaumont, like other schools, was beginning to generate income by hiring out its facilities. The Bursar preferred wealthy corporations running conferences. The Second

Master favoured educational institutions running summer schools. The High Master wanted to involve the local community to satisfy a condition for their charitable status.

'Good afternoon, gentlemen,' said Stanley Garnet. 'Have I come at a bad time?'

'I've just suggested we raise the school fees by 11.5% for the coming year,' said Anthony Parker-Smythe.

'Ouch! The parents won't like that,' said Stanley. 'Still, you haven't much choice unless you find other sources of income.'

'That's something we'd like to discuss with you, Stanley,' said Llywelyn.

'First off, you need to take a look at your investments. Thanks to Margaret Thatcher, you have benefited from interest rates as high as 17%. But beware! That won't last.'

'Why were interest rates pushed up?' asked Reg

'Usually to reduce inflationary pressure,' said Stanley. 'More recently to protect the value of Sterling in the ERM.'

'Exchange Rate Mechanism,' explained Anthony, seeing the look on Reg's face.

'The ERM is nothing for you to worry about. I'm sure Britain we'll pull out next year.'

'So that won't affect us?' said Llywelyn.

'I didn't say that,' said Stanley. 'It *will* affect you *if*, actually more likely *when*, we pull out of the ERM because the Government will cut interest rates to counter the inevitable recession. Your Bursar can tell you how much interest you'll lose on your investments if they cut today's rate from 15% to 10%.'

'You're painting a rather bleak picture,' said Reg.

'It's often what I have to do,' said Stanley.

'Aside from investments, what other sources of income should we consider?' said Reg.

'Draw upon your major asset. Make better use of your facilities and extensive grounds.'

'Hire out the swimming pool, tennis courts and sports fields, is that what you're saying?' said Reg. 'You know we are already doing that, don't you?'

'Yes, I know that. Haven't you got a British Medical Association conference booked to use the great hall sometime this term?'

'Yes, Stanley, you know jolly well we have. I am most grateful to you for recommending us to the BMA,' said Llywelyn.

'I was thinking more of your extensive grounds rather than your facilities,' said Stanley.

'We get a tidy rental income from the farm,' said Anthony. 'We raise the rent every year but it hasn't quite kept up with inflation.'

'Have you considered applying for planning permission to build on some of your land?'

'Actually,' said Llywelyn, 'we have submitted plans to build a sports hall.'

'I was thinking more of building some houses and a small shopping centre,' said Stanley.

'Would we get permission for that sort of project?' Anthony asked, his mind racing at the financial possibilities.

'I have no idea,' said Stanley, 'but it would be worth looking into. You'll need to do something imaginative to keep Beaumont Abbey afloat. Truth be told, you never know what disasters are waiting to befall you.' The Head of Banwell, Garnet and York never spoke a truer word.

After tea and cakes, brought in by Mary at a strategic moment, the meeting concluded. Anthony and Reg departed giving Stanley a chance to have a quiet word with Llywelyn.

'It's only a vague suspicion at this point, High Master. That's why I wanted to have your assessment of the work our Robert York has been doing for Beaumont. As I understand it, he and your Bursar work very closely together. Has that proved satisfactory?'

* * * * *

31

CHAPTER 6

"Life is nothing without friendship." Marcus Tullius Cicero

* * * * *

'More tea?' said Llywelyn.

'Yes. Thank you, High Master,' said Stanley Garnet, FCCA.

'Milk? Sugar?' said Llywelyn, knowing full well Stanley would refuse both.

'No thank you. Not in Earl Grey,' replied Stanley, carefully placing the bone china cup and saucer on the coaster protecting the polished top of the table alongside his chair.

'Do you like my latest acquisition?' said Llywelyn, seeing Stanley, an avid collector of antiques, gently running his finger around the rim of the circular table top.

'Absolutely splendid wine table!' said Stanley. 'George III oak, circa 1780, I'd say. Probably fetch at least £400 at auction.'

'I was pleased to pick it up for £380,' said Llywelyn. 'Now then Stanley, what's the concern about the work your Robert York has been doing for us? Something suspicious been going on, I think you said.'

'No, I didn't say that exactly. I said I'd like your opinion of Robert's work.'

'You're asking the wrong man, Stanley,' said Llywelyn. 'I read Philosophy not PPE at Oxford. Consequently I know little about Politics, even less about economics and nothing at all about accounting. That's why I consult you Fellows of the Association of Chartered Certified Accountants. I'm certainly no bookkeeper but as far as I can tell, York keeps Parker-Smythe on the straight and narrow.'

'May I ask you about your Bursar?' said Stanley. 'What's your opinion of him?'

'A bit stand-offish but he's alright, I suppose. Seems to have everything under control.'

'What's his background?'

'Army man. Major in the Pay Corps, so I'm told. He showed me one of his ledgers on one occasion. It didn't mean much to me but I was impressed by his calligraphy.'

'Confidentially, we are looking into Robert York's background. Would you mind if we looked into your Bursar's?'

'You'll be discreet?'

'Very! This is a delicate matter. They will be quite unaware of our inquiries.'

* * * * *

Both men were deep in thought and said nothing to each other when they stepped out of the High Master's study into the main corridor. Even if he had not had something on his mind, the Second Master, Reginald de Vere, would not have exchanged pleasantries with Anthony Parker-Smythe. Reg had little time for Nosey Parker and the Bursar had little or no time for the academic staff save for one.

Nosey turned right and made a bee line for his office. As far as he was concerned the meeting had been satisfactory. Stanley Garnet, of Banwell, Garnet & York, thankfully had not asked awkward questions about the accounts or the financial statements. Keeping the school out of the red or, more to the point, *appearing to be in the black* was the key to the success of his own personal finances. Nosey prided himself on his mastery of double entry bookkeeping but relied completely upon his pal, Bob York, for his mastery of corporate accounting or, more to the point, *creative accounting.*

As soon as he had locked his manila folder in his personal filing cabinet, he breathed a sigh of relief and started on his way back to his bachelor quarters. The only thoughts in his mind now were of a glass or two of whisky – doubles of course – and putting his feet up in front of the television. He could not have anticipated the chance observation he was about to make that would significantly affect his future.

Reg turned left and made a bee line for the side door into the fresh air. As far as he was concerned the meeting had been unsatisfactory. Stanley Garnet had not questioned Nosey Parker's figures and the High Master had all too easily agreed to raise the school fees. The increase would hit some parents very hard. Some might be obliged to move their sons into the state system. Reg was thinking of two boys in particular; Blaine and Gosling in the Fourths. Both had won scholarships. Both were Oxbridge material. Both had supportive parents who were hard pressed to cover the substantial expenses not met by the scholarships. These boys needed Beaumont. Beaumont would come to need them.

As soon as he felt the sunshine on his face, Reg took some deep breaths and turned his thoughts to tennis – doubles of course - and partnering Mary Cranborne. Madeleine, his late wife, and Mary had been good friends. Madeleine and Mary had often played tennis together against Louise, the High Master's wife, and Celia, the Chaplain's wife. It was Madeleine who persuaded Reg to take up tennis again. He had learnt to play when he was a boy but stopped playing when went up to Oxford and was thrashed 6-0, 6-0, 6-0 by his room mate who became a professional after graduating and returning to Australia.

* * * * *

'Good afternoon! Mary Cranborne.'

'Hello Mary. Reggie here.'

'Oh! Hello,' said Mary, holding the telephone to her left ear and fiddling with the string of pearls around her neck with her right hand.

'Any chance of a game of doubles before high tea, d'you think?'

'That would be nice. Have you been in touch with Louise and Arthur?' said Mary.

34

'No!' said Reg. 'I called you first. There wouldn't be much point if you were unavailable.

'Right!' said Mary, 'I'll call Louise and you call Arthur. Ring me back in five minutes.'

Reg telephoned Arthur Matthews, Head of Geography who, according to both boys and staff, ran his department with a rod of iron and extreme efficiency. He was an inspiring teacher whose enthusiasm for his subject bordered on the fanatical and whose occasional eccentricities made him all the more popular with the pupils. Arthur was a few years younger than Reg, slightly shorter but similar in build. Unlike Reg, Arthur had a beard and moustache. He kept the hair on his face neatly combed and trimmed but he had long given up the battle to control the tousled mop of brown hair on the top of his head. On one occasion he made the mistake of allowing a barber to trim his eyebrows. As a consequence, his eyebrows grew long and became entangled to form a dense line across the base of his high, furrowed forehead. 'Mixed doubles against you and Mary?' said Arthur. 'Certainly as long as Louise Pugh-Jones is on my side. See you at Gower in twenty minutes.'

Mary telephoned Louise Pugh-Jones who, according to her husband, the High Master of Beaumont, could be found most days during the summer either gardening or playing tennis, unless of course it was raining; then she could be found in their sun room with her nose in the Telegraph crossword. Louise met Llywelyn at Oxford in the summer of 1963. She was in her second year reading Philosophy, Politics and Economics (PPE). He was writing his dissertation (*The Moral Foundations of Crime and Punishment*) for his DPhil. They happened to sit next to one another in the Gulbenkian Theatre to hear the first in the series of six weekly talks – known as the John Locke lectures - to be given by Bertrand Russell on *the Elements of Ethics*. 'Mixed doubles against you and Reggie?' said Louise. 'Love to. Who? Mad Arthur! That'll be fun. Why is he called Mad Arthur? Remind me, Reg, to tell you the story over coffee sometime. See you shortly.'

Twenty-five minutes later, all four players were dressed in white and on the tennis court at the back of Gower House. The women wore plimsolls, plain tennis dresses (modestly covering their thighs to just above the knees) and white headband visors (sensibly keeping their hair and the sun out of their eyes). The sweat band on their left wrists and their healthy suntans completed the picture of two very fit ladies who took their tennis very seriously. The men played tennis for a bit of exercise and mostly just for fun. Nevertheless they always took care to dress properly. They wore shorts, short-sleeved cotton shirts, cotton socks and tennis shoes. They should have worn sweat bands but they never did; they used the sleeves of their cotton shirts.

Mary spun her racquet, Louise correctly called smooth and elected to serve. Arthur, standing close to the net, heard the hum and felt the wind in his right ear as the ball sped past him. Before he could gather his wits, the ball shot back past his left ear. At Mary's command, Reg lunged towards the net to volley Louise's return, stuck out his racquet, made contact and deflected the speeding ball straight at Arthur.

'Sorry old boy,' said Reg, as the ball thumped his opponent in the midriff.

'Well played Reggie.' said Mary, moving up to the net. 'Love fifteen.'

'You sure you're alright, Arthur?' said Reg.

'Yes. I'm fine. Didn't feel a thing,' lied Arthur. 'Might have been a different story if…'

'You ready, Arthur,' said Louise, impatiently bouncing the ball on the ground.

'Sorry!' said Arthur, scuttling across the court and placing himself at the net.

'Out!' Reg said with relief as the ball sped from Louise's racquet in a vicious curve towards his backhand and bounced outside the line.

'Second service,' said Mary. 'Ready Reggie?'

'Ready as I shall ever be, Mary,' said Reg.

* * * * *

Rupert knew exactly where he would find his tutor on that first Sunday afternoon. He opened the main door to the science block and strolled in. The block, fondly referred to as the Cavendish, had been built with money from donations and a substantial grant from the Nuffield Foundation. Inside and directly opposite the main door was the staircase leading up to the Chemistry Department and two Physics laboratories. To the left of the stairs was a short corridor and a door at the end. Rupert opened the door, marked *Staff Only*, and sauntered in to use the toilet.

Inside the Cavendish and to the left of the main entrance was a heavy fire door. Rupert, now suitably relieved, opened the door and stepped into the long central corridor running the length of the building. On the right were the three laboratories and prep room of the Biology Department. On the left was the language lab, the computer room, the electronics lab and the science prep room. Rupert peered through the small glass porthole before opening the door and stepping into the computer room.

'Hello! When did you get back?' said Colin Harper, Jardine's tutor and computing science teacher.

'Yesterday afternoon,' replied Rupert. 'I did look for you, you know.'

'Ah, well yesterday afternoon I was in a meeting with the High Master, the Second Master, Dr Heilbronn, Dr Newbold and your Housemaster,' said Colin, not stammering.

'Let me guess,' said Rupert. 'You were deciding my future, right?'

'No, not really,' said Colin. 'Only you can decide your future, Rupert.'

'But the meeting was about me, wasn't it?'

'Yes it was. We all agreed you have the brains to win an Oxbridge scholarship and to excel in whatever you put your mind to but…'

'But I have the wrong attitude. I'm not serious enough, right?'

'That's about it,' said Colin. 'Your last prank nearly got you thrown out. If I had been injured, I'm pretty sure the High Master would not have let you come back.'

'You were as much to blame as I was, you know,' said Rupert.

It began when Rupert saw two men in dinner jackets rappelling down the outside of the school clock tower late one night. Arthur Matthews, Geographer and mountaineer, and Philip Carratt, Head of Chemistry, had attended the annual black tie dinner of their Old Boys Association. It was about 11:30 p.m. when the taxi mistakenly dropped them off at the main entrance to Beaumont. Both men had probably drunk one port too many. Arthur asked Philip if he had ever climbed to the top of the school tower. When Philip foolishly said he had not, Arthur took his arm and led him under the arch and through the small door to the steep staircase inside the tower. Two-thirds of the way up, the stone steps ended and the two men, still in their bow ties and dinner jackets, had to climb the rest of the way to the top using the rungs of an iron ladder attached to the stone wall.

The fresh night air did little to restore their sanity. Arthur asked Philip if he had ever experienced the thrill of descending a vertical mountainside on a rope. When Philip foolishly said he had never been climbing, Arthur persuaded him (actually dared him) to abseil with him down the tower. The next morning when Philip woke up with a slight hangover but otherwise none the worse for wear, he thought their rappelling had been just a dream. When he saw the marks on his dinner jacket and the scuffs on his shoes, he remembered the limerick

There was a young named Ball
Who dreamt he jumped off the town hall.
Halfway to the ground

He woke up and found
It wasn't a dream after all.

Impressed by the stunt, Rupert persuaded Colin Harper to climb the steps and ladder to the top of the tower on some pretext or other. Once at the top, Rupert threw out the two ropes (left in the tower by Arthur Matthews), grabbed one and clambered over the edge of the parapet. He then announced he was going to abseil down the outside and persuaded his frantic tutor and only friend in the school to come with him. During the descent, Colin twice nearly lost his grip and would have fallen if Rupert had not grabbed his arm. Unfortunately, E. Gordon Hamilton, Rupert's Housemaster, witnessed the event and reported it to the Second Master.

The Bursar was making his way back to his whisky and television when he spotted Rupert Jardine entering the Cavendish. He knew the boy and he knew his father had heavily subsidised the computer room and language laboratory. Nosey Parker wondered what the boy was up to and how he managed to get into the building without a key. Curiosity got the better of him. He walked over to the Cavendish and, guessing the boy had been going to the computer room, Nosey walked along the outside of the building and looked through one of the windows.

'I don't know what got into me,' said Colin. 'How did I ever let you persuade me to...'

'You know how persuasive I can be,' said Rupert. 'Anyway, what are friends for.'

'You say we're friends,' said Colin, 'but you make me wonder sometimes.'

'We are friends,' cooed Rupert, putting his arm around Colin's shoulders. 'We'll always be friends.'

'Rupert, please,' said Colin, 'somebody might see us.'

'Who cares?' said Rupert, pulling Colin even closer.

Nosey was flabbergasted by what he saw. Here was the one member of the academic staff for whom he had some time. Colin Harper and a Sixth Former in an embrace. It was downright indecent. He could hardly

39

believe his eyes. Harper of all people. The one friendly member of staff. The one who had been so helpful fixing his bookkeeping and accounting programs on the computer in the Bursar's office. The one teacher he thought of as his friend. Nosey turned on his heel in disgust. Now he really would need his whisky. By the time he reached home and poured his first drink, he had decided he would have a friendly word with Colin Harper.

* * * * *

At two sets all, Reg suggested they should call it a day. He and Arthur had to get ready for supper then evensong in the Chapel. They all shook one another's hands and said how much they had enjoyed the afternoon. Reg would have liked to walk Mary home but Arthur wanted a word. The ladies walked some way together and before going their separate ways, Louise said, 'When would you like to meet for coffee, Mary?'

'Greg Watson has been badgering me about salaries.'

'I'm not surprised,' said Reg. 'He latched onto me outside the Long Room yesterday morning after the meeting. I'm afraid I had to tell him I didn't know anything about salary increases for next year.'

'Ah, but you had your annual meeting this afternoon with the High Master and Parker-Smythe,' said Arthur. 'You know something now, don't you?

'Yes I did. And yes I do but you'll have to wait until after the Governors have approved the High Master's proposals. They meet on Wednesday.'

'Actually,' said Arthur, 'I wanted to know if Walter Barnes has given his official notice to the High Master.'

'To tell you the truth, Arthur, I'm not sure.'

'I presume the old boy is retiring,' said Arthur.

'I assume so,' said Reg. 'If he is, then he'll need to give the High Master his notice today if he hasn't done so already.'

'Will Greg be made Head of PE or will money be wasted on advertising the post?'

'As to Greg Watson being offered the post...'

'I hope he gets it,' said Arthur. 'He's finding things a bit tight having two young children and his wife no longer working.'

'He's well qualified and very keen. No doubt about that,' said Reg. 'What would you do if he's put in charge of PE? Who would cover the geography he teaches?'

'Good point,' said Arthur. 'What did Kathy Watson teach before they started a family?'

'Geography, I think,' said Reg.

'Ah, there's my answer,' said Arthur.

'But you yourself just said she has two young children. What about them?'

'We'll get Louise Pugh-Jones to look after them,' Arthur said, then roared with laughter.

'Kathy Watson on the staff,' said Reg. 'The first woman to teach at Beaumont. Next thing you know, we'll be letting girls into the Sixth Form. Jardine would have a field day!'

'Rupert keen on girls, is he? That's not quite what I heard,' Arthur said with a wicked grin on his face.

* * * * *

CHAPTER 7

"Few sinners are saved after the first twenty minutes of a sermon." Mark Twain (1835 – 1910)

* * * * *

For the staff at Beaumont, the last day of their Easter holiday was the Wednesday. The Thursday and Friday were two of the five statutory INSET (in-service training) days introduced in 1988 by Kenneth Baker, the Conservative Minister for Education.

Quentin Waite, who probably considered himself the elder statesman of the Common Room, pronounced these days to be a waste of time and as ill-conceived as the National Curriculum his contemporary at Oxford, the Right Honourable MP for Mole Valley in Surrey, had introduced in his 1988 Education Act. They came to be known as Baker Days. The normally refined Quentin on one occasion referred to an in-service training day as a B-day. He was overheard by a young confused French Assistant who spent the rest of the day wondering why he had no bidet in his accommodation.

Gregory Watson, who probably considered himself the natural successor to the elderly Walter Barnes, Head of Physical Education, regarded these Baker days as an opportunity to broaden his horizons, bring himself up to date and, perhaps more importantly, to further his career. He particularly enjoyed spending time in the computer room trying out the latest software to teach his speciality – physical geography.

Colin Harper, who probably considered himself the staff dogsbody, detested these Baker days because he was obliged to show his reluctant non-mathematical and non-scientific colleagues how computers might be used to teach subjects like geography and history. He still remembered his embarrassment at being trapped between Arthur Matthews extolling the merits of some *good* software for geography and Quentin Waite disparaging some *bad* software for history. As a mere junior member of staff, Colin felt powerless to point out they were not comparing like for like.

For the boys at Beaumont, the last day of their Easter holiday was the Friday. With the exception of those few on delayed flights from the Far East, most boarders would return to school on Saturday or on Sunday morning. All boys, including day boys, would be in school on Sunday for lunch, dinner and evensong.

For the chaplain, the term always began on Sunday at seven o'clock with evensong. He believed the Trinity term sermon should be inspirational and set the tone for the weeks ahead and for the examinations after Whitsuntide. Dr Fiddle DD meant well. Unfortunately he tended to forget the advice of a professor of theology from Texas who was visiting Oxford during Fiddle's undergraduate days. Lecturing on how to deliver sermons from the pulpit, Professor Elmer P. Calhoun, declared in a Texan drawl: *if you haven't struck oil after five minutes, stop boring.*

* * * * *

Dr Fiddle thought a lot about his sermons but, kindly soul though he was, he gave too little thought for his congregation. When planning a sermon, he liked walking. Unfortunately he usually walked with his eyes more on the heavens above than on the earth beneath. Celia, his long suffering wife, despaired when his strolling took him across the pastures of Beaumont Farm, especially where cows had been grazing.

On one occasion, the portly chaplain's habit of gazing upwards led him to bump into the Head of Geography who was gazing downwards. Arthur Matthews was studying the gravel path and thinking the stones might provide material for a geology lesson. 'Look where you're going,' said a slightly dazed Arthur who was almost knocked to the ground. When he swung round and saw it was old Fiddle-dee-dee, Mad Arthur laughed and said, 'Sorry old man. My fault. You probably were looking where you'll be going one day.'

The chaplain apologised and went on his way to the walled garden, all the while struggling to put a name to the vaguely familiar face of the man he had just encountered; the man with glaring eyes, striking eyebrows and a mop of tousled-hair.

The Reverend Dr Humphrey Fiddle, DD was in his twelfth year at Beaumont and he was about to start his twelfth Trinity term with evensong at seven o'clock. As he swept along like a ship in full sail, his ankle-length black cassock shrouding his substantial hull and stern and his colourful academic hood billowing behind him like a disoriented spinnaker, the rays of the setting sun reflected off his bald pate and the wisps of silver hair around its rim. The eyes behind his gold-rimmed spectacles were like those of a ship's navigator scanning the darkening sky above to plot his position by the stars and navigate his way to the chapel.

The chaplain had dotted the 'i's' and crossed the 't's' of his sermon but he still had not decided on a passage from the Bible. With the run up to exams after Whitsuntide, he thought he might stress the value of revision. He had considered 1 Corinthians 13:12 - *Now we see things imperfectly as in a cloudy mirror, but then we will see everything with perfect clarity*. No, not suitable, for according to Celia there were some boys who would never see anything clearly. He had considered Proverbs 10:13 *Wise words come from the lips of people with understanding, but those lacking sense will be beaten with a rod*. Again, not suitable, for Celia reminded him the abolition of corporal punishment in independent schools had come into effect on the 1st November 1989.

On his way to the chapel he was considering Proverbs 19:20 when he was brought back to earth by the chorus of a small group of Lower Thirds. He almost bumped into them. *Good Evening, Dr Fiddle, sir*. He stopped, said *Good Evening, boys* and turned to walk slowly on. He caught snatches of their conversation. *I got Black Magic for my birthday* (actually a box of chocolates). *I read about the Prince of Darkness* (a 1987 film starring Donald Pleasance) and *knew we'd be bored* (sounded like new ouija board).

A few minutes later, a somewhat worried chaplain stepped into the vestry where the assistant chaplain, Donald Meeker, MDiv, himself already enrobed, was supervising the choirboys putting on their cassocks.

'Good evening, sir!' chorused Meeker and the boys in unison.

'What? Oh, yes. Good evening, boys!' responded Dr Fiddle.

'Everything alright?' asked Meeker, not used to seeing a frown on the chaplain's face.

'Yes. No, I'm not sure,' said the chaplain. 'No, I think everything may not be alright.'

* * * * *

Donald Meeker had been at Beaumont almost four years. His sister, Janet, was working as a nurse in England when the post of assistant chaplain became vacant. She saw the 'invitation to apply' in the Times and sent Donald the details. It was at the interview that he had his first sighting of the chaplain whose mind seemed to be elsewhere most of the time.

'Sorry, I missed that,' said Dr Fiddle. 'Where did you say you read for your degree?'

'King's College, sir,' said Donald

'King's College, London?'

'Yes, sir,' said Donald.

'Ah! Corpus Christi man, myself,' said Dr Fiddle. 'Ever consider Oxford, Mister... er?'

'No, not really, sir.'

'May I ask why not?' said Dr Fiddle.

'Rather too far away from my home town, to be honest,' said Donald.

'Your home town being?'

'London, sir,' said Donald, a little puzzled by the question.

'Oxford too far away, you say?'

'Yes, sir,' said Donald become even more puzzled.

Donald was offered the post and he accepted on the spot. Three months later, during the summer holiday, he moved into the school's bachelor accommodation. One weekend that summer, Janet visited her brother to see how he was settling in. While they were looking around the school they met Joyce Plaister SRN, the senior matron.

'Good afternoon, Miss Plaister,' said Donald. 'This is my sister, Janet.'

'Pleased to meet you,' boomed the formidable Joyce. 'Settled in have we?'

'Yes, matron, I have,' said Donald.

'What about you, young lady?' said the Senior Matron.

'Oh, no! I'm just here for the weekend,' said Janet. 'I have to be back in the hospital on Monday.'

'Nothing serious, I trust,' said Joyce, her face softening.

'Oh, I see,' said Janet. 'Oh, no. I have to be back at work. I'm on a sabbatical at Barts.'

'The London Children's Hospital?' said Joyce.

'Yes, that's the one,' said Janet. 'I'm a nurse.'

'Splendid! Absolutely splendid,' boomed Joyce. 'How much longer will you be there?'

'Actually,' said Janet, 'I finish next month. On August 31st.'

'Excellent!' boomed the Senior Matron. 'So you could start here on the 1st of September.'

'I'm sorry,' said Janet. 'I don't understand.'

'The assistant matron in Wedgewood is leaving. Actually she is retiring. I'm looking for someone to take her place. Interested?'

'Yes!' said Janet, 'but I'd like to know more about…'

'Of course! Of course!' boomed Joyce. 'Come on, let me show you your quarters in Wedgewood and explain your duties.'

'May I join you?' said Donald, feeling a bit left out.

'Of course!' boomed Joyce. 'Follow me.'

* * * * *

Even after nearly four years at the school, Humphrey Fiddle and Donald Meeker had still not managed to fathom one another but they had become used to one another. Donald had come to appreciate Humphrey – whom he always respectfully addressed as Dr Fiddle – for the amiable, kindly, yet head in the clouds fellow that he was. Humphrey had come to appreciate Donald – whom he sometimes variously addressed as Duncan or Dylan – for the dependable, worthy, feet on the ground fellow that he was.

'What passage have you chosen for your sermon this evening, Dr Fiddle?'

'I was thinking of Proverbs 19:20.'

'Hear counsel, and receive instruction, that thou mayest be wise in thy latter end,' said Donald, quoting from the King James Bible.

'Actually, Duncan, I prefer the NLT version you persuaded me to consider.'

'Get all the advice and instruction you can, so you will be wise the rest of your life,' said Donald, quoting from the New Living Translation and wondering this evening why he was being called Duncan.

'Yes, that's it,' said Dr Fiddle, thinking his assistant chaplain sounded more Scottish than Welsh this evening. 'That's the passage I'll use if…' Before he could say any more, Peter Morrison, Head of Music, began a voluntary on the organ in the chapel and Donald glanced at his wrist watch.

'Come along boys,' said Donald, 'let's get ready. Tompkins! Hair!'

'Yes, sir. Sorry, sir,' said Tompkins borrowing a comb and tugging at his tangled locks.

'Thank you kindly, Tompkins,' said Donald.

Beaumont Chapel is really too grand an edifice to be called a chapel. It was built near the end of the 19th century in the gothic perpendicular style of architecture, with the apex of its fan vaulted ceiling 100 feet above the floor. A stained glass window fills the space above the 45 feet wide stone altar and faces the Harrison and Harrison three manual pipe organ and gallery at the other end of the 150 feet long nave. There are eight similar windows on either side of the nave. Each window fills the space between a pair of stone columns supporting the arched roof.

On the south wall beneath the first window is the doorway into the vestry. Donald opened that door so he could hear Peter Morrison's improvisations more clearly and watch for the Second Master's sign for the choir to enter. The doorway beneath the eighth window opens into the cloister connecting the chapel to the school library and a courtyard. Staff and boys were filing through this doorway to their allocated seats. The staff and any distinguished visitors sat in canopied wooden seats recessed in niches in the long south and north walls. Mary Cranborne, the High Master's secretary, was in the niche furthest from the organ and nearest to the chancel and the wrought iron floor candelabra. The boys sat in the four tiered rows of pews, on either side of the nave, in front of and parallel to the staff seats. The staff seats are padded. The pews are not.

'The High Master has arrived, Dr Fiddle,' said Donald, seeing the signal from the Second Master. 'Ready Tompkins? Ready Sutton?'

'Yes, sir,' the head chorister and deputy head chorister said in unison.

'Very well, lead on.'

The choir boys processed two by two into the chapel. As the first two boys appeared from the vestry and in front of the chancel, Peter Morrison launched into J S Bach's Prelude in C Major BWV 547 and everyone stood up. The forty strong choir, followed by the assistant chaplain with Dr Fiddle trailing in his wake, made its way slowly down the nave towards the choir stalls. When Dr Fiddle came alongside a spiral staircase, he stopped, did an about face, bowed to the altar and took his place at the canopied seat next to the pulpit under the fourth window on the south wall. When the last notes of the Prelude had faded away, everybody except the choir and the assistant chaplain sat down.

When every choirboy's eyes were fixed on him, Donald Meeker raised his hands and nodded to Peter Morrison to play his introduction to Roger Quilter's setting of the poem Rudyard Kipling wrote for the 1934 London Pageant.

Non Nobis, Domine!
Not unto us, O Lord,
The praise and glory be
Of any deed or word.
For in Thy judgement lies
To crown or bring to nought
All knowledge and device
That man has reached or wrought

And we confess our blame,
How all too high we hold
That noise which men call fame,
That dross which men call gold.
For these we undergo
Our hot and godless days,
But in our souls we know
Not unto us the praise.

O Power by whom we live
Creator, Judge and Friend,
Upholdingly forgive,
Nor leave us at the end.
But grant us yet to see,
In all our piteous ways,
Non Nobis, Domine,
Not unto us the praise.

At the end of the anthem, the Second Master stood up and addressed the assembly. 'I remind you all, but Upper Fifths and Sixths especially, of the importance of this first half. Whitsuntide is just a few weeks away and the examinations will be upon us before we know it. There must be no slackening of effort. Your futures are in your own hands and the good name of Beaumont Abbey rests on your shoulders. We put our trust in you. Do not let us down.' As he turned to sit down, Reginald de Vere gave Rupert Jardine the benefit of a stony glare.

Donald Meeker announced the hymn. The choir and congregation stood up. The organist played the introduction. Then the chapel was filled with the sound of a favourite:

> *Holy, holy, holy, Lord God Almighty,*
> *Early in the morning our song shall rise to thee.*
> *Holy, holy, holy, merciful and mighty*
> *God in three persons, blessed Trinity!*

During the singing of the fourth and last verse, Dr Fiddle climbed the spiral iron staircase into the pulpit.

* * * * *

'In the name of the Father, the Son and the Holy Ghost. Amen.' The chaplain paused, took off his spectacles and polished the lenses. He cast his eyes over the serried ranks to look for the boys he had encountered on his way to chapel, squinted and realised he still had his spectacles in his hand. He put them back on his nose and looked at his sermon. The sun had set. The moon was full but hidden by a blanket of heavy black cloud. A thunderstorm threatened. Inside the chapel the glass in the windows was made darker by the glow from the electric candles along the choir stalls and from the electric wall lights in the organ loft. The brightest light came from the seven wax candles on the wrought iron candelabra standing on the floor by the chancel.

'The Second Master reminded us of the imminence of Whitsuntide and the examinations that will follow. This evening I had intended to take as my text Proverbs 19 verse 20: *Get all the advice and instruction you can, so you will be wise the rest of your life,* and to encourage your efforts in the coming weeks. I cannot do that now. I must talk to you about something far more important.' Dr Fiddle polished his spectacles again and took a deep breath. 'I must tell you about the Prince of Darkness and the occult.' At that precise moment the flash of lightening that lit up the windows was followed by a clap of thunder. Before the chaplain could continue, an owl swooped past the east window hooting loudly.

For the next twenty minutes Dr Fiddle subjected his audience to the dangers, the very real dangers, of dabbling in Black Magic. 'Some of you,' he said, scowling at some Lower Thirds who were sniggering, 'may think it a game to play with ouija boards. It is not. You will be meddling in matters…' One of the boys he had encountered on the way to chapel had a broad grin on his face. The chaplain caught his eye and let fly with a quotation from Hamlet, scene v, 'there are more things in heaven and earth, Horatio, than are dreamt of in your philosophy.'

Having built up a good head of steam, the chaplain lost all track of the time. Drawing upon 1 Peter 5:8, he urged them to *be sober, be vigilant; because your adversary the devil, as a roaring lion, walketh about, seeking whom he may devour*. The Lower Thirds were the first to become restless. What's that board game he's talking about? Why does Old Fiddle-Dee-Dee think your name's Horatio? What's all that about a roaring lion? A member of the Upper Fourths had to clap his hand over his mouth when the boy next to him whispered *the lion shall lie down with the lamb… but the lamb wouldn't get much sleep*.

Just after the chaplain began to describe the physical smell of evil, Mary Cranborne quietly rose from her seat, picked up the candle snuffer and approached the candelabra. One by one the seven flames were extinguished, allowing the gutted candles to add their smell to the chapel. Dr Fiddle took the hint and ended his sermon by drawing upon Ephesians 6:11 to urge everyone to *put on the whole armour of God, that ye may be able to stand against the wiles of the devil*. 'In the name of the Father, the Son and the Holy Ghost, Amen.' Peter Morrison launched into J S Bach's Fugue in C Major BWV 547. The congregation came to its feet and remained standing whilst the choir processed back to the vestry at a slightly faster rate than usual and nearly left Dr Fiddle behind.

'That was a stroke of genius, Mary,' said the Second Master to the High Master's secretary outside the chapel. 'You deserve a medal. What made you do it?'

'Really, Reggie,' said Mary with a wry look on her face. 'I don't know what you mean. Anyone could see those candles were spluttering.'

'I'm sure the High Master was impressed by your selfless act,' said Reggie.

'The candles *were* spluttering,' insisted Mary, 'I just happened to be nearest to them.'

'If you say so,' Mary. 'Anyway, as a token of my gratitude, let me offer you a glass of sherry. We have a bottle of Jerez de la Fronteira 'Fino' in the Common Room.'

'Mary. It's Mary. Our saviour,' exclaimed Arthur Matthews as Reginald de Vere led her into the Common Room.

'The candles *were* spluttering,' said Mary.

'Of course they were,' said Arthur pouring three glasses of sherry. 'That's what we were all saying just before you came in. Mary Cranborne snuffed out those candles in the nick of time... which reminds me... speaking of Nick. What was old Fiddle-Dee-Dee talking about? Black Magic in the Lower Thirds? The Prince of Darkness. Putting ideas into the boys' heads I shouldn't wonder. What'll happen next?'

'That, my dear Arthur, is a very good question,' said the Second Master. 'What will happen next?'

In the vestry, a puzzled assistant chaplain could not refrain from asking the chaplain why he changed his sermon. When Dr Fiddle told him what he had overheard some Lower Thirds talking about, Donald could hardly believe it. And when he pressed the chaplain for details and was told that one boy confessed to having a box of Black Magic, Donald could not suppress a laugh. 'I'm sorry if you think it funny, Dylan,' said Dr Fiddle. 'With Wales having a history of magic and witchcraft, I should have expected you of all people...' Donald frowned, wondering why his boss had started talking about a part of Britain he and his sister Janet had not even visited. 'Yes, yes,' muttered Dr Fiddle, He paused then said, 'Stonehenge! All that sandstone came from Wales more than five thousand years ago! You know that of course. Stonehenge! That stone in the centre of the circle... you know it's called the slaughter stone. An evil place.' As the chaplain turned to leave the vestry he said, 'Some boys are capable of great evil. Vigilance, Dylan.'

Donald was not surprised to find Dr Fiddle's sermon the main topic of conversation when he arrived back at Wedgwood. Most of the boys were joking about it. One or two boys asked him what Ouija boards were and how they worked. One boy wondered if he would be allowed to make one in his craft and design lesson. Donald did not rise to the bait. Instead he reminded everyone of the Second Master's message.

On his rounds later that evening Donald noticed Rupert Jardine sitting by himself. He was pleased to see he had his nose in a book. Had he noticed the title of the book he might not have been pleased. He might even have remembered Dr Fiddle's parting words: *some boys are capable of great evil.*

* * * * *

CHAPTER 8

"Today is the tomorrow we worried about yesterday."
Anon

* * * * *

Angus MacKay stepped into the office and quietly closed the door behind him. Stanley Garnet, the head of Banwell, Garnet and York, Chartered Accountants, waved the Scotsman into an easy chair, handed him a cup of coffee then settled himself into the easy chair on the other side of the coffee table. These two men had minds as sharp as razors but the Presbyterian MacKay often found it expedient to let his razor appear dull-edged compared to that of his Anglican boss.

The two men differed in their physical appearance. Angus had a wiry, sinewy physique he kept in shape by fell running and long-distance cycling. Stanley had long given up badminton, squash and tennis to keep physically fit; he now relied on a tailor and bespoke suits to create the illusion of his being in shape. Angus had sandy-coloured eyebrows and hair, piercing blue eyes, a sharp nose, thin lips and boyish freckles that made him seem younger than a man in his mid-fifties. Stanley had thick, steel-grey hair, brown eyes and an avuncular face that made him seem older than a man in his mid-fifties.

Angus connected Stanley's surname with the abrasive mineral used in grindstones and not with the garnet gemstones used in jewellery. In his opinion, Stanley Garnet was hard; and he was fair but definitely not a man to cross. Angus checked his watch - nine o'clock – and waited patiently for his boss to say why he was summoned to this meeting behind closed doors so early on Monday morning.

'You've probably guessed why…'

'Och, aye,' said Angus. 'Internal or external?'

'Both, actually,' said Stanley. 'So the utmost discretion, understood?'

'I ken,' said Angus. 'Names?'

'Anthony Parker-Smythe,' said Stanley. 'Bursar at Beaumont Abbey.'

'That's his real name?'

'Probably not but that's for you to find out. Supposedly a Major in the Army Pay Corps.'

'Is that so?'

'That's what he led the High Master of Beaumont to believe, anyway,' said Stanley.

'The internal?' said Angus.

'Robert York.' Stanley almost whispered his junior partner's name.

'Utmost discretion then,' said Angus. 'When do you want me to start?'

'Immediately,' said Stanley.

'How long have I got?'

'Shall we say four weeks?'

'Four weeks!' said Angus. 'No doubt you'll be wanting a result in two.'

'Let me know as soon as you have anything interesting,' said Stanley.

'Right enough,' said Angus. 'Best to start with the internal.'

* * * * *

Most teachers and pupils at Beaumont did not relish the first period on the first Monday of term. Dr Philip J Carratt and his Lower Thirds chemistry class were the exceptions to this rule. The boys hurried into the laboratory as quickly and as silently as they could; Jasper (his nickname amongst the boys) would not tolerate running or noise on *their* part. They donned their safety goggles and white lab coats, sat on their stools, opened their notebooks and waited patiently.

'Those buttons on your lab coat are there for a purpose, Jenkins,' Jasper barked.

'Yes, sir. Sorry, sir,' said the boy, hastily doing up his buttons.'

'I trust we all enjoyed our Easter break?'

'Yes, sir. Thank you, sir,' chorused the twenty boys.

'Everybody refreshed and ready for hard work?'

'Yes, sir. Thank you, sir,' they chimed.

'Excellent. Let's get started. Look at the blackboard and tell me what you see.' Jasper paused then scanned the shower of hands in the air. 'Jenkins! Suffering from jet lag, are we?'

'No, sir.'

'I should hope not. You could probably have walked to Beaumont.' Jasper knew very well Jenkins came up from London by car on Sunday morning. 'So, what do you see on the blackboard?'

'A word equation, sir.'

'Good. Anything odd about it?'

'Yes sir. It's not finished,' said Jenkins.

'Would you be kind enough to finish it for us?'

'Yes sir. Hydrogen plus Oxygen equals water,' Jenkins said seeing hydrogen + oxygen = written on the board.

'Sir! Sir!' All hands were now in the air.

'Yes, Boardman,' said Jasper, looking at a star pupil.

'Hydrogen reacts with oxygen to form water,' said Boardman.

'Excellent!' said Jasper, writing the word water on the blackboard. 'Now I need an assistant with nerves of steel. Any volunteers?'

'Fully awake now, are we Jenkins?' said Jasper. 'Good. If the rest of you would all be kind enough to move the back of the lab.'

Dr Carratt handed Jenkins a metre ruler. Strapped to one end was a wax taper which the boy lit with the nearby Bunsen flame. Dr Carratt removed the cap from a small plastic bottle (which he had previously filled with a mixture of hydrogen and oxygen in the ratio of two volumes to one) and used it to blow a soap bubble. The bubble floated into the air and burst before Jenkins could reach it with the burning wax taper. The class groaned. Dr Carratt blew another slightly smaller soap bubble. Jenkins missed again. Another groan from the back of the lab. 'Last chance, Jenkins,' said Dr Carratt and blew a large bubble. The noise was deafening even to the boys at the back of the lab. 'Well done Jenkins. I think that was louder than last year.' With their ears still ringing, the boys returned to their seats.

'What else is on the blackboard that needs to be finished?'

'Yes. Jenkins?'

'The chemical equation for the reaction, sir,' said Jenkins. On the blackboard Dr Carratt had written

$$H_2(g) + O_2(g) \rightarrow$$

'Good.' Dr Carratt paused then said, handing the boy the chalk, 'Very well, Jenkins. Finish it.' Jenkins wrote $H_2O(l)$ after the arrow. 'Not bad, Jenkins. Have you finished?' Jenkins thought for a moment then put a '2' in front of the $H_2(g)$ and the $H_2O(l)$. 'Well done!' said Dr Carratt. 'We'll make a chemist of you yet.'

The lesson was almost over when Dr Carratt sent all the boys to the back of the lab again. This time he was on his own at the front. He had filled an antique glass bottle (known as a torpedo or Hamilton bottle after its inventor, Paul Hamilton) with 200 ml of hydrogen and 100 ml of oxygen and wrapped the bottle in a very thick towel. Standing at one end of the long demonstration bench, Dr Carratt called out. 'Ready, gentlemen?' The boys put their fingers in their ears. Dr Carratt removed the rubber stopper and held the mouth of the flask close to the flame of the nearby Bunsen burner.

The noise of the explosion was so loud it was heard in the main building of Beaumont. A sheet of flame shot from the bottle, blew out the Bunsen flame and almost reached the other end of the demonstration bench. 'Prep for tonight, gentlemen. A full account of this morning's demonstrations and experiments.'

* * * * *

'Mr Trevanion is here, High Master,' said Mary Cranborne. 'Shall I show him in?'

'Yes, please.'

'What time shall I bring in coffee?'

'Oh, yes. In about a half an hour, I think,' said Dr Pugh-Jones. 'About ten thirty.'

Mary ushered the school solicitor into the High Master's study, closed the door behind him and returned to her office. Henry Trevanion, LLM of Trevanion, Doyle and Root, had looked after Beaumont Abbey's legal affairs for longer than he cared to remember. He promised Christopher Doyle he would hand over the reins in two years time when he retired at age sixty-five; and so he would. Henry was a man who kept his promises.

'So, Llywelyn, the Governors will meet this coming Wednesday?'

'Yes, Henry. Same as always. 10 o'clock in the small library.'

'Anything on the agenda out of the ordinary? Anything I should know about?'

'No. No, not really,' said Llywelyn, hesitatingly as he recalled his meeting with Stanley Garnet. *This is a delicate matter. They will be quite unaware of our inquiries.*

'Are you sure? Absolutely sure?' said Henry. 'No barrister likes surprises.'

'Actually,' said Llywelyn, 'Stanley asked me yesterday what I thought of the work Robert York does for us.'

'Stanley Garnet?' said Henry. 'He wanted to know what you thought of his junior partner.'

'What I thought of his work,' said Llywelyn. 'Not what I thought of Robert.'

'What did you say?'

'What could I say? It's no secret I'm not an accountant.'

'Just as well you told me this,' said Henry. 'Will York be at the meeting on Wednesday?'

'Yes, of course, unless Stanley attends instead,' said Llywelyn. 'Parker-Smythe will be there as well.'

'I saw that look on your face. Something else I should know?'

'Stanley asked if I'd mind... They want to look into our Bursar's background.'

'So,' said Henry pursing his lips, 'Anthony Parker-Smythe and Robert York are going to be investigated.'

'I didn't say that, Henry. Anyway, Stanley said it will all be very discreet. The men won't know they are...' There was a knock on the door and the High Master's secretary entered. 'Ah, coffee. Thank you, Mary.'

Henry Trevanion sipped his coffee and mulled over what Llywelyn had just told him. Over the years, Henry had lost the impetuosity of his youth. Experience had taught him patience. In the eyes of his younger colleagues he was now the wise counsellor to whom they could turn for advice. He was indeed a shrewd old bird.

Being somewhat underweight for his age and height, Henry Trevanion, LLM seemed rather frail; his silver-handled walking stick contributed to this illusion of frailty. His head, trunk and legs were sensibly proportioned but his neck was scrawny and a trifle too long. In a particular light and from a distance he appeared bald; but with the light behind him, close inspection of the top of his head revealed fine, short golden hairs reminiscent of the stubble on a cornfield after harvest. The skin of his upper eyelids had begun to sag and partially hide his grey-green eyes magnified by the large lenses of his tortoiseshell spectacles perched precariously on his small beaked nose. Even in his youth, Henry had never experimented with a moustache or beard so there was no hair on his face to hide the wrinkles. He had never had a loud voice but like a good actor or teacher, Henry could whisper and be clearly heard in every corner of the courtroom.

'So there's trouble ahead,' said the shrewd and extremely tough old bird. 'Perhaps we should launch our own inquiry into Major Anthony Parker-Smythe.'

'I wish you wouldn't sound so pleased about...'

'Come, come! Llywelyn. When's the last time you had any excitement at Beaumont?' Just at that moment the sound of Dr Carratt's final demonstration shook the air. 'It seems I spoke too soon, old boy. Was that gunfire?'

'Carratt!' said Llywelyn. 'Dr Carratt as usual. Starting the term with a bang.'

'I trust he didn't reduce your number of boys or damage...'

'Why did you say that?' said Llywelyn.

'Say what?'

'You hope he didn't reduce the number of boys.'

'I was just being flippant. I'm sorry,' said Henry.

'What was behind your flippant remark about the number of boys?'

'Your major endowment and your charitable status," said Henry. 'If I remember correctly, the number of pupils currently at Beaumont fulfils the conditions of the trust. Lose just one boy and you'll lose the endowment and maybe your charitable status. A disaster for you and probably the end of Beaumont Abbey.'

* * * * *

Dr Carratt was still wearing his laboratory coat when he walked into the Common Room for the mid-morning coffee break. He checked his pigeonhole then scanned the notice board. There was note from the Second Master reminding everyone that the Governors were meeting on Wednesday and therefore the small library would be out of bounds. Quentin Waite, Head of History, was in his usual corner in his usual chair hurrying through the Times crossword at his usual speed. Greg Watson, PE and Geography, was having an animated conversation with Reginald de Vere, the Second Master.

'Did Walter forget to give the High Master notice?' asked Greg.

'I really couldn't tell you, Greg. All I know is... Walter has not officially resigned.'

'So I've absolutely no hope of taking over the PE department in September.'

'Why don't you talk to Walter?' said Reg.

'What good will that do,' said Greg. 'It will just make things awkward.'

'Cheer up,' said Reg. 'He'll have to retire next year.'

'Yes, I know but it means I'm stuck on my present salary for another year.'

'Don't forget there should be a pay rise in September. That's the main item on the agenda for the Governors' meeting on Wednesday,' said Reg.

'Any idea how much we'll get?'

'Sorry, Greg,' said Reg, excusing himself. 'I must have a word with Dr Carratt.'

'Hello Reg,' said Phil. 'Greg giving you a hard time again?'

'You know Greg. Asks me questions I can't answer.'

'It'll be about money or Walter retiring or more computer room time for his geography. My guess is money today,' said Phil. 'I mean... even if Walter retires this year and Greg gets his job, he won't get much more as head of department. I mean... things are pretty tight at the moment, so I don't reckon the Governors will give us much of a pay rise.'

'You could be right,' said Reg.

'If Greg is short of cash he should rob a bank,' said Phil. 'I know... Greg and the staff should form a league of gentlemen... like in that 1958 film with Jack Hawkins and Nigel Patrick. I'll provide the explosives to open the safe...'

One member of staff who overheard Phil left the Common Room deep in thought.

* * * * *

CHAPTER 9

"I had a terrible education. I attended a school for emotionally disturbed teachers." Woody Allen

* * * * *

At nine thirty on Tuesday morning, Angus MacKay entered his security code for the current week and pushed open the door of the three-story building, an unprepossessing fortress of grimy sandstone to which passers-by never gave a second glance, if indeed they ever gave it a first glance. In sharp contrast to the bleak outer walls and relatively small windows, the interior was surprisingly light, airy and modern; or, one should say, as modern as Stanley Garnet would allow in the designs prepared by the company awarded the contract for refurbishing the offices of Banwell, Garnet and York.

The heavy main door had hissed shut and secured itself before Angus reached the curved marble-topped desk and the elderly receptionist holding the fort behind it.

'Good morning, sir. Nice morning,' said the gnarled ex-serviceman.

'Aye. It's going 't be a grand day, Jack, right enough,' said Angus.

'Not going to be too warm for you, I hope, Mr MacKay.'

'No. Not for me, Jack,' Angus said. Then without a trace of a smile on his thin lips, he said, 'It might just turn out to be a bit too hot for some.'

'By the way, sir,' said Jack apologetically as though it was his fault, 'the lift is on the blink again.'

'Never use it unless I have to,' said Angus.

'Part of your keep fit plan for your fell running?'

'Every little helps, Jack,' Angus said. 'Mr York in yet?'

'No, not yet, sir. He's usually in by 10 o'clock if he's coming in. His secretary, Mrs Woods, came in fifteen minutes ago.' said Jack, getting the lady's name and title wrong.

Angus took the stairs two at a time to the third floor and knocked on the outer office door. Robert York's personal assistant, Sheila Forest, stopped work on her computer and looked up as soon as she heard the knock. Before she could say *come in*, Angus was inside and closing the door behind him. Sheila smiled nervously and said her boss was not in yet. The nervous smile was replaced by a frown that wrinkled her forehead when Angus said it was her he had come to see.

'Actually,' said Angus, 'it's your computer I have come to investigate.'

'My computer?'

'Yes,' said Angus, 'and the one on your boss's desk.'

'I don't understand,' said Sheila.

'It's a security issue. Nothing for you to worry about, lassie,' said Angus. 'I need a wee bit of time on your machine just now. So meantime, I'm afraid you'll just have tae find something else to do. OK?'

'Can I just finish this report?' said Sheila.

'Aye. I don't see why not,' said Angus. 'Mind if I help myself to a drop of coffee?'

'No. Of course not,' said Sheila. 'Do you take milk and sugar?'

'No thanks, lassie. Black will do just fine.'

When she had printed out the report and put it on her boss's desk, Sheila told Angus she would go and make herself useful in another office and leave him in peace. At the doorway, she turned and asked if Mr York had been informed that the computers were going to be examined. When Angus shook his head and told her it was a just minor routine not worth bothering her boss about, she disappeared down the corridor without closing the door and without divulging her password.

In his role as Forensic Accountant and Forensic Technologist – titles more in vogue in America than Britain – he was used to navigating computer systems to recover data that have been deleted, encrypted, hidden or otherwise lost. He found Sheila's password in the all too common place. It was pencilled on the inside cover of the computer's instruction manual in the top drawer of her desk. As soon as he was logged in, Angus looked at the file structure. It was more or less as he expected. This computer was used mainly for routine office work. Nevertheless, he connected it to equipment he carried in his case and began making a disk image file of the hard drive.

'Good morning, Angus,' said Robert York striding in through the open doorway.

'Good morning, Mr York. Nice morning for a change.'

'I think it's going to be too warm for my liking,' said Robert.

'Aye, it could be,' said Angus. 'It could be, right enough.'

'Sheila said you were here. Is there a problem with her computer?'

'Hopefully not,' said Angus. 'No, I've been asked to take a look at our entire system. That means the servers in the basement and every computer in the building, yours and Sheila's included.'

'So what are you looking for exactly?' Robert asked.

'Potential security breaches in the firewalls. Bugs in the software for potential malfunction. Physical errors on hard drives. The usual sort of stuff,' said Angus.

'I thought that's what we pay IT maintenance for,' said Robert. 'Aren't they supposed to keep an eye on things for us.'

'Aye, right enough,' said Angus, ' but somebody has to keep an eye on those IT fellows.'

'Are you going to be much longer? Sheila has work to do for my annual meeting with the Governors at Beaumont Abbey tomorrow,' Robert said tetchily.

'Och, sorry, I dinnae know that,' Angus lied smoothly. 'I'm nearly finished here. I'll come back and do yours tomorrow, if that's alright.'

'Yes. Yes. That'll be fine,' said Robert. 'Routine, you say?'

'Absolutely pure routine,' lied Angus. 'Nothing for you to be concerned about.' When he had finished, Angus popped his head around the door of Robert's inner office to signal his departure. 'I'm off then,' said Angus. 'See you tomorrow. Och, no! You'll be away.'

'Governor's meeting at Beaumont,' said Robert. 'Bit of a bore to tell the truth but I can rely on Jean-Pierre, their chef, to do us proud.'

'That's nice to hear,' said Angus. 'You're lucky if you've somebody you can rely on.'

* * * * *

The academic gown had seen better days but it still served to protect Dr Heilbronn's two-piece brown tweed suit from chalk dust. It also reinforced the picture young boys had of the Head of Mathematics; a large, fierce bear, from the Black Forest, standing on its hind legs, growling gutturally, pawing the air and failing totally to communicate.

The sixteen members of his Lower Sixth top maths class habitually moaned about the amount of work he dished out and the high standard he set them but not because they had genuine grounds for complaints; it was their way of asserting their superiority over the other classes and, in their own roundabout way, expressing their admiration for the brilliant mathematician that their teacher was.

'Good morning, gentlemen,' said Dr Heilbronn, extracting a sheaf of papers from his briefcase. 'If you have no objection, I should like that we begin this morning with those simple geometrical problems I posed for your entertainment during your Easter break.' If you would be so kind, Mr Brett, to take a sheet and pass the rest around.'

Centred at the top of the page was the heading: THEOREMS IN GEOMETRY. Centred immediately below the heading was: [Who? Where? When? What?

How?] Underneath and well spaced out were five names: Apollonius, Feuerbach, Menelaus, Pappus and Thales. Dr Heilbonn allowed a short time for everyone to look at the sheet then said, 'Any questions before we begin?'

'Why no why, sir?'

'A good question, Mr Brett, but I do not intend to be digressed into philosophy today,' said Dr Heilbronn. 'Mr Chéng! You have a question?'

'Please! I have question.'

'Very well, let's hear it,' said Dr Heilbronn.

'Why names important? Apollonius called Apollonius of Perga but he not born in Perga. Why when important? Nobody knows birth and death of Apollonius for sure; maybe born 262 BC; maybe died 190 BC.'

'What's your point, Mr Chéng?'

'I think only what and how important. Please!' The bright student held his breath.

'I agree, Chéng of Singapore. Fortunately, you had the good sense to do what I asked. I presume you know the who and why of the others on my list.' Before Chéng could reply, Dr Heilbronn said, 'Be so good as to tell us the what, Mr Chéng.'

'Apollonius theorem, sir?'

'If you please.'

'In any triangle, sum of squares on any two sides equals twice the square on half the third side plus twice the square on the median bisecting third side.'

'Thank you, Mr Chéng,' said Dr Heilbronn. 'Now would one of you rephrase that.'

'If BM is a median of a triangle ABC,' began Brett, 'and if AB = c, BC = a, AC = b, and BM = m, the median, then $a^2 + c^2 = 2.m^2 + b^2/2$.'

'Thank you, Mr Brett. Mr Zháng!' said Dr Heilbronn, 'Would you be so kind as to share with the rest of us what you are whispering to Mr Chéng?'

'Please, sir, I agree with Chéng. Who and when not important.'

'I see. So you did not bother to find out the who and when for Thales?'

'Thales of Miletus was Greek like Apollonius. Maybe born 624 BC. Maybe died 546 BC. We not know for sure,' said Zháng.

'I agree, Zháng of Hong Kong. And the Thales theorem.'

'If A, B and C are points on a circle where the line AC is a diameter of the circle, then the angle ABC is a right angle.'

'Thank you Mr Zháng... You wish to make another point?'

'Yes, please. If they had computers in time of Thales, we know all about him now for sure. Computers have good memory. Keep accurate records. Do not lie.' Rupert Jardine almost laughed out loud when he heard that.

'Mr Jardine!' said Dr Heilbronn, seeing the look on his star pupil's face, 'You have a question?'

'Did you know Feuerbach personally, sir?' Rupert asked, keeping a straight face as he saw the good doctor rise to the bait.

'I may look old to you, Mr Jardine, but I am not that old. Karl Feuerbach died on the 12th March in 1834. He was not quite thirty-four years old. Even if he had died only last year, I probably would not have known him. Karl was born in Jena and lived in Ansbach where his father was president of the appeals court. Karl studied at the universities of Erlangen and Freiburg. Those were not my universities. He published his elegant theorem in 1822. It was his only success. The rest of his life was a failure. The wretched fellow couldn't even commit suicide. He once threw himself out of a window only to land unhurt in a bank of soft snow. Ach, ein dummkopf!'

'The authorities let him teach at Hof and,' Dr Heilbronn paused, closed his eyes, pinched the bridge of his nose then continued, 'when they thought he had recovered from a nervous breakdown, they let him teach at Erlangen.' Dr Heilbronn opened his eyes, took his hand away from his face and went on, 'However, they made him retire when he took a sword into a classroom and threatened to cut off the head of any student who could not solve a problem he had set.' Dr Heilbronn paused again, blinked and, looking sternly at Jardine, said, 'Ach, so. Perhaps he was not a complete dunderhead.'

Realising he had been, as he would put it, *digressed*, he stroked his beard, ran his finger down the scar on his left cheek then said, 'So, Mr Jardine, Feuerbach's theorem if you please.'

'For any triangle, the nine-point circle is tangent to the incircle and to each of the three excircles of the triangle.'

'Thank you, Jardine of Princeton. Gentlemen, I shall expect to see your statements and proofs of all five theorems at our next lesson.'

* * * * *

Any meeting of the Governing Board of Directors gives Beaumont staff extra work. The meeting on the first Wednesday of Trinity supplements this extra work with a large helping of anxiety, with uncertainty causing the greatest concern. The High Master's report on the academic year to date and on the school's future prospects should go hand in glove with the Bursar's report on the school's financial position. Dr Llywelyn Pugh-Jones and Mr Anthony Parker-Smyth had their own reasons to be anxious this year.

Henry Trevanion's remark about pupil numbers, endowments and charitable status was still gnawing at Llywelyn's stomach when Mary entered his study.

'Would you look this over, High Master' said Mary Cranborne, handing Llywelyn a copy of the report he had drafted and printed out. 'I have marked in the margin some sections you might want to reconsider.'

'Thank you, Mary.'

'It's almost ten thirty. Would you like your decaffeinated coffee now?'

'Yes, please,' said Llywelyn, thinking decaffeinated was little better than none at all. 'Would you bring a cup for yourself, Mary.'

'If you insist, High Master,' said Mary, hiding her surprise.

Mary brought the coffees and took her seat in front of Llywelyn's desk. She took a sip from her cup and waited.

'I'd like your candid opinion of this report to the Governors.'

'This is a rather unusual request, High Master, and a bit awkward,' she said.

'Why awkward?'

'Well, you see. I'm not sure it's my place to...'

'How long have we worked together now, Mary? What is it? Eight years.'

'Yes, High Master, I have been your secretary for nearly eight years.'

'And how many of my reports have you prepared for the Governors?'

'None, actually. You prepare the reports. I simply type and print them.'

'Not quite true,' said Llywelyn. 'No, not quite true. I have always relied upon you to check them for grammatical errors.'

'Yes but...'

'And from time to time I think, no I *know*, you make small changes; little clarifications, shall we say.'

'High Master, I'm sorry if...'

'No need for you to be sorry. On the contrary, I am sorry not to have...' Llywelyn hesitated. 'The thing is, Mary, just correcting my grammar is hardly making proper use of your experience and qualifications. No. No. You should do more, much more...'

'I'm not sure that...'

'Mary, I want you to tell me what message you think I'm going to be sending to our Governors tomorrow with this report. Is it the right message or the wrong one?'

Mary Cranborne, BA, put down her empty cup, picked up her copy of the draft report. In all her years at Beaumont she had never been asked to comment upon, no not comment upon, to *criticise* a High Master's report to the Governors. She was flattered. She was anxious. She was honoured. She was in fact delighted.

'You do want me to be frank, High Master?'

'Absolutely. Perfectly frank. Tomorrow's meeting may be the most important one ever.'

'Very well. I'll be frank,' said Mary. 'If you deliver this report tomorrow after one of Jean-Pierre Escoffier's lunches, I fear even the Rt Hon Lord Crispin Bartholomew in the chair will find it hard to keep his eyes and ears open.'

'It's too long, is that it?' said Llywelyn.

'Yes, I think it's too long but it's also rather…' Mary paused then blurted out, 'dull.'

'Have all my reports been *dull*?' Mary nodded. 'Oh dear!'

'I'm sorry, High Master, but you ask me to be frank.'

'Yes, I did. So how would you have written it?'

'Perhaps the best way to answer your question would be for me to redraft it.'

Later that afternoon the High Master sighed with relief when he finished reading Mary Cranborne's redraft. The first page began with a concise summary of the school's achievements to date and the plans for the future. This was followed by a numbered list of topics for discussion: (1) Staffing, (2) Building, (3) Finance, (4) Charitable Status and (5) Directors. The details, necessary and sufficient for the Board of Governors to make informed decisions, were given under the relevant topic headings on the subsequent pages comprising the body of the report.

* * * * *

'Just one moment, Mr York,' said Mrs Susan Taylor, 'I'll see if he is free.' She put the accountant on hold and rang through to Anthony Parker-Smythe. 'I have Mr York on the line for you, Bursar. Shall I put him through?'

'Hello Bob,' said Nosey Parker. 'All set for tomorrow?'

'Yes,' said Robert York, junior partner in Banwell, Garnet and York. 'What about you?'

'Just putting the final touches to my report now,' said Nosey.

'Any problems?' said Bob.

'Not really. There'll be the usual fuss over the proposed increase in staff salaries and arguments about finding the money for the sports hall. What about you?'

'No problems at my end, although...'

'What?' said Parker-Smythe, his nose sensing something might be up.

'Angus MacKay was in my office this morning.'

'Who's he when he's at home?' asked Nosey.

'Angus is a canny Scot. Stanley Garnet calls him our trouble shooter. This week he's checking on the work of our IT department. Claims it's routine checking on security; firewall security, software malfunction, hard drive errors. He was inspecting my PA's computer this morning. He'll be looking at mine tomorrow. I shouldn't be surprised if he doesn't turn up at Beaumont and take a look at your system.'

'Why would he do that?' asked Nosey.

'We're your accountants, don't forget. Angus will probably want to make sure your systems are sound. We couldn't have faults in your system feeding false data into our systems and generating errors in the accounts we produce and audit for you,' said Bob.

'So it's just routine stuff?' said Nosey suspiciously.

'Pure routine, old boy. Absolutely nothing to worry about,' said Bob. 'Relax. We've got you covered.'

It was another dry, sunny morning when the Bursar stepped out of the main building and headed for the Cavendish. Tony Smith had not received much in the way of a formal education and, unlike Colin Harper and

Rupert Jardine, would not have been elected to Mensa, the high IQ society. But the Bursar was no fool. He kept his wits about him. He lived by the words on a poster in his secretary's office; a poster displaying a photograph of a barn owl and the caption *half of being smart is knowing what you're dumb at.*

The brilliant, shy, somewhat reclusive and, in Tony Smith's opinion, quietly attractive Colin Harper was alone in the computer room when the Bursar knocked on the door and walked in.

'G-good m-morning, Bursar,' stuttered Colin. 'W-what brings y-you h-here?'

'No need to stand on ceremony, Colin,' said the Bursar. 'Please. Call me Anthony.'

'S-sorry, B-b-bursar, b-b-but…'

'Don't upset yourself, Colin. Please. I don't like to see you get upset.'

'Th-thank you,' said Colin. 'It's j-just th-that…'

'I understand,' said Tony. 'Look, I just dropped in to ask you a question about computers. About my computer actually.'

'W-w-what about it?'

'How secure is it?'

'P-pretty secure, I'd say,' said Colin, stuttering less as their conversation moved into his area of expertise. 'You use a strong password and change it regularly, right?'

'Oh, yes,' said Tony. 'Just the way you taught me. But what about my files?'

'I showed you how to hide and password protect your files, right?'

'Yes. Yes, you did,' said Tony. 'I'm really thinking about some sensitive files…'

'Files you don't want anybody to know about, right?'

'Yes. That's right. Are they secure?'

'As secure as I could make them,' said Colin. 'They're hidden, password protected and encrypted.'

'So only I can access them?'

'Pretty much,' said Colin after a slight hesitation.

'When you say pretty much, you mean…?'

'I suppose I could get access,' said Colin, 'but then, I'm an expert.' Just at that moment Rupert Jardine came into the room. 'Speaking of experts.'

When the Bursar had left the room and closed the door, Rupert gave Colin a bear hug and asked him if he could use his master computer. When Colin asked why, Rupert explained, 'Old Klaus wants us to prove five geometry theorems.'

'Don't be disrespectful, Rupert,' said Colin, 'It's Dr Heilbronn to you.'

'Anyway,' said Rupert shrugging his shoulders, 'he wants us to prove the theorems of Apollonius, Feuerbach, Menelaus, Pappus and Thales.'

'Feuerbach's theorem?' said Colin. 'That's tricky. How are you going to prove that one?'

'With a computer.'

'Tell me more,' said Colin.

'I'll use co-ordinate geometry to transpose the problem into a system of equations and apply algebraic elimination theory. The only difficulty will be reducibility. As long as I choose the right variables, I should be able to avoid large polynomials in the elimination algorithms.'

'I see,' Colin said, even though he did not. 'Well, you'd better get on with it.'

'Should be finished before lunch,' said Rupert. 'No time this afternoon.'

'Ah, yes. You'll be out on the cricket pitch.'

'Just a warm up practice game,' said Rupert. 'You should come and watch.'

'I'd like to but I think I should take a look at the Bursar's computer.'

'Worried about security, is he? Got files he doesn't want anybody to see, I'll bet.'

* * * * *

The sun was still shining but there was a light easterly breeze cutting across the pitch as Rupert began his smooth, flowing fifteen yard run up to the wicket. Washbrook, the opening batsman, raised his bat and kept his eye on the ball in Rupert's hand. When Rupert reached the crease, he arched into the classic side-on position so his entire body was like a tightly coiled spring. Washbrook moved onto his back foot the instant the ball left the bowler's hand. He judged it perfectly. As the ball swung away, Washbrook angled the face of his bat and guided the ball wide of the three slips to the boundary for four.

As he walked back to the start of his run, Rupert polished one side of the ball on the side of his white flannels. He turned to face the batsman and began his run, again holding the ball in an outswinger grip. Rupert's second ball was even faster than the first but Washbrook again timed his shot perfectly, cutting the ball past the slip fielders for another four. No bowler, least of all Rupert, likes to be treated in such a way. The instant Washbrook saw this third ball leave Jardine's hand, he moved onto his back foot but slightly across the wicket. He misjudged it badly. The ball did not swing away. Instead it dropped short, broke back and caught Washbrook a savage blow in his midriff.

Jardine joined the other players gathering around Washbrook doubled up on the grass.

'Sorry old chap,' said Rupert who was smiling inwardly and not sorry at all. 'You OK?'

'Yes. I'm fine,' said Washbrook who was inwardly cursing himself and not fine at all.

'Are you fit to carry on?' said Edrich, the coach and former professional cricketer.

'Yes, sir. I'm fine, really,' said Washbrook.

Rupert's next ball proved otherwise. It was a very fast but very obvious inswinger that uprooted leg stump. 'Well bowled!' said Washbrook sportingly as he trudged off the field, less confident than he had been four balls earlier. He may have been the first this season but he would not be the last person to be hurt by Rupert Jardine.

* * * * *

CHAPTER 10

"This is only my suggestion," said the chairman of the board to the directors. "It's for to you to bear in mind whose suggestion it is." Anon

* * * * *

It was Wednesday morning and eight thirty. Angus MacKay punched in his security code and entered the sandstone fortress protecting the offices of Banwell, Garnet and York, Chartered Accountants. He waved to Jack, the ex-serviceman behind the reception but hurried to the stairs before the old fellow could engage him in conversation. As usual, Angus took the stairs two at a time and, not even slightly out of breath, quickly reached Robert York's lair on the third floor.

He unlocked the door and entered the empty outer office; he was fairly certain it would be another half hour before Sheila Forest arrived. He took a set of special keys from his case and, at the second attempt, found one to unlock the filing cabinet standing in the corner by the door into York's inner sanctum. The labels on the suspension files simplified his search. It took him less than twenty minutes to photograph all the interesting documents and re-lock the cabinet. When Robert York's PA arrived at five minutes to nine, Angus was in her chair at her desk sipping a cup of black coffee.

'Oh!' Sheila said, obviously startled. 'You gave me a turn.'

'Och, sorry lassie,' said Angus. 'I dinnae mean tae startle ye.'

'How did you get in here? I thought I'd locked the door when I left yesterday.'

'I hoped you wouldn't mind,' said Angus, 'I made myself a cup of coffee.'

'No. No, of course not,' said Sheila, still somewhat flustered. 'Help yourself.'

'It's a wee bit cloudy this morning. We might be getting some rain.'

'What? Cloudy… Rain… Yes, I suppose so,' said Sheila. 'Can I help you, Mr MacKay?'

'Aye, you could,' said Angus. 'Would you mind unlocking the door into your boss's room. I need to take a look at his computer.'

'Oh! Yes. Yes, of course. You looked at mine yesterday. Any problems?'

'If you'd just unlock the door, please lassie,' said Angus.

The Forensic Accountant and Technologist entered the inner sanctum and closed the door quietly but firmly. He had made it crystal clear that he should not be disturbed and, when Sheila had asked, he said no, he would not want any more coffee.

He knew Robert York would not have left his passwords lying around so he did not waste time looking for them. With his not inconsiderable amount of experience and the help of a little gadget, it took him less than two minutes to log in and start plumbing the depths of the two hard drives. Angus ignored the visible, unprotected files; he was after the hidden, encrypted files. It took him most of the morning to find all of them but find them he did.

When Sheila tapped on the door to say she was going for lunch and to ask if he would like anything, he thanked her - he rarely bothered with lunch - and asked what time she would be back. When she said she usually took an hour for lunch and would be back by half past one, Angus nodded and wished her *bon appétit*. He used the hour she was out of the office to sift through Robert York's personal filing cabinet and photograph some very interesting documents that cross-referenced some encrypted files on the computer. The most intriguing documents and files made mention of a Tony Smith, some off-shore companies and some accounts in Guernsey in the Channel Islands.

* * * * *

'Mrs Taylor and I have finished in the small library, High Master.'

'Thank you, Mary.'

'Do you really want both of us there during the meeting?'

'Yes please. I'd like both of you to take notes. I know you do shorthand. What about Susan?'

'I don't know,' said Mary. 'Probably. She's very competent at most things.'

'I'd also like both of you to join us at high table to... how shall I put it?' said Llywelyn.

'Keep our eyes and ears open to get a sense of what the Governors are really thinking?'

'Yes. That's it,' said Llywelyn, 'People often drop their guard over a glass of wine and a good lunch, especially one prepared by Jean-Pierre.'

'Is Mrs Pugh-Jones coming to lunch?'

'I'm afraid so... Oh, dear, that doesn't sound... What I meant was that Louise will be there to keep an eye on me,' said Llywelyn. 'Watching what I eat and drink, you know. I have pointed out to my good wife that I only attend one Jean-Pierre feast per term.'

'Perhaps,' said Mary, 'I could arrange for her to take lunch next to the Cultural Attaché from the American Embassy, Warren Cooper. He's quite engaging.'

'Ah, what a splendid idea,' said Llywelyn. 'Just the diversion I might need, Mary.'

Lawrence St John Beecroft, the Head Boy (or PD - Potissimus Discipulus), together with three other senior prefects, hovered in the main entrance to greet the Governing Board of Directors. As usual, the first to arrive was the Chairman, the Rt Hon Lord Crispin Bartholomew of Temple Meads, PC, MA, DPhil. Handing his tightly rolled black umbrella and leather briefcase to the PD the Privy Counsellor said, 'It might rain on your parade this afternoon, St John (pronouncing it sinjin).' The Chairman never forgot a name or a face. He also remembered the Head Boy was an officer in the

RAF contingent of the Beaumont Combined Cadet Force and the CCF assembled for drill and training on Wednesday afternoons.

'Good morning, Lord Bartholomew,' said Mary. 'Coffee? Black with one spoonful of brown sugar, I believe.'

'And how is the High Master's Secretary today?' inquired the Chairman. 'Still keeping Beaumont running as smoothly as a Swiss watch, I dare say.'

One by one the other eight Board members arrived to be met by the senior prefects who ushered them to the small library where Mary Cranborne dispensed coffees or teas and ignored various flattering remarks about her capabilities.

'Everyone of the directors has arrived, Bursar,' said Susan Taylor poking her head into the Bursar's room.

'As soon as you've finished your coffee then, Robert,' said Anthony Parker-Smythe.

'Any idea what's on the luncheon menu?' the school accountant asked.

'Mrs Taylor! Do you have the luncheon menu for high table today?'

'Here you are, Bursar,' said Susan handing him a card bearing the school crest.

'Thank you, Mrs Taylor,' said Parker-Smythe, handing the menu to Robert.

'Right! Let's see what we've got to look forward to…'

Soupe à l'Oignon
Poulet au Cidre Breton
avec
des Petits Pois et des Pommes Frites
Crêpe Suzette

'Don't keep me in suspense,' said the Bursar. Robert read out the menu and Parker-Smythe said, 'What's that in English?'

'Onion soup. Chicken, peas and chips followed by pancakes,' said Robert. Neither man noticed the look on Susan Taylor's face when she heard the word *pancakes*.

* * * * *

The Rt Hon Lord Crispin Bartholomew opened the meeting of the governing Board of Directors at 10:30 a.m. precisely. He sat at the head of the table to see clearly everyone present and to let everyone clearly see who was in charge.

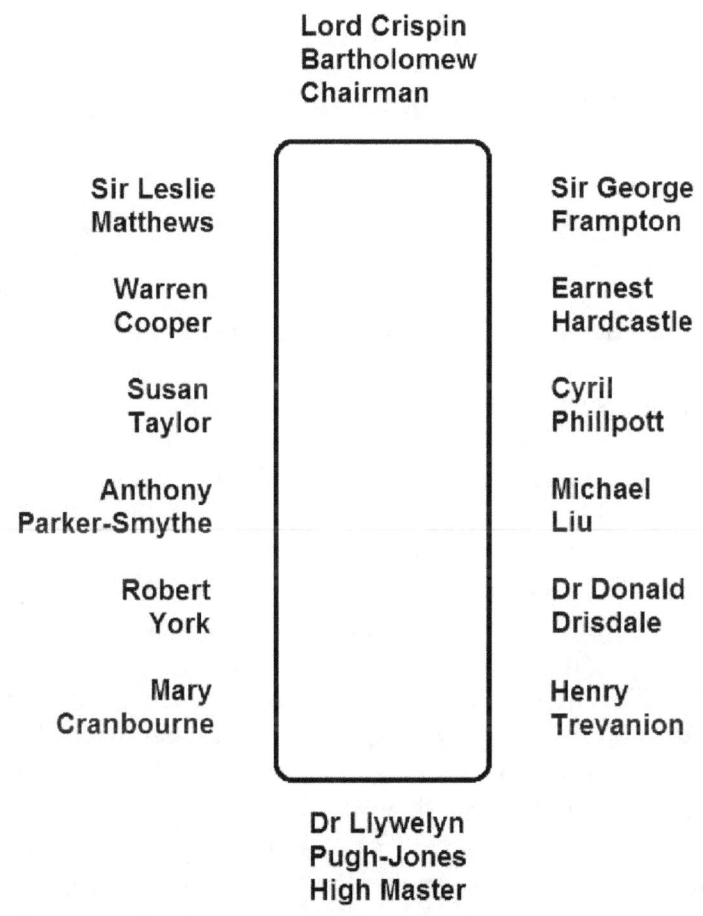

Lord Crispin Bartholomew Chairman

Sir Leslie Matthews	**Sir George Frampton**
Warren Cooper	**Earnest Hardcastle**
Susan Taylor	**Cyril Phillpott**
Anthony Parker-Smythe	**Michael Liu**
Robert York	**Dr Donald Drisdale**
Mary Cranbourne	**Henry Trevanion**

Dr Llywelyn Pugh-Jones High Master

On the chairman's immediate right and left were Sir Leslie Matthews, OBE and Prof Sir George Frampton MA, PhD, FRS. Warren Cooper from the American Embassy sat next to Sir Leslie and Earnest Hardcastle, MA, FioD, regional manager of the National Westminster Bank, sat next to Sir George.

At the other end of the polished walnut table, facing the chairman, was Dr Llywelyn Pugh-Jones, the High Master. On his immediate right was Henry Trevanion, LLM, the school solicitor, and on his immediate left was Mary Cranborne, BA.

Robert York sat next to Mary and Dr Donald Drisdale, MB, ChB representing the parents sat next to Henry. The remaining seats were occupied on the one side by the Bursar (next to Robert) and Susan Taylor (next to the Bursar) and on the other side by Michael Liú, FRCS, representing the Old Boys, and Cyril Phillpott, representing the DES (Department of Education and Science).

'First item on the agenda,' said the chairman. 'Apologies for absence.' Then looking up and down the table, he said, 'None! Thank you all for coming.' After a pause, he looked at Dr Pugh-Jones and said, 'Second item. The High Master's report.' Llywelyn cleared his throat.

'Thank you, Lord Bartholomew. May I begin by publicly expressing my thanks to Mary Cranborne for her invaluable help in the preparation of this report.' After pausing and smiling at his secretary, Llywelyn continued. 'As you can see, we have listed the five areas of concern on the first page.' Another pause while the Directors found the list.

'The first issue is *Staffing* for the next academic year. Our two language assistants will leave at the end of term having completed their year with us. We have two suitable replacements lined up but I need your authority to engage them. You may wish to postpone your decision until I have spoken on section 3 of my report - *Finance* - and you have received the Bursar's report.

Two junior members of staff are leaving us in the summer, taking their next steps up the ladder. I need your authority to replace them.'

'You said two *junior* staff, High Master.'

'Yes, Mr Chairman. Billington from the History Department and Osgood from Biology.'

'Walter Barnes staying on another year then?'

'Yes, Mr Chairman.'

'Bit long in the tooth for physical education, I'd have thought,' mused the Lord.'

'I guess the guy is in good shape and can still do the job, right?' said the American.

'He's in excellent condition,' said Llywelyn, 'and he has a first class second in Gregory Watson.'

'This guy Watson,' continued Warren Cooper. 'Hoping to get his boss's spot, was he?'

'So, to be clear,' said Lord Bartholomew cutting short the interchange, 'We are well staffed but we need two replacement junior teachers and we must discuss whether or not to replace the two language assistants. Pray continue High Master.'

'Section 2 – *Buildings*. Aside from the usual maintenance and running repairs, the costs of which are rising as our Bursar will no doubt confirm, we are looking to build a new sports hall. This is an ambitious project. The Bursar's report will include a proposed budget. We shall need your authority to pursue this.'

'What's wrong with the present gymnasium?' asked Michael Liú, an Old Beaumontian and eminent cardiac surgeon.

'Did they play basketball here in your time, Dr Liú?' asked Warren Cooper.

'No. No we didn't,' said Michael Liú.

'I'm not surprised. There's hardly room in the gym for the badminton court,' said the American.

'What facilities will the proposed sports hall offer that the present gymnasium does not?' asked the chairman.

'You will find a detailed answer to that question, Lord Bartholomew, in Section 2 in the body of our report. May I now move on to Section 3 – *Finance*?'

'Please do,' said the chairman.

'As the Bursar's detailed report will show, our expenditure increases because of increases in teachers' salaries, utility bills and obligatory NI contributions. We have no control over National Insurance costs and there's little we can do to reduce utility bills. The major factor over which we do have some control is salaries.'

'Teachers in State schools hoped for a twelve percent increase next September. Their pay rise will probably be...' He hesitated and looked at Anthony Parker-Smythe.

'Ten and a half percent, High Master,' said the Bursar,

'Ah, yes. Thank you, Bursar,' said Llywelyn. 'This is a matter for serious discussion.'

'Indeed it is,' said the chairman. 'This is just my suggestion, of course, but I propose we defer this discussion and deal with it after the Bursar has reported?' All heads nodded in agreement. 'Good. I should like to hear what you have to say on the topic of *Charitable Status*, High Master.'

'We have set out the details in Section 4 of the report. I might summarise our concern by saying that to retain charitable status and the considerable tax benefits arising therefrom, we must satisfy the conditions of the Charities Act...' The chairman interrupted.

'Beaumont is legally required to demonstrate that its *aims* are for the *Public Benefit* and that its *purposes* are *charitable* according to the Charities Act. You already do this, High Master, by providing bursaries and scholarships to people who cannot afford your fees. Your major uncertainty rests with the Charity Commission not being willing or able to suggest the percentage of bursaries that you should offer.' Anthony Parker-Smythe interrupted.

'If I may, Lord Bartholomew. Bursaries are really subsidies we draw from the higher fees being paid by the wealthy parents and from our endowments.'

'Yes. Yes. Thank you Bursar,' said Llywelyn. 'A major concern, Lord Bartholomew, is that if we raise fees...'

'When we raise fees,' the Bursar interrupted again. 'There's no if about it.'

'Thank you, Bursar,' said Llywelyn with a scowl. 'If and when we raise fees, our numbers could fall below the minimum needed to satisfy a key condition of our major endowment.' Henry Trevanion, the school solicitor, nodded his head in agreement.

'If I may, Lord Bartholomew,' said Robert York, interrupting the High Master. 'Beaumont meets the Charity Commission's *Public Benefit Requirement* by making its facilities available to the local community. The proposed new sports hall will provide a public benefit just like the swimming pool, tennis courts and playing fields do now.'

'But you charge the public for using the facilities, I hope,' said Sir Leslie.

'We certainly do,' said the Bursar. 'And that doesn't stop them being a public benefit.'

Cyril Phillpott caught the chairman's eye and said, 'Schools recently granted charitable status awarded from five to fifteen percent of their income in means tested bursaries.'

'Beaumont?' said the chairman looking at Anthony Parker-Smyth.

'About ten or eleven percent, Lord Bartholomew.'

'Very good. Thank you for that information, Bursar,' said the chairman. 'May we move on to your final section, High Master. Lunch draws near.'

'Certainly, Lord Bartholomew,' replied Llywelyn. 'Section 5 – *Directors*. May I start by expressing my thanks to you, Sir Leslie, for your services to the school over the years. Beaumont owes you a great debt of gratitude. On behalf of the staff and pupils, past and present, I wish you and Lady Matthews a long a happy retirement.'

'May I, Lord Bartholomew, on behalf of the parents, past and present, formally propose a vote of thanks?'

'Thank you, Dr Drisdale. Seconded? Thank you Sir George. All in favour? Unanimous.'

'It will be extremely difficult, if not impossible, for anyone to fill your shoes, Sir Leslie, but I should like to recommend Randolph Jardine as your replacement.'

'Is that the guy who founded Jardine International?' asked Warren Cooper.

'Yes it is,' said Llywelyn. 'Do you know him?'

'Not personally,' said Warren, 'but I know of him. He has quite a reputation back in the States. His wife's British. She was a successful actress before she married. I've seen her face in the high society magazines. Very good looking.'

'Their son is in the Lower Sixth,' said Llywelyn. 'A brilliant mathematician according to our Dr Heilbronn.'

'Unless any member of the Board objects, I suggest we accept the recommendation of the High Master. All in favour? Excellent. Let's adjourn for lunch,' said the chairman.

* * * * *

The High Master led the way into the grand dining hall, a grade I listed building, and showed his guests to their seats at high table. Lawrence Beecroft, the PD, said the ante cibum Grace: *Benedic nobis, Domine, et omnibus tuis donis* and the school remained standing until everyone on high table had sat down. Llywelyn could not see his wife. She was sitting at the far end of the table and hidden behind Warren Cooper. The Bursar and the school accountant were opposite them. Mary Cranborne had Dr Drisdale on her left. Susan Taylor was on her right, sitting next to Dr Liú. Sir Leslie Matthews and Earnest Hardcastle were on the other side of the table, directly opposite the two secretaries.

'How long have you been in the pork pie business, Sir Leslie?' asked Earnest Hardcastle.

'Nigh on fifty-five years,' replied the owner and head of Matthews Meat Products. 'A bit longer than you've been in banking, no doubt. My granddad started the business. Dad took it on when granddad died. Dad started showing me the ropes when I was still at school. I must have been only ten the first time he showed me around the factory.'

'Will you miss it?' asked Susan Taylor.

'I might. Then again I might not. Edna – that's my second wife – wants us to cruise around the world. We might. Then again... Ah, here comes the soup. What is it?'

'It's French onion soup. Jean-Pierre prepares it the traditional way with beef stock; he puts the cheese on top then bakes it in the oven. Our chef always serves the soup with croutons,' said Mary Cranborne. '*Soupe à l'Oignon* is one of my favourite dishes.'

The soup was followed by the delicious main course of breast of chicken, roasted with Breton cider, garden peas delicately flavoured with fine herbs and French fried potatoes.

The regional manager of the National Westminster Bank held his glass to his nose, sniffed and said, 'French white Burgundy, if I'm not mistaken. The Chardonnay grape. A good choice with roast chicken.'

'Do you think the meeting is going well, Sir Leslie?' asked Susan.

'Yes. Lord Bartholomew keeps a firm grip. I like that. I can't abide time wasting.'

'Time is money,' said Susan. Sir Leslie, his mouth full of soup, nodded in agreement.

'What did you think of the meeting, Dr Drisdale?' Mary asked, turning to the representative of the parents sitting on her left.

'It's going very well. I thought the High Master's report was rather better... er... um. I thought his report was most informative. Clear and succinct,' said the doctor. 'I shall be most interested to hear what the Bursar has to say about next year's fees.'

At the other end of the table, Warren Cooper was trying to convince Louise Pugh-Jones that the Metropolitan Museum of Art in New York was the greatest art museum in the world; but of course Louise knew that the Victoria and Albert Museum was the greatest. They neither heard nor cared what Nosey and Bob were discussing. In the middle of high table, Llywelyn and Henry, sitting either side of Lord Bartholomew, were discretely informing the chairman of their concerns over the school's charitable status and the conditions of the major endowment. While on the subject of finances, they mentioned the inquiry being conducted into the background and activities of the bursar and the accountant.

'No thank you,' said Susan Taylor, waving away the desert. 'I never eat pancakes.'

'Surely you're not weight watching,' said Mary Cranborne.

'Not at the moment,' said Susan.

'So how can you possibly refuse Jean-Pierre's *Crêpe Suzette*?' said Mary.

'I just never eat pancakes, *ever*,' said Susan.

'Why on earth not?' asked Dr Liú.

'It's a long story,' said Susan.

'Come on. Let's hear it,' said Sir Leslie. 'I like a good story.'

Susan Wellborn was born in England but moved with her parents to South Africa when she was still a child. She grew up in Cape Town and was educated at Herschel Girls School, a private Anglican establishment for girls only. She was an undergraduate in the Faculty of Commerce at UCT, the oldest university in South Africa, where her studies included accountancy and business. When she was twenty-five, she met and married Roderick Taylor, a wealthy car dealer and amateur racing driver who turned professional after they had been married five years. He began driving Formula

One cars and, known as Hot Rod Taylor, became a major attraction on the Killarney track in Cape Town. In the next five years, her husband had several accidents on the circuit - one quite serious which put him in hospital for several weeks. During that time, Susan's parents died and there was growing unrest in South Africa. After nearly ten years of a childless and loveless marriage, Susan left Roderick and South Africa for good.

'Why do I never eat pancakes? I was at a dinner party in Cape Town. We were served pancakes for desert. It was Shrove Tuesday. The pancakes were delicious. Someone said so to our hostess and made the particular point that the pancakes were surprisingly warm - a change from the usual cold stodge. The hostess accepted the compliment graciously and then led us all into the kitchen so we could thank the cook.'

'Lefu was a large, fat, sweaty black man, naked from the waist up except for the apron covering his front. He beamed with delight when one of the guests asked him to make some more pancakes. Lefu – his African name means *sickness* or *death*, by the way – did as he was asked. While he was cooking the first pancake, another guest asked how he managed to keep the pancakes warm. He beamed again and, when he had tossed the first pancake a couple of times, he took the pancake out of the pan and slipped it under his armpit! I, and I believe most of the guests, have never eaten pancakes since that evening.'

The High Master rose to his feet. The guests on high table and the rest of the school stood up. Lawrence Beecroft, the PD, said the post cibum Grace: *Benedictus sit Deus in donis suis. Sit nomen Dei benedictum* and the school remained standing until everyone on high table had left the dining hall.

Back in the small library with everyone comfortably seated, Sir Leslie Matthews said, 'Before we begin, Lord Bartholomew, may I say how much I have enjoyed my time as a Director on the Board, particularly under your chairmanship. As a token of my esteem and with the agreement of the High Master, I have arranged for every member of staff and boy at Beaumont to receive, once a year, a complimentary pork pie. The *free* pies will be delivered, fresh of course, on the 21st of September which I hope will become known as Matthews Day.'

'What a cute idea,' said Warren Cooper. 'Great advertising too, Sir Leslie.'

'I don't deny it's good for business as well as the school,' said Sir Leslie, 'What you Americans call a win-win situation, I believe.'

'The High Master confided over lunch that your generosity does not stop with these pork pies,' said Lord Bartholomew, allowing himself the ghost of a smile.

'Sir Leslie has set up a trust fund to provide each year a full scholarship for a deserving pupil taking Business Studies, Economics or Mathematics in the Sixth Form,' said Llywelyn. 'The award will be known as the Lady Edna Matthews Scholarship. We are all most grateful to you, Sir Leslie.' When the *hear, hears* from all present had died down, Lord Bartholomew called upon the Bursar to present his report.

Anthony Parker-Smythe began confidently enough. He drew everyone's attention to the papers which Susan Taylor had thanklessly distributed and expressed his appreciation to Robert York for his expert help. Just before the Bursar started to bore the Board, Mary Cranborne stood up and closed the windows. She shut out the noises of the Combined Cadet Force but unfortunately cut off the supply of fresh air to the room.

'You should have three documents. A balance sheet, a statement of financial activities (SOFA) and an income and expenditure account. The balance sheet,' he said, before everyone had found it, 'shows our recognised assets, liabilities and fund categories.'

'I don't seem to have... Ah, sorry. Yes, I have it,' said Prof Sir George Frampton.

'The SOFA,' continued the Bursar without pausing, 'shows all incoming and expended resources, with all changes in the funds reconciled. You will note we have clearly distinguished unrestricted funds, restricted funds and endowment funds.'

'The SOFA includes all gains and losses, does it not?' said Earnest Hardcastle.

'Yes. Yes it does,' said Parker-Smythe, glancing in Robert York's direction.

'So why bother with a separate income and expenditure account?' asked the Nat West regional bank manager.

Before either Parker-Smythe or York could reply, there was a grunt from Professor Sir George Frampton. His eyes were closed, his head was tilted forward, his chin was on his chest and his hands, clasped together and resting across his waistcoat, moved gently up and down with each breath he took. The Bursar was still staring at Sir George when Earnest Hardcastle repeated his question.

'Why do we need a separate income and expenditure account?'

'If the Income and Expenditure Account cannot be clearly distinguished within the Statement of Financial Activities, unrealised gains and losses may be challenged because as you well know, Earnest,' snapped Sir George, to everyone's surprise, coming alive and staring hard at the regional bank manager, 'unrealised gains and losses are not allowed in an Income and Expenditure Account.'

For the next forty-five minutes, Anthony Parker-Smythe and Robert York had to answer some rather awkward questions. Warren Cooper, being relatively new to the Board, wanted a breakdown of the investment. This prompted Sir Leslie Matthews to ask for a breakdown of the expenditure on food. Earnest Hardcastle wanted to know why the rent from Beaumont Farm was so low. Michael Liú queried the income from the Old Beaumontians; he thought they had donated significantly more than the accounts showed.

When Lord Bartholomew finally declared the meeting closed, the Board had sanctioned a ten percent increase in schools fees, an eight percent increase in the salaries of the academic staff, a six percent increase for non-academic staff (the bursar, the matrons and secretaries) and a four percent increase for other ancillary staff. The Board had also authorised the one-year appointment of two language assistants, the full-time appointment of two junior members of staff and the pursuit of a new sports hall.

When Mary Cranborne reopened the windows, she let in fresh air and the shouts of the NCOs still drilling the CCF. 'It's about time you saw the cadets doing their stuff,' Sir Leslie said to Warren Cooper sitting next to him. 'Follow me.' As it turned out, Michael Liú, Dr Drisdale and Cyril Phillpott also followed Sir Leslie onto the parade ground.

* * * * *

'These guys look really sharp in their uniforms,' said the American. 'I guess their cost is included in the school fees.'

'Actually it isn't,' said Sir Leslie. 'The Ministry of Defence provides them. Ah, here's the Sergeant Major. He'll be able to answer your questions. Good afternoon, Stanley.'

'Good afternoon, Sir Leslie,' SMI Batters barked as he came to attention and saluted.

'I'm right to say the MOD provides the uniforms for the boys free of charge?'

'Correct, Sir Leslie,' said Stanley still standing at attention. 'All except their boots. The CCF supplies them but the boys have to pay for them.'

'What kind of boots are they?' asked Warren Cooper.

'Strictly regulation boots!' said Stanley, with a quick twist of his head to set his Adam's apple exactly in line with his tie. 'Boots! Black! Responsive to polish!'

'May I ask you about the striped tie you're wearing, sir?' said the American.

'Prince of Wales's Own Regiment of Yorkshire, sir,' barked Stanley with pride.

'Would I be right to guess you did a tour of duty with your battalion in Northern Ireland?' said Dr Drisdale.

'Sir! Two tours,' barked Stanley.

'What was it like?' asked Dr Drisdale.

'Nor much fun, sir,' said Stanley rather quietly. 'I preferred my stint in Cyprus.' Ending on that note, the sergeant major led the group across the now almost deserted parade ground to show them the rifle range. On their way, he explained for Warren Cooper's benefit the background to the CCF.

'The main aim of the Combined Cadet Corps is to *"provide a disciplined organisation in a school so that pupils may develop powers of leadership by means of training to promote the qualities of responsibility, self reliance, resourcefulness, endurance and perseverance"*. It does encourage boys interested in becoming Regular Officers or officers in the Reserves but it is not a pre-service organisation. Most contingents are in Independent Schools like Beaumont where the aim is to instil qualities of leadership, self-reliance, teamwork and citizenship. We achieve this by a combination of military and adventure training.'

'Are all the boys at the school in the CCF?' Warren asked.

'It's compulsory for the main school and voluntary for the sixth form, sir.'

'There may be one or two exceptions on medical grounds,' said Dr Drisdale.

'Or if parents object on religious grounds,' said Michael Liú.

'Were you in the CCF, Mr Liú?' Sir Leslie asked.

'Oh, yes,' said the Old Beaumontian. 'And I was an Air Force Cadet Under Officer when I was in the Sixth. It was great fun. We had a great time in our summer camp in Cyprus. I even learnt to fly.'

'Statistically,' said Cyril Phillpott, 'the Army is the most popular Corps.'

'Here we are gentlemen,' said SMI Batters. 'The rifle range. It's probably the most popular activity. It's used by all three contingents – not just the Army.'

'Do they use live ammunition?' asked Warren Cooper.

'Yes, sir,' said Stanley, 'but under strict supervision. We don't want them shooting one another now, do we sir.'

'No indeed, sergeant major,' said Sir Leslie. 'That would never do. We can't afford to lose any boy at the moment, and certainly not by being shot to death.'

* * * * *

CHAPTER 11

"The opportunity for doing mischief is found a hundred times a day, and of doing good once in a year." Voltaire

* * * * *

After helping Fiona with the supper dishes, Angus gave his wife a kiss on the cheek and headed for his study where he poured himself a glass of 15-year old Glenfiddich Solera Reserve. Fiona – the Gaelic word for *wine* – gave him the single malt whisky for Christmas. It was *single* because it was made at *one* distillery and it was *malt* because it was made from *one* malted grain - barley. Angus took a sip, let the liquid rest a wee while on his tongue then swallowed. Thus fortified, he sat at his desk and switched on his computer. It was time to study what he had collected from Robert York's hard drive and filing cabinet earlier that Wednesday.

Jersey, Guernsey and Sark are three islands lying in the English Channel off the north west coast of France. Sark is the smallest of these Channel Islands with its population of about six hundred. Unlike Jersey and Guernsey, it has neither reciprocal tax arrangements nor disclosure of information agreements with Great Britain or any other country for that matter. Sark has no income tax, no capital gains tax, no inheritance tax and no company register. A company can have its business address on Sark and can trade from there using Sark's sophisticated electronic and telegraphic communication systems.

So, Angus was both surprised and relieved to discover Tony Smith and Bob York had set up off-shore accounts in Guernsey and *not* Sark. It had made, and would make, his life much easier. Before he left his office that afternoon, he had placed a few telephone calls to Guernsey to reliable contacts who owed him favours. Tomorrow, Thursday, he would gather more pieces of the puzzle when he visited Beaumont.

* * * * *

'I thought the meeting went quite well, Bob' Nosey said, as he poured his co-conspirator a glass of late bottled vintage port.

'Oh, really?' said Bob. 'There were too many awkward questions for my liking.'

'Sir Leslie seemed satisfied when I told him the approximate cost of breakfast, lunch and supper per boy' said Nosey.

'Wanting a breakdown of the cost of food wasn't one of the awkward questions,' Bob said. 'No, it was that American wanting details of the investment income.'

'I thought you dealt with that very well,' said Nosey. 'I liked your line about Common Investment Funds (CIFs) set up by the Charity Commission under section 22 of the 1960 Charities Act and being available only to charities in England and Wales.'

'Ah,' said Bob, taking a sip from his glass, 'this is a rather nice drop of port. What is it?'

'Barros Colheita 1975,' said Nosey. 'Glad you like it. 1975 was the year they harvested the grapes. After they fortify the wine and before bottling, they mature it for up to seven years in oak casks. Smell the wood... in with the aroma of ripe red fruits and dry figs?'

'Now you come to mention,' said Bob, 'no I can't... but then, I'm no connoisseur.'

'Getting back to Warren Cooper,' said Nosey, 'I think what shut him up was your point that CIFs reduce our risks by diversifying our investment, that they are inexpensive to administer and that they enjoy the same tax benefits as other charities.'

'You noticed I didn't mention that the Charity Commission does *not* promote CIFs as safe, risk free or necessarily suitable for charities generally,' said Bob, taking another sip.

'Have one of these,' said Nosey, handing Bob a large open box of Belgian chocolates.

'They go well with this port.' Then before starting on his second chocolate, he said, 'Susan Taylor informed me your Angus MacKay is coming to see me tomorrow. Tell me again. Who is he and what does he do *exactly?*'

'To be honest, I'm not sure,' confessed Bob. 'He was part of the furniture when I joined the firm and before I became a junior partner.'

'He's been there a while then.'

'Yes! Quite a while. He and Garnet go back a long way,' said Bob. 'It's odd now I come to think of it.' He took another sip of port and another Belgian chocolate. 'The day I came to be interviewed for a position with the firm, I spent most of the day with MacKay. He was the one who showed me round and took me to lunch. I don't remember much about that day but I remember a joke – at least I supposed it was a joke – MacKay told me when the waiter brought the soup.'

'Let's hear it,' said Nosey.

'Well,' said Bob, 'the waiter put the soup in front of me. And just as I picked up the salt cellar, MacKay put his hand on my arm and said: *When Andrew Carnegie saw a man, seeking a place in his company, shake salt onto his soup before tasting it, he told the man he wouldn't give him the job. When the man asked why not, the billionaire Scottish immigrant told the man he didn't want anyone who took anything for granted.*'

'Anyway, Mackay's coming here tomorrow morning to see me,' said Nosey.

'He'll probably just want to take a look at your computer. Sheila told me he looked at mine this morning and hers yesterday. He assured me it's just routine.'

'Did you believe him?'

'It doesn't matter what I believe,' said Bob. 'The important thing is your computer is secure and your off-shore companies and accounts encrypted and hidden.'

'So Colin Harper and Rupert Jardine tell me,' said Nosey.

'Do you trust them?'

'I trust Harper. I'm not so sure about Jardine but Harper's his tutor and vouches for him.'

'You usually have to trust somebody at sometime of other.'

'You're probably right,' said Nosey who trusted nobody.

'Tell me again why you picked Guernsey out of the Channel Islands,' said Bob who, unbeknown to Nosey, had most of his accounts on Sark.

'Kill two birds with one stone, old boy. I can have a pleasant holiday there and manage my accounts at the same time,' said Nosey. 'Ever been to Guernsey? Very pleasant. I usually stay at La Collinette Hotel. It's a bit expensive but very comfortable. Excellent sea food. Close to St Peter Port and the night life to suit all tastes, mine included.'

* * * * *

Louise had clearly decided her husband would need very little for supper. It was rather much as he feared. Llywelyn cast a gloomy eye over the lettuce leaves, radishes, celery, beetroot and grated raw carrot on his plate. It was a colourful sight but, unlike the repast Jean-Pierre had provided at lunchtime that Wednesday, it failed to stimulate his gastric juices. Mayonnaise, even the low fat kind, was out of the question. Husband and wife sat facing one another across the kitchen table – Llywelyn refused to eat such food in the dining room – each waiting for the other to break the silence.

'I'm sorry,' said Llywelyn whose hearing was impaired by the noise of the celery he was crunching, 'I missed that.'

'I didn't say anything,' said Louise.

'Oh, right!' said Llywelyn. 'My mistake.'

'There's something on your mind, Llew. What is it?'

'Well,' said Llywelyn, 'a number of things actually. Let's go into your sunroom.'

Dr Llywelyn Pugh-Jones was no fool and, in spite of outward appearances, was neither aloof nor supercilious. He never forgot his grandfather's maxim *two heads are better than one* and Llywelyn knew Louise's head was often better than his own.

'Now then,' said Louise, settling herself into her favourite chair, 'what seems to be the problem?'

'Let me begin with the school fees,' said Llywelyn. 'The Board authorised a ten percent increase.'

'Isn't that the same as last year?'

'Yes. Exactly the same percentage,' said Llywelyn. 'but the increase is actually bigger, d'you see, because last year's annual boarding fee went up by ten percent of £6,410...'

'£641,' said Louise, 'but you set this year's fee at £7050, if I remember correctly.'

'Yes, that's right, not £7051. And now the new increase will be ten percent of £7,050.'

'£705 instead of £641,' said Louise. 'So, what's an extra £64 to most parents?'

'It's not *most* parents I'm worried about,' said Llywelyn. 'It's the parents of scholars like Blaine and Gosling. Things are tight for them even with our bursaries. They might take their sons away. Beaumont needs bright boys like these. They're Oxbridge material.'

'Well, if the parents do take them away,' said Louise, 'you'll just have to dream up some replacements.'

'Funny you should put it that way,' said Llywelyn. 'It's reminded me of the two ideas I had over breakfast last Saturday. Yes, I remember. I was listening to some Prokofiev on BBC Radio 3 Breakfast Hour and...'

'What were these two ideas of yours?'

'Oh, one was just fanciful. Not worth mentioning,' said Llywelyn. 'The other was quite practical and endorsed by the Board today.'

'And that was?'

'I had the idea to recommend Randolph Jardine as Sir Leslie Matthews' replacement.'

'What else is worrying you?' asked Louise.

'The staff,' said Llywelyn. 'I'm worried about the staff.

97

'Why? What have they been up to now?'

'Oh, no. They haven't been up to anything as far as I know,' said Llywelyn. 'No, it's their salaries. The Board would only agree to an eight percent increase for September. And Parker-Smythe said teachers in State schools are going to get ten and a half percent.'

'Eight percent is still pretty good,' said Louise. 'I assume they will still get their various non-taxable expense allowances for entertainment, telephone and the like.'

'Yes they will *and* I shall press Parker-Smythe to increase those by eight percent as well.'

'Then I shouldn't worry about the staff if I were you. It's not as if they will go on strike or do something silly, is it?' said Louise, unaware certain discussions were taking place that same evening in the Common Room.

'No, you're quite right as usual. I don't need to worry about the *academic* staff.'

'Do you have reason to worry about the other staff?' said Louise, frowning.

'Well,' said Llywelyn, hesitating, 'Stanley Garnet confided on Sunday that... I can't remember his exact words but it seems he has initiated an investigation... They have some concerns about their junior partner, Robert York.'

'Concerns about Robert York?' said Louise. 'That's hard to believe.'

'They also want to take a close look at Parker-Smythe.'

'Nosey Parker? Now that doesn't surprise me,' said Louise. 'What he's been up to?'

'Nothing I hope,' said Llywelyn. 'I gather Stanley Garnet's trouble shooter, Angus MacKay, is coming to Beaumont tomorrow to see Nosey... er... Parker-Smythe.'

* * * * *

Initially Rupert Jardine did not want to join the CCF. He did his best to avoid it. He tried medical grounds but was unsuccessful because he was physically fit and healthy and always had been. He tried religious grounds but was unsuccessful because his father was an atheist and thought the military discipline would do his wayward son some good. He was right. Jardine came to like the Air Corps.

When he returned home at the end of his first year at Beaumont he started flying lessons. He passed the Private Pilot Knowledge Exam as soon he reached the minimum age requirement – on his fifteenth birthday. He flew his first solo when he reached the minimum age requirement - on his sixteenth birthday. Rupert intended to qualify for his Private Pilot's Licence as soon as possible after he reached seventeen - the minimum age. When he entered the Lower Sixth he became a cadet flight sergeant and intended to become a Cadet Under Officer in the Upper Sixth.

Sergeant Major Instructor Stanley Batters had some reservations but when he was asked for his opinion by Jardine's Housemaster, E. Gordon Hamilton, SMI Batters said, quoting from the aims of the CCF, that the lad was developing *self reliance, resourcefulness, endurance and perseverance.* However, he tactfully omitted *qualities of responsibility.* SMI Batters couldn't keep Rupert away from the rifle range but then again he did not want to. Rupert had become the best shot in the Air Cadet Rifle Team. It was just regrettable that SMI Batters and PSI Morton, permanent staff instructor i/c the armoury, had always to watch Rupert's comings, shootings and goings like hawks.

'Where's my cocoa, you little tick?' said Rupert. It was Wednesday evening and he was still annoyed with Stan Batters for not letting him near the rifle range that afternoon.

'Sorry, Jardine,' squealed Chén as Rupert twisted his ear. 'I do prep. Just finish now.'

99

'I don't want your excuses, you little toad,' Rupert hissed into Chén's ear. 'I want my cocoa, you savvy?'

'Yes. Yes, Jardine. Please, let go ear. I get cocoa now.'

'Quick about it,' said Rupert giving Chén's ear a final twist. 'Don't spill any! And bring me a chocolate biscuit while you're at it.'

Chén returned in double quick time, put the hot cocoa and chocolate biscuit on the table and, before Rupert could twist his other ear, beat a hasty retreat not stopping to close the door behind him. Fagging for prefects in the independent schools had been abolished by about 1980. Rupert was not a prefect. So on both counts, Chén should not have been Rupert's fag or *boots* as they were once called.

'I'd like a word with you, Jardine,' said Zháng.

'If it's about Feuerbach's theorem,' said Rupert, 'I've got better things to do with...'

'No, it's not about geometry,' Zháng said softly. 'It's about young Chén.'

'About my boots? What about him? Want him to fag for you, do you?'

'No I do not want him to fag for me,' said Zháng. 'And I don't want him to fag for you or anybody else. From now on you will leave Chén alone.'

'What if I don't, Mr Stephen Zháng?' said Rupert.

'Then you will have to answer to me,' said the short, stocky lower sixth former.

Rupert hauled his tall muscular frame out of his chair and sauntered into the corridor to confront Stephen who was almost five inches shorter and quite a few pounds lighter. Rupert then made three mistakes. Firstly, he invaded Stephen's personal space by standing only eighteen inches away from the young man from Singapore, and said, 'So I'll have to answer to you, will I?'

'You will,' said Stephen in a very quiet voice.

'Alright,' said Rupert, 'here's my answer to you. Chén is my boots and he fags for me.'

'Perhaps I did not make myself clear,' said Stephen, 'Chén will not fag for you, for me or for anybody ever again. Chén is now under my protection.'

'Maybe I didn't make myself clear. Chén is my...' At this point Rupert made his second mistake. To emphasise his point, he poked at Stephen's chest with the index finger of his right hand. Rupert never made contact, never finished the sentence he had started and never quite worked out how he came to be flat on his back staring up at Stephen.

Only slightly dazed, Rupert got to his feet and made his third mistake. He decided to teach Zháng a lesson. He lunged forward. Stephen pivoted and sent Rupert head over heels onto his back again. Ten minutes and many painful falls later, Zháng twisted Rupert's ear and said, 'Have I made myself clear now? Chén is nobody's boots.'

When Stephen had walked off, Rupert had picked himself up off the floor and went to see Janet Meeker, the House Matron, for a couple of aspirins.

'My goodness,' said Janet, 'what have you been up to, Rupert Jardine?'

'I think I overdid it on the CCF training circuit this afternoon,' he lied.

'That's the trouble with you young athletes. You don't know when to stop. I must say you do look a ghastly colour. Sit down and roll up your shirt sleeve.'

'What are you going to do?' asked Rupert. 'Give me a fatal injection?'

'Nothing so dramatic,' she said, putting a thermometer in his mouth to shut him up. 'I'm going to check your blood pressure.' When she took the thermometer out from under his tongue, she saw his temperature was normal.

'How's my temperature?' asked Rupert.

'A perfectly healthy 37.0 °C. So you're not running a fever,' said Janet.

'That's odd,' said Rupert. 'I expected my temperature to be high.'

'Dare I ask why,' said Janet.

'I always get hot and bothered when I see you, Janet.'

'Matron! I'm *matron* to you, young man,' said Janet blushing.

'I'll bet my blood pressure will be high as well,' said Rupert. 'You send everybody's blood pressure sky high when…'

'Stop it. Just stop talking, please.'

'Well,' said Rupert. 'What's the verdict?'

'You're an impudent young man,' said Janet.

'I know that,' said Rupert. 'I was asking about my blood pressure.'

'The diastolic is a healthy 75. The systolic is 129. That's a shade high but I suppose you ran up the stairs to get here,' said Janet. 'Perhaps I should take it again.' She did and this time the systolic was 119. 'Your blood pressure is fine. Be off with you.'

'What about something for my headache?' said Rupert. 'Perhaps your soothing hand on my brow.'

'Here,' said the still blushing Janet, handing him a glass of water, 'swallow these two aspirins and take your mischievous self back to your room before you overstep the mark. You'll get yourself into serious trouble one of these days.'

* * * * *

It was quite late on Wednesday afternoon. All the governors had departed, including those who had kept Jardine out of the rifle range by monopolising SMI Stanley Batters. Mary Cranborne knocked, entered the Common Room, pinned the notice on the board and left. Quentin Waite did not see her come and go. He was dozing in his favourite chair, his face covered by the Times newspaper. The staff who had spent their afternoon helping with the CCF were relaxing in a corner on the far side. Except for Gregory Watson, they did not notice Mary come and go.

'Damn!' said Greg. 'That's all I need.'

'What's up?' said Arthur Matthews, Head of Geography.

'The High Master's notice,' said Greg. 'The Board's raising the school fees by ten percent but our salaries by only eight percent.'

'Eight percent?' said Keith Bradley. 'Are you sure?'

'That's what is says here,' said Greg. 'Come and look for yourself. Eight percent!'

'I thought we'd get the same as the teachers in the state schools,' said David Swann.

'What? Twelve percent?' said Keith.

'No!' said David. 'That's what the unions asked for. No, ten and a half percent.'

'What about our entertainment and telephone allowances?' asked James Jackson.

'They're going up by eight percent as well,' said Greg.

'Well that's alright then,' said James. 'Those allowances and the increases we've had for the last three years still keep us ahead of the teachers in the state system.'

'They do. They do,' said Geoffrey Rusbridge, Head of Economics, 'but only just.'

They stood around for a while studying the notice then drifted back to their seats in the corner. Someone tried to look on the bright side but Greg would have none of that. He slouched in his chair, his gloomy face reflecting his inward misery at Walter Barnes staying on for another year and the prospect of telling his wife, Kathy, they would be on a tight budget for another year. They sat in silence for a while until 'Mad' Arthur Matthews piped up and said, 'Let's drown our sorrows in drink, chaps. My treat.'

Thirty minutes and several drinks later, the mood had lightened. When he saw Greg still looked exceedingly glum, Arthur suggested they should put their minds to the task of keeping their colleague out of the workhouse. 'What we need to do,' said Arthur with a slight slur in his voice. 'What we need to do is...'

'Have a whip round?' said Keith Bradley who taught woodwork and metalwork.

'No, no, no,' said Arthur. 'What we need to do is...'

'Win the lottery?' said James Jackson who taught maths and physics.

'No, no, no. Listen!' said Arthur. 'What we need to do is...'

'I know a good joke about the lottery,' said David Swann who taught history.

Isaac went to the synagogue on Saturday and prayed. I'm in terrible trouble, God. Please let me win the lottery. No use. His prayer wasn't answered. He didn't win.

The following Saturday Isaac went to the synagogue. He went down on his knees and for the second time prayed. Oh God I'm in terrible financial trouble. Please help me and my family. Let me win the lottery. No use. His prayer wasn't answered.

On the following Saturday, Isaac went to the synagogue for the third time. Wailing loudly, Isaac fell prostrate in front of the bimah and prayed. I'm in terrible trouble, God. Please help me, my family and the people that work for me. Let me win the lottery.

This time Isaac heard the voice of God. *Isaac! Meet me half way. Buy a ticket!*

A few more drinks were consumed. A few more jokes were told. The mood lightened even more. But Greg still looked glum. Then someone said, 'I know! Let's rob a bank.' Greg laughed. Everybody laughed. Everybody, that is, except one member of staff. He just smiled and gave thought to the plan forming in his mind.

* * * * *

CHAPTER 12

"A man is usually more careful of his money than of his principles" Oliver Wendell Holmes, Jr

* * * * *

He was not ashamed of his past. In his own way he was quite proud of it; well parts of it. But his past was *his* past. Not something to dwell upon; rather something to recollect and perhaps even to relive in his mind. As he cut a swathe through the soap, he looked at his weather-beaten face in the mirror and remembered his first shave and how those cuts on his face stung when his father rubbed an alum block over them. He also remembered not flinching and his father saying: 'You're a true highlander, laddie, and I'm proud of you.'

Angus MacKay was born in the parish of Halkirk, He attended the village primary school up to the age of eleven and then for his secondary education, up to the age of seventeen, he bicycled to a school seven miles away in the market town of Thurso. With his father's permission, he enlisted into The Black Watch five months before his eighteenth birthday.

He rose rapidly to the rank of major and saw service in Korea where he was awarded the highest award for gallantry – the Victoria Cross. To the surprise of his comrades and his father, Major Angus MacKay VC mysteriously signed off and officially left the army just before his battalion began its first two-year peace-keeping tour of Northern Ireland. Two years later he quietly signed on to Stanley Garnet's firm of chartered accountants.

Fiona MacKay always knew, from the way he dressed, when her husband was on one of his *special assignments*. This Thursday morning was no exception.

Jacket: Harris Tweed green/oatmeal mix with buttons - leather.

Shirt: cream.

Tie: striped - Black Watch regimental.

Trousers: Cavalry twill – beige, worsted.

Socks: green/oatmeal mix.

Shoes: dark brown - polished.

She once made the mistake of referring to his *trews*. She was rebuked. Lowlanders wear those close-fitting tartan trousers. Highlanders wear the kilt.

'Where's the battlefield today, Major?' said Fiona when her husband appeared.

'Beaumont Abbey School, Colonel,' replied Angus.

'Who's the target?'

'A weasel of a bursar going by the name of Anthony Parker-Smythe.'

'Another one of Stanley Garnet's discreet inquiries, is it?' said Fiona.

'Och, aye!' said Angus. 'Another kid glove job.'

'Softly, softly! Catchee monkey?'

'That's about the way of it, lassie,' said Angus.

At precisely eight-thirty on Thursday morning, Angus knocked on Mary Cranborne's door and moments later he was shown into the adjoining room for a confidential word with the High Master of Beaumont Abbey, Dr Llywelyn Pugh-Jones. When ushered into the presence, most people, parents and pupils alike, became rather nervous and felt somewhat intimidated. It was a novel experience for the boot to be on the other foot.

'Ah, Major MacKay,' said Llywelyn, 'so good of you to… that is to say…'

'*Mister* MacKay will do just fine,' said Angus. 'I left the army a long time ago.'

'Sorry. Yes. Quite so,' bumbled Llywelyn. 'Mister MacKay it is then. Er… coffee. May I offer you some coffee? Perhaps you would prefer tea?'

'Coffee. Black. No sugar. Thank you.' Mary was amused. She had never seen the High Master so nervous. She poured a black coffee for Angus, a cup of Earl Grey tea for Llywelyn then left the room, quietly closing the door behind her.

'Stanley Garnet told me you were awarded the Victoria Cross on active service in…'

'Och,' said Angus, waving his hand as if to brush a mosquito away from his face. 'that was a long time ago when I was very young and idealistic.'

'Be that as it may,' said Llywelyn, 'I must say...'

'We're busy men,' interrupted Angus. 'and time is short. I'd be grateful if you'd tell me what you know about your bursar.'

Ever since last Sunday afternoon when Stanley Garnet, the senior partner in the firm of chartered accountants, Banwell, Garnet and York, had confided that their junior partner, Robert York, and Beaumont's bursar, Anthony Parker-Smythe, were to be discreetly investigated, Llywelyn had been on edge. Yesterday evening he became even more edgy when, on mentioning the investigation, his wife, Louise, showed no surprise but simply wondered what Nosey Parker had been up to. To make matters worse, she had asked her husband the same question: *What do you know about your bursar?*

After a restless night, he was tired and not really in a fit state to face Angus MacKay VC, a former major in the Black Watch. As he had confessed to Louise over breakfast, what little he knew about Mr Parker-Smythe was really what he had been told by Mr Parker-Smythe himself. 'I shouldn't worry,' said Louis, clearly concerned for her husband's health. 'If Stanley's investigator asks what you know about Nosey Parker, tell him that you never pry into the private lives of your colleagues, that he seems competent and that the Governing Board of Directors appointed him to the post of Bursar, so it was their responsibility to check his credentials.' And that's exactly what Llywelyn told him.

* * * * *

Tony Smith was born in 1947 in London. The Second World War had ended. Bread and potato rationing had started. When the munitions factory closed, his mother had lost her job and his father had left them. To make ends meet, his mother took in washing

107

and discreetly provided some other services at their two-bedroom terraced house in Camden Town. He tried his best to forget his early childhood.

From the age of five he went to a local primary school run by war-weary teachers in a prefabricated building. He was unfortunate to achieve only a borderline pass in the eleven plus exam but he was fortunate to be given a place in one of the few technical schools. He proved to be particularly good with numbers. He left school at sixteen and worked as a cashier in the local Co-op store until he was seventeen.

With his mother's permission – she was glad to see the back of him – he enlisted. After he had completed one year of service, he was transferred to the Royal Army Pay Corps. He took three years to become corporal but shortly after achieving that rank Tony Smith was obliged to sign off and leave the RAPC whose motto, ironically, is *Fide et Fiducia* (faith and trust). Actually, he was to all intents and purposes court-martialled.

'Corporal Smith,' said his commanding officer, ' do you know why you have been called to appear before me?'

'Sir!' said Corporal Smith, 'Yes, sir.'

'You are charged with embezzling public money.'

'Sir!'

'*Public* money, Smith. Money for which I, as your commanding officer, was responsible. Do you understand, Smith?'

'Sir!'

'You know we're not talking about a couple of quid out of the petty cash box, Smith?'

'Sir!'

'No, Corporal Smith, we're not, are we?'

'No, sir!'

'Just how much *are* we talking about?'

'Sir! I'm not sure, sir.'

'You're not sure,' said Captain Gravestone. 'You're not sure.'

'No, sir!' said Corporal Smith. 'I'm not sure, sir.'

'Well then, Smith, perhaps you'd be kind enough to give me your best estimate.'

'Sir!' said Smith, desperately trying to arrive at his best answer; too low a figure and Gravestone wouldn't believe him; too high a figure and Gravestone would stop this summary hearing and have him tried by a Regimental Court-Martial.

'I'm waiting, Smith.'

'Sir! About nine thousand pounds, sir.'

'D'you take me for a fool, Smith?'

'No, sir!'

'It might be nearer to fifteen thousand pounds, sir.'

'Fifteen thousand, you say,' said Captain Gravestone, pursing his lips. He had called this summary hearing on the basis of a claim, by one of Smith's disgruntled cronies, that the corporal had embezzled about seven thousand pounds. Gravestone investigated and put the figure nearer to ten thousand pounds. 'You're quite sure, are you Smith?'

'Sir!' said Smith, 'That's just an estimate, sir. It might be a little more.'

'An estimate! It might be a little more. Look here, Smith,' said Gravestone, 'I don't want your estimates. I want to know exactly how much we're talking about and, more to the point, how much you're going to hand back. Understood?'

'Sir!' said Smith, still standing rigidly to attention and feeling weak at the knees.

'Right,' said Gravestone, 'pushing his cap, leather gloves and swagger stick to one side to clear a space on his table for his notepad. 'How much did you take and how much am I going to get back?'

'Eighteen thousand, nine hundred and fifty-four pounds and sixteen pence taken, sir.' Gravestone wrote on his pad: £18,954.16 debit. 'Sixteen thousand, four hundred and thirty-two pounds and 73 pence to be returned, sir.' Gravestone wrote on his pad: £16,432.73

credit. Then he subtracted the credit from the debit to get £2,521.43.

'What did you do with the two thousand, five hundred and twenty-one pounds and forty three pence, Smith?'

'Sir! I spent it, sir.'

'You're an utter disgrace, Smith. By rights I should have you tried by a Regimental Court Martial and sent to prison. That would, of course, reflect badly on the regiment but it's what you deserve. Am I right, Smith?'

'Sir!' said Smith, knowing Gravestone was really thinking of his own reputation.

'Well, I am not going to bring the RAPC into disrepute. No, Smith, I am going to do what I can to protect the reputation of the Corps in general and my men in particular,' said Gravestone. 'I'm going to let you off lightly. Within the next twenty-four hours, Smith, you will return to me the £16,432.73 *in cash* and you will officially request my permission to *sign off*. Understood, Corporal Smith.

'Sir! Understood, sir. Thank you, sir.'

Several weeks later, Captain Gravestone was in the officers mess having a drink at the bar when Major Frobisher sidled up. 'Everything under control, Gravestone?'

'Yes, Major.'

'I gather Corporal Smith has left the Service.'

'Yes, sir. Personal grounds. Mother very ill and on her own. Needs his support.'

'Quite a reliable chap when it came to money, I believe,' said Major Frobisher.

'Oh, yes!' said Gravestone with a smile, thinking of the £16,432.73 Smith had returned *in cash* and the £6,755 left over after he had deposited the missing £9,677.73 back into the accounts, 'Smith certainly knew how to handle money. I shall be ever grateful to him for the work he did.'

* * * * *

Major Anthony Parker-Smythe fortified himself on a full English breakfast. Afterwards, he took his time over his ablutions and gave careful thought to his attire. He decided on a hand-tailored, three-piece suit – grey, pinstriped – a white shirt and Royal Army Pay Corps striped tie, grey socks and polished black shoes. He folded a white handkerchief into his top breast pocket and he fixed into his lapel a Rotary International badge, even though he was not a member and not entitled to wear it.

'Good morning!' said Susan Taylor, '*Major* MacKay? Is that right?'

'Yes!' said Angus. 'And you're Mrs Taylor, no doubt. The Bursar's secretary.'

'Yes, I'm Susan Taylor... or Parker-Smythe's PA if you prefer.'

'I'd prefer Mrs Taylor, if that's alright by you.'

'And how do you prefer to be addressed?' Susan asked.

'*Mister* MacKay to you, Mrs Taylor but keep to Major when Mr Parker-Smythe arrives.'

'I understand, Mr MacKay,' said Susan. 'Yes, I quite understand.'

'How long did you live in South Africa?'

'How did you... Ah! My accent. Of course,' said Susan. 'Long enough I should say.'

'Did you go to school in South Africa?'

'Yes. Herschel Girls Anglican School'

'And after that?'

'University of Cape Town.'

'To study...?'

'Commerce.'

'Did that include business studies and accountancy?'

'Yes it did as a matter of fact,' said Susan. 'This might sound a little odd but I really enjoyed the accountancy part of the course.'

'So you're a qualified accountant,' said Angus. 'That's very interesting.'

'Oh, here he is now. Good morning Bursar,' said Susan. 'This is *Major* MacKay.'

As they shook hands, Angus remembered the first time his father took him fly fishing for salmon in the river Thurso. It was a cold, damp morning in March. He landed a fish weighing eleven pound. It was big enough to take home and eat. His father showed him how to kill the salmon humanely - by breaking its neck with a sharp, heavy blow – and how to drain out the blood and clean it. In Angus's steely grip, Anthony Parker-Smythe's hand felt was just like that dead salmon – cold, clammy and limp.

'I hope you've not been waiting long,' said Anthony. 'I thought our meeting was for half past nine.' It was already 9:35 a.m.

'Nine o'clock,' Angus lied. 'It dinnae matter. I've had a wee chat with Mrs Taylor.'

'Oh, sorry. I really thought it was half past nine.'

'If you'll excuse me, Major MacKay. I must get on,' said Susan smiling to herself. She knew jolly well the meeting really was for half past nine and not nine o'clock. 'What time would you like coffee, *Major* MacKay? Would half past ten suit you?' He nodded.

'Oh,' said Anthony. 'Is this going to be a long meeting? I am rather busy and…'

'The sooner we get started, the sooner we'll be finished,' said Angus. 'Your room is through here, I assume. Would you mind leading the way?'

Angus pulled up a chair and waited impassively until Anthony was ensconced behind the other side of his desk. Without saying a word, Angus produced a fountain pen and black leather-bound notebook from the inner pocket of his jacket. He took the lid off the pen then slowly and deliberately opened the notebook. Anthony squirmed in his seat then nervously opened his large desk diary.

'That's very odd,' said Anthony, looking at his entry for Thursday. 'I definitely have your appointment down for half past nine.'

'Och, mistakes are easily made,' said Angus. 'And just as easily discovered, ye ken.'

'I'm not in the habit of making mistakes. No. that wouldn't do at all, not for a man in my position. Far too much at stake,' said Anthony, fingering his tie.

'RAPC tie, I see,' said Angus quietly.

'What? Oh, yes,' said Anthony. 'Royal Army Pay Corps. Quite right? What was yours?'

'What was your rank when you signed off?' Angus asked, ignoring Anthony's question.

'Is that relevant to your inquiries?' asked Anthony, somewhat flustered.

'Just a friendly question from one ex-army man to another,' said Angus.

'Yes, of course,' said Anthony. 'It's just that…'

'For the record, from one ex-army man to another,' said Angus, 'I was a major in The Black Watch when I signed off.'

'Would you mind if my PA brought the coffee in now?'

'Let's leave it till ten thirty. We've a lot to get through,' said Angus firmly.

For the next three quarters of an hour, Anthony squirmed in his seat while Angus plied him with questions. What accounting software do you run? How often do you back up your files? Where do you keep the backup files? What hard copies do you make? Where do you store these copies? Do you encrypt your files? What firewalls and anti-virus software do you run and how often do you upgrade them? Do you operate online banking? Which physical banks hold your accounts? How frequently do you meet with the school accountant? When was the last time you went over your accounts with him?

When Susan Taylor brought in the coffee tray and saw how ashen the Bursar looked, she felt moved to ask if he was alright.

'As a matter of fact, I feel rather under the weather,' said Anthony, pulling his white handkerchief out of his top pocket and mopping his brow.

'Here,' said Susan, 'a cup of your favourite coffee may be just what you need.' Then turning towards Angus, she asked, 'How do you take your coffee, Major?'

'Black. No sugar, thank you, Mrs Taylor.'

'Biscuit?'

'Not for me, thank you,' said Angus. Then turning to Anthony, said, 'What about you?'

'No! No thank you,' said Anthony, refusing a chocolate biscuit probably for the first time in his life. He never noticed the wry look on Susan's face.

Angus did not wait for Anthony to finish his coffee. He pressed on with his questions. By eleven o'clock, Anthony could take no more and asked to be excused. Angus, forever impassive, simply put away his notebook and pen, saying, 'I'll examine your computer now and come back tomorrow when you're feeling better.'

* * * * *

When Susan heard the Bursar's door to the main corridor open and close, she decided to go and collect the coffee tray. As she stood up, the connecting door opened and Angus appeared carrying the tray. 'I think your boss has gone to lie down for a wee while, Mrs Taylor. He's not feeling too grand.' Susan smiled and took the tray from Angus. 'Would you like a hand with the washing up?' he asked.

'No thank you Mr MacKay. Dolly Brown will take of it,' said Susan. 'What now?'

'If you can spare me a wee bit o' time, I should like to talk to you.'

'Certainly,' she said. 'What do you want to talk about?'

'Let's start with the work you do here,' said Angus.

'Well, for what it's worth, I am the Bursar's personal assistant,' said Susan.

Over the next hour, Susan Taylor explained what she did. She began with her official duties as personal assistant. Angus MacKay listened carefully. The list was very long and sounded more like the duties of the bursar himself rather then his assistant. She took responsibility for premises management and for the support staff - catering, cleaning and ground staff - and the costs related to maintenance, supplies and wages. She kept records and dealt with invoices and receipts for goods and services. She ensured that financial deadlines were met. She reconciled the accounts each month.

It was her unofficial activities that interested Angus. He uncovered these by an occasional smile, a word of encouragement and a seemingly innocent question.

'You do all that *and* fetch him his coffee and chocolate biscuits,' said Angus. 'I'd like to think he appreciates you, Mrs Taylor, but somehow I rather doubt that.'

'The satisfaction I get from what I do here is thanks enough.'

'I notice the school has a bookshop and an outfitters. Who looks after their accounts'

'They keep their own ledgers but I check them once a month.'

'You don't find that tedious?'

'As I told you, Mr MacKay, I like working with figures and accounts,' said Susan. 'I keep a weather eye on all the accounts both official and unofficial... Oh, perhaps I shouldn't have said that.'

'Now you really do have my fullest attention,' said Angus. 'Tell me more.'

'Oh, dear,' said Susan. 'Look, Mr MacKay, it's time for lunch. Would like to join me at high table?'

'I don't usually eat lunch,' said Angus, 'but I'll make an exception today.'

Over lunch, Susan talked about her parents, about growing up in Cape Town, about her time at school and university, about her marriage and separation. All the while Angus smiled, nodded and listened carefully.

Never before had she talked so much about herself even to her close friends. She felt at ease with this Major MacKay. In contrast to her boss, the so-called Major Parker-Smythe, this Scotsman was a man she felt she could confide in and trust. She hoped she was right.

'I hope you enjoyed your lunch, Mr MacKay,' said Susan. She could not help but notice the contrast between Angus who ate moderately and Anthony who ate greedily.

'Thank you, Mrs Taylor. I did,' said Angus, 'but not as much as I enjoyed your company.'

'I did prattle on rather,' said Susan, suddenly realising Angus now knew almost everything there was to know about her but she knew next to nothing about him.

'If you'll excuse me now,' said Angus when they were back in her office, 'I need to take a look at Parker-Smythe's computer. I may also want to peek into his filing cabinet. Do you have a key?'

'Officially, no!' said Susan, handing him her duplicate. 'You might want to talk to me again when you've finished in there.'

'I might well, Mrs Taylor. Thank you for your help. May I use your photocopier?'

'Of course,' she said, 'but I could save you time by doing the photocopying for you.'

'Och, that would grand. I was hoping you'd offer.'

'If you could give me some idea of what you're looking for,' said Susan, 'I might be able to…'

'Och, that's just it, Mrs Taylor. I'll not know until I find it. I usually start with bank statements, credit statements, financial statements, that sort of thing, you know.'

'How about… Oh, please call me Susan, Mr MacKay.'

'Very well, Susan it is, but not in front of your boss or anyone else. Agreed?'

'Right! Understood, Angus. May I call you Angus?'

'How about Stewart?' said Angus, 'Just between the two of us ye ken?'

'Is that your name?'

'No! It was my father's name. I usually use it when I need to be incognito.'

'I understand. So if I am speaking to you on the telephone and anyone is in earshot, I should address you as Stewart?'

'Aye, that's about it,' said Angus. 'Now you started to say…?'

'Oh, yes! You said you weren't sure what you were looking for,' said Susan. 'How about Special Purpose Vehicles and off-shore accounts?'

While Parker-Smythe was trying to calm his nerve with another glass of port back in his rooms, Angus and Susan were, in her words, the mice at play while the cat was away. She should, of course, have guessed Angus would never qualify as a mouse under any circumstances. And if she had known the extent of his knowledge, she might not have prattled on about SPVs and off-shore accounts.

'A Special Purpose Vehicle is a legal entity - a trust or a limited company. You can use it legally or illegally (embezzling, concealing losses, laundering money, misstating earnings by disguising loans as revenue, etc.) because it is usually private, bankruptcy remote and off-balance sheet. Even when you use SPVs legitimately, you may be skating on very thin ethical ice. Guernsey is a good off-shore place for SPVs; it levies no tax on company profits and has no exchange controls or withholding taxes on payments.'

'I'm impressed, Susan. You obviously didn't waste your time at the university.'

'So you'd be interested in his off-shore accounts?'

'Aye, I would that,' said Angus. 'By the by, is his name really Anthony Parker-Smythe?'

'That is the name on one of his passports,' said Susan

'*One* of his passports,' said Angus. 'He's got two?'

'I *think so*. I've only seen the one but I came across a document referring to him as Tony Smith. I wouldn't be surprised if he's managed to get one in that name as well.'

'It's possible,' said Angus. 'If he used his birth certificate in the name of Tony Smith and later changed his address and then legally changed his name by deed poll to Anthony Parker-Smythe…'

'Then took a driving test as Parker-Smythe and used his driving licence…'

'That might work,' said Angus. 'Probably easier to buy a passport on the black market.'

'I thought it was illegal and impossible to have two passports,' said Susan.

'Illegal? Yes! Impossible…' Angus said softly, thinking of those two years he officially never spent in Northern Ireland.

The time flew by. Susan went through the filing cabinet and did the photocopying. Angus navigated the computer, uncovering hidden, encrypted and 'deleted' files. Just before he finished for the day, he used the equipment he carried in his case to make disk image files of the hard drives on Susan's computer and her boss's computer. Susan walked with Angus to the main entrance and was delighted when he asked her to keep her eyes and ears open for anything she thought might further his investigation. Anthony Parker-Smythe, alias Tony Smith, alias Nosey Parker, might have emptied his bottle of port if he had realised he was going to be *under surveillance* from now on.

* * * * *

'Pull yourself together,' Robert York hissed into the telephone. 'Those were just the sort of questions he asked me. It's routine.'

'He asked me what my rank was when I left the army. What's routine about that?'

'Probably just idle chat. What were you doing at the time?' asked Bob.

'I don't remember,' said Nosey.

'Did you tell him?'

'Tell him what?'

'Your rank when you left the army.'

'Yes. No. Oh, God. I don't remember,' Nosey almost whimpered. 'There was just something about him... He just... His eyes seemed to...'

'Calm down,' said Bob. 'He's just checking to make sure we are following proper security procedures. Using impenetrable firewalls, strong passwords and good encryption techniques. That's all. What are you worrying about?'

'What if he finds my off-shore accounts files?'

'He's not looking for those but what if he does? All those SPVs are perfectly legal.'

'Are you sure?' said Nosey.

'Of course I'm sure,' said Bob. 'After all, it's your own money in those accounts, isn't it? It's just yours. It's nobody else's, right?' Silence. 'Are you still there?' asked Bob.

'Yes. Yes, I'm still here.'

'Are you alright?' asked Bob.

'No. I'm not feeling too good,' Nosey croaked. 'I'd better lie down.'

* * * * *

CHAPTER 13

"Contentment makes poor men rich; discontentment makes rich men poor." Benjamin Franklin

* * * * *

It had been cloudy and threatening rain all day but by five o'clock the sun broke through and shone down on the tennis court at the back of Gower House. Shortly thereafter, Louise Pugh-Jones began telephoning. Mary Cranborne was available. Reggie de Vere and Arthur Matthews were not available; something about a meeting in the Common Room. She telephoned the chaplain's wife. Celia Fiddle was available. Louise telephoned Mary again.

'We need one more for doubles, Mary. Any ideas?'

'I wonder if Susan Taylor plays tennis,' said Mary.

'Oh, dear me,' said Louise, 'I feel awful. We've never ever asked her, have we?'

'No we haven't. I can't think why not.'

'I suppose when Madeleine de Vere was alive, we had our regular four and it never crossed our minds to invite anyone else,' said Louise.

'Yes but after Madeleine passed away, why didn't we think of Susan to make up the four?' said Mary.

'It's no excuse,' said Louise, 'but she has tended to keep herself very much to herself.'

'Agreed,' said Mary. 'Although strangely enough, she was very chatty about an hour ago after she had spent the day looking after that Major MacKay.'

'Oh, really!' said Louise. 'Very interesting!'

'Would you like me to give Susan a ring?' Mary asked.

Susan Taylor was delighted to be asked to make up the four. 'It's quite a while since I've played, Mary. So don't expect too much. I know how seriously you and Louise take your tennis.' Mary did not contradict Susan because they *were* serious players. She simply said they would be on the court at the back of Gower House at six o'clock.

Louise and Mary were warming up when Susan arrived dressed in white culottes, white short-sleeved cotton shirt, white socks and tennis shoes. And like them, Susan wore a white headband visor and sweatbands on her wrists. Just as Susan was taking her racquet out of its case, Celia Fiddle, garbed in whites, arrived to complete the foursome. They spun racquets for partners and Susan found herself paired with Mary. Louise spun her racquet, Mary called *rough* and Louise chose to serve.

'Fifteen love,' said Celia, when Louise served an ace to Mary. Susan moved back from the net to the base line to receive the next service. Louise aimed for Susan's backhand and hit the ball as hard as she could. It should have been another ace.

'Good return, partner,' said Mary.

'Fifteen all,' said Celia.

Mary and Susan took the match by two sets to one in three very close sets. As they walked off the court, Mary said to Susan, 'When was the last time you played tennis?'

'Oh, three years ago at the historic Palm Springs Tennis Club in California.'

'Gosh! That sounds rather grand,' said Celia. 'What was the weather like? Did it rain?'

'Actually,' said Susan, 'it was a bit like Cape Town in December but without the cooling sea breeze. The Palm Springs Club is at the foot of the San Jacinto (Hyacinth) mountain range in the Coachella Valley, so it tends to be rather too hot and dry.'

'How many courts does the Club have?' asked Louise.

'Ten or eleven, I think,' said Susan. 'It also has three outdoor swimming pools.'

'How long did you go for?' asked Celia.

'Two weeks,' said Susan.

'Gosh! Two weeks! How wonderful!' Celia twittered. 'Humphrey couldn't afford to treat me to a holiday like that on his chaplain's salary. I don't know how you could afford it… Oh, dear. I'm sorry. That was very prying of me, wasn't it?' Susan did not take offence.

'It wasn't all that expensive,' said Susan, 'but I did have to sell some of my ICI shares.'

'Ah!' said Louise who had read Philosophy, Politics and Economics at Oxford, 'so you play the Stock Market, do you?'

'No, not really,' said Susan. 'My portfolio is rather humdrum – mostly Blue Chip stocks.'

'Perhaps we should get together and pick your brains, Susan,' said Louise. 'What d'you say, girls?'

'Susan can tell us how to make money on the Stock Market and why she never eats pancakes,' said Mary, 'And Louise can tell us why Arthur is called 'Mad' Arthur.'

'Who's that?' asked Susan.

'Arthur Matthews. Head of Geography and a mountaineering fanatic,' said Louise.

'Ah, yes. Now I know who you mean,' said Susan. 'I didn't know he went climbing.'

'Absolutely *mad* keen,' said Louise, 'He's probably been up and down most mountains. He also shins around the walls of the Common Room at least once a year but that's not why he's known as 'Mad' Arthur.'

'I wonder if he's been to Tahquitz Rock in the San Jacinto Mountains,' said Susan. 'That's quite a famous rock climbing area in Southern California.'

'I wouldn't be surprised,' said Louise. 'I'll ask him next time I see him.'

* * * * *

By six o'clock every afternoon, Dolly and Tom Brown will have tidied the Common Room in time for the teaching staff to untidy it with their presence. This Thursday was no exception. The assistant caretakers had barely left the CR when in walked Greg Watson (P.E. and geography) with Keith Bradley (woodwork and metalwork). Both men were in their first teaching post.

Both were married with young children. Both were disappointed by the forthcoming salary increase of 8% instead of the expected 10½%.

'Thanks for helping out yesterday afternoon, Keith.'

'My pleasure, Greg. It would have been nicer if it had been a bit warmer. Still, when you come to think about it, what a great job we've got. Standing around in the fresh air, watching boys playing cricket and getting paid for it.'

'What are you drinking?'

'Oh, I'll have a cup of Dolly's coffee, thanks,' said Keith. 'Milk and two sugars.'

'Ham and egg sandwich?'

'Please.'

'White or brown bread?'

'White.'

'Here you are,' said Greg, putting the cup, saucer and plate down on a table.

The door opened and in walked James Jackson (chemistry) followed by David Swann (history). They helped themselves to tea and sandwiches before joining Greg and Keith around the small table. James was in his first teaching post and his wife, Julia, was pregnant with their first child. David was engaged to be married.

'How was the cricket practice yesterday?' asked James.

'Fine. Just another practice,' said Greg, 'not that you'd know from the way those chaps played.'

'Good were they?' said David.

'Pretty good but... I'm not complaining... but they treated the practice more like their annual needle match with Brindle College,' said Greg.

'I say!' Keith said. 'What's going on between Hammond and Jardine?'

'Those two have been rivals on the field from the first,' said Greg. 'Len Hammond is one of the few batsmen who's not frightened by Rupert Jardine's fast bowling.'

'What about off the field?' said James.

'Daggers drawn most of the time,' said Greg. 'Fortunately, Hammond is Upper Sixth and a first class batsman whereas Jardine is Lower Sixth and a first class opening bowler. And even more fortunately, Hammond is an excellent captain the whole First Eleven respects, and that includes Jardine, I suspect.'

The door opened several more times to admit members of staff looking for coffee, tea, sandwiches and cake. Arthur Matthews (geography), Geoffrey Rusbridge (economics), Alan Radford (English), Dr Herbert Newbold (physics) and Dr Philip Carratt (chemistry) – all heads of department – formed their own group around a nearby table. When Quentin Waite, Head of History, arrived a little later, he helped himself to a piece of Dolly Brown's cheese cake, poured himself a dry sherry from the drinks cabinet then settled into his favourite armchair within earshot of both groups.

Two other members of staff entered separately and quietly. First was Colin Harper (maths and computing science). He was spotted by James Jackson and persuaded to join the group. Second was Reginald de Vere (Second Master) who followed Quentin's example with a sherry and a slice of Dolly's cheesecake. Reg settled into an armchair alongside Quentin to eavesdrop on the conversations of the two groups.

* * * * *

'When did you say you're getting married, David?'

'This August, Greg. Saturday the 11th at 11 a.m. to be precise,' said David.

'Not having second thoughts then?' said Keith.

'Good Lord, no,' said David, with a wicked smile on his face. Penelope wouldn't hear of it.' When the laughter had subsided, Greg turned to James.

'When's Julia due?'

'June.'

'Sorry, my mistake,' said Greg. 'When's June due?'

'In exactly forty-one days, three hours, sixteen minutes and... five seconds,' said James.

'Come off it,' said Keith. 'I know you teach chemistry and not biology but you know as well as I do, the term of any pregnancy can vary by a day or two...'

'Several days, actually,' interjected David.

'I know that,' said James, smiling and looking closely at his watch, ' but June's due in precisely forty-one days, three hours, fourteen minutes and... twenty-five seconds. My wife, *Julia*, however, is due around the middle of June.'

'I thought your wife's name was... Oh, *very* funny,' Greg said wryly. 'Well I hope you'll be able to feed three mouths on next year's salary.'

'Four mouths,' said James.

'Three,' said Greg. 'Yours, Julia's and the baby's. That's *three*.'

'It's *four*' said James. 'That's the trouble with you Geographers. You can't count. My mouth – one. Julia's mouth – two. And... the twins – three, four.'

'Twins!' exclaimed Keith. 'Congratulations, old boy. You'll have your arms full.'

'Now you really *will* find it tight on next year's salary,' said Greg. 'That I do know.'

In the first few weeks after his wife died, Reg struggled to contend with the waves of grief and despair that overwhelmed him. Now four years later, he still suffered bouts of sadness especially when he heard his young colleagues talking about their wives and their children. Reg carried in his wallet three photographs, all of Madeleine. They never had children. They had tried. Madeleine became pregnant twice but miscarried each time. After the second miscarriage, the doctors – they actually consulted three specialists – warned against a further pregnancy and advised a hysterectomy.

'What are we doing here, Arthur?' asked Phil Carratt. 'I thought you'd have been out on the tennis court.'

'Normally, yes, you're right. I should be out playing tennis, Phil,' said Arthur Matthews, taking a bite out of his ham and egg sandwich.

'Well, you're obviously not,' said Phil. 'So why are you here and why did you drag us along this evening?'

'Something I overheard my Greg Watson say to your James Jackson,' whispered Arthur, taking another bite.

'Well, what did you hear Greg…'

'Keep your voice down,' hissed Arthur conspiratorially.

'What did you hear Greg Watson say,' whispered Phil.

'He said…' Arthur glanced across to the other group and then hunched closer to Phil. 'He said they should rob a bank.'

'Rob a…'

'Shush!' said Arthur, 'Keep your voice down.'

'You're not serious?' said Geoffrey Rusbridge scornfully.

'Deadly serious, old boy,' whispered Arthur. 'Look at them over there. They're planning a bank robbery.'

'You're off your rocker,' said Geoffrey. 'I reckon you had a fall in the Cairngorms and hit your head. Rob a bank for goodness sake. Why would they want to do that?'

'Just keep quiet and listen. You'll see,' said Arthur.

Quentin and Reg did hear every word 'Mad' Matthews and 'Moneybags' Rusbridge said. Quentin polished his glasses and shifted in his seat so he could better see and hear what the junior members of staff were saying.

'You're quite right, Greg. Things will be a bit tight especially when the twins arrive but I have a contingency plan,' said James. 'I'm banking on marking exam papers.'

'Which Boards?' asked David.

'Joint Matriculation Board and Cambridge.'

'What levels?' asked Keith.

'GCSE with JMB and A-level with Cambridge.'

'Crikey! Two lots of papers in the same three weeks,' said David.

'And new-born twins,' said Keith. 'You'll never cope.'

'The A-level papers should come to me a week or two before the GCSE papers.'

'Why d'you say that?' asked David.

'Well, the GCSE results are published about two weeks after the A-levels, so...'

'The results might come out at different times,' said David, 'I shouldn't bank on marking the papers at different times.'

'How much will you get for all this marking?' Greg asked.

'I estimate about fifteen hundred pounds,' said James.

'Don't bank on that,' said Greg.

'And that's before tax,' said Keith.

'I don't care,' said James, 'It will put money in the bank and that's what counts.'

'Sounds like slave labour to me,' said Keith.

'Do you know an easier way for me to get my hands on some extra cash?' asked James.

'Of course we do,' said Greg. 'We rob a bank.'

None of the five heads of department could hear every word of the conversation but they heard the words *bank* and *banking* clearly enough. It was the last straw when they heard Greg Watson say *rob a bank*; their curiosity got the better of them. Phil Carratt, the Head of Chemistry, led the way and the other four somewhat agitated heads followed.

'Do you mind if we join you fellows?'

'Please do, Dr Carratt.' said James, breaking the uneasy silence. The men shuffled their chairs in a wide circle around the two tables which they had pulled together and sat down; all except Phil Carratt.

'I'm ready for a proper drink,' said Phil, still standing by his chair. 'What can I get everyone?'

Quentin and Reg watched and listened to all this with interest and a not inconsiderable amusement. Over the years the relationship between heads of department and junior staff had become more cordial. Nevertheless, an intangible barrier, between senior and junior, still existed and revealed itself through certain formalities and codes of behaviour.

'Red wine for me, Phil,' said Arthur.

'Same for me, Phil,' Geoffrey said.

'Alan! Herbert! What about you?'

'White wine, Phil,' they said.

'And what about you chaps?' said Phil, turning to the junior staff. 'Wine or beer?'

'A light ale, please, Dr Carratt,' said James. The rest, including Colin Harper, followed suit. All five respectfully ordered a light ale from the beneficent Dr Carratt.

'Fifteen love to the senior team,' said Reg to Quentin.

'Agreed!' said Quentin. 'He threw them so off balance that none had the wit to jump up and stand the first round. I wonder who will ask the first question and how they'll deal with it.'

'So,' said Geoffrey Rusbridge, 'why are you going to rob a bank?'

'Probably for the same reason Mr Matthews will climb a mountain,' James, the humorist in the group, said nonchalantly. 'For a bit of a lark and because it's there to be done.'

'So,' said Geoffrey, 'you're not interested in the money then?'

'I didn't say that. All five of us would be interested in the money. Isn't that right chaps?' said James. He looked at Colin Harper who hadn't said a word all evening. 'Isn't that right Colin?'

'Y-yes. Th-that's right, J-James.'

'Why the concern with money?' Geoffrey Rusbridge asked. 'Not got enough of the stuff, is that it?'

'Since you asked, Mr Rusbridge,' said Greg. 'No, we don't have enough of it. And things are going to get tighter next term with the salary increase at eight percent instead of the expected ten and a half percent.'

'So you're serious about robbing a bank, are you Greg?' asked Arthur Matthews.

'Absolutely! Unless,' said James, smiling wryly across the table at the Head of Economics, 'Mr Rusbridge could suggest other quick ways to make some easy money.'

'Thirty fifteen to the junior team, I think,' said Quentin to Reg.

'Very nicely played,' said Reg. 'But I'll lay odds the juniors have opened themselves up to one of Geoffrey's disputations.'

'I have to agree with you, Reg. The question is which one?'

'My money – sorry, Quentin – I'll wager he'll give them his Rockefeller anecdote.'

'Let's consider why you *think* you don't have enough money. It's probably because you are concerned about people who have more than you and unconcerned about people who have less than you. In other words, you are unhappy about the unequal distribution of wealth in the world. You're like the Red Bolshevik who, one day in late October, 1929, just after the Black Tuesday Stock Market Crash, stormed into the Rockefeller Center on Fifth Avenue, New York, complaining about the unequal distribution of wealth. John D. Rockefeller, overhearing the man rant and rave, turned to his secretary and said, "What is the current estimate of my wealth?" The secretary replied, "Two hundred million dollars." Then Rockefeller asked, "What is the current estimate of the world population?" The secretary replied, "Two billion men, women and children." The Rockefeller asked, "What do you get if you divided my wealth by the world population?" The secretary replied, "$200,000,000 ÷ 2,000,000,000 = $0.10, sir." Finally Rockefeller said to his secretary, "Give this guy 10 cents and throw him out!"

'Thirty all!' said Reg.

'Agreed!' said Quentin. 'Junior team to serve. A bit of care needed now to avoid another disputation.'

'I fear someone will make the mistake of asking Geoffrey directly how to make money.'

'Indeed,' said Quentin. 'That would be folly. He's bound to give them homework to do.'

'That he will,' said Reg. 'And he'll pour scorn on any useless idea.'

'You never know. They might have one sensible idea between them,' said Quentin.

'You never know. They're a pretty bright bunch,' said Reg, 'And that Colin Harper is a genius. A bit odd, mind you, but a genius all the same. If anyone is going to produce the goods, my money's on Colin. One thing's for sure, he'll never be a bank robber.'

* * * * *

'Seriously, Mr Rusbridge,' said David, 'what can *we* do to make money?'

'I assume you want to make it legally, quickly and safely,' said Geoffrey, looking at his watch. 'It's getting late. Let me suggest the five of you have a brainstorming session and write down all the ways *you* can think of to make money. Then we'll get together in a few days time and… well, we'll take it from there.'

'That will mean putting our bank robbery on hold for a while, chaps,' said James, grinning broadly. 'Is that alright?' All but one nodded in agreement. 'We're agreed, Mr Rusbridge. Thank you for your help.'

'Think nothing of it,' said Geoffrey. And that's exactly what one of them thought.

'I'm ready for another drink,' said Keith, standing up. 'What can I get everyone?'

* * * * *

"Money can't buy you happiness but it does bring you a more pleasant form of misery." Spike Milligan

* * * * *

In 1557 in the April section of his *one hundred good points of husbandry*, Thomas Tusser wrote *Sweet April showers Do spring May flowers*. Almost four centuries later, in 1921 to be exact, Louis Silvers composed the music, B. G. De Sylva wrote the lyrics and, on Broadway, Al Jolson sang the now well-known song *April Showers*.

Though April showers may come your way,

They bring the flowers that bloom in May.

Nowadays, psychiatrists tend to regard Tusser's words to be less about farming and more about the human psyche; the suffering of unpleasantness (the rain in April) for the later reward of pleasure (the flowers in May).

The April showers at the start of the Trinity term at Beaumont Abbey had been neither more heavy nor more frequent than usual. Only once were the ladies forced to scamper for cover from the tennis court behind Gower House. Only once was the First Eleven forced to abandon their cricket match, much to the chagrin of Jardine who was on a hat trick. And only once was the CCF forced to parade in the pouring rain, much to the delight of Jardine who wangled extra time on the rifle range.

Nosey Parker was *not* a man of the outdoors, so the unpleasantness he had to endure in April was certainly not rain. Angus MacKay *was* a man of the outdoors and liked the rain, so the unpleasantness he had to endure in April was the tedium of trawling through a mountain of files and documents for signs of wrong doing by men like Parker-Smythe.

'I've some good news and some bad news,' said Angus MacKay over the telephone. 'What d'you want first?'

'Since when have you ever been the bearer of good news,' said Stanley Garnet. 'I'll take your bad news first.'

'I'll not complete this investigation in one month,' said Angus. 'And I'll be needing to spend a wee bit o' time in Guernsey, so that'll cost you a pound or two.'

'Nice place for a holiday, Guernsey. A bit warmer than your Scottish Highlands.'

'I ken,' said Angus. 'but it'll be no holiday I'll be taking.'

'What's the good news?'

'It's a wee bit early to be sure,' said Angus, 'but so far I've no evidence of malpractice on yon Robert York's part.'

'Well that's a relief,' said Stanley.

'Did you not hear what I said? I've no evidence *so far*. I'm not giving Bob a clean bill of health yet,' said Angus. 'He might be up to his neck in the mire with Beaumont's bursar.'

'Oh!' said Stanley, 'What's Parker-Smythe been up to?'

'Let's just say he seems to have pretty sticky fingers.'

'Have you said anything to Pugh-Jones?'

'Och, no. I'm just letting you know I'll be working from home for the next few weeks.'

'Except when you're taking Fiona on holiday to Guernsey at the firm's expense.'

'You know Fiona,' said Angus. 'She'll not be left at home.'

'So you're putting her on my payroll, are you?' said Stanley.

'Och, no. She'll settle for expenses,' said Angus, smiling to himself at the thought of Stanley's face when he sees the bill for their stay at La Collinette Hotel. 'The point is Mr Anthony Parker-Smythe – by the way, his real name is Tony Smith – knows me by sight but he has never seen Fiona. So she'll be able to keep an eye on him in Guernsey.'

'How do you know he's going to Guernsey?' asked Stanley.

'A wee birdie,' said Angus, thinking of Susan Taylor.

'Knowing the way you work,' said Stanley, thinking of Ireland, 'you'll have a spy in the Beaumont camp. I won't waste my time asking who that is. I won't even guess.'

'Good for you.'

'Will you be going back to Beaumont in the near future?'

'Aye, maybe if only to keep Smithy on his toes,' said Angus. 'I'd prefer to drop in when Bob York's there with him. Find out when he plans to go there and warn me, will ye?'

'Of course. Leave it to me,' said Stanley. 'By the way, I shall be interested to know what drops out of the tree when you give it one of your shakes. Keep me posted.'

* * * * *

The four ladies were on court at least one evening each week in April but rarely managed three sets because they were so evenly matched. They always spun their racquets for partners and it never seemed to matter who partnered whom. They were enjoying one another's company and getting on well; so well in fact that after their third evening session they booked the court to play on the Sunday afternoon. They were in the middle of their first set that afternoon when the heavens opened and they had to dash for shelter. When there was no sign of the rain letting up, Louise invited them back for a cup of tea.

'I do *love* your sunroom,' gushed Celia. 'So warm and...'

'Sunny?' Mary said with a twinkle in her eye.

'Yes, yes,' said Celia, ' So warm and sunny.'

'Would you hand round the cakes, Mary?' said Louise as she poured out the teas.

'You do eat cake, don't you?' Mary said, grinning and holding out the plate to Susan.

'Especially this chocolate fudge cake. Thanks,' said Susan.

'Why did you ask Susan if she…? Oh, now I remember,' said Celia. 'Susan never eats pancakes. That's right, isn't it?'

Susan yielded to their pressure. She told them about Lefu, the sweaty cook, whose name meant *sickness* or *death* and who put pancakes under his armpit to keep them warm. She told them about her childhood in South Africa. She told them about her student days at the University of Cape Town. She even told them about the racing driver she married and deserted. Susan felt more at ease and more at home than ever she had since coming to England. She felt she was among friends at last.

'Now then, Susan,' said Celia. 'You must tell us how we can make money. I really do want to travel but I can't do that on Humphrey's salary. I'd *love* to go to California.'

'Yes, come on, Susan,' said Mary. 'How do we play the Stock Market?'

'Susan does not *play* the Market,' said Louise, 'She *invests* in stocks and shares.'

'Well, whatever Susan does,' said Celia, 'I'd like to do the same so I can afford to travel.'

'I think you'll need some money to start with,' said Louise, 'Money you can risk and afford to lose. Isn't that right, Susan?'

'Yes, I suppose so,' said Susan. 'You usually need money to make money.'

'How much did you have when you started playing… sorry,' said Celia, 'When you started *investing* in the Stock Market, if you don't mind my asking?'

'No, I don't mind. As a matter of fact, I never bought my first lot of shares,' said Susan. 'I inherited them from my father. He had shares in De Beers, the diamond mining company Cecil Rhodes formed with the financial help of the Rothschild family.'

134

'But you did buy your second lot of shares, though,' said Celia. 'How did you do that?'

'I saved up my dividends. And when De Beers looked like losing their monopoly of the diamond trade, I rather foolishly sold my shares. That's when I used my dividend savings and the money from the sale of the De Beers shares to start investing seriously.'

'So there's not much hope for me,' said Celia. 'I haven't got any money.'

'I've not much,' said Mary. 'but I think I could find some if I looked hard enough.'

'Come to think of it,' said Celia, 'I do have some premium bonds I could cash in.'

'If you're serious,' said Susan, 'you could form an investment club. You wouldn't need a lot of money to do that.'

'What's an investment club and how would we form one?' asked Celia. Susan explained.

'An investment club is just a small group of people pooling their money to buy and sell stocks. You'd need a constitution, a set of rules, one or two officers – a treasurer and maybe a secretary – and an official address to give your local tax office. You'd divide the income and profits between you according to your club rules. You'd each pay tax on your share even if the club keeps your share of the income and gains for re-investment.'

'I propose we form a club now,' said Celia. 'Mary could be secretary. Susan could be treasurer. Oh... Oh, yes. And Louise could be president. I'll be a member. All in favour?'

'Whoa, Celia!' said Louise. 'Let's not be too hasty. Mary and Susan work full-time.'

'Oh, yes. You're right, of course. Sorry. I should have realised they'd be too busy.'

'Actually,' said Mary, 'I'd be happy to be the secretary. I don't think it would take up that much time. The treasurer would have the hardest job.'

'What do you say, Susan?' said Celia. 'Would you be the treasurer of our club?'

There could have been school photographs even before 1900 when the *Brownie Camera* appeared on the mass market. Beaumont Abbey has plenty of photographs. Distinguished Old Boys hang in the main corridor on the stone wall facing the High Master's study. Groups of past pupils, some distinguished, others not so distinguished, hang in the hallways of the four houses: Armstrong, Burdett, Gower and Wedgewood. Past teams - cricket, hockey and rugby – hang in the pavilion waiting to be moved to the new sports hall. Past groups of academic staff, framed behind glass, hang on the common room walls, surviving Dolly's dusting and Arthur Matthews's annual mountaineering escapade.

A keen observer would notice that academic staff photographs in general will have certain characteristics in common. For example, they will have been taken outdoors on a dry but sunless day to minimise the risk of staff shutting their eyes and appearing to be asleep. All staff entitled to do so will be wearing an academic gown over a suit and tie.

The staff will be divided into three or four rows. Those in the front row will be seated. The High Master will have the centre seat. The Second Master will be on his immediate right. On his immediate left will be the most senior, and oldest by age, Head of Department. The rest of the chairs will, as far as possible, be occupied by the other department heads - the longer their service, the closer they will sit to the centre.

The second row – those standing immediately behind the chairs - will comprise the shorter members of staff. The third row will be the taller staff. The back row will be the youngest, most agile staff perched precariously on benches of dubious stability. The entire group will be photographed on a lawn which, like the hair of the staff, will have been especially trimmed for the occasion. And the photograph's background will, of course, be the building's most impressive stone wall and/or stained glass windows.

136

Close examination, perhaps with a magnifying glass, will reveal that the photographs share other common characteristics. For example, staff sitting in the front row generally bear what might best be described as a supercilious smile. Senior staff standing behind the seats will have put on a brave face; an honest smile being out of the question for a number of reasons not the least of which is the rather long time they have been forced to stand still. Any senior or aged member of staff with a genuine smile will likely be in his retirement year.

The junior members of staff in the photographs fall into one of three groups: those having nothing to smile about; those with false smiles hoping for promotion; and those with broad grins responding to a ribald joke just dispensed by one of their number.

One other common characteristic in academic staff photographs is the receding hairline. This usually distinguishes the seniors from juniors. Eye glasses could also distinguish the young from the not so young but they are rarely worn, the favourite but flimsy excuse being that the lenses would reflect sunlight into the camera and spoil the photograph.

In the Beaumont staff photographs, the Head of Economics and Business Studies was the only person to wear a black gown over a white cotton, single-breasted, two-button blazer. This was Geoffrey Rusbridge, BA (Oxon), a clean-shaven man of medium build and height, with well receded dark brown hair always carefully brushed and shiny. One might describe him as compact and even go so far as to call him dapper. A colleague did once say, somewhat unkindly, that Geoffrey, in his white straw hat, white blazer, white shirt, red and white striped (Merton College) tie and light grey flannels, looked like the captain of the local lawn bowling club. Someone must have overheard that colleague's remark because the boys had nicknamed Geoffrey *lawn bowler*.

'Good afternoon, gentlemen,' said Geoffrey addressing his Lower Sixth Economics set, causing the hubbub in the room to subside. 'I trust your noisy arguments concerned your assignments which as usual thoroughly ruined my evening.' As he returned their papers, he said, 'Mr Zháng! Since you seem to be the only person to have done any work, would you kindly explain to the rest of this so-called top set the difference between fiscal policy and monetary policy.'

'The difference between them is their way of influencing the economy,' said Zháng.

'Good. So far I believe you have everybody's attention, including that of Mr Lucas. Pray continue.'

'The Government carries out a fiscal policy to control its borrowing by controlling taxation and its own spending. The Bank of England, or the Federal Reserve in America, carries out a monetary policy by setting interest rates and controlling the money supply.'

'Very good. Thank you Mr Zháng,' said Geoffrey. 'So, Mr Lucas, what might be the effect of the Bank of England adopting an expansionary monetary policy?'

'The old lady of Threadneedle Street would print more pound notes and we'd have more money to spend, sir,' said Lucas.

'Would we be any better off, Mr Lucas?'

'I wouldn't sir,' said Lucas.

'I probably shouldn't ask. Oh, well.' sighed Geoffrey. 'do tell us, Mr Lucas, why you wouldn't be any better off?'

'Because my father wouldn't increase my allowance, sir.'

'How can you be sure he wouldn't increase your allowance, Mr Lucas?'

'Well, sir, last year when I was in Cyprus with the CCF, I sent him a really nice picture postcard of Limassol Castle... You know, sir, where Berengaria of Navarre is supposed to have married Richard the Lionheart in 1191 to become Queen of England...'

'What did you write on the card, as if we couldn't guess?' said Geoffrey.

'*No mon, no fun, your son*,' said Lucas.

'And how did your father reply?'

'My father sent me card with a cartoon of a moth flying out of an empty wallet, sir. He'd drawn a balloon coming out of the moth's mouth and written in the balloon the words: *Too bad, how sad, your dad.*' The giggling subsided. Geoffrey turned to his star pupil.

'Yes, Mr Zháng, you have something sensible to contribute?'

'According to the Quantity Theory of Money, $dP/P = dM/M$.'

'For the benefit of Mr Lucas and others,' said Geoffrey, 'would you care to translate your mathematics into ordinary language, Mr Zháng.'

'If the Bank of England prints more money, we may have more to spend but we won't be able to buy more because prices will inflate or the value of the money will fall. dM is the increase in M, the money, so dM/M is the fractional or percentage increase in the money supply. dP is the increase in P, the price, so dP/P is the fractional or percentage increase in prices. Money supply increases so prices increase.'

'Thank you, gentlemen,' said Geoffrey at the end of the lesson. 'Your assignment for this evening – a co-operative assignment on this occasion – is to list as many ways as you can devise to make money quickly. And please, Mr Lucas, do not include counterfeiting.'

* * * * *

Ever since his most unnerving and unpleasant encounter with Major Angus MacKay, an experience he had no wish to repeat, Nosey Parker had not been quite himself. Bob York had not helped by telling him he had nothing to worry about *as long as the money* in the Guernsey accounts *was only Nosey's own money*. Nosey was sure Bob knew he was feathering his nest but this was the first time Bob, or anyone else, seemed interested in knowing where the feathers came from.

Ever since her encounter with Angus, an experience she would be happy to repeat, Susan Taylor had not been herself. She was now keeping an even closer watch on

Tony Smith's activities. She was playing tennis regularly. She was enjoying the company of friends. In short, her days in South Africa were becoming a distant memory and she was beginning more fully to enjoy life.

Ever since his unnerving but not unpleasant encounter with James Jackson and others in the Common Room that Thursday evening, Colin Harper had not been quite himself. The more he had tried to think up ways to make money, the more convinced he became that the only *quick* way was to steal from the wealthy. Bank robbery was a possibility. Banks were usually rich. And nowadays computers ought to ensure the theft would be swift, silent, non-violent and, more importantly, go undetected for a considerable time. Colin decided to keep what he called his *cat* (computer-assisted theft) *burglary* to himself for the time being. He also decided to ask for help with the assignment Geoffrey Rusbridge had set him and his confederates.

'Mr Harper would like a word with you, Bursar,' said Susan. 'Are you available?'

'Certainly. Please send him straight in.'

'Please come in, Mr Harper,' said Susan, looking the picture of health and radiating confidence. The sunshine had made her natural fair hair even fairer and had tanned her face and arms to the point where the freckles were almost invisible. The young maths and computing science teacher, by sharp contrast, looked drawn, white-faced and ill at ease. Susan felt sorry for him. 'Would you like something to drink, Mr Harper?'

'Y-yes. Th-thank you. Yes, if that's no t-trouble.'

'Colin! How nice to see you' said Nosey, after Susan had left and closed the door, 'I was just thinking about you.'

'Oh, r-really,' said Colin, sitting in the chair Angus MacKay had occupied a few days earlier.

'Yes, I was,' said Nosey, worried about the hidden files on his computer. 'I'll explain why later. What can I do for you?'

'I h-hope you w-won't mind m-my asking,' said Colin. 'I n-need your help.'

'How can I help?' Nosey asked warily.

'I w-would l-like you t-to t-tell me how t-to m-make m-money qu-quickly.'

At that moment there was a knock on the door and Susan entered with coffee, tea and chocolate biscuits. It was a timely interruption. It allowed Nosey the breathing space to wonder why Colin would want money quickly and to consider whether or not to help him. As she poured out the drinks and handed round the biscuits, Susan wondered why this man wanted money and why he had come to Tony Smith for help. After she left the room, she paused outside the closed door to eavesdrop a second time.

'I'm flattered you have come to me for help, Colin,' Nosey said. 'May I ask how much money you need and how soon you need it?'

'Th-that's hard to s-say,' stuttered Colin, thinking about his four junior colleagues and their salary increase for next term. Teachers in the state system were going to get a rise of 10.5%. He and his colleagues were going to get a rise of 8.0%. He rapidly estimated that the 2.5% difference would represent a shortfall on each annual salary of £400 to £500. So all five of them would be short by a total of £2,500 or thereabouts.

'Two thousand five hundred pounds, you say?'

'Th-that's just a rough estimate,' said Colin.

'And how soon would you want it?' asked Nosey.

'Th-that's also hard to s-say. P-probably by n-next S-September.'

'In three months time,' said Nosey. 'Well now Colin, I think I could manage that but I wouldn't do this for anybody else. You do understand that, don't you?'

'Oh no!' said Colin. 'You m-misunderstand. I d-don't want y-you to l-lend m-me m-money. I w-want y-you to tell m-me how y-you m-make it.' Then it suddenly dawned on Colin. The Bursar had off-shore accounts in Guernsey and was probably very wealthy.

Do teachers have a cushy life? Someone outside of the profession might say yes because teachers seem to work short hours, take long holidays and have enviable job security. Do teachers in the independent boarding schools have an easier life than teachers in the state day school? Some teachers at Prescott Manor, the state-maintained school down the road, might envy the higher salaries and longer summer holidays at Beaumont Abbey. Some staff at Beaumont might envy the teachers at Prescott Manor not having to teach on Saturday morning and being able to leave school behind them every afternoon. That said, few would actually be prepared to change schools.

The work of a teacher is never confined just to the classroom or laboratory. This was true at Beaumont. During term time, staff felt they were on duty twenty-four hours a day for the seven days of the week. The calls upon their time were such that quite a few days went by before those five junior staff could meet Geoffrey Rusbridge in the Common Room. Colin Harper on this occasion was first to arrive. James Jackson, Gregory Watson, Keith Bradley and David Swann soon followed.

'Right,' said James, 'Whose turn is it to sign the chit for drinks?'

'Mine I believe,' said Colin without a trace of a stammer. 'What are you chaps having?'

'I say!' said David, 'Old Colin's coming out of his shell, don't you think?

'Definitely!' said Keith. 'I mean… last time we didn't get a peep out of him.'

'Bit of an odd bloke if you know what I mean,' said Greg, tapping the side of his nose.

'I wouldn't say that,' said James. 'I think he's just a bit shy, that's all. He's a first class mathematician and an absolute wizard when it comes to computers. Why only the other day… Ah, there you are. Well done Colin.' Then turning to Keith, James said, 'See that! All the drinks exactly as ordered. Now why can't you ever do that, Mr Bradley?'

During the next ten minutes or so, Arthur Matthews, Alan Radford, Dr Herbert Newbold and Dr Philip Carratt arrived and seated themselves at a nearby table. Quentin Waite and Reginald de Vere appeared shortly afterwards. They settled themselves into their comfortable armchairs in time to observe and listen to the *gang of five* telling jokes. After the fourth joke, it was Colin's turn. At this point, even the four heads of department stopped talking amongst themselves. 'Come on, Colin,' said James. 'It's your turn to tell one.' To everyone's amazement, Colin put down his glass and told his joke confidently.

'Four teachers were stuck in a car that had stopped and wouldn't restart. The driver taught chemistry,' said Colin, looking straight at James. 'He said the car wouldn't start because they put in the wrong fuel; leaded instead of unleaded. The front seat passenger taught metal work,' continued Colin, looking at Keith. 'He said the car wouldn't go because the big end had broken. One of the two passengers in the rear taught history,' said Colin now looking at David. 'He said the car wouldn't go because it was the history of inferior Italian cars repeating itself.' Colin drained what little was left of the red wine in his glass, then continued. 'The other passenger in the rear seat taught computing science. He said he didn't know why the car stopped but said it would restart if they all got out of the car and got back in again.'

Geoffrey Rusbridge was completely taken aback by the roar of laughter from the *gang of five* confederates just as he entered the Common Room. And he found it hard to believe Dr Carratt who said Colin Harper and not James Jackson caused the laughter. When he realised Quentin had not understood the joke, Reg made the mistake of trying to explain it. 'A computer can crash for no apparent reason, so the quickest way to get it working again is to log out and boot it up again.' The Head of

History was completely lost. How could a computer *crash*? It does not move about. And where do logs and boots come into it? As far as Quentin was concerned, crash, log out and boot up belonged to a language quite foreign to his ears. When he realised his cause was a lost one, Reg said, 'Another glass of red?' That was a language Quentin thoroughly understood.

'Our mentor has arrived at last,' said Greg. 'Time for our lesson.' The five junior staff took their drinks and chairs to join the five heads of department.

'Good evening Mr Rusbridge,' said Colin. 'May I get you something to drink?'

'A glass of white would be nice, Colin,' said Geoffrey. When he noticed the colour of the wine in his colleague's glasses, he said, 'I think there's a Chardonnay in the refrigerator.'

'I hope this is chilled to your liking, sir,' said Colin, handing Geoffrey a glass of Chablis.

'Thank you, Colin,' said Geoffrey, taking a sip. 'Perfect. Santé!'

'I expect you know,' said Dr Carratt, 'that this Chardonnay, Chablis or White Burgundy got its big buttery taste from malolactic fermentation. Perhaps James would explain.'

'Fifteen love to the seniors,' whispered Reg to Quentin.

'What? Oh, yes. Right,' said the young chemistry teacher stalling for time. 'It's a secondary fermentation process to improve the wine. Since wine making is your speciality, Dr Carratt, perhaps you would explain further.'

'Fifteen all,' whispered Quentin to Reg.

'Malo refers to malic acid which confers a harshness to a wine. Lactic refers of course to lactic acid which confers a softness. In the secondary fermentation, Lactobacillus bacteria convert malic acid into lactic acid. The diacetyl derivative of lactic acid is responsible for the buttery character of the wine.'

'Thirty fifteen to the seniors,' said Reg.

144

'So you see,' said James, holding up his glass, 'this wine is not so acidic as Chardonnays that have not undergone secondary fermentation.'

'Thirty all,' said Quentin.

'Quite right,' said Dr Carratt. 'Unfortunately, the secondary fermentation has reduced the fruitiness of this Chardonnay.'

'Forty thirty to the seniors,' said Reg.

'As a compromise,' said James, 'you could split a batch of wine into two parts, secondary ferment one part to reduce the acidity and then blend the parts to produce a wine with a reasonable fruitiness and acidity.'

'Deuce,' said Quentin.

* * * * *

'Now then gentlemen,' said Geoffrey, turning to the junior staff and trying to take a firm hold on the meeting. 'how do you propose to make money? Who's going to start?'

'I scribbled down some of our ideas,' said David. 'They're just our initial thoughts and they're not in any priority order you understand.' He read out the list.

Brew and sell beer, wines and spirits (James - chemistry)

Organise educational touring holidays (David - history)

Tennis coaching rich widows (Greg – physical education)

Car and motor cycle hire and maintenance (Keith – metal work)

Run an import/export business (Colin – maths and computing)

'I like the first idea,' said Phil Carratt. 'I have all the equipment you'll need in my lab but I don't think your suggestion is legal, James. You'd better ask Quentin.

'Home made wine is not illegal,' said Quentin, after he and Reg had joined the gathering. 'You can brew as much as you like for your own consumption or to *give away* to friends. If you wanted to sell it, you would have to apply for a wine producer's excise licence and comply with all the rules and regulations pertaining to the Alcoholic Liquor Duties Act of 1979 and the Weights and Measures legislation *and* satisfy the various conditions concerning bottling, health and hygiene, labelling, storing, shipping, et cetera, et cetera.' He raised his glass to his lips, took a sip, swirled the amber liquid over his tongue and swallowed.'

'Every year I have to sign a Customs and Excise form to declare the two stills in chemistry are used to produce distilled water only,' said Phil Carratt. 'And without warning, an official will drop in to inspect them. So, if we distilled home made wine…'

'Don't even think about it,' said Quentin. 'Totally illegal!'

'Could we apply for a licence and do it legally?' asked James.

'You could but you'd be wasting your time. As part of your application you would have to provide a plan – it's called an entry of premises – to show the position and description of each vessel or other piece of plant you intend to use in the production of wine. If you intend to distil, then your premises must be a fortress: thick concrete walls, windows secured by one inch thick steel bars spaced a certain distance apart and buried a certain distance in the concrete,' Quentin said with a shudder. 'Not a legal option, young man.'

The discussions continued. David tried to sell his educational tours, Greg his coaching of rich widows and Keith his vehicle hire and maintenance. The consensus of opinion was they would take too long and too much effort for too little return. Colin tried to explain the profitability of an import export business but the others thought it would be too complicated for them. Alan Radford, the Head of English, who was getting tired and wanted to leave, attempted to summarise their discussions.

'It seems to me,' he said, 'that you haven't properly defined your goals and considered the consequent principle courses of action. How much money do you want to make and how quickly? How much time and effort can you devote to the task? Do you want to make it legally or illegally?'

'I estimated £2,500 before the first of September,' said Colin, going on briefly to explain his reasoning.'

'I'm definitely *not* going to rob a bank for a measly five hundred pounds,' said Keith.

'So how much do you want, Keith?' asked Greg.

'I don't know *exactly*,' said Keith. 'A lot more than £500, that's all I can say.'

'I take it,' said Alan, 'that you don't mind making your money illegally, Keith?'

'I think of myself as Robin Hood and these chaps as my merry men,' said Keith. 'We'll rob the rich and give to the poor... that's us of course.'

'Oh, please. Not that old chestnut again,' said Quentin. 'If, and I stress *if*, there was a Robin Hood, I doubt if he was a sainted knight of the realm. More than likely he was just a common poacher and highway robber with a not so merry band of cut throats.'

'W-well,' said Colin, his stammer returning, 'h-he p-probably had the right idea. If w-we w-want to m-make a l-lot of m-money qu-qu-quickly, w-we'll have t-to r-rob the r-rich.'

* * * * *

CHAPTER 15

"We succeed only as we identify in life, or in war, or in anything else, a single overriding objective, and make all other considerations bend to that one objective."
Dwight D. Eisenhower

* * * * *

Dr Llywelyn Pugh-Jones, High Master of Beaumont Abbey, would hesitate to nominate his favourite colour, food or drink but would not hesitate to name his favourite month. In Wales, the land of his birth, May is the sunniest month of the year. In England, May comes a close second to the sunniest month - July. During the month of May, Dr Pugh-Jones never has any difficulty following his doctor's orders to take a daily brisk walk.

In the corner of his extensive garden, Llywelyn paused in the sunshine to enjoy the fragrance of the blossom from a whitethorn tree. Shortly after he had been diagnosed with a heart condition, he read of medical evidence supporting the use of the leaves, flowers and fruit of the crataegus monogyna to treat cardiac insufficiency. So for three years, Llywelyn had made it his business to collect from his favourite tree in late Spring, the white petals (after pollination by the midges) and in late Summer, the red haws.

Louise, his wife, brewed herbal tea from the whitethorn petals. Edna, their house keeper, used the fruit to make jam. When Llywelyn was young he learned to associate food that was good for him with food that he disliked. Boiled cabbage was one of his mother's favourite 'good for him' foods. He still hates boiled cabbage but he enjoys the petal tea and haw jam even though they are 'good for him'.

On his medically prescribed brisk walk, Llywelyn tried not to think about the problems waiting for him in his study. He had heard nothing from Stanley Garnet or Major MacKay regarding their inquiries into the bursar and the school accountant, so he feared the worst. Some parents had already complained about the increase in the school fees and asked for a detailed explanation; although none had yet threatened to withdraw their son, he again feared the worst. He dreaded to think what some disgruntled staff were planning in response to their lower than expected salary increase; he feared the worst as usual.

'Good morning Mary.'

'Good morning, High Master. What a beautiful morning. Perfect for tennis.'

'Ah, yes. I gather Mrs Taylor has joined your ranks. She's pretty good I hear.'

'Very good, actually,' said Mary. 'She's certainly raised our standard of play.'

'Really? I shouldn't have thought that possible.' He put on his glasses. 'The post?'

'Another five letters from parents,' said Mary. 'More complaints about the fees increase. Two threatening to withdraw their boys.'

'Oh dear!' sighed Llywelyn. 'Who are they? Not the Blaines and Goslings I hope?'

'No!' said Mary. 'The parents of Jepson in Lower Third and....' She paused to sift through the letters, 'and the parents of Harrington in Upper Fifth.'

'Not scholarship material either of them,' said Llywelyn, 'but both decent enough boys, none the less.'

'No doubt you'll want to respond fairly soon to all these letters, High Master. Would you be ready to start dictating at half past ten?' Llywelyn nodded and Mary left him to think.

The High Master was still undecided on how best to reply to all the letters when Mary knocked and entered with his morning cup of Earl Grey tea and her shorthand notebook. Remembering how helpful she had been with his report to the governors, Llywelyn decided to ask for her advice and help.

'If I may be frank, High Master,' said Mary, 'you should not reply to these complaining letters until you have clarified your position on certain fundamentals.'

'For example?'

149

'For example,' said Mary, 'how do you regard Beaumont Abbey in relation to, say, Eton, Harrow and Winchester on the one hand and, say, Prescott Manor, Weasel Secondary Modern and Crowbridge Comprehensive on the other hand?'

'I'm not quite sure what you're driving at,' said Llywelyn. 'but I suppose I'd start by confessing that Beaumont is not in the same league as Eton, Harrow or Winchester. They never have to worry about pupil numbers. It's well known that Old Etonians put their grandchildren's names down for Eton at birth.'

'So why do *we* have to worry about pupil numbers?' said Mary.

'Well I suppose it's because we cannot offer what Eton offers?'

'I think Beaumont offers much the same as Eton but on a smaller scale,' said Mary, 'but I think there is a more important difference.'

'And that is?'

'It's much easier to get into Beaumont and much harder to get into Eton,' said Mary.

'So we should make our entrance exam harder, is that what you're saying?'

'No, not necessarily,' said Mary. 'but you should build Beaumont's reputation as a school that's hard to get into. That way, money will be a secondary consideration.'

'What does this have to do with how I reply to these latest letters?' asked Llywelyn.

'Think of Beaumont as being like Eton. Then the parents who take their boys away would simply be making room for the boys on your waiting list.'

'Very interesting,' said Llywelyn. 'Now, why did you ask how I regard Beaumont in relation to the state schools like Prescott Manor down the road?'

'Well, where will a boy go if his parents take him away from Beaumont?' said Mary.

'An independent school with lower fees?' said Llywelyn.

'Perhaps,' said Mary, 'but I think a state school with no fees at all is more likely. In which case, we should ask what the parents are buying with the Beaumont fees that their boys could not get for free at Prescott Manor?'

'Ah, I see,' said Llywelyn. 'So in my reply to these letters, I should tell the parents what they would be denying their sons if they take them away from Beaumont?'

'No, not quite, but you might *hint at* the benefits of boarding and being under the care of a first class staff twenty-four hours a day; of the all-round education we provide, including the wide range of sporting facilities and extra-curricular activities such as the Combined Cadet Corps,' said Mary. 'And don't forget Beaumont Abbey's ancient tradition - something the secondary moderns and comprehensives cannot call upon.'

'Splendid!' said Llywelyn. 'I don't suppose you'd be willing to...'

'I'd be delighted, High Master. I'll have some drafts ready for you to consider early this afternoon.'

'Thank you, Mary. I'm most grateful,' said Llywelyn. 'Would you see if the Second Master is free. I must to discuss this with him right away.'

* * * * *

When he was headmaster of Uppingham School, the Reverend Edward Thring founded, in 1869, the Head Masters' Conference (HMC) - an association of the headmasters of the prestigious Public Schools but not those of lesser standing. In 1904, the HMC introduced the first Common Entrance Examination (CEE) for the members of the association.

Dr Llywelyn Pugh-Jones, like the High Masters of Beaumont before him, is a member of HMC and all boys applying to enter his school must sit the CEE English, Mathematics and Science papers in January or early February. In June, the successful boys would sit Beaumont's own scholarship entrance examination, taking papers in at least four subjects chosen from

151

Geography, History, French, German, Greek, Latin and Religious Studies. No matter where the boys sit the two examinations – in most cases in their preparatory schools at home or abroad – both sets of papers would be sent to Beaumont for marking.

Each year Beaumont awards five scholarships which remain valid for the whole time the holders attend the school. The scholarships for classics, mathematics, modern language and science, are awarded solely on the examination results; applications by parents are not needed. In the case of music however, parents must apply on behalf of their son who will be auditioned. Each scholarship may cover up to fifty percent of the school fees.

Each year Beaumont also awards ten bursaries covering from 10% to 100% of the school fees. Unlike a scholarship, the value of a bursary is based on the family's wealth and is reviewed every year. Every boy who passes the Common Entrance and the Scholarship Entrance is called to Beaumont for an interview. If he needs financial help, the boy's parents must apply for a bursary before they attend with their son for the interview. Each application is considered by a committee of the governing board of directors.

'The Second Master is here to see you,' said Mary, putting her head around the door.

'Ah, Reg! Come in, come in,' said Llywelyn.

'Good morning, High Master,' said Reginald de Vere. 'Nice day for tennis.'

'What? Oh, yes, tennis! Of course, you're one of the enthusiasts,' said Llywelyn.

'I enjoy the odd game of mixed doubles,' said Reg, 'but Arthur and I have only had one game so far this season. Your wife and your secretary seem to prefer doubles with Susan Taylor and Celia Fiddle.'

'Ah, well,' said Llywelyn, 'you and Arthur aren't up to their standard, d'you see. You'll have to raise your game to an higher level before they'll let you in… which brings me neatly to why I wanted to see you.'

'My standard of tennis?' said Reg.

'Good lord, no. Nothing to do with your tennis. No, no. I'm talking about our standard here at Beaumont.'

'Oh, I see,' said Reg, even though he didn't see what the High Master was getting excited about. 'Well, this year's tennis team is not as strong as last year's but they should...'

'No, no, no! I'm not talking about tennis. I'm talking about the standard we set for boys to get into Beaumont Abbey.'

'Ah! You mean our entrance exams,' said Reg. 'We're making them too hard.'

'No! Yes! No! Look,' said Llywelyn, 'I am in a way talking about our entrance exams but I'm really concerned with how Beaumont is perceived and how that perception affects our intake.'

'You want to make entry easier so we'll have more applications for places?'

'Not exactly,' said Llywelyn. 'I want to make entry harder so more will apply for places.'

'I'm sorry, High Master, but you've lost me, I'm afraid,' said Reg.

The High Master did his best to explain his thinking. Eton was so hard to get into that grandparents put their grandchildren's names on the waiting list at birth. Beaumont was so easy to get into that grandparents were not entering their grandchildren at birth.

The Second Master responded. Beaumont had all the pupils it could handle. Building the school's reputation as hard to get into would take time. Raising the standard of entry might well mean unfilled places in the short term.

'*In the short term*, perhaps,' Llywelyn said excitedly. 'But, in the *long term*, we'd see a growing waiting list and an end to our worries over pupil numbers and rising fees.'

Reginald de Vere had seen Dr Llywelyn Pugh-Jones with bees in his bonnet before but this bee was buzzing more loudly than all the previous bees put together; its

153

buzz was interfering with the High Master's sense of reason.

Reg pointed out this year's Scholarship papers had already been dispatched; it was too late to change them. He also pointed out that of the eighty or ninety boys who pass Common Entrance and apply to Beaumont, few ever fail the Scholarship Entrance.

'That's my point,' said Llywelyn. 'More than just a few should fail. I'm sure Eton, Harrow and Winchester fail more than we do.'

This latest bee had buzzed so loudly that the High Master completely forgot to ask the Second Master if a group of disgruntled staff were really planning to rob a bank. More importantly, the buzzing had driven out of his mind the warning of Beaumont's solicitor, Henry Trevanion, LLM of Trevanion, Doyle and Root: *lose just one boy and Beaumont could lose its major endowment and its charitable status.*

* * * * *

Louise Pugh-Jones called to order the fifth meeting of the BALI Club. Agenda item 1 - apologies for absence. None. All ten members were present. Item 2 - minutes of the fourth meeting. Approved. Item 3 – report from the secretary, Mary Cranborne.

'BALI - the Beaumont Abbey Ladies Investments - has now been registered as a legal partnership. The local tax office has been notified of our existence and given my name and address for all correspondence. Three of these copies of our constitution and rules,' said Mary, placing the documents on the table, 'must be signed by every member of BALI and returned to me. Please keep an unsigned copy for your records.'

'Could you remind me, Mary, why we registered BALI as a legal partnership?' said Celia Fiddle, wife of Dr Humphrey Fiddle, the school chaplain.

'Our Treasurer will…'

'It's simpler, less expensive and more tax efficient than registering as a corporation,' said Abigail Rusbridge, interrupting Mary.

'Thank you for that, Abigail,' said Louise rather sharply. 'Thank you, Mary, for your report. Concise and to the point, as usual. Will someone propose we accept the Secretary's report.' Celia proposed, Abigail seconded and Mary's report was accepted unanimously. 'Agenda item 4 – Treasurer's report.'

'Mrs Rusbridge is quite right, of course,' said the Treasurer. 'Our partnership was legally formed the moment we formally adopted our Constitution and Rules...'

'The Partnership Agreement!' interrupted Abigail, 'that's what they should be called.'

'Thank you Abigail,' said Louise. 'Please continue Madam Treasurer.

'Thank you, Madam President. As I was about to say, forming a company is much more complicated and BALI would have to pay corporation tax and the individual members – properly known as share holders - would be taxed on the income and capital gains.'

Abigail interrupted the Treasurer again, 'If we were a company, none of us would get the £5,000 capital gains allowance.'

Geoffrey Rusbridge, the Head of Economics, was dapper. Abigail, his wife, was not. By no stretch of the imagination could she be said to meet dictionary definitions of dapper: *trim, neat and spruce in dress and bearing* and certainly not *small and nimble*. She was a large woman albeit neither short nor tall, She was in fact 5 ft 3½ ins tall - the average height of adult females in England. She qualified as chubby, because she was plump and round, but not as cuddly, because she was imperious to the point of being arrogant.

Abigail graduated in law at Oxford but chose the altar rather than the bar. She married Geoffrey, bore four children and practised being a wife and mother instead of a lawyer. When her fledglings left the nest, she took

155

to reading anything and everything, usually critically and often, like a proof-reader, scouring the pages for errors. She also became a *connaisseuse* (she disliked the term *connoisseur*) of dark chocolate and fine liqueurs which she digested along with whatever she happened to be reading.

The Chaplain's wife felt sure the wife of the Head of Economics would know a lot about the Stock Market. She was right. Celia also felt sure Abigail would prove to be a valuable and valued member of the investment club. She hoped she was right but she was beginning to fear she may have been wrong.

'Yes, thank you Abigail,' said Louis sounding anything but grateful. 'May we please hear the treasurer's report without further interruption. Time marches on.'

'We opened an Abbey National plc business account with Mary and myself as the two signatories. The balance is £990.00 as at noon yesterday. If, Mrs Rusbridge, you would be kind enough to give me your cheque today that will bring the balance to exactly eleven hundred pounds.'

'I thought the Abbey National was a building society,' said Maureen, wife of Dr Philip Carratt, Head of Chemistry.

'It *was*. But as Mrs Rusbridge probably knows, the Abbey National Building Society recently demutualised and became a bank listed on the London Stock Exchange (LSE). We shall use NatWest as our brokers.'

'Why don't we use Abbey as our brokers?' asked Elisabeth, wife of Alan Radford, Head of English.

'It doesn't offer brokerage services,' said Abigail sharply.

'Why don't we have our bank account with NatWest,' asked Maureen. 'Wouldn't it be better than dealing with two banks.'

'We did consider that,' said Mary, 'especially since the school banks with National Westminster and the regional manager, Earnest Hardcastle, is one of our governors but..'

'Abbey National offers free banking for investment clubs, no doubt,' said Abigail.

'Quite correct, Mrs Rusbridge,' said the Treasurer. 'Abbey will also pay interest on the account. NatWest pays no interest, charges a monthly fee *and* charges for just about every transaction.'

'Could we pay our ten pound monthly subscription directly into the Abbey account by standing order?' Maureen asked.

'Certainly,' said the Treasurer. 'It would be very helpful if everyone did that.'

'Will someone propose we accept the Treasurer's report?' said Louise. Mary proposed, Celia seconded and Susan Taylor's report was accepted unanimously. 'Agenda item 5 – unfinished business. Perhaps Mary would recapitulate.'

* * * * *

'We were discussing voting and share ownership,' said Mary. 'On voting for administrative matters such as admitting new members, we agreed each member has one vote. We have not agreed on voting for investments or on share ownership. We asked Susan to explain the Unit Valuation System (UVS) and proportionate voting.'

'Susan, you have the floor,' said Louise.

'Thank you, Louise. Let me start by recapping on why we should not use an equal share ownership scheme,' said Susan, glancing at Abigail. 'It can be a nightmare to keep track of accounts if, say, members pay late, miss, reduce or increase their monthly subscriptions, or if they need to withdraw money. There's also the problem of new members; they would have to pay all their missed monthly subscriptions as well as the joining fee.'

'So if somebody wanted to join in six months time,' said Maureen, 'they would have to pay sixty pounds on top of the one hundred pounds joining fee?'

'Seventy pounds, not sixty,' said Abigail. 'You've forgotten this month's subscription.'

'Sorry!' said Maureen. 'Abigail's right. They would have to find one hundred and seventy pounds.'

'Gosh!' said Celia. 'I can think of someone who wants to join but if they had to...'

'That's why we shouldn't use an equal share ownership scheme,' said Abigail. 'The unit valuation system is complicated but much better.'

'Mrs Rusbridge is right again. The Unit Valuation System, or UVS for short, solves the problems I mentioned *and* it is very flexible. The UVS lets members vary their subscriptions and their share of the club's investments. But this raises the question of proportionate voting.'

'What do you mean by proportional voting?' Elizabeth asked.

'Proportionate!' said Abigail. 'Being in proper proportion. Almost but not quite the same as proportional which also has precise meanings in mathematics.'

'What proportionate voting means, Liz,' said Susan, raising her eyes towards heaven before looking at Elizabeth, 'the more money you have invested, the more weight your vote should carry. With the Unit Valuation System, the more units you hold, the more votes you would have.'

'That sounds reasonable,' said Elizabeth, 'but wouldn't that mean the club could end up being run by one member?'

'Oh, yes,' said Susan, glancing at Abigail, 'but not if we set a limit: no member can hold more than one third of all the voting rights put together.'

After a lengthy discussion in which Susan tried to explain how the number of units for each member would be calculated and Abigail never once interrupted, Elizabeth proposed and Maureen seconded the motion that BALI adopt the Unit Valuation System.

After a short discussion in which Susan pointed out that if Mrs Rusbridge pays £110, then all ten members will to date have paid the same subscription and have equal voting rights, Mary proposed and Celia seconded the motion that BALI adopt the proportionate voting system for investments. Both motions were passed unanimously.

Louise was aware that three members of the club had, apart from raising their hands to vote, contributed nothing throughout the meeting. 'Item 6 on our agenda will normally be Education. I think Susan and Abigail have covered item 6 for this meeting.' A few heads nodded in agreement. 'I should like to ask Rosemary to be responsible for item 6 at our next meeting.' All eyes focussed on Rosemary, wife of Dr Herbert Newbold, the Head of Physics.

'You do realise I know very little about...'

'Join the club,' said Celia, giggling at her own little joke.

'Perhaps somebody else would...'

'Forgive me for pressing you,' said Louise, glancing in Abigail's direction. 'but we all agreed to learn and to share what we learn.'

'Yes. Of course. Sorry, Louise. It's just that I know so little about the Stock Market. I'm not sure where to start.'

'I've heard about bears, bulls and stags but I have no idea what they've got to do with...' twittered Celia.

'Please!' said Louise, holding up her hand to stop Abigail in her tracks. Then turning to Rosemary she said, 'Why don't you and Mrs Dawson put your heads together and tell us about those animals at our next meeting. Would that be alright Gladys?'

'Why not?' said the School Librarian and widow of the former Head of English.

'Splendid!' said Louise. 'Now I'd like to ask you, Janet, to present at our next meeting a proposal for our first investment. Would you be willing to do that?'

'Yes, I don't see why not?' said Janet Meeker, matron of Wedgewood House and sister of Donald Meeker, the assistant chaplain.

'Excellent! That's the spirit,' said Louise. 'Actually that will appear as agenda item 8 – Portfolio. For agenda item 7 – Economic Report, I propose Mrs Rusbridge should be our permanent economic reporter. Would you mind, Abigail? Splendid!' Louise was about to close the meeting when Susan caught her eye. 'Any other business?'

'May I remind members,' said Susan, 'that BALI will be exempt from the provisions of the Financial Services Act of 1986 as long as we run the club democratically and have control over our investments. And as long as we do *not* advertise, give investment advice to non-members and pay any member for services to the club.'

'What would happen if…'

'If we did not comply, Celia, then BALI would be classed as an *investment business*. The club would have to be authorised by the Financial Services Authority (FSA) and if we broke any of their rules, the FSA could impose very stiff penalties,' said Susan.

* * * * *

CHAPTER 16

"Where secrecy or mystery begins, vice or roguery is not far off." Samuel Johnson

* * * * *

The High Master would never have revealed, even to his wife, how much he depended upon Mary. And the High Master's Secretary had been, and would continue to be, the epitome of discretion. So Reginald de Vere could not have known that Mary Cranborne had released the latest bee in the Dr Llywelyn Pugh-Jones' bonnet. And although he was the Second Master, he would not necessarily have been privy to their correspondence with complaining parents or with the parents of potential new boys.

'Good afternoon, Mary.'

'Good afternoon, Reggie,' said Mary. 'Anything the matter?'

'As a matter of fact there is,' said the Second Master. 'Is the High Master available?'

'He's not back from lunch yet,' said Mary. 'Is it something I might help you with?

'No, I'm afraid not. I really wish you could,' said Reg. 'When do you expect him back?'

'Any minute now, I imagine,' said Mary, comparing the clock on the wall with the watch on her wrist. 'He said he would be back at half past two. Why don't you take a seat.'

Reg perched on the edge of a chair and mumbled under his breath as he thumbed through a collection of papers. Mary caught snatches of the conversation he was having with himself. 'I must stop him. Make Beaumont hard to get into. Grandparents will enter their grandsons at birth. Set the pass mark high. Sixty new boys for the Lower Thirds.

'Is it about the new entrants?' said Mary

'I'm sorry, Mary. What was that you said?'

'You seem to be concerned about the new intake?'

'Yes, in a way,' said Reg. 'I'm worried that…'

'Oh, I think the High Master has arrived. Just a moment.' Mary knocked on the door. 'The Second Master is here to see you, High Master.' She stepped inside Llywelyn's study and whispered, 'He's worried about something. Next term's new intake I think.' With that she returned to her office, leaving the study door ajar. 'The High Master will see you now, Second Master.'

'Something worrying you?' said Llywelyn.

'Yes,' High Master. 'It's about this year's scholarship entrance exams.'

'What about them?'

'It's the pass mark,' said Reg. 'If we put it too high...'

'Fewer boys will pass,' said Llywelyn. 'That's good.'

'No. I don't think it is,' said Reg.

'Why not?'

'In the first place, we could find ourselves calling fewer than sixty boys for interview.'

'Good,' said Llywelyn. 'That will show Beaumont's hard to get into.'

'Who? Who will it show? We'll just be preaching to the choir,' said Reg. 'And in the second place...' He paused to scratch his head. 'In the second place...'

'What's wrong with interviewing fewer than sixty potential new boys?' asked Llywelyn.

'What's wrong?' said Reg, taking a deep breath and counting slowly up to ten in his head. 'It's obvious what's wrong. If we interview fewer than sixty, we'd never fill our sixty places. That's what's wrong.'

There was a knock on the door and Mary Cranborne entered with the afternoon tea tray. The two men watched in silence as she poured a cup of Earl Grey for Llywelyn and a cup of coffee for Reg. 'Would you like a slice of fruit cake, Second Master?' she said. Reg shook his head. 'High Master?' Llywelyn also shook his head. As soon as Mary had left the study and closed the door behind her, Reg took up where he left off.

'I was under the impression, High Master, we were obligated to admit a minimum of sixty boys into the Lower Thirds and award a minimum number of bursaries and scholarships,' said Reg.

'You could be right,' said Llywelyn. 'Actually it's been a while since I perused the terms and conditions of our major endowment.' He picked up the phone. 'Mary, would you be kind enough to bring me the file on our major endowment?' With her usual ruthless efficiency, his secretary appeared in less than no time and handed him the file. 'Very good. Thank you, Mary.' Reg waited patiently whilst Llywelyn sifted through the file. 'Ah, here we are. Yes, you're right, Reg. Beaumont must admit a minimum of sixty new boys every year but...' He continued scanning the page. 'It does *not* state that the sixty new boys must enter the Lower Thirds. Interesting.'

'That means we could admit fewer than sixty to the Lower Thirds as long as we make up the number with new entries higher up in the school,' said Reg.

'That's right. So let's set the pass mark high and pass fewer than sixty.'

'How many would you want us to pass?' asked Reg. 'Fifty-eight? Fifty-five? Forty?'

'If we pass sixty the same as last year, how could anybody tell we are making Beaumont harder to get into?' said Llywelyn. 'How about fifty-eight?'

'So you want us to adjust the boundary mark to pass fifty-eight boys?'

'Do you see a difficulty with that?' asked Llywelyn.

'Oh, no difficulty with the pass mark,' said Reg. 'We can adjust it to do whatever you want. That's what we've always done anyway. No, the difficulty is that all fifty-eight boys might not get through the interview.'

'I don't follow,' said Llywelyn.

'We might pass them but some of them, or more likely their parents, might not pass us.'

'Oh, I hadn't thought of that.'

163

'Let me make a suggestion, High Master?' said Reg. 'Let's pass sixty-five or seventy and thin the number of entries to sixty at interview. Then at the interview we can give sixty-five or seventy parents the impression that Beaumont is very choosy.'

'What a good idea, Reg. I Like it.'

* * * * *

'How was your meeting yesterday?' asked Geoffrey, opening his Financial Times.

'I was just about to ask you the same question,' said Abigail, spooning a generous helping of Old English Thick Cut Marmalade on to her breakfast plate.

'I was first,' said Geoffrey. 'It was the fourth meeting this month, wasn't it?'

'The fifth, actually. But as I told you before, these meetings are not really *meetings* in your sense of the word. They're just gets-together.'

'Just a few women getting together for a chat, is that it?'

'Yes, that's about it,' said Abigail, carefully applying a liberal helping of marmalade to a piece of buttered toast and popping it into her mouth.

'What do you find to talk about?' asked Geoffrey, taking a sip of fresh orange juice.

'Anything and everything,' said Abigail, preparing to insert another piece of buttered toast and marmalade. 'What about your meeting?'

'Mostly the state of the economy, personal finance, investing… that sort of thing.'

'Sounds pretty dull. Do many staff attend?'

'There's usually ten staff who actively participate and a couple who sit on the sidelines.'

'These meetings of yours… Fairly formal, are they?'

'Oh, I shouldn't say that. No, definitely not formal. We prefer a relaxed atmosphere.'

'I expect drinks from the Common Room bar help the informality,' said Abigail wryly.

164

'How many come to your gets-together?' asked Geoffrey.

'About ten. Yes, usually ten,' said Abigail, assembling another bite size portion of toast for her taste buds and digestive system. 'A few more might be joining in the future.'

'Oh, really! What's the attraction?' asked Geoffrey, taking another sip of juice.

'I suppose it's a social thing,' said Abigail who, in her husband's estimation, had never been much of a social animal. 'However, I do try to raise the level of conversation above the mundane and share my knowledge with the club members.'

'Club members?' said Geoffrey. 'Ah, you women have formed a book club. That's why you've had your nose stuck in so many books lately. I see.' But much to his wife's relief, Geoffrey did not see at all. He had certainly never noticed many of her books were about the Stock Market, stocks and shares, trading and the law.

* * * * *

It was only a small flag, two centimetres long and one centimetre tall, tattooed high up on the skin covering the deltoid muscle of her left arm. In her youth, it was considered 'cool' and patriotic to have a red maple leaf flanked by two red bars somewhere on your body. Now at her age it was a constant reminder of youthful foolishness. She was able to keep the tattoo hidden under her nurse's uniform except when she went for a swim.

On hearing the knock, the young matron opened the door of her office in Wedgewood House to find Rupert Jardine standing there pressing a blood-stained handkerchief to his forehead. 'Well I never,' said Janet Meeker, 'you're just the person I wanted to see but not in this state. What have you been up to?'

'Net practice,' said Rupert.

'I don't understand,' said Janet.

'Cricket practice... In the nets.'

'What happened?'

'I misjudged a bouncer from Hammond and paid the price,' said Rupert.

'Let's have a look at you,' said Janet, removing the handkerchief to reveal a nasty cut. 'You're lucky. It won't need stitches.' She bathed the wound and applied an antiseptic dressing. Then she made Rupert sit while she wrote in a book. When Rupert asked what she was writing, she said, 'A brief report for the records, that's all.'

'You're from Canada, aren't you?' said Rupert.

'Yes! How did you guess?'

'Your accent's not American and... I saw your Canadian flag when you were in the pool the other day.' When Janet blushed, Rupert said, 'Very daring! Do you have any other tattoos?'

'Now you're being impertinent,' said Janet. 'But for your information... No, I do *not* have any other tattoos. Let's change the subject.'

'Alright,' said Rupert, 'Why did you want to see me?'

Janet had already learned a great deal about the Stock Market from Stephen Zhǎng, a very bright lower sixth former in Wedgewood who was in the top sets for economics and maths. When she told him she was looking for a company to invest in, Stephen told her she should find out as much as she could about any company before buying its stock. He thought Rupert, who was in his maths set, might be able to tell her about his father's company, Jardine International. Zhǎng was right. Rupert could tell her everything she should know about his father's business and something she ought not to know.

Randolph Jardine was twenty-four when he began working for Computer Identics Corporation, a company developing helium-neon lasers to scan barcodes at a distance and cope with damaged labels. When Computer Identics began to develop complex computer based operational control systems (CBOCS) with their optical scanners as the cornerstone of those systems, Randolph left the company. Using all the knowledge he had gained legitimately and some secrets he had gathered illegitimately, he started his own business that grew to become Jardine International Corporation (JIC), a company now making, selling and maintaining networks and systems for data collection and processing. From its initial public offering (IPO) the JIC stock rose from $15 to an all-time high of $245 mainly as a result of a variety of crafty mergers and slick acquisitions.

'Are you a stockholder in the company, Rupert?'

'Yes. Mother insisted on giving me a thousand shares for my sixteenth.'

'A thousand shares! That sounds rather a lot,' said Janet.

'It's just a drop in the ocean,' said Rupert. 'I'll probably get a lot more this year.'

'Even so,' said Janet, 'a thousand shares. That's a lot of money, isn't it?'

'I suppose so,' said Rupert. 'Stock prices go up and down, you know. Yesterday my stock was worth about one hundred and twenty-six thousand dollars. Today it could be less or it could be more. Still, if all goes well, my stock might be worth a lot more in a few weeks time.'

'Oh, why is that?'

'My father's got his eye on SIGEM Ltd.'

* * * * *

Colin snatched the note from his pigeonhole and glanced at it as he hurried to his waiting class. *Mr Harper, please come to my office at your earliest convenience. Thank you. ST.* Colin was a little surprised; the Bursar usually appeared unannounced at the door of the computer room whenever he wanted help. It was only after Colin had dismissed his class he noticed the note was signed ST.

'G-good afternoon, M-Mrs T-Taylor,' stuttered Colin. 'Y-you wanted t-to s-see m-me?'

'Yes Mr Harper. Please come in.' Colin shuffled in and closed the door. 'Please sit down,' said Susan. 'I was about to make some tea. Would you like a cup?'

'Y-yes, p-please.'

'Do you take milk and sugar?'

'Um, yes. Thank you.' Susan left the room and Colin waited nervously for her return. In the five minutes that seemed more like half an hour, he had time to notice Mrs Taylor's office was as neat and orderly as his computer room. He also had time to wonder why he was sitting in her office.

'Sorry I took so long,' said Susan. 'A watched kettle never boils.' She put down the tray and poured out two teas. 'How many lumps of sugar, Mr Harper?'

'T-two please.'

'There you are,' said Susan, putting the cup and saucer on a small table. 'Now, how about a sandwich or a slice of Mrs Brown's fruit cake?' Before Colin had a chance to reply, she handed Colin a plate and made him take a sandwich and a slice of cake. While Colin did his best to avoid dropping crumbs or spilling tea on himself and the carpet, Susan explained why she had asked to see him.

'The Bursar will be away for the next three or four days,' said Susan. 'Something to do with the Independent Schools' Bursars Association.' She paused to take a sip of her tea. 'Anyway, I'd like to use this time to improve my computer skills… So I thought of you.'

'I'm n-not s-sure…'

'Am I right in thinking you installed the computer programs the Bursar uses?'

'Y-yes. B-but…'

'So you could install the same programs on my computer,' said Susan.

'Yes, I could,' said Colin. 'That's easy.'

'Good!' said Susan. 'What about the data base the programs manipulate?'

'I'd have to check the size of your hard drive,' said Colin, losing his stammer now he was in his element. 'I could do that now if you like.'

'Wonderful,' said Susan, jumping up from her chair.

'It's not too bad,' said Colin, 'but it would better if I fitted a second hard drive to keep the data separate from the programs.'

'When could you do that?'

'What about this evening?'

'I've arranged to play tennis this evening,' said Susan. 'but I could…'

'As long as I know what you want and I can get into your office,' said Colin, 'I can do it this evening while you're playing tennis.'

'Wonderful,' gushed Susan. 'That's very kind. If you tell me what time, I can let you into the office before I go to Gower House.'

'I could be here at half-past five,' said Colin. 'I'll fit a second hard drive and load a copy the Bursar's programs and data. Would you want the data updated?'

'Yes,' said Susan, after a slight hesitation. 'but I wouldn't want to impose on you.'

'Oh, it wouldn't be an imposition,' said Colin. 'You're on the school network, so I could program your computer to automatically update the data daily.'

'Would my computer be secure?'

'Oh, yes,' said Colin. 'I'll make sure your computer has its own firewall and for extra security, I'll route everything through the computer room which has a heavy firewall.'

'Wonderful!' said Susan. Then placing a hand on his arm, she said, 'One other thing, may I trust you to keep all this a secret? Just between you and me?'

'Yes, certainly,' said Colin, who by nature had always been a secretive person.

'Thanks,' said Susan. 'We'll not say anything to Mr Parker-Smythe. He has enough on his plate already. I'm sure you understand.'

Susan persuaded Colin, against his better judgement, to have another cup of tea and a second slice of Dolly Brown's fruit cake. While he was eating and drinking, she said she had a friend who wanted to computerise the records of an investment club. She asked Colin if he could help. It just happened Rupert Jardine had produced a suite of programs that could be adapted for the purpose.

That evening while Susan, Celia, Mary and Louise were enjoying a game of doubles, Colin Harper was installing a second hard drive, copying all the Bursar's data onto it and setting up the automatic updating. Rupert appeared at Susan's office three days later.

'Mr Harper sent me, Mrs Taylor.'

'Ah, yes. Rupert Jardine, I presume,' said Susan. 'Is this about your…'

'Small business records and accounts program. Yes. Could you do without your computer for about half an hour?'

'Oh, my goodness. Is it ready to be installed?' asked Susan.

'Yes, it is,' said Rupert.

'Then I'd better get out of your way.' She got out of her chair to make way for him. The tall, good-looking, self-assured teenager reminded her of Roderick Taylor, the handsome young car dealer she met and married when she was twenty-five and deserted ten years later before she came to England.

'Do you mind if I watch what you're doing?' Susan said, offering him her chair and holding on to its back.

'No, of course not Mrs Taylor,' said Rupert, sitting down on the seat and noticing how warm it was. 'Here's the manual I wrote to cover the basic functions.'

'This looks very professional, Rupert. May I call you Rupert?' said Susan.

'Yes, of course, ma'am. Rupert is fine by me,' said Rupert.

When she leant forward to take the spiral-bound book, her bare arm touched the back of his neck and sent

170

a tingle down his spine. Rupert was able to concentrate on installing his software while Susan was studying the manual but when she put it down on her desk and placed her hands on his shoulders, his mind started to wander. Susan was just old enough to be his mother but her youthful figure, fair hair and sun-tanned freckled face prevented Rupert from thinking of her in that way. By the same token, his manliness, self-assurance and good looks prevented Susan from thinking of him as a son.

Once the software was installed, Rupert ran the program and showed Susan how she could use it to track each member's subscriptions and calculate their individual capital gains and tax liabilities. He also explained how she could use the program to store the club's portfolio of shares and automatically handle the Unit Valuation System. Rupert also showed her how to customise the program by, for example, entering a specific name for the investment club.

'Rupert, you're a genius,' said Susan. 'How did you learn so much about computing? Not by studying Computing Science here at Beaumont under Mr Harper. You probably know more than he does.'

'Actually, ma'am, Colin's a very good teacher but...'

'There's not much he knows that you don't.'

'Well I did start messing about with computers almost as soon as I was born.'

'Ah, your father...'

'Randolph gave me the components so I could design and build my own computer even before IBM started marketing the personal computer in 1981.'

'Goodness! How old were you then?' said Susan.

'Five or Six,' said Rupert. 'I don't remember for sure.'

'You're a very clever young man,' said Susan, squeezing his arm. 'I very lucky to have met you.'

'Thank you, ma'am,' said Rupert. 'I'm glad to have met you and I hope we'll...'

'Before I forget,' interrupted Susan. 'Please don't tell anybody about this. Let's keep this a secret between the two of us.'

'What about Colin?' said Rupert. 'He already knows.'

'Yes, yes. Mr Harper. Of course. He's bound to know what you have been doing for me. But please don't tell anyone else.'

'You can rely upon me, ma'am,' said Rupert. 'I'm yours to command.'

* * * * *

No one, least of all Geoffrey Rusbridge, kept count of the number of times they gathered in the Common Room and failed to come up with practical ways of making their fortune through team work. On one occasion, James Jackson, the young assistant chemistry teacher said they should learn card counting and win money playing blackjack at a casino. When David Swann, the young history teacher, was foolish enough to ask about card counting, James explained.

In about 1980,' said James, 'a maths professor and some of his students at MIT (Massachusetts Institute of Technology) devised a method of keeping track of the cards in blackjack to improve their odds. They won a lot of money in Las Vegas.'

'What did they do?' asked David. 'Take in turns to memorise the cards that had been played?'

'No, nothing like that,' said James. 'They gave each card a score. Low cards, from 2 to 6, favour the dealer and scored +1. Cards 7, 8 and 9, are neutral and scored 0. The remaining cards, the high cards – ten, jack, queen, king and ace, favour the player and scored –1. From that they could tell if the remaining cards to be dealt favoured the dealer or the player.'

Needless to say, one or two, who practised card counting and became quite proficient, did visit one casino once and came away the poorer for it. Colin Harper should have told them every game in a casino has a built-in edge in favour of the house and no mathematical betting system can beat that edge. But then, Colin Harper had his own plan to get rich. He would use his skill with computers and the knowledge he had recently acquired from the Bursar's office; a secret he shared with no one, not even Susan Taylor.

* * * * *

CHAPTER 17

"Wee, sleekit, cowran, tim'rous beastie, O, what a panic's in thy breastie!" Robert Burns

* * * * *

Colin did not know Robert Schifreen personally but he knew about him. He knew he was arrested in 1985 for hacking into a British Telecom computer and reading the emails of Prince Philip. He knew Schifreen was the first person charged with illegal access of a computer system. And he knew Schifreen was acquitted because there was no specific law against what later came to be known as hacking.

Robert Jonathan Schifreen was, however, convicted and fined £750 under the Forgery and Counterfeiting Act of 1981 - for the offence of using a false instrument.

It is an offence for a person to use an instrument which is, and which he knows or believes to be, false, with the intention of inducing somebody to accept it as genuine, and by reason of so accepting it to do or not to do some act to his own or any other person's prejudice.

Colin had never considered a computer to be a *somebody*, so he was tickled by the thought of his computer being somebody and decided to call it Teddy? After all, the autopilot in an aircraft is called *George*! He was also amused by Schifreen's fine of £750; a small price to pay, he thought, for being caught accessing other people's computers.

He might not have been so amused if he had known that the English Law Commission's *Computer Misuse Act* was on the brink of becoming law. In just a few months this Act would *make provision for securing computer material against unauthorised access or modification; and for connected purposes*. It would introduce three criminal offences carrying a prison sentence of up to five years or a fine of up to £5000.

Colin was so taken by his idea of transferring money from other people's accounts into his own and so engrossed in the technicalities to achieve those transfers that he failed to consider the legal consequences. It occurred to him that he was about to commit statutory and common law offences; but then he would never have considered that he might be found out. His mind was focussed on methods not outcomes. He would panic later.

'Hello, Colin,' said Rupert. 'You wanted to see me?'

'Yes, Rupert. I want to pick your brains.'

'OK. Shoot,' said Rupert.

'How much do you know about Access Control Software?'

'I suppose you mean like the stuff we've developed at Jardine International to prevent unauthorised access to data,' said Rupert.

'Yes, exactly,' said Colin. 'I assume your software interfaces with the operating systems and serves as a control centre for all security measures.'

'It sure does,' said Rupert. 'The software we gave you for Beaumont is a slimmed down version of the software we supply to world banks.'

'I see! Could you get me a copy of the full-blown version? I'd like to study the code.'

'I don't see why not,' Rupert said then smiled. 'Planning to rob a bank, are you?'

* * * * *

Louise called the sixth meeting of the BALI club to order. There were no apologies for absence – agenda item 1. The minutes of the previous meeting were approved without discussion – item 2. The secretary had nothing to report – item 3. Under agenda item 4, the treasurer announced all ten members had now paid their initial fee of £100 and their first month's subscription of £10. There was no unfinished business – agenda item 5.

It took under ten minutes to reach agenda item 6 – education. 'Rosemary and Gladys. Are you ready to tell us about those animals?' said Louise. Gladys Dawson, widow of the former Head of English and now

Beaumont's librarian, nodded at Rosemary, wife of Dr Herbert Newbold, the Head of Physics.

'If we buy shares and expect to sell them at a higher price, we are *bulls*. If we sell shares and expect to buy them back at a lower price, we are *stags*.'

'No, Rosemary,' said Gladys, the school librarian, 'we are *bears*.'

'Oh, yes. Sorry! *Bears*. Slip of the tongue We are *bears* if we expect to buy shares back at a lower price,' said Rosemary. 'We are *stags* if we buy and sell shares in a short period of time to make a quick profit.'

'Deplorable!' snorted Abigail. 'It's always the *male* of the species.'

'Well, actually,' said Gladys diffidently, '*bear* applies to the female as well as the male member of the *ursidae* family, doesn't it?'

'Let's not get side-tracked,' said Louise. 'Please continue, Rosemary.'

'In a *bear market* the stock prices fall. In a *bull market* they rise.'

'Excuse me,' said Celia, 'but what's the difference between a stock and a share?'

'Not much as far as I could tell,' said Rosemary. 'Stock is the capital raised by a company by issuing shares. When we buy shares in a company, we receive a certificate – called a stock or share certificate – showing our share of that company's stock.'

'A *Stock Market* or *Stock Exchange*,' said Gladys, 'is where stock brokers and traders buy and sell shares in stock.'

'Stock exchanges are companies run for profit and traded just like other companies,' said Rosemary. 'If we wanted to, we could buy shares in the London Stock Exchange itself.' That was something even Abigail did not know.

Rosemary and Gladys impressed everyone not only with what they had learned but also with the information sheets they gave out. All the ladies were surprised to learn there were more than sixty major stock exchanges, with the London Stock Exchange being the fourth largest and the Toronto Stock Exchange the sixth largest. The NASDAQ (National Association of Securities Dealers Automated Quotations) stock exchange opened in New York on the 8th February, 1971 to be the world's first electronic stock exchange.

'That was absolutely splendid,' said Louise. 'I think Rosemary and Gladys deserve a round of applause.'

'They've earned another glass of wine,' said Abigail, reaching for the bottle.

Abigail refilled the glasses and Mary handed out the vol-au-vents that Jean-Pierre, Beaumont's resident chef, had prepared at Louise's request. During the interval between items 6 and 7 on the agenda, the ladies sat quietly digesting the food, the drink and the information Rosemary and Gladys had given them. When everyone seemed ready, Louise recalled the meeting to order. 'Item 7 – economic report. Abigail.'

'Since the 19th October 1987, so-called Black Monday, when the footsie all-share index lost more than 26%, falling from about 1100 to 800, the market's been having its ups and downs.'

'Footsie!' giggled Celia. 'I thought that was flirting by touching somebody's legs under the table.'

'F-T-S-E,' said Abigail tetchily. 'It's an index produced by a company owned jointly by the Financial Times – FT – and the London Stock Exchange – SE.'

'Sorry,' said Celia. 'It must be the wine.'

'The *footsie* is the best indicator of the British market, accounting for more than 95% of eligible companies with a total capitalisation of almost two trillion pounds,' said Abigail.

'So when the *footsie* is rising we're in a bull market,' said Elisabeth, wife of Alan Radford, Head of English.'

'Yes, yes. Of course!' said Abigail impatiently.

'Is the *footsie* rising or falling now?' Elisabeth asked, ignoring Abigail's impatient tone.

'For the past six months it's been falling,' said Abigail, 'but in the last week or so it has been rising. I believe we're seeing the start of a...'

'Bull market,' chirped Celia.

Abigail went on to say much the same about three other indices: the Dow Jones in America, the Nikkei in Japan and the Standard & Poor TSX in Canada. She believed they were at the start of a bull market. Now was the time to buy shares. The question was, of course, shares in which company. 'Thank you, Abigail,' said Louise. 'That brings us very neatly to agenda item 8 – our first investment. Janet.' The sister of Donald Meeker, the assistant chaplain, took a deep breath.

'I propose we buy shares in SIGEM Ltd. It's a small California based company specialising in the purification of silicon and germanium to make semiconductor discs. It has a market cap of 9.5 million dollars, a P/E of 1.2 and the SIGE share price was $1.05 when the NASDAQ closed today.'

'What do you mean by market cap?' asked Maureen, wife of Dr Carratt, Head of Chemistry.

'Market capitalisation. It's the cost of acquiring the company,' said Janet.

'Share price multiplied by number of outstanding shares,' said Abigail.

'So SIGEM must have about nine million shares,' said Louise.

'Yes, Louise. About nine million,' said Janet.

'And P/E?' said Elisabeth. 'What's that all about?'

'It's on the sheet we gave you,' said Gladys. 'It's the ratio of the price of the share to the earnings.'

'Why is that important?' asked Maureen.

'Think of two companies with the same share price, say $10,' said Janet. 'Company A has a P/E of 6 and company B has a P/E of 3. All other things being equal, which share do you think we should buy? Company A or company B?'

'Company A?' guessed Celia.

'No, Celia. Company B,' said Janet. 'With company A we'd be paying twice as much for the same earning power.'

'What made you pick SIGEM Ltd?' asked Rosemary. 'I mean… there are so many companies to choose from?'

'I had a lot of help,' Janet confessed. I talked to Stephen Zháng. He's in Wedgewood. Very clever. Studying economics in the sixth form. Father's a stockbroker in Hong Kong. Stephen told me what to look for when choosing a company. That's how I knew about market cap and price to earnings ratio. Stephen said the best way to find out about a company is to talk to people in the company. He suggested I talk to Rupert about his father's company, Jardine International. I was a bit surprised because I didn't think those two boys liked one another. Well… Rupert was very helpful and I learned a lot from him. It was he who mentioned SIGEM Ltd. He said his father had his eye on that company. So I thought I should take a close look at it. And there you are.'

'Thank you, Janet,' said Louise. 'The matter is now open for discussion.'

'Actually,' said Susan, 'Janet had mentioned she was looking at SIGEM Ltd, so I did some homework. It's a small company but not really a penny-stock. Silicon is essential for computer microchips and Germanium is used in lasers. Jardine International is based on computer systems and laser scanners but I don't know why Randolph Jardine's got his eye on SIGEM Ltd…' She paused then said, 'Unless of course it's a case of Randolph the blue shark sizing up a tasty mackerel.'

'Anybody else want to comment?' said Louise. 'No. Very well, shall we invest in SIGEM Ltd? All in favour?' Everyone nodded. 'Anyone against? Good. Now we need to agree on our level of investment.'

'If we set aside £100 for various expenses,' said Susan, 'then we'll have £1000 available to buy shares.

The rate of exchange is approximately $2 to £1. So we could buy about two thousand shares at $1 each.'

'All our eggs in one basket? No! Too risky,' said Abigail. 'I suggest we buy one thousand shares.'

'I agree,' said Celia.

'Any other proposal?' said Louise. 'Very well. All in favour of buying one thousand shares in SIGEM Ltd. Unanimous. Thank you ladies.' Louise shuffled her papers and asked, 'Any other business?'

'Mary Cranborne leant across and whispered in Louise's ear.'

'Ah, yes. Thank you Mary,' said Louise. 'Our next meeting will be held at Susan's place. The High Master and I will be in Bournemouth attending the annual HMC meeting, so I'd be grateful if you, Celia, would take the chair. I declare this meeting closed.'

* * * * *

The gathering in the Common Room had opened, without any formal declaration as such and, unusually, long before Keith Bradley arrived. It had become routine for the five heads of department and the five junior members of staff to form a large circle around a pair of tables. According to Colin Harper, the mathematician, they actually formed an ellipse with the two tables at its foci. Quentin and Reg occupied their usual armchairs to observe the proceedings from a short distance outside the oval.

'Maureen and I bumped into Albert Cockle a while ago,' Dr Philip Carratt said, apropos of nothing in particular. 'He's moved up in the world since he was here.'

'Old Bertie Cockle?' said Arthur Matthews, Head of Geography. 'Bowler hat and white cotton gloves?'

'The very same,' said Phil. When he saw the puzzled looks on the faces of his young colleagues, he decided an explanation was in order. 'A few years back, Peter Morrison, Head of Music, spent his Easter holiday somewhere in India studying Hindustani classical music.'

'I remember,' said Alan Radford, Head of English, 'He'd been driving us all mad in Gower with his Ravi Shankar recordings. I think he brought a sitar back with him.'

'That's not all he brought back,' said Phil. 'Apparently he left it a bit late getting his first hepatitis A vaccination. He was supposed to get it at least four weeks before his trip.'

'Hepatitis. Inflammation of the liver, if I'm not mistaken,' said Alan.

'Quite correct,' said Phil. 'HA is one of three common viruses. HB and HC are the other two and are more serious. Even so, the HA put poor old Peter in the hospital and out of action for the whole of the Trinity term. The High Master was in a fair old flap until somebody – I forget who – came across Bertie Cockle.'

'Wasn't that you, Reg?' whispered Quentin.

'Guilty as charged, your honour,' said Reg. 'Madeleine and I were celebrating our wedding anniversary in the Gower Heights Hotel.'

'Gower Heights! I've heard they do an excellent luncheon but an overpriced dinner.'

'We went there because, according to my dear late wife, their French chef knew how to prepare moules marinières: *dans une grande casserole, mettez l'oignon et les échalotes finement hachés, ajoutez le vin blanc puis les moules,*' said Reg with a certain sadness in his voice. 'Anyway, after we finished our meal, we took coffee in the lounge and listened to the resident pianist. It was Albert Cockle. Madeleine was so impressed with his playing, especially when he rattled off the Anniversary Waltz. Later when Peter was taken ill, I thought of Bertie and we engaged him for the Trinity term.'

Do you remember the first day Bertie appeared here in the Common Room, Arthur?' said Phil Carratt.

'Rather,' said Arthur. 'Looked as though he'd come straight off the Music Hall stage. Black jacket, pin-striped trousers, pink and white striped shirt with a white collar… Oh, yes, yes… and he was wearing white cotton gloves and carrying a black bowler hat.'

'Music Hall,' explained James in a whisper, 'was where people went for entertainment before they had television to keep them at home.'

'Who could forget that bowler hat,' said Phil. 'You know… when he told me he was standing in for Peter… I think he actually said he was our *acting* Head of Music… and I asked him, as one does, where he'd been teaching, he gave a little cough into the white glove on his left hand and said, in true theatrical fashion, *I have been resting.*'

'Absolutely in character,' said Alan Radford, Head of English and celebrated Director of Beaumont's school plays.

'I suspected from his complexion he might enjoy a glass or two,' said Phil, moistening his larynx with some red wine, 'so I was the first but certainly not the last to stand our new member of staff a round. It loosened his tongue. Bertie, as he became known to his colleagues, confided that in his youth he had established a bit of a name for himself on the Variety stage.'

'First time I clapped eyes on Bertie's profile from a distance,' said Alan, 'I thought it was Anthony Parker-Jones and started to wonder who on the staff had invited him into the Common Room.'

'D'you know, Alan's quite right,' said Reg to Quentin. 'Not quite peas in a pod but Albert Cockle and Anthony Parker-Smythe were similar in build. And they had a similar dress sense but… how can I put it?'

'Polonius put it rather well in Hamlet Act 1 Scene III,' said Quentin. 'If memory serves…
Costly thy habit as thy purse can buy,
But not expressed in fancy—rich, not gaudy,
For the apparel oft proclaims the man…'

182

'That's about it,' said Reg. 'In Bertie and Anthony's case, their clothes maketh *not* the men.'

'Then there's their names,' said Quentin. 'Albert Cockle. Anthony Parker-Smythe. I'm inclined to say they sound... what's the word? Fraudulent?'

'Bogus?' suggested Reg.

'Ah, yes. Bogus would do,' said Quentin. 'Poorly chosen aliases, I'd say.'

'Both men were fond of their tipple,' said Reg.

'Indeed. I recall one cynical colleague suggesting gin would flow from their ears if he squeezed their necks.'

'Who said that?' asked Reg when he had stopped chuckling.

'It wouldn't do for me to say,' said Quentin. 'I've no desire to be dragged into court on a charge of slander.'

'Bertie was only with us for a term,' said Phil, 'but he left his mark. He could play just about anything, all without music, but he specialised in popular songs, dance music and light classics. The boys loved him. The first time they heard him play was in the Chapel. All the boys and most of the staff were in their seats awaiting the arrival of the High Master and choir when Bertie, seated at the Harrison and Harrison three manual pipe organ, launched into *I do like to be beside the seaside*. It was like listening to Reginald Dixon playing his signature tune on the Wurlitzer organ in the Blackpool Tower ballroom.'

'Must have been a bit of a shock for the High Master,' said James, grinning widely.

'Actually,' said Phil, 'Dr Pugh-Jones probably never heard a single note of it because at exactly the right moment, Bertie segued into Lead us, Heavenly Father, Lead us.'

'Do you remember the Summer music concert at Parents' Weekend?' said Alan.

'Memorable. We'd heard nothing quite like it before and, with all due respect to Peter, nothing like it since,' said Phil. 'No orchestra. No solo instrumentalists. No Bach, no Beethoven and no Mozart. No classical music of any weight whatsoever.'

'What intrigued me,' said Alan, 'was the High Master's reaction. The horror on his face at the start and, if you'll pardon the expression, the change in his tune when Bertie and the boys received a standing ovation at the end.'

'So, what sort of concert was it?' asked David.

'In his annual address to the parents the High Master referred to it as a *choral concert*,' said Phil. 'Fifty or sixty boys from the Lower Thirds and Fourths assembled on the platform. They were immaculately turned out; white shirt, school tie, grey trousers and, as our Sergeant Batters might say, shoes, black, responsive to polish! Bertie appeared dressed as usual but *sans* bowler hat and posed theatrically alongside the grand piano until the applause subsided. Then with a flourish, he removed his white gloves, sat down and played an introduction to *The Happy Wanderer*. The whole concert was devoted to medleys of popular songs. It was a huge success.'

'During the interlude,' said Phil, 'Sir Leslie Matthews congratulated the High Master and said what a change it was to hear some decent tunes for once. Apparently the first song was one of Lady Matthews' favourites but Sir Leslie couldn't remember what the song was called. When Dr Pugh-Jones said he thought it was *Der fröhliche Wanderer*, Sir Leslie gave him a funny look and hurried off to refill his glass.'

'Bertie never ate school lunch. One day, my wife was doing a bit of early afternoon shopping in the village and met Bertie coming out of the Crown and Anchor. On another occasion Maureen and I were in town waiting to catch a bus back to Beaumont when Bertie turned up. My wife was tickled by the old-fashioned way he accompanied his *good evening Mrs Carratt, Dr Carratt* by doffing his bowler hat at each of us. We couldn't help overhearing the conductor say, *Why, bless my soul, if it isn't the pianist from Gower Heights. Good evening Mr Cockle. How are you this evening?* And we couldn't help but notice Bertie's face flush with pride at being recognised.'

'You said Bertie's moved up in the world,' said Alan.

'Yes. The last time Maureen and I bumped into him, he proudly told us he had been appointed Head of the Lower School in a Comprehensive.'

* * * * *

'Stick 'em up!' said Keith, pointing a large revolver at James Jackson's chest.

'Steady on,' said James, raising his hands in the air but not standing up.

'Is that thing loaded?' said David Swann, the young history teacher.

'This is a forty-four Magnum. It's the most powerful handgun in the world. It would blow your head clean off. You've got to ask yourself one question: *Do I feel lucky?* Well, do you, punk?' Keith snarled in his best impersonation of Clint Eastwood.

'Inspector Harry Callahan!' said Greg Watson, the young PE and geography teacher. 'Dirty Harry in the 1971 film.'

'Where on earth did you...' David did not finish his sentence. Keith was now pointing the gun at his chest.

'Empty your pockets... Now!' snarled Keith, pointing the gun at James again.

'My pockets are already empty, Harry,' said James. 'That's why we're having these meetings... or had you forgotten.'

Keith stared hard in turn at James, David, Greg and finally Colin who was looking paler than usual. Then he burst out laughing, handed the gun to James and trotted over to the drinks cabinet. James weighed the gun in his hand. After he had looked down the barrel, he passed the gun to David who quickly handed it to Greg. Keith

185

returned with his glass of beer in time to see Greg point the gun at Colin's chest.

'Careful, old boy,' said Keith. 'That's not a toy.'

'Is it l-l-loaded?' stammered Colin.

'Let's find out, shall we,' Greg said. And in the same breath he pulled the trigger.

The white-faced Colin Harper was the only one who didn't laugh when a metal rod came out of the barrel and the word *BANG* appeared in white letters on a red flag.

'Fantastic!' said James, ever ready for a practical joke. 'Where on earth did you buy it?'

'I didn't buy it,' said Keith. 'I made it in the workshop.'

'You made it?' said David. 'Really?'

'Of course I did.'

'*You? You* actually made it?' said Greg. '*Really?*'

'Are you doubting my ability?' said Keith. 'I'm rather offended.'

'Why? Why did you make it?' a red-faced Colin asked now he had stopped shaking.

'Obvious!' said Keith. 'We'll need guns if we're going to rob a bank but if we're caught, we don't want to be charged with armed robbery, do we?'

'Does Keith know what he's talking about, Quentin?' asked Reg.

'Yes and no,' said Quentin Waite MA (Oxon) LLM, Head of History. 'If he took that RIF...' A puzzled look appeared on Reg's face. 'Realistic Imitation Firearm, old boy.'

'Ah,' was all the Second Master could say while his companion took a sip of port.

'If he took that RIF into a bank to collect cash not belonging to him,' said Quentin, carefully putting down his glass, 'he might *put a person or persons in fear of being then and there subjected to force.* That would constitute intimidation and the theft would be aggravated robbery.'

'It wouldn't matter that he didn't have a real gun then?' said Reg.

'No,' said Quentin, 'It would be enough to *have the appearance of being a firearm, whether capable of being discharged or not.*'

'Pretty serious crime then?' said Reg.

'Yes indeed,' said Quentin, Bachelor of Law. 'If he were found guilty of robbery, or of an assault with intent to rob, he could be imprisoned for life.'

* * * * *

CHAPTER 18

"A man's most open actions have a secret side to them."
Joseph Conrad

* * * * *

The Bursar told Susan Taylor he would be away *four* days at the annual conference of the Independent Schools' Bursars Association (ISBA). She was certain it was a *three*-day event but she neither knew nor cared how Tony Smith intended to spend the extra day in Torquay. Susan was just pleased to have an extra day to complete the first phase of her plan. Thanks to Colin Harper and Rupert Jardine, she had the wherewithal to scrutinise the school accounts and to manage the investment club accounts. She would, however, need Rupert's help before she could check on Tony's own secret accounts.

'Hi! Donald Meeker here,' said the assistant chaplain, pressing the telephone to his ear.

'Good morning Mr Meeker,' said Susan. 'Mrs Taylor... from the Bursar's office.'

'Mrs Taylor. Ah, yes. Good morning. What can I do for you?'

'Would you be kind enough to give Rupert Jardine a message?'

'Yes, of course,' said Donald. 'Is it urgent?'

'No, not really. He's been helping me with my computer and I'd be grateful if he could pop in to see me as soon as he's free. Lunchtime if possible.'

The Reverend Meeker simply said Mrs Taylor had telephoned and for Rupert to see her as soon as possible, preferably at lunchtime; something to do with her computer apparently. Rupert's imagination was beginning to run riot. He remembered seeing *The Graduate* - a film about an older woman, played by Anne Bancroft. seducing a young man, played by Dustin Hoffman – and now he wondered if Mrs Taylor might be seeing herself as Mrs Robinson and seeing him as Benjamin Braddock.

'You wanted to see me, ma'am?'

'Yes, Rupert. Please come in,' Susan said in what Rupert imagined a rather silky voice.

'Is it about your investment club accounts program?'

'No, not really,' purred Susan. 'I'm having trouble accessing some files. Something to do with passwords. Could you take a look?' She gave Rupert her seat at her desk and stood behind him, putting her warm hands on his shoulders to send a shudder down his spine.

'Which files can't you access?' asked Rupert. When Susan leant forward to point at the computer screen, he felt the heat from her body on the back of his neck. Another shudder shot down his spine. He clicked on the file name and a window appeared asking for a password. 'You're right, ma'am. You do need a password,' he said in a croaking voice.

'I'm not very good at passwords,' Susan confided in a silky whisper. 'Is there any way I could get into these files without passwords?'

'I could probably install a backdoor.'

'What's that?' asked Susan.

'It's a program to bypass normal authentication. It would let you into any part of the computer without a password,' said Rupert. 'It may take me a bit of time to do.'

'How long?' said Susan, squeezing his shoulders and massaging the nape of his neck with her thumbs.

'If you'll let me take your computer to the Cavendish, I could probably be done within the hour.'

'Wonderful,' said Susan silkily, giving his neck and shoulders a squeeze. 'Could you have it back by three o'clock?'

'Sure can, ma'am,' said Rupert, beginning to feel hot all over.

'There was one other thing you might be able to help me with,' Susan said softly.

'Anything, ma'am,' said Rupert, his imagination going into overdrive.

'I want a computer in my living quarters. I'm not sure what to buy. Could you help me?'

'What will you use it for?' asked Rupert, his body on fire as if he had just completed a twelve-over spell of fast bowling against Brindle College 1st Eleven.

'Your investment club accounts program…' said Susan, still gently massaging his neck, 'but… I'd also like to have a duplicate of my office system to play with.'

'You wouldn't need to buy… Look, ma'am. I'd be happy to replicate this office system for you,' said Rupert. 'I could even set it up so your home and office systems handshake.'

'Wonderful!' said Susan. 'Would my home system also have a backdoor?

'Sure,' said Rupert, more excited than he would ever have thought possible.

When the crimson-faced young man left her office carrying her computer, Susan locked the door behind him and returned to her desk. She dialled 9 for an outside line then rang the local branch of the National Westminster Bank.

'Good afternoon. NatWest Bank. Tracy Hodder speaking. How may I help?'

'Good afternoon, Tracy,' said Susan. 'I'd like to speak to Mr Baker.'

'Who shall I say is calling?'

'Susan Wellborn.'

'Just one moment,' said the new girl on reception. 'Mr Baker… I have Susan Wellborn on the line. Shall I put her through?' Tracy pressed the correct buttons to put Mr Baker on hold and return to the in-coming caller. 'Sorry to keep you waiting, Miss Wellborn. I'm putting you through to Mr Baker now.'

Susan was impressed by the receptionist's efficiency. Tracy had not been impertinent or time-wasting by asking why Susan wanted to speak to Daniel Baker. She had not cut Susan off accidentally or made her listen to a recording extolling the services claiming to make NatWest second to none. And she genuinely apologised for keeping her waiting even though she took less than thirty seconds to connect Susan to her investment broker.

'Good afternoon, Miss Wellborn. How are you today?'

'I'm fine, Mr Baker,' said Susan. 'And you?'

'Very well, thank you,' said Daniel, quietly pressing a key on his computer keyboard to reveal Susan's accounts on the screen.

'I'm ringing to check on the status of the orders I placed with you recently.'

'Haven't you received your trading statement?' Daniel asked.

'No,' said Susan. 'There was nothing in the post when I opened it this morning.'

'Oh, dear. I do apologise. We did send it out *First Class*,' said Daniel apologetically.

'Perhaps you could tell me over the phone where I stand,' said Susan.

After more apologies and numerous identity verification questions which he was obliged to ask her and which he attempted to justify – customer security, anti-money laundering and so on – Daniel Baker told Susan he had acquired for her ten thousand shares of SIGEM Ltd at $0.95 per share. He was also able to tell her, as Mrs Taylor, the secretary of the BALI investment club, he had acquired one thousand shares for the club at the same time and at the same price: $0.95 per share.

Just before 3 o'clock, there was a knock on her office door and Rupert returned with her computer. He showed Susan how to enter her computer through the backdoor and how to access all the data files. Rupert also mentioned he had installed a small screen blackout program. 'So if someone comes into my office,' said Susan, 'I just tap the F11 key to turn the screen black and press F10 to get the screen back again. Wonderful!'

Before leaving her office, Rupert asked Susan if she would like him to come to her quarters at the weekend to install her home computer system. His heart missed a beat when, caressing the left side of his face with her right hand, she whispered, 'Wonderful!'

* * * * *

As far as Anthony Parker-Smythe was concerned, this year's ISBA conference was on the whole as dreary those he had attended in previous years. The best part of the seminars was for him the coffee and light refreshments served in the mid-morning breaks.

He always avoided seminars on topics such as *Health and Safety Policy*, *Asbestos in Schools*, etc., and usually attended seminars on specific financial topics that might make his life easier. This year he probably saved himself hours of work by collecting handouts at the seminar providing *Guidance on Bursaries* with up-to-date template forms for *confidential statement of parental financial circumstances* and *grant assessment*.

The afternoon plenary sessions were meant to inspire and motivate the delegates. As far as Anthony was concerned they were hot air events to help sleep off his buffet lunches.

The exhibitions were mostly a waste of time. This year Anthony was drawn to a stand where a young company representative was enthusing about contract compliance audits, compensation audits and exit audits to three female delegates. At one point, the young man baited his hook with an illustrated brochure which he handed to his audience of four. Just as Anthony accepted his copy with a big smile and a sickly *thank you, dear boy*, and just as the handsome young rep thought he was about to reel in a new client, a young lady took the young man's place on the stand. Anthony slipped off the hook and swam away.

On his fourth morning, the day after the conference had ended and the exhibitors had cleared their stands, Anthony slept in and had a full English breakfast tray delivered to his room by an attractive waitress in whom he showed no interest and to whom he proffered neither a grateful word nor a gratuitous coin.

When he had shaved, showered and dressed, he left his suitcase with the concierge and took a stroll down to the harbour in the warm sunshine of the so-called English Riviera. An onshore breeze, filled with the smell of the ocean, chilled the air and provided what little persuasion Anthony needed quickly to turn his back on the water and head to 6 Park Place for lunch in *The Hole in Wall*, purportedly Torquay's oldest pub. Over a delicious fish pie and a bottle of Muscadet, Anthony tried to focus on the holiday he was planning to take in Guernsey but his mind kept drifting to the work waiting for him at Beaumont and to the likelihood of another visit from the steely-eyed major, Angus MacKay.

'Good morning, Bursar. How was the conference?'

'Pretty much the same as last year, Mrs Taylor. Any problems while I was away?'

'No, Bursar,' said Susan. 'Nothing I couldn't handle.'

'That's a relief. So... what's on the agenda for today?'

'The High Master would like to you to see him at ten o'clock. He wants to talk about his plans regarding the new entries. It may have something to do with awarding bursaries and scholarships.'

'Right. Could you photocopying these template forms,' said Anthony. 'I should like to give them to the High Master when I see him. I fetched them from the conference.'

'Yes of course,' said Susan, 'I'll do them straight away. Anything else?'

'Not for the minute,' said Anthony.

'Mr Harper would like to see you this afternoon. Would two o'clock be convenient?'

'Yes, I suppose so. Did he say what it's about?'

'No he didn't but I got the feeling it's a personal matter.'

'Personal you say?' said Anthony.

'Oh, I nearly forgot,' lied Susan, 'Major MacKay telephoned. He'd like to see you again.'

* * * * *

The High Master of Beaumont had, for the past week, been preoccupied with the forthcoming HMC annual conference. He had been asked to deliver a paper on a topic of his own choosing. When the HMC Chairman invited Dr Llywelyn Pugh-Jones to address the assembly in a plenary session, he had suggested as a topic the question of whether or not philosophy might be usefully and properly taught in the independent schools.

For the third and last time, Llywelyn checked through his paper then carefully placed it in his brief case. It was his secretary, Mary Cranborne, who dutifully word-processed, printed and bound the paper and suggested the cover page:

Philosophy in the context of personal and social education (PSE)

Dr Llywelyn Pugh-Jones

High Master of Beaumont Abbey

Abstract

There is empirical evidence that children can develop reasoning skills through philosophical inquiry and thereby improve their cognitive and academic skills. This paper describes a course in ethics drawing upon familiar situations to initiate discussion of concepts such as courage, willpower, friendship, happiness, rights, crime and punishment.

Now that he could stop worrying about his talk, he could get back to worrying about other matters. His phone rang. 'I have Mr Trevanion for you, High Master,' said Mary.

'Henry. Thank you for returning my call. How are you?'

'Fine. Just fine, Llywelyn. Thank you for asking.'

'Good. Good. I'm glad to hear it,' said Llywelyn, struggling to remember why he had called the school solicitor in the first place.

'You were right to ask about the conditions for charitable status,' said Henry.

'Ah, yes. Charitable status!' said Llywelyn.

'I must apologise,' said Henry. 'The number of your new entries each year is directly tied to your major endowment but only indirectly tied to your charitable status.'

'Yes, I understand about the endowment, Henry. I've been, as you might say, *perusing* the file. As long as we take in sixty new pupils each year, we won't have a problem.'

'Correct,' said Henry.

'I also understand the sixty new pupils need not all be into the Lower Thirds.'

'Correct again,' said Henry. 'And of course they need not all be boys.'

'Oh, really?' said Llywelyn. 'Now that's interesting.

'As to the matter of your charitable status, I am in a position to tell you this,' said Henry. 'Firstly, the purposes of a charity for the advancement of education are *necessarily* for the public benefit. Secondly, a charity does not have to show it is providing public benefit in the way in which it carries out its activities; it merely has to show it is carrying out its purposes.'

'So?'

'So,' said Henry, 'should you be asked to state how Beaumont has been satisfying public benefit in carrying out its purposes, you could respond simply by stating the school has been satisfying public benefit in that its purposes are charitable for the public benefit, and that it has been carrying out its purposes. You then list Beaumont's activities.'

'Is it that simple?' said Llywelyn, even though the lawyer lost him after his first sentence.

'Probably,' said Henry, 'but I strongly advise you to pay careful attention to the percentage of income distributed in bursaries and scholarships.'

'Thank you, Henry. I shall do just that.'

At exactly ten o'clock, Mary Cranborne ushered the Bursar into the High Master's study and returned almost immediately with tea, coffee and biscuits on a silver tray. She poured a cup of Earl Grey tea for Dr Pugh-Jones and a cup of coffee with cream and two sugars for Anthony Parker-Smythe. When the High Master refused a biscuit she smiled approvingly. When the Bursar took two chocolate biscuits, she gave him her severest frown of disapproval.

Llywelyn thanked Mary then sipped his tea while she left the room and closed the door behind her.

'How was your conference, Anthony?'

'Very informative, High Master,' lied Anthony. 'Four days well spent. I brought these templates back.' He leant forward and handed Llywelyn the copies of the forms for *confidential statement of parental financial circumstances* and *grant assessment*.'

'Most timely, Anthony. Bursaries and scholarships. The very thing I wanted to see you about,' said Llywelyn, putting the papers on his desk and reaching for his cup of tea.

The Bursar managed to finish his two chocolate biscuits and his cup of coffee while the High Master explained his intention to establish Beaumont as a school that's hard when it comes to gaining entrance and scholarships but generous when it comes to awarding of bursaries to successful applicants.

'If I understand what you are saying, High Master,' said Anthony, 'you want to increase the percentage of income allocated to bursaries.'

'Yes. Yes I do.'

'We currently award about ten or eleven percent,' said Anthony.

'Yes, I remember that's what you told Lord Bartholomew at our governing board of directors meeting last month,' said Llywelyn. 'I should increase that to… oh, let's say fifteen percent. Could we?'

'Not without *drastic* cost cutting,' said Anthony, worrying about his expenses. 'May I suggest twelve percent for the next academic year and thirteen percent for the year after that?'

'Well, I…'

'If you remember, High Master, Mr Phillpott said at the meeting that charitable status has been awarded to schools granting as little as five percent of their income in means tested bursaries.'

'Yes, indeed,' said Llywelyn, ' but if I remember correctly he said *between five and fifteen percent.*'

'I really could not support increasing Beaumont's percentage to fifteen, High Master.'

'Before I'll consider twelve percent,' said Llywelyn, 'I need you to describe in detail what drastic cost cutting would be needed to award fifteen percent of our income in means tested bursaries.'

'Very well, High Master,' said Anthony. 'May I assume that in September Beaumont will have its full complement of pupils?'

'I see no reason why not,' said Llywelyn.

'You don't sound… if I may say so, High Master… You don't sound completely sure.'

'I have every confidence in the staff in charge of our scholarship examinations… But of course we can never know what the future has in store for us,' said Llywelyn.

'My point exactly,' said Anthony. 'What if some pupils do not return? What then?'

'A shortfall of one or two would not affect our charitable status but we might have a problem with our major endowment.'

'You would have a problem,' said Anthony, 'especially if it was a last minute decision and it didn't give you time to recruit replacement pupils.'

'Actually,' said Llywelyn, 'if we had a waiting list for places at Beaumont, we could…'

'Yes, you could fill the gaps from a waiting list but only if you had a waiting list and those on it were still waiting,' said Anthony. 'And you could still find yourself starting the new year with a few gaps in the registers.'

'I hadn't looked at it that way,' said Llywelyn. 'How could we bridge that gap?'

'Make up some names,' said Anthony. 'After all, to the authorities the pupils at a school are just names and numbers on a piece of paper or on a computer data file. They might just as well not exist.'

'Yes, indeed. How true,' said Llywelyn.

The bursar's words reminded the High Master of the tale of the non-existent *Lieutenant Kijé* and the two ideas fluttering into his brain over breakfast on the first Saturday of Trinity term. One idea had already been acted upon; Randolph Jardine would replace Sir Leslie Matthews on Beaumont's governing board of directors. The other idea – actually more of a fleeting thought sparked off by *Troika*, Prokovief's sleigh ride tune – would, if acted upon, likely lead to tragedy.

* * * * *

'Would you join me for lunch today, Mrs Taylor? I'd like to try a new local *bistro*.'

'Oh,' was all an extremely puzzled Susan could manage.

'A Monsieur and Madame Escoffier run it.' Said Anthony.

'That's interesting,' said Susan. 'Are they anything to do with Beaumont's chef?'

'Yes, they are Jean-Pierre's brother and sister-in-law. It was Jean-Pierre who told me they were opening *La Cave Gourmande*.'

'Are you sure it's *Gourmande* and not *Gourmet*?' asked Susan

'Yes, yes. I wrote it down. It's definitely *La Cave Gourmande*,' said Anthony whose knowledge of French was extremely limited even when it came to *le menu*.

'Is there any other reason why we are not having lunch at Beaumont?' Susan had really wanted to ask why they were having lunch in *The Greedy Cellar* but thought better of it.

'No, not really, Mrs Taylor.' And then with an oily smile said. 'This is my treat.'

In Susan's eyes the man seated opposite could never be Anthony Parker-Smythe, the *gourmet*; he would always be Tony Smith, the *gourmand*. In contrast to the substantial meal the bursar ordered and in keeping with her habit of controlling her weight by eating only a light lunch, Susan began with *Anchoïade camarguaise* - an assortment of crisp vegetables cut into sticks with an anchovy sauce – followed by *blancs de poulet à la sauce aux cèpes* – slices of chicken in a mushroom sauce with an aroma of truffles – accompanied by roasted vegetables.

'How was your meeting with the High Master?' Susan asked by way of conversation.

'He wants to put more money into means-tested bursaries,' said Anthony. 'He asked for fifteen percent of the school income.'

'That's quite an increase on our present allocation, isn't it?'

'Too much,' said Anthony. 'I suggested twelve percent this coming year and thirteen percent the year after.'

'That sounds sensible,' said Susan. ' What did he say to that?'

'When I told him we'd have to make some pretty drastic cuts if we allocate fifteen percent of our income to means tested bursaries, he instructed us to provide full details of those cuts before he would consider allocating only twelve percent to bursaries.'

'Ah, I see,' said Susan. '*We* shall have to prepare an accurate balance sheet showing all the current bursaries throughout the school to calculate the percentage allocated now and *we* shall have to keep a running check on the bursaries awarded following next month's interviews. That's a lot of work for *us*.' She swallowed her last piece of chicken then said, 'What are these drastic cuts *we* shall have to make?'

'Ah, yes. Those cuts,' said Anthony. 'I'd like your suggestions on cuts, Mrs Taylor.'

* * * * *

Back at Beaumont, Colin Harper sat on a seat in the main corridor waiting patiently. He had come to the conclusion he should open an off-shore account and that it would suit his purpose best if the account were in a particular branch of a bank in Guernsey. He looked up when he heard footsteps in the corridor leading from the front entrance of the school and was a little surprised to see the bursar and his PA come around the corner side by side.

'Good afternoon, Mr Harper,' said Susan. 'Have you been waiting long?'

'N-no, M-Mrs T-Taylor, n-not l-long.'

'Please come and wait in my office. I'm sure Mr Parker-Smythe won't be long.'

'H-how are y-you g-getting on with your c-computer?' asked Colin, genuinely interested.

'Fine! Thank you, for asking,' said Susan. 'Rupert Jardine has been a great help.'

'T-that's good,' said Colin. 'He's my s-s-star s-s-student, you know.'

'Hello,' said Susan, answering the telephone after the first ring. 'Yes, very well. I'll send him right in.' She put the phone back on the hook and said, 'The Bursar will see you now, Mr Harper.'

'Sorry if I kept you waiting, Colin,' said Anthony glancing at his watch. 'Our lunch meeting took longer than expected. Now then, what did you want to see me about?'

'I'd like your advice on off-shore accounting,' said Colin without a stammer.

'Off-shore accounting, you say. That's not something I know much about,' lied Anthony.

'Forgive me, Bursar, but I thought you told me you had off-shore accounts in Guernsey.'

'Did I?' said Anthony. 'When did I tell you that?'

'Earlier this term. It was when I came and asked you how to make money quickly.'

'That's when I told you?'

'Yes!' said Colin. 'You said making money is only part of becoming rich. You said keeping hold of your money is just as important as getting hold of it and that's why you keep yours in off-shore accounts in Guernsey.'

'I see. Well I do have a little money in a Guernsey off-shore account but...'

'Well then,' said Colin, 'could you help me open an account in your Guernsey bank?'

'Do you really need me to help you open an off-shore account?'

'Yes, I do,' said Colin. 'I'd like you to be my referee.'

'Would you be able to be in Guernsey during the mid-term break?'

'Yes, certainly.'

'And you're sure you will need an off-shore account?' said Anthony.

'Definitely,' said Colin. 'You see, I'll be coming into a large sum of money very soon.'

'Well that is good news,' said Anthony. 'You won't want to borrow from me then.'

'No, Bursar,' said Colin. 'We studied Hamlet at school and I remember Polonius said *Neither a borrower nor a lender be; For loan oft loses both itself and friend, and borrowing dulls the edge of husbandry*. No, Bursar, it's never been my intention to *borrow* from you.'

* * * * *

CHAPTER 19

"In the long history of humankind (and animal kind, too) those who learned to collaborate and improvise most effectively have prevailed." Charles Darwin

* * * * *

The two disinterested observers had been enjoying their sherry and cheese cake for ten minutes before the Head of Geography arrived to disturb the Common Room quietude.

'Ah, there you are, Reg,' said Arthur Matthews. 'Thought you might be here. By rights we should be out on the tennis court with Louise and Mary.'

'I fear, Arthur, they've relegated us to reserves in case Celia and Susan can't play.'

'Shame! Never mind,' said Arthur, 'we'll have to organise a men's doubles. How about it Quentin? Care for a game of tennis?'

'When I was called to the bar,' said Quentin Waite, putting down the Times crossword, 'I was advised never to ask a witness a question to which I did not know the answer. In the light of that advice, how would you regard your question?'

'Without wishing to offend, old boy,' said Arthur, 'I'd expect you to say no.'

'In that case,' said Quentin, 'I just might surprise you. I'd be delighted to join you for doubles. I used to enjoy a game of tennis, you know.'

'Really?' said Arthur.

'Yes, really!' said Reg. 'He's not kidding. As a young barrister, Quentin probably spent as much time on the tennis courts as he did in the law courts.'

'Hello chaps!' said Dr Phil Carratt, Head of Chemistry, breezing into the room with Alan Radford, the Head of English and Housemaster of Gower.

'You're just in time,' said Reg. 'I think Quentin is about to regale us with a tennis story.'

'One Sunday morning I had a telephone call from Sebastian Walker. We played tennis together when we were up at Oxford. Johnny – an inevitable nickname in view of his surname and fondness for the Kilmarnock nectar – had quite a decent backhand as I recall. Anyway, out of the blue, Johnny telephoned to ask a favour. Apparently he had wangled himself a minor post in the Foreign Office and got himself into a bit of fix. Under the influence of one glass too many at an official reception, he had agreed to play tennis with his opposite number from the Russian Embassy.

The next morning, the Sunday morning when he rang me, Johnny said the Russian Embassy had called to confirm a game of *doubles*, not singles, at eleven o'clock. Johnny needed a partner. Luckily I still had my whites, tennis shoes and racquet, so I agreed to play. By the way, this all happened quite a few years ago when I just a young barrister - cutting my teeth on the bar you might say.'

'When Johnny and I arrived, the two Soviets – Johnny had referred to them as Russian diplomats - were already on court warming up. Both were taller than either Johnny or myself. Both looked fitter than we had been even as undergraduates at our peak. Both looked disconcertingly like a pair of agents of the Committee for State Security - Komitet Gosudarstvennoj Bezopasnosti or KGB, if you will – readying to interrogate us. Now old Johnny had assured me this was just a friendly game to promote *l'entente-cordiale* between him and his Russian counterparts. Well, during our short warm up, drops of rain began to fall onto my glasses from the dark clouds hiding the sun. I sensed we were in for a storm in more ways than one.'

'Unaccustomed to spinning racquets and calling rough or smooth, one of the Soviets tossed a coin for service. To Johnny's consternation, I correctly called heads and, more to his dismay, I elected to serve. Now old Johnny may have had a pretty good backhand but, though I say it myself, I had an even better first serve. Just as I took up my position, Johnny suggested in a loud voice that we retire to the pavilion before the rain became heavy. The burly Soviets shook their heads and chorused *niet! niet!*'

'I threw the ball high in the air, arched my back and produced the best serve of my life. The ball sped from my racquet in a vicious curve, dipped, landed just inside the corner of the forecourt and singles service line, then fizzed into the netting surrounding the court. It was an ace to end all aces. One of the square-jawed, muscular, thickset Soviets who claimed to be *Cultural Attachés*, snarled "Advantage Great Britain" and glowered at us.'

'Johnny looked despairingly at me and then turned to the Soviet and said, "It's actually fifteen-love." Unfortunately, even to my ears it sounded like *Sorry, it's fifteen, Love*! I forget how the match ended but there was a great deal of rain and very little cordiality. I haven't seen or heard from Johnny since.'

* * * * *

One by one the junior members of staff comprising the *gang of five* arrived. Dr Newbold, Head of Physics and Geoffrey Rusbridge, Head of Economics, were the last of the senior staff to drift in. When all ten men were seated, Geoffrey steered the conversation to finance and in an attempt to establish some kind of common ground said, 'Well chaps, how are you going to make your fortune?' Although he was careful not to use the plural *fortunes*, it made no difference. None of the five was in a collaborative mood.

'I've heard from Cambridge and the Joint Matriculation Board,' said James, the chemist.

'Good news, I hope,' said Greg, PE and geography.

'Yes and no,' said James. 'The good news is I shall be marking about 300 A-level scripts for Cambridge and about 500 GCSE scripts for JMB. I should make about one thousand five hundred pounds before tax.'

'What's the bad news?' Greg asked.

'I'll have to do all that marking in the same three weeks and do my teaching.'

'It shouldn't be too bad,' said Phil Carratt. 'Get your wife Katherine to open all the scripts to the first question and mark that one first. After you have a done a few, you won't need to refer to the mark scheme and you'll rattle through. Do the same for all the other questions. It's a piece of cake.'

'What about the twenty sample scripts I'll have to send to the chief examiner?'

'You're in luck,' said Phil. 'I'll be your chief examiner for Cambridge.'

'I've had a bit of luck as well,' said Greg.

'Exam marking?' said David, the historian.

'No thank you,' said Greg emphatically. 'I've landed a job as an instructor at the Body Zone Fitness and Gym in the Beau Sejour Leisure Centre in Guernsey.'

'In Guernsey?' said the computer scientist, Colin, becoming more anxious than usual.

'Yes,' said Greg. 'Six weeks in the sun for me and the family, all expenses paid. And I'll probably earn as much as James slaving over eight hundred exam papers.'

'What have you got up your sleeve, Keith?' said David

'Spare parts,' said Keith, the design and technology teacher.

'Sorry, old man. You've lost me,' said David.

'Braines! I'm making money with Braines,' said Keith.

'Since when did you have any brains,' said James, grinning all over his face.

'No. Not my brains. Charlie…'

'Who are you calling a…'

'No. Charlie Braines. You know. The chap who owns a chain of repair garages. His son's in the Upper Fourths,' said Keith. 'Charlie can't get the spare parts for his older cars so I'm going to supply him.'

'How?' David asked. 'Steal them?'

'No, not really,' said Keith. 'I've an arrangement with a couple of scrap yards. They'll let me know when an old car comes in and we'll strip it.'

'We? And who might *we* be?' said David.

'I should have said *I*,' said Keith, 'but of course, if *I* can get the vehicles back to school then some of my lads can help. Good practical experience for them.'

'I suppose your lads will machine the parts as well, will they?' said Greg.

'Oh, yes,' said Keith. 'According to the aims and objectives of CDT - Craft, Design and Technology to you - I have to *give boys the confidence and competence to identify, examine and solve practical problems* and *encourage the flexibility and openness of mind necessary to meet challenges.* Just doing my job, d'you see.'

'That just leaves you and Colin,' said Geoffrey, addressing David. 'Are you two going to rob a bank?'

'I can't speak for Colin,' said David, 'but no, I will not. Penelope wouldn't approve.'

'She'd worry you might get caught, is that it?' said James.

'Oh no. She knows I'm too smart to get caught,' said David, keeping a straight face. 'No, it's not that. Penny is very particular about what I wear. She'd just die if I donned a ski mask and blue denim overalls.'

'So how do you plan to get rich quick?' said Greg, grinning from ear to ear.

'He's going to marry into money,' quipped James. 'The banns have been called giving notice of the marriage of the Honourable Penelope FitzGibbon... only daughter of Viscount Percival FitzGibbon, sole heir to his estate and Spinster of this parish... to the dishonourable David Swann, impoverished Bachelor of Arts and...'

'As a matter of fact,' said David, cutting James short, 'with Mr Radford's help, I'm going to make a killing in the market.'

'Oh, really,' said Geoffrey, putting down his glass of white wine. 'How exactly? A bit of insider trading?'

'No, no! Not the Stock Market, Mr Rusbridge. The fruit and vegetable market. I'm going to grow *organic* tomatoes at Gower House. I've got it all worked out.' David fished a piece of paper out of his inside coat pocket and read aloud:

One packet of 100 tomato seeds	£0.45
One bundle of 100 5 ft. canes	£7.95
One ball of garden twine	£0.75
Total outlay	£9.15

Yield of tomatoes @ an average of 10lb per plant will be 1000lb

1000lb of *organic* tomatoes @ £1.95 per lb. will return £1,950

Gross Profit £1,950 minus £9.15 = £1,940.85

When the applause died down, David said, 'I bought the seeds today.' When everybody had stopped laughing, David turned and said, 'It's up to you now Colin to rob a bank.'

* * * * *

After three hard fought sets in the warm afternoon sunshine, the four ladies were content just to sit on the grass and talk. In response to Mary's question, Louise said the High Master's talk at the HMC Conference had gone down very well. In response to Louise's question, Celia said she thought the BALI meeting had gone well. In response to Celia's question, Susan explained that an illegal insider trade is buying or selling stocks to make a profit based on information not available to the general public. In response to Susan's question, neither Celia nor Louise nor Mary knew what David Swann was doing on the patch of earth running in front of the long south-facing wall of the walled garden.

* * * * *

When Fiona called him to the telephone she saw he was already dressed for one of his special assignments. Keeping her hand firmly over the mouthpiece, she said, 'There's a lady calling herself Susan asking to speak to a man calling himself Stewart. I take it she means you and not your father.' When Angus nodded, she said, 'Is Stewart in or out?' As Angus straightened his Black Watch tie, his wife uncovered the mouth piece and said, 'Hold on. He's just coming.'

'Good morning Mrs Taylor,' said Angus, waving his wife away into her kitchen.

'Good morning, Stewart,' said Susan. 'I hope I've not caught you at an inconvenient moment.'

'Och, no!' said Angus. 'I am just on my way out but it's nae bother.'

'Oh, dear,' said Susan. 'Well you see, I thought you'd like to know Mr York's coming here today.'

'Any idea what time?'

'Half past ten.'

'Right. Thank you for letting me know, Mrs Taylor,' said Angus and hung up.

'Was that your mole?' asked Fiona reappearing from the kitchen.

'Aye. It was,' said Angus.

'So, a change of plans?' said Fiona. 'You'll be going to Beaumont.'

'Aye, I'll be going to the school but there's no change of plan. Stanley Garnet telephoned me yesterday to say his Robert York was seeing yon Anthony Parker-Smythe today.'

'Ah, I see,' said Fiona. 'That's why were dressed for battle.'

When Susan entered carrying the tray of coffee and chocolate biscuits, the Bursar noticed it was almost half past ten but did not notice there were three cups and saucers on the tray. Susan left the room and reappeared almost immediately to announce the arrival of Robert York. The two men exchanged formal greetings while Susan poured two coffees. When she had left the room and closed the door behind her, Robert raised his eyebrows and gave Anthony a quizzical look.

'You sounded more anxious than usual over the phone,' said Robert. 'What's up?'

'The High Master wants to increase the percentage of income awarded to bursaries.'

'So, is that a problem?'

'In theory, no,' said Nosey Parker. 'But the more income we give away, the less we have for running this place and the less we have in the reserve fund to generate investment income. How safe are those Common Investment Funds (CIFs) you recommended?'

'No investment is *safe*, old boy. You know that as well as I do,' said Bob.

'You know what I'm getting at,' said Nosey.

'Let me put it this way,' said Bob, 'your CIFs are as safe as those Special Purpose Vehicles (SPVs) you've got in Guernsey.'

'I'm not sure I find that particularly reassuring.' There was a knock on the door and Susan entered. 'Yes, what is it, Mrs Taylor?' said Nosey.

'Major MacKay is here to have a word with you and Mr York.'

'Thank you Mrs Taylor. You'd better show him in.'

'Coffee, Major MacKay?' said Susan.

'Please, Mrs Taylor. Black. No cream. No sugar. Thank you,' said Angus. She smiled as she handed him his coffee and he gave her a conspiratorial wink as she left the room.

Angus said he was sorry to trouble them but both men sensed he was not in the least bit sorry. Angus said he could come back another day but both men felt sure he had no intention of leaving. Angus said he had a few simple questions to ask them but both men knew in their bones his questions would not be simple.

Nosey said he would be happy to help but Angus knew he would try to hinder him. Robert said, in a superior tone of voice, he would have a word with Stanley Garnet about these security checks but Angus knew he would not. Both men said they were prepared to answer his questions but Angus was sure they were quite unprepared when he asked, 'How secure are your accounts here in Beaumont and off-shore in Guernsey?'

* * * * *

CHAPTER 20

"Travelling makes a man wiser, but less happy."
Thomas Jefferson

* * * * *

Travellers to and from Beaumont Abbey were generally spoilt for choice. Lying within a forty mile radius of the school were three small railway stations on the mainline from Carlisle to London, an airport for international flights and two access roads onto the M1 motorway. But travellers from Beaumont heading for the Channel Islands had little choice; they had to reach Portsmouth by early evening to catch the night sailing on either the *Corbière* operated by British Channel Island Ferries (BCIF) or the *Earl Granville* operated by Sealink British Ferries. And these two ships sailed on almost identical timetables to arrive in St Peter Port at around seven o'clock in the morning.

The MacKays boarded the early morning train from Carlisle to London at the first small station which, from their house, was a gentle stroll for Angus and a brisk walk for Fiona. Gregory Watson tried to stay calm as Colin Harper raced through the narrow country lanes to the second small station where, with plenty of time to spare, he parked his black Ford Fiesta and joined his somewhat shaky colleague on the platform. Angus recognised the slightly-built Colin, Beaumont's computer genius, but not the well-built Gregory, as the two young teachers entered the neighbouring second class compartment at the rear of the train. Anthony Parker-Smythe went by taxi to the third small station which was large enough to merit a porter to carry his luggage and show him to his reserved seat in the first class compartment, next to the restaurant car near the front of the train.

When the refreshment trolley appeared, Angus bought a black coffee and sandwich but wanted Fiona to take lunch in the restaurant car. On her return, she automatically handed Angus the receipt and said, 'Are you sure it's alright? Seems a bit pricey to me.'

'Och, aye. Stanley will set expenses against tax, you can be sure o' that.'

'How was the sandwich?' Fiona asked, knowing full well what he would say.

'I dinnae know what's inside it but it's no *salmon* from Thurso water,' he said, wrapping the remnants back in the cellophane and dropping it into the waste bin. 'How was lunch?'

'Actually rather good,' said Fiona. 'I had the place to myself except for one chap who almost put me off my lunch. Talk about greedy.'

'I think,' said Angus, after she described the man, 'you've seen our quarry.'

Anthony Parker-Smythe took a taxi from Euston to Waterloo station where a porter he neither thanked nor tipped helped him to his reserved first class seat on the train to Portsmouth harbour. The other four travellers took the London Underground and made their separate ways to unreserved seats in second class carriages on the same train.

On the overnight crossing to St Peter Port in Guernsey, Anthony tossed and turned in his cabin on the *Earl Granville*. On the *Corbière*, Angus snored and Fiona slept in their cabin whilst Colin dozed and Greg snored in reclining chairs in the passenger lounge. The *Earl Granville* docked at St Peter Port ten minutes before the *Corbière*.

A young and inexperienced cabin steward performed the unrewarding task of carrying the heavy suitcase off the *Earl Granville* ferry and directing the driver of a waiting taxi to take Anthony to La Collinette Hotel by the quickest route.

'Good morning, sir,' said the good-looking porter. 'Welcome to La Collinette.'

'Good morning,' said Anthony, waving the taxi away without tipping the driver.

'Is this your first visit to Guernsey, sir?'

'No. I have been here many times and I always stay at La Collinette,' said Anthony. 'I've not seen you before. What is your name?'

'My name is Kristian,' said the young man. 'Kristian at your service, sir.'

'Well, Kristian, would you give my luggage to the concierge for safekeeping while I'm in the dining room,' said Anthony, slipping the young man a generous tip accompanied by a sickly smile. 'I'll expect you to show me to my room after I've had breakfast.'

* * * * *

Fiona and Angus, making light of their suitcases, left the ferry and strolled the few hundred yards along the St Julian's Emplacement to the North Esplanade and the very short distance to Le Pollet for a typical French breakfast in the Boulangerie Victor Hugo.

The *café* was freshly brewed from a mix of Arabica and South American beans. Angus drank his without cream, milk or sugar. Fiona took a little sugar. The *jus*, from freshly pressed Valencia oranges, was not chilled. The freshly baked *croissants* and *petits pains au chocolat* were still warm. Only the *confiture d'orange et de fraises* had not been prepared on the premises.

'Apparently,' said Fiona, 'Victor Hugo exiled himself when Napoleon III seized power.'

'That the fellow who wrote *Les Miserables*?' said Angus, feigning ignorance.

'Och, aye!' said Fiona, mimicking her husband's voice. 'He wrote it here in Guernsey. The Hugo family lived in St Peter Port for seventeen years.'

Angus ate a leisurely *petit déjeuner* to avoid checking into La Collinette Hotel at the same time as Anthony Parker-Smythe. For the same reason, he and Fiona walked to the hotel via Le Truchot and the Candie Gardens, passing the South Africa War memorial and the statue of Victor Hugo *en route*. For a fell-runner like Angus MacKay, the half mile uphill from the Boulangerie was literally just a stroll in the park even carrying two fairly heavy suitcases. Fiona had no trouble keeping up but, unlike her husband, was perspiring and slightly out of breath when they finally arrived at reception.

'Is Mr Parker-Smythe in his room?'

'No, I believe he has gone out, Mr MacKay,' said André, the receptionist, glancing at the key rack to confirm his answer. 'Would you like me to inform you when he returns?'

'Och, no,' said Angus, picking up their suitcases. 'I'll nae doubt bump into him sometime or other today.'

'Your room is in the West Wing. I'm sure you will like it, Mrs MacKay,' said André, handing Fiona the key. 'It has a splendid view of our gardens and swimming pool.'

'D'you want me to unpack?'

'Would you mind, Colonel?' said Angus.

'No, I don't mind,' said Fiona. 'I'd rather unpack than go with you to the bank.'

'You'll be taking a dip in the pool?'

'Och, aye,' said Fiona, grinning at her husband. 'Now away about your business, Major.'

* * * * *

Colin and Greg were not far behind the MacKays but at the end of the St Julian's Emplacement they turned right onto the Glategny Esplanade and trudged another seven hundred yards around the coast road to the St Georges Bed & Breakfast.

Greg left their lodgings before Colin and jogged the 180 yards up Piette Road and the three hundred yards through Cambridge Park to the Beau Sejour Leisure Centre. The assistant manager, Sophie-Mae Guallianne, offered a firm handshake and apologised for her English which was far better than Greg's French then whisked him away on a whirlwind tour of the buildings and grounds.

'This is our main indoor sports area,' she said, leading Greg into the Sir John Loveridge Hall. 'As you can see, it's marked out for Badminton, Basketball, Five-a-Side Football and Volleyball. We also hire out the hall for conferences, concerts, entertainment and sporting events.'

'Is this where I'll be working?' asked Greg.

'Here, yes… or in the fitness centre or in the pool or out on the tennis courts... we'll see.'

Throughout the tour, the assistant manager listed changes she wanted but feared might be a long time coming: improved ventilation and changing rooms for pool users, modernised catering facilities and shopping area, better flooring in the sports hall. She ended the tour at the café. 'Well, Greg, what do you think of my little centre?'

'I'm impressed. Very impressed. But *little*? I'd hardly call it *little*,' he said. thinking of the somewhat smaller sports hall they hoped to build at Beaumont one day.

'Good. I'm glad you like it,' she said. 'There are many improvements to be made but as it stands, my centre is still better than that horrible concrete bunker next door.'

'Concrete bunker?' said Greg with a puzzled look on his face.

'The two-storey underground fortress. Headquarters of the 584th German regiment in the second world war. I can't understand why anyone would want to preserve it, can you?'

'No,' said Greg, shaking his head, not understanding in the least what she was talking about. Then after a pause he said, 'Could you suggest where we… I mean, where my wife and I and our children could stay when I'm working here in the summer?'

'A self-catering cottage at La Collinette about four hundred metres from here as the crow flies. Go and book one now. Mention my name and tell them you'll be working for me in the summer. They'll give you a very good discount.'

* * * * *

'Good morning,' said Anthony, tapping the young man lightly on the shoulder. 'I see you found the place.

'Yes I did,' said Colin, turning to face his referee from Beaumont. 'Yes, very straightforward. Your directions were very clear, thank you Bursar.'

'Anthony! You must call me Anthony.'

'If you insist,' said Colin.

'I do, dear boy. And I shall call you Colin if you've no objection. Now let's go inside.'

The Pierson, Heldring & Pierson bank could not claim a pedigree as far back as the late eighteenth century when Mayer Rothschild established European banking but it did claim to trace its tradition of confidentiality and respectability back to the late nineteenth century when the two brothers, Jan and Henri Pierson, established the bank in Holland.

Tony Smith felt at home when he walked into the Guernsey branch of the Dutch bank. He had wanted to become a banker. He fancied an oak-panelled office in an edifice steeped in ancient traditions. He dreamt of power over other people's money. As the Bursar of Beaumont Abbey, he now had an oak-panelled office and he now controlled the school's money but in his mind a banker and a bursar were worlds apart. He took his eyes off the imposing glass chandelier when he heard footsteps on the bank's marble floor.

'Good morning, *Monsieur* Smith. How are you today?' said the manager.

'A little tired from my journey,' said Tony, 'but it's nice to be back in Guernsey.'

'And this is the gentleman of whom you spoke?' said the manager, turning to Colin.

'Yes, this is my friend and colleague, Mr Colin Harper.'

'*Enchanté*, Monsieur,' said the manager. 'Welcome to Guernsey. Permit me to introduce myself. Arnaud le Tissier, *à votre disposition*.'

'Pleased to meet you,' said Colin, as they clasped hands briefly and limply.

'This is your first visit to Guernsey, Monsieur Harper?'

'Yes,' said Colin. 'My first visit.'

'But not your last, I hope,' said the manager. '*Bon*! I understand you wish to open an account with us, that is correct, yes?'

'Yes,' said Colin.

'*Parfait*!' said the manager. 'We shall attend to the matter *immédiatement*.'

* * * * *

Fiona tucked her auburn hair into her white bathing cap, adjusted her goggles then sprang from the tiled edge of the pool to enter the water with barely a splash. She sliced through the cool water with a stylish front crawl, breathing on alternate sides at every third stroke and tumble turning at each end of the pool. With the water at 25°C, an ideal temperature for serious swimming, Fiona was pleased to have the pool to herself. As she swam back and forth the piscine, Fiona wondered what havoc her feline Angus would wreak among the avian bankers.

'I have an appointment to see Monsieur Arnaud le Tissier,' said Angus.

'There is a Monsieur MacKay to see you, sir,' the young lady behind the enquiries desk whispered into the telephone. '*Oui, Monsieur le Tissier. Toute suite*.' She put down the telephone, came from behind her desk and said, 'Follow me, Monsieur, if you please.'

'Monsieur MacKay, please. Take a seat. May I offer you something to drink?'

'Un café, s'il vous plaît,' said Angus

'You speak French, Monsieur MacKay?'

'Only a little,' lied Angus, 'but I'd prefer English just now.'

'*D'accord, Monsieur*. Your business… it is of a delicate nature, is it not?'

'Let's just say my enquiries should be discreet and treated in the strictest confidence.'

'But naturally,' said the manager, stroking his neat, grey moustache with the forefinger of his left hand. 'Our customers must have the utmost confidence that Pierson, Heldring & Pierson (Guernsey) Ltd maintains the strictest confidentiality, you understand.'

'Of course,' said Angus. 'There would be little point, would there not, in holding an offshore account here if one could not rely upon your confidentiality.'

'Ah, here is our coffee,' said the manager. 'Allow me to offer you *un petit-beurre.*'

Angus accepted the tiny cup of black coffee and broke his golden rule; he accepted a biscuit bearing the impression LU – PETIT-BEURRE – NANTES. According to the manager, LU was *l'emblème* for Louis Lefèvre-Utile who invented the famous French biscuit in Nantes in 1886. When Le Tissier had finished nibbling his biscuit and drained his coffee cup, he dabbed his moustache and lips with a napkin before turning his attention to his visitor.

'I'd like to examine the accounts of a man going by the name of Anthony Parker-Smythe or Tony Smith,'

'I regret,' said the manager, 'that our policy of...'

'Strict confidentiality. Yes, I understand,' Angus said in a soft voice. 'Under *normal* circumstances, you should deny me access but circumstances are *not* normal, you see.'

Angus showed Arnaud le Tissier one of his leather bound identification cards before handing him one of his official-looking documents. The manager took pains to match his visitor's face with the photo on the card before carefully studying the document.

'This man Smith or Parker-Smythe as you also name him,' said the manager, 'he is...'

'My enquiries are strictly confidential and in the early stages.' said Angus, raising his hand, with the palm facing le Tissier, as though he were a policeman on traffic duty. 'I shall as far as possible proceed with the utmost discretion, you understand.'

217

'I understand, Major. You may rely upon me,' said Le Tissier, hand on head.

'Good!' said Angus. 'Now, I should like to start with account records and any documents relating to Smith's various companies.'

'Of course, Major,' said the manager. '*Par hasard*, Mr Smith was in here a short while ago with a colleague but he left about fifteen minutes before you arrived.'

'Do you happen to know the name of his colleague?'

'But certainly,' said Le Tissier, 'Mr Harper. Actually, he may still be in the bank talking to Monsieur Fournier... the man in charge of our security systems.'

'Really,' said Angus. 'I must have a word with Monsieur Fournier.'

* * * * *

The situation at Pierson, Heldring & Pierson was little different from other banks. It was reliant upon a developing Information Technology (IT) and still struggling with choices of operating systems. The IBM mainframe with its remote access control facility (RACF), introduced in 1976, competed with other systems that processed financial transactions and secured its banking data with its own access control software. Consequently, the central operating system for all the banks had to synchronise with different computer platforms and had thereby to expose them to greater risk of hacking.

Monsieur Fournier was delighted to tell Colin in great detail not only what Colin already knew about security systems in general but also what he did not know about this bank's security systems in particular. Fournier's explanation of the format of the 5-bit coding on track 2 of the magnetic strip on the PH&P bank's debit card was cut short by the appearance of Arnaud le Tissier and Angus MacKay.

'Monsieur Fournier! Permit me to introduce Major MacKay,' said the manager. 'Major MacKay, this is Mr

218

Fournier. He is our IT specialist in charge of our security systems.'

'Pleased to meet you,' said Fournier.

'And this is Mr Harper,' said Le Tissier. 'A fellow countryman I believe.'

'Hello,' said Angus, shaking Colin firmly by the hand. 'Another Scotsman?'

'No, English. Born in Cambridge actually.'

'In Guernsey on business, Mr Harper?' said Angus.

'Holiday mostly,' said Colin. 'And you?'

'Business mostly,' said Angus.

'Very well,' said Le Tissier, 'I shall leave you in Monsieur Fournier's capable hands.

'You are interested in our security systems, Mr MacKay?'

'I'm thinking of opening an off-shore account here,' lied Angus. 'Just wanted to know how safe it would be.'

'As I have explained to Mr Harper, we take great pride in our security.'

'So if I put money in an account here, nobody but myself can take it out. Is that so?'

'I do not believe I have met anyone who could bypass our security,' said Fournier. 'Now, as I was saying to Mr Harper, the coding on the magnetic strip of our debit cards…'

* * * * *

Greg strolled the one-third of a mile from Sejour Leisure Centre across Cambridge Park to Fosse André, then along Coronation Road and St Jacques to the building that began as a doctor's home and surgery in the 19th century, became a signals headquarters for the German High Command during the second world war and was now La Collinette Hotel.

'Good afternoon, sir,' said Éloïse.

'Good afternoon,' said Greg, giving the *receptionniste* an admiring look. 'My name is Watson… Gregory Watson.'

'What can I do for you, Mr Watson?'

'I'm here to book a self-catering cottage for six weeks in the summer when I shall be working for Sophie-Mae Guallianne at the Beau Sejour Leisure Centre.'

'For how many persons?' said Éloïse.

'Four,' said Greg. 'My wife, myself and our two children.'

'How old are your children?'

'Mark is almost five and Tracy is just three and a half years old.'

'Will Tracy be able to sleep in a single bed?'

'Yes. Why do you ask?' said Greg.

'There is no charge for children under ten years of age if they can sleep in the beds we provide,' said Éloïse. 'Would you like to see a cottage?'

'Yes, please,' said Greg.

'Kristian! Show Mr Watson a two-bedroom cottage.'

Greg knew at once Kathy would be thrilled: a modern kitchen with a dishwasher, fridge and a microwave oven as well as a normal oven. The lounge diner was large and there was a television for the kids. There were two bedrooms; one with a double bed and one with twin beds. There was even a picnic table on the terrace. The only thing that might trouble Kathy was that the cottage overlooked the pool.

'Did you like the cottage, Mr Watson?' said Éloïse.

'Rather,' said Greg. 'I can't wait.'

'Which one would you like to reserve? One by the pool or one of the two a bit further away, overlooking the gardens?'

'By the pool, please.'

'You will keep a close eye on your children, yes?' said Éloïse.

'Of course,' said Greg, sounding not quite as confident as usual.

'Very well. I shall need a non-refundable deposit of one hundred pounds, please.'

'Colin! What are you doing here?'

'I was about to ask you that,' said Colin Harper.

'I'm reserving a cottage for the summer… Actually, old boy, I wonder… They want a deposit of a hundred pounds. I don't suppose you could…'

'Of course,' said Colin. 'We'll use my new debit card.'

'Thank you, sir,' said Éloïse, swiping the PH&P card through the reader.

'Thanks, old man,' said Greg. 'Bit of luck you turning up when you did. So, what brings you here?'

'I've been invited for afternoon tea.'

* * * * *

The man enjoyed a quick 500 metre swim then relaxed on a pool-side lounger. He rarely derived pleasure from basking in the sunshine but delighted in looking at Fiona's well-proportioned figure filling the one-piece swimming costume. He was lying on his left side propped up on his left elbow enjoying this view when movements in front of the cottages at the far end of the pool caught his eye. It was Greg and Kristian. He watched them walk past and enter the main building. Not long after, he saw Colin arrive.

'That's very interesting, lassie,' said Angus.

'How long have you been lying there?' said Fiona.

'I lose all track o' time when I'm enjoying myself.'

'What's caught your eye?' said Fiona.

'Apart from yourself, you mean?' said Angus. 'I saw yon fellow who was with Harper on the train and just now saw Harper himself. I wonder what those two are doing here.'

Angus barely noticed the sun go behind the cloud but Fiona shivered. 'I'm away to our room, Major. Are you going to join me?

'Is that some kind of offer I shouldn't refuse, Colonel?' he said, side-stepping a lash from the end of her towel.

'Mind your manners, Major, or you'll find yourself on a charge.'

'I noticed the Colonel was shivering, sir. Permission to warm the Colonel up, sir,' said Angus, wrapping his towel around his wife.

'At this time in the afternoon, the Colonel would prefer a nice hot cup of tea, thank you, Major,' said Fiona.

As they entered the dining room, about a half an hour later, Angus gripped his wife's arm and pulled her towards a table in a corner recess. On the far side of dining room by a window with a view into the gardens, Anthony Parker-Smythe was conversing with Colin and Greg. The Bursar was facing the window.

'What's that all about?' said Fiona.

'Parker-Smythe alias Smith,' said Angus quietly. 'The fellow you saw in the dining car on the train to London. Over there… Chatting to Harper and that other fellow.'

'The fellow with his back to us?' said Fiona. 'Are you sure it's him?'

'That's our quarry… or I should say *your quarry*, Colonel,' said Angus. 'I'm going to slip away. You go and sit on that table next to them and enjoy your pot of tea. I'll see you back in the room.'

Angus was stretched out on the bed with his hands clasped behind his head and his eyes closed when he heard the key in the lock. When Fiona walked in, he was sitting in the chair by the window writing in his black leather-bound notebook. The bed cover was smooth and flat the way the maid had left it. He smiled and ignored her frown when he said, 'Interesting eavesdropping?'

'That always sounds like something nasty coming off the roof,' said Fiona. She kicked off her shoes and flopped onto the bed. 'I see you have your notebook and pen ready, Dr Freud, so I'll close my eyes and begin.'

'The greedy fellow called the puny fellow Colin and the gorgeous fellow Mr Watson. The puny fellow called the gorgeous fellow Greg, so…'

'Ah, Greg Watson. I think he teaches PE at Beaumont,' said Angus.

'What's the greedy fellow called?'

'He calls himself Anthony Parker-Smythe but he was born Tony Smith.'

'Right. Well Tony did most of the talking... usually answering Colin's questions. Greg hardly said a word. I got the impression he was an uninvited guest. The gist of it seemed to be that Colin wanted to know how Tony made money.'

'Did he now,' said Angus, making a note in his black book.

'Seems your Tony is a director of a number of companies here in Guernsey. One company finances property development in Spain. Another makes money from vending machines... I wasn't sure how. A third company is into financial investments... again I never picked up any details. Do you know anything about his companies?'

'Oh, yes,' said Angus.

'Before I forget,' said Fiona, 'Tony is going to show Colin a bit of Guernsey's night life this evening. I don't know if Greg's going. Are we going to tag along in the shadows?'

* * * * *

They sat in a dark corner of the lounge where they were less likely to be seen but from where they had a clear view of the main entrance. When Anthony Parker-Smythe appeared and handed in his key at reception they barely recognised him. In place of his suit and Army Pay Corps tie, he was wearing a short-sleeved multi-coloured floral shirt open at the neck, a pair of lightweight cream slacks, pale purple socks and tan-coloured slip-on suede shoes. Around his neck hung an oval St Christopher medal on a gold chain.

Anthony glanced at his watch. The taxi was late and he was getting hungry. Just as he was about to return to reception, Fiona came outside and stood next to him under the awning. She was wearing a close-fitting black dress and a pair of black high-heeled shoes. As she pulled the white silk shawl around her shoulders, she turned and smiled, 'It's chillier than I thought.' Anthony nodded but did not speak. 'Ah, good,' said Fiona, 'my taxi.'

'Excuse me,' said Anthony, 'but I think it's the one I ordered.'

'Oh, dear! Really?' said Fiona. Then before Anthony could reply, she opened the door and spoke to the driver. 'Who ordered you?' When the driver said he had come for a Mr Parker-Smythe, she said, 'Bother. Where are you going?' When the driver told her he was going down into the town, she turned to Anthony and said, 'Would you mind if I shared your taxi? Thanks awfully.'

'Where to?' said the driver.

'The Golden Parakeet, if you please,' said Anthony. 'On Le Pollet.'

'That's lucky,' said Fiona. 'That's just where I'm going. One of the better night clubs, so I'm told.'

'They do a rather good buffet meal and offer a good selection of wines,' said Anthony.

'Ah,' said Fiona, 'but do they have live music?'

'Yes, I believe so,' said Anthony.

'A jazz trio. Piano, double bass and drums,' said the driver, 'Call themselves the Downbeats. They're pretty good. Not noisy. You can at least hear yourself think.'

Fiona hopped smartly out of the taxi and hurried inside the night club leaving Anthony to pay the driver the exact fare showing on the meter. She disappeared into the ladies room and used her cell phone to contact Angus. 'I'm at the Golden Parakeet night club on Le Pollet. Harper was outside the main entrance when we arrived. Get moving, Major.'

Anthony and Colin sat at a table in one corner of what they regarded as the half-empty room. Angus and Fiona sat at a table in another corner of what they regarded as the half-full room. Both tables were partially hidden from one another but had quite a good view of the rostrum and the Downbeats playing their jazzed up versions of Anything Goes, Night and Day, I Get A Kick Out Of You and other Cole Porter hit tunes.

The three musicians were in their early fifties and dressed like men in their early twenties. Shiny white leather yachting caps hid grey hairs or bald heads – it was hard to tell which. Tight-fitting black leather trousers concealed their varicose veins. The long-sleeved, tight-fitting red polo-necked sweaters and the white leather open waistcoats – two sizes too small and lacking in buttons and button holes – actually drew attention to their paunches. The dark sunglasses covering their eyes made Fiona think of the nursery rhyme: three blind mice.

'What are we doing here?' said Fiona.

'Having a wee bit of a night out, I'd say,' said Angus. 'The food's good to eat. The music good to listen to. And you're very good to look at.'

'You know what I mean.'

'We're just keeping a wee eye on yon Parker-Smythe. With a bit o' luck we'll run across one or two of his Guernsey business partners.'

'Like that fellow who's talking to him now?'

Colin did not like the look of Marcel Durand, a heavy-set man whose hair was glossy with brilliantine and whose breath reeked of nicotine. He was rather glad when his host excused himself and led Marcel away from the table. Colin had just finished his *entrée d'escargots gratinés* when Anthony returned red-faced and agitated.

'He doesn't look too happy,' said Fiona.

'D'you mean Parker-Smythe?' said Angus.

'Yes. Look how he's shovelling food in his mouth. Seems to be in a hurry.'

'Anything the matter?' said Colin. 'You look all hot and bothered.'

'I'm sorry, dear boy, to spoil your evening but...'

'Was it that chap? Is he the problem?'

'No. Well, yes, in a way,' said Anthony. 'He's a sort of business partner.'

'To do with one of your companies?'

'Yes. Trust-o-matic Vending Ltd. Marcel runs the Guernsey side of our operation.'

'He seemed a bit put out,' said Colin. 'Annoyed I might say.'

'Yes, well, we've had a little disagreement over money. I'm sure I can make him see reason but with him in his present frame of mind, I think I'd better be getting back to my hotel. Will you excuse me, dear boy?' said Anthony, placing some notes on the table. 'This should cover the meal.'

'Looks like he's leaving,' said Fiona. 'I wonder where he's going?'

'My guess is he's on the run from that heavyweight who came to his table. He didn't look best pleased,' said Angus. 'Parker-Smythe may be mixing with the wrong people... like those two thugs who've met him at the door.'

Colin watched the Bursar head for the door and saw him encounter two burly young men. When one of them grabbed Anthony by the arm, Colin became alarmed. By the time the waiter had arrived and Colin had settled the bill, the Bursar was nowhere to be seen. Outside the Golden Parakeet, Le Pollet was almost free of pedestrians. The noise from a passing scooter momentarily deafened Colin but as his hearing returned he heard the sound of voices coming from the alley alongside the night club. Angus and Fiona reached the front door just as Colin dashed in, white-faced and out of breath. When he saw Angus he blurted out 'Parker-Smythe's in trouble... In the alley... Quick.'

'Look after our friend. Get him a brandy or something and stay here,' said Angus. 'An alley is no place for ladies and young school teachers.'

* * * * *

In all walks of life there are amateurs and there are professionals. One definition of the amateur is a person unskilled in or having only a superficial knowledge of a

226

subject or activity. Marcel Durand's young thugs, Paco and Zack, who were laying into Anthony Parker-Smythe, were two amateurs about to meet one professional.

Paco was standing behind Anthony, his back to one side of the alley. Zack was standing in front of Anthony, his back to the other side of the alley. Paco held Anthony's arms behind his back while Zack broke Anthony's ribs. Anthony's nose was bleeding and his lips were swollen. He had long since ceased to be in any state to cry for help.

Another dictionary definition of amateur is a person who engages in an activity as a pastime rather than for gain. These two thugs were so enjoying the activity which Marcel Durand had commissioned, they did not notice the former Black Watch commando in the dark alley until it was too late.

Paco was first. Angus took the right wrist in a steely grip and twisted. All in the same smooth movement, he slipped in behind the slightly heavier, taller man and kicked him behind the right knee. As Paco was falling to the ground, Angus delivered a vicious blow to the carotid artery just under the right ear.

Zack was next. Released from Paco's grip, Anthony fell forward against his attacker then slumped to the floor. Before Zack could regain his balance, Angus took his left wrist in a vice-like grip and twisted the man through a half-circle and propelled him against the brick wall of the alley. The punch under the right ear made sure Zack, like his accomplice, would be unconscious for some while.

'What service do you require?'

'Ambulance and police,' said Angus. 'A man has been attacked by two men in the alley alongside the Golden Parakeet in Le Pollet.' He shut off his cell phone and went back into the night club.

'Everything alright?' Fiona asked.

'Mr Parker-Smythe has been mugged,' Angus said to Colin. 'An ambulance is on the way.' Then he said to

Fiona, 'You take a taxi back to the hotel. I'll join you as soon as I have given my statement to the police.'

* * * * *

It took less than five minutes to escort the dazed and bewildered Paco and Zack to the Police Headquarters at Hospital Lane to be examined by a police surgeon and thereafter to be questioned by officers of the law in the Bailiwick of Guernsey. Colin Harper and Angus MacKay volunteered their statements in two other separate rooms.

'Now then, sir,' said the avuncular sergeant, placing the single sheet of typewritten paper on the table in front of Colin, 'I'd be obliged if you would check this carefully. When you are satisfied as to its correctness, I'd be obliged if you would sign and date it.'

I was Mr Anthony Parker-Smythe's guest at the Golden Parakeet. At about a quarter to eight, Mr Parker-Smythe left the table to speak to a man he said was Marcel Durand, a business partner in Trust-o-matic Vending Ltd. When Mr Parker-Smythe came back to our table he seemed agitated and said that he and Durand had "had a little disagreement over money." Mr Parker-Smythe then excused himself and said he was going back to his hotel. I saw two men meet him at the door and leave with him. I thought something was wrong so I followed. When I saw the two men fighting with Mr Parker-Smythe I ran back into the Golden Parakeet for help.

....
signature
....
date

If there had been any fells in Guernsey, Rhys Tostevin and Angus MacKay might have a run a close race. As it was, Rhys spent what little time he had to himself sailing single-handed around the Channel Islands. Both men had been weathered by the elements and hardened by their encounters with society's lower

228

forms of life. Tostevin's eyes followed the point of his pencil across MacKay's statement.

I noticed Mr Anthony Parker-Smythe sitting at a table with Mr Colin Harper when my wife and I arrived at the Golden Parakeet. At 19:46, a thick-set man came to Mr Parker-Smythe's table. About one minute later Parker-Smythe got up from his table and went with the man to the bar. At 19:58 Parker-Smythe came back to his table and cleared his plate; he seemed to be in a hurry. At 20:04 Parker-Smythe left his table and hurried to the door where he met two men. They left with him. Three minutes later Harper got up from his table and left the night club. Two minutes later Harper ran back into the Golden Parakeet very upset saying Parker-Smythe was in trouble. I went outside and saw three men lying in the alley alongside the night club. One of them was Parker-Smythe. He seemed to be hurt so I used my cell phone to call for an ambulance and the police.

....

signature

....

date

'Would you mind clarifying one or two points for me?' said the inspector languidly. Seeing Angus give an almost imperceptible nod, he continued, 'You know Parker-Smythe and Harper, I believe.'

'Aye. I know Parker-Smythe. He's the bursar at Beaumont Abbey School. Ex-army man.'

'Harper?'

'I know of him. A teacher at Beaumont.'

'No idea why they're here in Guernsey, I suppose?' said the inspector.

'No. On holiday like my wife and myself perhaps?' said Angus.

'So you've no idea why Parker-Smythe was attacked?'

'No, none at all.'

'You say you *went outside and saw three men lying in the alley.*' Angus gave another almost imperceptible nod. 'According to one of my officers at the scene, Parker-Smythe was in a bad way… Lying in a pool of blood. Can you corroborate that?'

'Too far away for me to see that,' said Angus.

'You didn't go into the alley and take a close look?'

'I'm not fond of dark alleys at night. Dangerous places wouldn't you say?' said Angus.

'Here's my problem,' said the inspector. 'Parker-Smythe badly beaten up, lying on the ground barely conscious and there's these other two lying there out cold with hardly a mark on them. Bit odd to say the least.'

'Parker-Smythe's ex-army,' said Angus. 'Perhaps he took a beating but held something in reserve and then surprised them.'

'From what my crime-scene officer tells me, Parker-Smythe doesn't look the type…'

'You can't always tell from appearances what a person is capable of, can you?' said Angus.

'No, you can't and that's a fact,' said Rhys.

* * * * *

It took the ambulance five minutes to deliver Anthony to the Princess Elizabeth Hospital emergency unit at Le Vauquiedor. It took much longer for the emergency team of doctors and nurses to stabilise him and much longer still before he was off the critical list. Zack had broken nine ribs, four on Anthony's right side and five on his left. As a result, Anthony suffered damage to his liver, his spleen and his kidneys. Serious enough as these injuries were, the head injury when Anthony fell to the ground caused a subarachnoid hemorrhage: bleeding in the area between the brain and the thin tissues covering the brain. Fortunately his skull was not fractured but the surgeons had to drill a hole into either side of his head to relieve the pressure.

* * * * *

'Good morning. Angus MacKay. I'm phoning from Guernsey. Sorry to trouble you at this hour but I thought you should be the first to know that your bursar, Anthony Parker-Smythe, has met with an accident... Yes, pretty serious I'm afraid... No he's off the danger list but he'll be in hospital for quite a few weeks... No, I'm sorry I couldn't say when he might be fit to return to duties... No, certainly not this term... Yes, you will... Yes, you will need an acting bursar... May I make a suggestion?'

* * * * *

CHAPTER 21

"I destroy my enemies when I make them my friends."
Abraham Lincoln

* * * * *

The notice on the board in the Common Room was brief and to the point.

Mr Anthony Parker-Smythe is temporarily indisposed. Mrs Susan Taylor BA, will act as Bursar during his absence.

The question James Jackson wished to ask Colin Harper was also brief and to a related point but David Swann momentarily side-tracked him.

'I'm surprised to see you here, James' said David. 'I thought you'd be marking those eight hundred chemistry scripts.'

'Not yet. I get my first batch of papers in two days time,' said James.

'Katherine all set to open all of them to the first question?' said David.

'Look here, can we forget exam marking this evening,' snapped James. 'I've a question to ask Colin… if you don't mind.'

Quentin and Reg were as usual in their armchairs. The other ten members of staff were as usual in their seats forming an ellipse around the two tables at the foci. 'Come on Colin,' said James, 'what happened in Guernsey?' All eyes and ears were on Colin Harper.

He told them about the night club and Marcel Durand. He told them about Paco and Zack mugging Parker-Smythe in the dark alley. He told them about giving his statement to the police. He did not tell them about the quiet Scotsman he met at the Pierson, Heldring & Pierson bank in the morning and later at the Golden Parakeet, the evening the Bursar was mugged. He did tell them about visiting the Princess Elizabeth hospital with Greg.

'Crikey!' said James. 'You were lucky they didn't mug you as well.'

'Nine broken ribs and a fractured skull!' said David. 'Crikey!'

'His skull wasn't fractured,' said Greg. 'but they had to operate on his head.'

'Subarachnoid hemorrhage. That's what the doctors told us,' said Colin.

'His liver, spleen and kidneys were damaged as well,' said Greg.

'How long is he going to be in hospital?' asked David.

'They couldn't say,' said Colin, 'but he won't be back this term.'

* * * * *

The report was brief and to the point. The junior partner in the firm of Banwell, Garnet & York, Chartered Accountants went beyond his accountant duties - controlling systems of records, auditing books, preparing financial statements, giving tax advice and preparing Beaumont's tax returns - but Angus found no evidence of wrongdoing or professional misconduct. Robert York had legitimate personal off-shore accounts in Sark but Angus found nothing to connect them with Parker-Smythe's companies in Guernsey.

Stanley Garnet glanced at the claim for expenses, raised an eyebrow then put down the file and turned to his friend. 'No need for me to be concerned about Robert then?'

'Maybe. Maybe not,' said Angus. 'No harm in keeping an eye on his work at Beaumont.'

'I heard from the High Master that Parker-Smythe is temporarily indisposed. What did he mean?'

'A couple of young thugs put Parker-Smythe into hospital,' said Angus. 'He'll be in the Princess Elizabeth for a wee while I shouldn't wonder.'

'*Temporarily indisposed*! Dr Pugh-Jones has a gift for understatement,' said Stanley. 'What happened to the muggers?'

'They helped the police with their inquiries,' said Angus, not giving Stanley the answer he was fishing for.

'I gather Parker-Smythe's personal assistant is standing in for him temporarily,' said Stanley. 'That Mrs Taylor strikes me as a very capable woman.'

'Och aye, she's that right enough,' said Angus. 'but she's nae his PA. And they'll find her a wee bit more than just capable. I'm seeing her next Tuesday. D'you want a report?'

* * * * *

During her interview with the High Master, Susan realised how well Angus MacKay had prepared the ground for her. So, after a calculated display of sham reluctance, she finally acceded to the High Master's request but on suitable terms and on conditions allowing her freedom to appoint an assistant.

'I don't know what to say. I'm somewhat lost for words.'

'Just say yes,' said Susan.

'It's so... well, unexpected. Perhaps I should take some time to think about it... you know, talk it over with my husband first.'

'What do you think he'll say?' said Susan. 'Will he object?'

'Oh no, I'm sure he won't object. He'll probably think it a bit... funny.'

'Why?' said Susan. 'What's funny about being the Assistant Bursar?'

'Nothing! Nothing at all.'

'Would he think you couldn't do the job?' said Susan.

'Certainly not. Geoffrey would know I could do it.'

'Good. So you'll say yes then?' said Susan.

'Oh... alright! Yes. I'll do it,' said Abigail. 'When do you want me to start?'

'Monday morning. Nine o'clock sharp. During office hours you'll be Mrs Rusbridge and I'll be Mrs Taylor, agreed?'

'Agreed!'

* * * * *

Louise Pugh-Jones called the investment club meeting to order. Item 1 – apology for absence: Elizabeth Radford. Item 2 – minutes of the previous meeting: approved. Item 3 – secretary's report: no change in membership. Item 4 – treasurer's report.

'The club bought one thousand shares in SIGEM Ltd at \$0.95 per share,' Susan reminded the group. 'That company is going to be taken over by Jardine International Corporation. The shares were trading today at \$1.95 and could go higher before the New York Stock Exchange closes at 9 p.m. our time. So the question is...' Susan paused and turned to the member sitting next to her.

'Do we sell our shares now or wait for the takeover?' said Abigail Rusbridge.

'Gosh!' said Maureen Carratt, 'We've doubled our money.'

'Let's not get carried away,' said Louise. 'We have to...'

'May I ask Susan a question?' interrupted Rosemary Newbold.

'Yes, of course, Rosemary,' said Louise.

'Why has the share price gone up?'

'Jardine International Corporation is offering to buy the SIGEM shares for more than their current market value,' said Susan. 'That kind of offer pushes up the stock price.'

'What happens if we don't sell our shares now?' asked Maureen.

'If we do nothing,' said Susan, 'then at takeover, we'll receive one JIC share for each share we hold in SIGEM Ltd *and* a cash payment of one dollar per share.'

'Isn't this exciting,' said Celia Fiddle to Gladys Dawson who was sitting next to her.

235

'We have three choices,' said Abigail, taking her cue from Susan. 'Sell all our shares now. Don't sell any of our shares now. Sell some of our shares now.'

'If we sell half our SGEM shares now,' said Janet Meeker, tapping on her pocket calculator, 'we'd get back most of the thousand dollars we invested... Yes... Five hundred times $1.95 would be $975... '

'Don't forget the selling fee,' said Abigail.

'What would that be?' said Janet.

'About twenty-five dollars,' said Abigail.

'Alright,' said Janet. 'So we would get back $950 dollars but after the takeover we would get another five hundred dollars and have five hundred JIC shares worth at least $500.'

'All in favour of selling five hundred shares now?' said Louise. 'Unanimous.'

* * * * *

'Good morning. NatWest Bank. Tracy Hodder speaking. How may I help?'

'Good morning, Tracy,' said Susan. 'I'd like to speak to Mr Baker.' The ever efficient receptionist did not ask questions or keep Susan waiting.

'Miss Wellborn. Good morning. How are you this morning?' said Daniel.

'I'm fine, thank you.'

'What can I do for you?'

'As Mrs Taylor, treasurer of the BALI investment club, I'd like to place a limit order to sell five hundred of our shares in SIGEM Ltd. at $2.00 per share or better.'

'I see SGEM was trading at $1.90 at close yesterday,' said Daniel, checking his computer screen. 'Any other orders?'

'As Susan Wellborn I'd like to place a stop limit order to sell five thousand of my SGEM shares at $2.50 or better.'

Susan strolled into her old office to see how the Assistant Bursar was coping on her first day. Mrs Abigail Rusbridge was wearing a pair of flat-heeled shoes of soft black leather, an ankle-length black skirt and a long-sleeved white blouse with buttons to the collar which was secured with a small enamelled brooch. Her well-brushed hair was parted down the middle and held back from each temple by hair grips matching the brown tortoiseshell of her large, square reading glasses. She was still rather plump for her height but she now concealed her plumpness. Her manner was still imperious but no longer to the point of arrogance.

To all outward appearances, Abigail Rusbridge had become a new woman and the perfect Assistant Bursar. Her desk was as neat and tidy as herself. She picked up the telephone on its first ring.

'A Mr Daniel Baker for you, Mrs Taylor,' said Abigail. 'Should I put him through to your office?'

'Yes please Mrs Rusbridge,' said Susan.

'I'm putting you through now, Mr Baker,' said Abigail.

'Good afternoon, Mr Baker,' said Susan. 'You have some news?'

'Yes indeed. We have filled your order to sell those five hundred SGEM shares for your investment club. We sold at $2.10 per share. Do you still want your five thousand shares on a stop limit of $2.50?'

'I think I'll risk it for a day or two longer, Mr Baker.'

'As you wish. I shall keep you informed. Good afternoon, Mrs Taylor.'

Susan returned to her old office to tell Abigail the good news. '$2.10 a share! Didn't we do well,' said Abigail. 'If we can keep this up, Celia Fiddle will be on holiday in California before she knows it.' While her Assistant Bursar was in such a buoyant mood, Susan asked Abigail if she would like to look after health and safety, ancillary staff employment, maintenance contracts and one or two other areas of responsibility with definite legal implications. 'Certainly. That sounds most interesting,' said Abigail. 'It's about time I put my law degree to some use.'

* * * * *

'This woman who calls you Stewart…'

'Which one would that be, Colonel?' said Angus, pulling on his pyjamas.

'There's more than one, Major?'

'I cannot tell a lie, Colonel. Maybe there is. Maybe there isn't,' said Angus.

'Come off it, Major. With a face like yours, you're lucky there's one,' said Fiona.

'Och, and there's me thinking the freckled, weather-beaten look was coming away back into fashion.'

'This woman…'

'You'll be meaning Mrs Taylor,' said Angus. 'Acting Bursar at Beaumont now yon Parker-Smythe is out of action.'

'Yes, that's her. Susan. First name Susan? Young? Attractive? Good Looking is she?'

'She's a bonny lass right enough,' said Angus. 'In the prime o' life. Husband's a racing driver back in South Africa. She's all alone here in England.'

'Looking for a shoulder to cry on, I don't doubt,' said Fiona. 'Sounds just the woman you should steer clear of, Major.'

'I dinnae think Susan does much crying. You could be right though… Maybe I should keep my distance. One woman's as much as I can cope with…' Angus never flinched when Fiona punched him playfully but hard in his abdomen; she hurt her wrist.

'Incidentally, I have to go to Beaumont tomorrow. Susan has asked to see me…' Fiona landed another hard punch and hurt her other wrist. Fortunately, once they were both beneath the sheets, Angus gently took Fiona's mind off the pain in her wrists.

* * * * *

Thanks to Rupert, who provided a copy of the Jardine International Corporation Access Control Software; and to Monsieur Fournier, the security systems chief at the Pierson, Heldring & Pierson bank in

Guernsey, who provided details of how they used the security software; and to Arnaud le Tissier, the manager at the bank, who authorised his opening of an account; and to Parker-Smythe who vouched for him, Colin Harper was almost ready to put his plan into action. He had just one simple problem to solve.

Muttering to himself under his breath, Colin expressed his problem, quite unnecessarily in the form of a mathematical equation on his computer:

$y = mx + c$

'I'll let y be the total amount of money to be transferred and x be the number of deserving colleagues. The rate, m, will be the amount of money per colleague and c will be my costs of the operation: subsistence and travel expenses to Guernsey.'

The value of x was 5 because Greg, James, Keith, David and Colin himself formed the *gang of five*. The value of c was 94 because Colin had spent a total of £94: petrol for his car, return train fares to Portsmouth Harbour, return ferry boat crossing to Guernsey, bed and breakfast at the *St Georges* and various meals and snacks. What was the value of m?

When he had asked the Bursar for advice on money and the Bursar had asked him how much he wanted, Colin had quickly estimated in his head that getting a rise of 8.0% instead of 10.5% would mean a shortfall of £400 to £500 on his annual salary.

He told Teddy, his computer, the value of m was 500.

Teddy told him $y = 2594$.

'Thank you, Teddy,' said Colin. 'Will you now please take £2594 from this account... [*He typed in the details of Anthony Parker-Smythe's personal account with the Pierson, Heldring & Pierson bank in Guernsey.*] '...and transfer it into this account' [*He typed in the details of his own account in Guernsey.*]

'Transfer complete,' said Teddy.

'Thank you, Teddy,' said Colin. 'Will you now please transfer from my Guernsey account £500 into each of the following accounts.' [*He typed in the British bank account details of his four colleagues.*]

'Transfers complete,' said Teddy.

'Thank you, Teddy,' said Colin. 'Now transfer £594 from my Guernsey account into this account.' [*He typed in his own British bank account details.*]

'Transfer complete,' said Teddy.

'Thank you, Teddy,' said Colin. 'Goodnight!' [*He patted the bobble hat sitting on top of the monitor and logged off.*]

* * * * *

He was not sure why but Angus decided to wear the shoes, socks, trousers, jacket, shirt and Black Watch tie that Fiona regarded as his battle dress for special assignments. It was not as though he was going to interrogate Anthony Parker-Smythe, that sly Bursar of Beaumont. He was going to see the delightful Susan Taylor.

When Angus knocked and entered the office, he did not expect to be confronted by the imperious Mrs Abigail Rusbridge LLB, ready to hold the fort against all comers. Abigail removed her reading glasses in order to scrutinise the man who entered her sanctum before she had uttered *come*!

His piercing eyes beneath his sandy-coloured eyebrows seemed to penetrate the façade of Abigail's outward appearance and drill down into her soul. She quickly put her glasses back on and looked down.

If Angus was surprised at seeing Abigail instead of Susan behind the desk, he did not show it. He stood relaxed and motionless, feet slightly apart and arms hanging loosely by his sides, while Abigail consulted the office diary.

'Major MacKay?' said Abigail looking up into his blue eyes. He nodded. She picked up the telephone. 'Mrs Taylor, Your two o'clock appointment is here.'

As she left her desk and ushered him into what had been Parker-Smythe's office, Angus observed the Assistant Bursar – her title was prominently displayed on the desk name plate – had very slender ankles and, for a woman clearly carrying too much weight, was surprisingly light on her feet. Mrs Abigail Rusbridge LLB had, he thought, the ears of a chiropteran and the eyes of a raptor; little would escape her notice.

'Would you like me to organise some coffee, Mrs Taylor?'

'Major?' said Susan, looking at Angus.

'If it's no trouble,' said Angus.

'No trouble at all,' said Abigail.

'Black, then. No sugar. Thank you, Mrs Rusbridge,' said Angus.

'I heard that Tony Smith and Marcel Durand were partners in Trust-o-matic Vending Ltd, that they fell out over money and that Durand had two men work Smith over. Is that true?' said Susan.

'Where did you hear that?' said Angus.

'A little bird told me,' said Susan. 'He also told me that you had gone outside the Golden Parrot...'

'Parakeet! The Golden Parakeet,' said Angus. 'Fiona and I were having a meal there...'

'Fiona's your wife?'

'Aye, that she is,' said Angus. 'Fiona and I were there when Parker-Smythe got mugged.'

'My little bird also told me you went outside, found Smith badly beaten up and called for an ambulance and the police.'

'Aye. Parker-Smythe was in a bad way.'

'I heard the police found his two attackers out cold,' said Fiona. 'Who...'

'I hope you dinnae get me here just to talk about Parker-Smythe being mugged.'

'No... No, of course not... I'm sorry,' said Susan. 'but it's to do with him. You see... I've uncovered some irregularities in his accounting... I thought you might be interested... ' When Angus merely took another sip of coffee, she continued, 'I wondered what you think I should do now.'

Angus put down his cup and saucer, took out his pen and black leather-bound notebook, sat back in his chair and gave the delightful Susan his full attention.

'Parker-Smythe is involved with three different companies: Channel Islands Credit & Loan Ltd, SpeConstruct Ltd and Trust-o-Matic Vending Ltd. All I know about the third one is that the company is making a tidy profit from whatever it is their vending machines dispense and that Marcel Durand may be his not so silent partner in Guernsey.'

When Angus told her he had seen one of the Trust-o-Matic machines on the wall in the men's washroom at La Collinette hotel, she remembered the machine on the wall in the women's washroom at the local restaurant where Parker-Smythe had taken her to lunch.

She raised her eyebrows, shook her head and said, 'Trust-o-Matic may be a perfectly legitimate company but in view of what their machines dispense, it may not be a company the Beaumont Board of Directors would consider fitting for their Bursar.'

'The first company - Channel Islands Credit & Loan – appears to be financing the second company - SpeConstruct Ltd. - a property development company in Spain. On the surface, nothing illegal about that,' said Susan, pausing to finish her coffee.

'But!' said Angus.

'But when we dig below the surface,' said Susan, 'and ask where the CI Credit & Loan money comes from...'

'We discover an irregularity,' said Angus.

'At this term's Board Meeting, when Warren Cooper asked Parker-Smythe some awkward questions about Beaumont's investments, Robert York tried to pull the wool over our eyes with talk of Common Investment Funds (CIFs) and the Charities Act.'

'Warren Cooper?' said Angus, raising an eyebrow.

'One of the Governors. American Embassy. Cultural Attaché I believe.'

'Warren Cooper,' said Angus under his breath. "Well, well. It's a small world.'

'I'm sorry. I didn't catch that,' said Susan.

'Nothing. Please go on.'

'First, putting money into Channel Islands Credit & Loan Ltd would not be investing in CIFs... they're designed to reduce risk by diversification and to provide tax benefits,' said Susan. 'Second, SpeConstruct Ltd is a high risk company. The bottom could drop out of the Spanish property market at any time and leave investors high and dry.'

'Let me guess,' said Angus. 'Parker-Smythe has put Beaumont money into SpeConstruct.'

'Yes but not directly,' said Susan. 'He put it into CI Credit & Loan which...'

'put it into SpeConstruct,' Angus paused then asked the question to which he already knew the answer. 'How much money are we talking about?'

'In round figures, one million pounds,' said Susan. 'Beaumont's reserve fund.'

The phone rang. It was Abigail. Daniel Baker from NatWest was on the line. She put him through. Susan listened to what he had to say, thanked him and hung up. Turning back to Angus, she said, 'Sorry about that. I hope you didn't think me rude.'

'No, of course not.' He noticed the look on her freckled face and said, 'Good news?'

'Yes, as a matter of fact,' said Susan, thinking of her five thousand SEGM shares Daniel Baker had just sold for $2.55 per share. 'Something to celebrate. I wonder... Would you be my guest for dinner this evening?'

* * * * *

243

The High Master had been shocked by the news of Parker-Smythe's accident and even more shocked when he learned from Colin Harper the extent of the Bursar's injuries and how they were inflicted. Being beaten up in a dark alley alongside a night club on an island off the coast of Normandy was not the sort of thing that happened to someone from Beaumont Abbey. Dr Pugh-Jones had never really liked Parker-Smythe and, somewhat to his shame, now found it difficult to feel sorry for the man.

'It was most thoughtful of Major MacKay to suggest Mrs Taylor might stand in as Bursar, don't you think, my dear?'

'An interesting man,' said Louise. 'I think Susan's taken quite a shine to him.'

'Bit of a dark horse in my opinion,' said Llywelyn. 'I confess I found him somewhat unnerving. Not a man to be trifled with. He was most matter of fact when he telephoned to tell me Parker-Smythe had been mugged.'

'I'm sorry, Llew, but I've little time for any man who frequents night clubs,' said Louise.

'What's your opinion of Mrs Taylor? Will she cope d'you think?'

'Have no fear on that score,' said Louise. 'Susan will cope. I shouldn't be surprised if she'll apply to be Bursar if Nosey Parker doesn't come back.'

'D'you think so?' said Llywelyn.

'I certainly do. Susan is a woman who knows what she wants and knows how to get it. I don't think she'll let much stand in her way.'

* * * * *

Angus moved to one side the lighted candle that interrupted his view of the bonny lass facing him across the table in the corner of La Cave Gourmande restaurant. In the best French tradition, they took their time over each course and talked. It was almost a repeat performance of the time when they had lunched together in the dining hall at Beaumont. Susan did most of the talking and Angus most of the listening.

'What interest did Beaumont get on its £1,000,000 investment?

'Here's the thing,' said Susan. 'Beaumont has been getting £8,000 a month... an interest rate of 9.6% which doesn't sound bad except... building societies have been paying 14% on *low risk* savings accounts. SpeConstruct Ltd has been paying CI Credit & Loan 18%; that's £15,000 a month. Parker-Smythe has been pocketing the difference... £7,000 a month squirreled away in one of his Special Purpose Vehicle accounts.'

'What do you think should be done about it?'

'Well,' said Susan, 'he's been skimming for the past three years and cheated the school of at least 4.4% interest on its reserve fund... That's if the money had been in a building society paying 14%. So he should pay at least £132,000 back to the school.'

'What about the £1,000,000 capital?'

'Tricky,' said Susan. 'It's tied up in land and property in Spain. However, if SpeConstruct Ltd was bought out...' She closed her eyes and gave thought to an idea that had just popped into her head. 'Suppose Trust-o-Matic Vending Ltd took a bank loan to buy SpeConstruct Ltd and clear the company's debt to CI Credit & Loan, then...'

'CI Credit & Loan could repay Beaumont its one million pound investment,' said Angus.

'How are you enjoying acting as Bursar?'

'I like it a lot,' said Susan. 'I want to thank you for your support... you know... putting in a good word to the High Master.'

'Och, I just pointed out the obvious solution to his problem, in case, like many people, he dinnae see what was under his nose,' said Angus.

'Well I *am* grateful to you,' said Susan, reaching across the table to touch his hand.

'And there was I thinking we were here because you had something to celebrate and all the time...' he said raising his wine glass and fixing her with his piercing blue eyes.

Angus drove Susan back to Beaumont and escorted her to the door of her one-bedroom cottage but declined her invitation for coffee. As he turned to leave, Susan said, 'Oh, goodness, I nearly forgot. I've been keeping an eye on Parker-Smythe's Guernsey accounts and I noticed something rather odd. Some money went out of his personal account. It wasn't recorded in the usual way as a debit. It just… well… £2,594 just disappeared.'

* * * * *

CHAPTER 22

"Success depends upon previous preparation, and without such preparation there is sure to be failure."
Confucius

* * * * *

Even in the best of health, Anthony Parker-Smythe had never been grateful for mercies, large or small. Lying on his back in agony, he felt no gratitude towards the man who had rescued him in the alley or towards the surgeons who had saved his life or towards the hospital staff who were taking care of him. He just wallowed in self-pity, cursing the world in general and Marcel Durand and his two thugs in particular.

He ignored the fact that his nose was unbroken and his face unmarked. He left untouched the basket of fruit on his bedside locker and scorned the card on which was hand-written *Get Well Soon - Mary Cranborne pp The High Master*. It did not matter that nobody may have felt sorry for him; Anthony Parker-Smythe more than made up the deficit by feeling immensely sorry for himself.

His arms and legs were bruised and sore but their aching was insignificant compared to the ceaseless throbbing in his head and the intense pain in his body. He pressed the switch. In response, the PCA infusion pump delivered 1 mg of morphine sulphate into his intravenous drip. He knew if he were to press the switch again his request for more analgesic would be denied; the Patient Controlled Analgesia would make him wait four hours for his next dose. Anthony closed his eyes and fell asleep.

The visitor sat in the chair at the side of the bed, brief case on his lap, and helped himself to a grape from the basket of fruit. He had not come to the Princess Elizabeth hospital out of friendship. He may have been an associate of Parker-Smythe but he had never been a friend. He had come not to cheer up his co-conspirator but to add to his misery. In fact, Robert York was in Guernsey at the request of his senior partner, Stanley

Garnet, and under an obligation to follow instructions from Angus MacKay.

'Hello, what are you doing here?' said Anthony, waking up and focussing on his visitor.

'An errand of mercy, old boy,' said Robert, taking a sheaf of papers from his brief case. 'I'm here to try and keep you out of goal.'

'They know all about your Channel Islands Credit & Loan company putting one million into your SpeConstruct company in order to buy land and build properties in Spain... Yes, yes! I know what you're going to say... I told you it was all perfectly legal. If you remember, I said it was alright *as long as the money belonged to you and nobody else*. Well it wasn't alright. You used Beaumont's reserve fund.'

'I invested their money and they got a good rate of return,' said Anthony. 'Why are they complaining?'

'They're complaining, old boy, because it was a risky investment *and* because the rate of return from a safe investment in a building society was fourteen percent... a tad higher than the nine point six percent your company paid them... and a lot lower than the eighteen percent your SpeConstruct company was paying your Credit & Loan company.'

'That's not illegal. That's just good business practice,' said Anthony.

'They don't think so,' said Robert. 'It's called misappropriation of funds. They say that over the past three years you skimmed at least £132,000 rightly theirs.'

'How did they reckon that?'

'You paid them 9.6% when building societies were paying 14.0%; you short-changed them by 4.4% on £1,000,000 over three years,' said Robert.

'I don't feel well,' moaned Anthony, pressing the PCA button to no effect.

Robert shuffled the papers and persuaded Anthony to sign them. The first set of papers were to legalise the cash purchase of SpeConstruct Ltd by Trust-o-Matic

Vending Ltd for a substantial sum. Anthony, coming apart at the seams, failed to notice these papers had already been signed by Marcel Durand. When he did notice, he felt even more unwell and cursed the PCA button for not responding.

'What's the matter?' said Robert. 'Something wrong?'

'How did you get Durand to sign?'

'It wasn't difficult. We... I just pointed out this was his chance to benefit from the boom in Spanish property development... and that he'd be foolish not to sign,' said Robert. In fact it was Angus MacKay who persuaded Durand not only to sign the papers but also to ensure that Anthony came to no further harm.

The second set of papers authorised the Channel Islands Credit & Loan company to pay into the Beaumont reserve fund £1,132,000 with immediate effect. On the one hand, Anthony Parker-Smythe never liked to part with money and certainly not on this scale. On the other hand, he liked even less the thought of spending time in prison.

'Just one more paper to sign,' said Robert. 'You'd better read it first.'

The High Master
Beaumont Abbey School
Westmoreshire
England
Dear Dr Pugh-Jones,

Owing to my recent accident and subsequent deterioration in my health, I write to tender my resignation as Bursar with effect the 31st June.

I have enjoyed my time at Beaumont and I am sorry to be leaving under these circumstances.

I have no hesitation in recommending Mrs Susan Taylor to the post of Bursar. She is a most capable lady and, should she be appointed, would serve Beaumont well.

Yours sincerely,
Anthony Parker-Smythe

'Forty fifteen!' said Susan, staying at the net but moving to the right-hand side of the court.

'Good serve!' said Susan. 'Game and set! Well played partner.' Celia beamed and mopped her brow with the sweat band on her left wrist.

'I propose we stop at one set all. Is that alright with you Mary?' said Louise to her partner.

'That's fine by me,' said Mary.

'Louise,' said Susan, 'may I invite everyone back to my cottage for drinks?'

'That would be very nice. Thank you,' said Louise.

Beaumont Abbey provided the one-bedroom cottage, tax free and partially furnished but Susan had added a few touches of her own. The wooden bay-window seat was covered by a cushion, upholstered in brocade and custom-made to fit. She had a large bookcase alongside the window hiding the leather-bound books - some first editions - from the damaging rays of the mid-day sunshine; and she had arranged her books according to the Dewey decimal system and *not* the common way according to height - tallest on the left and shortest on the right.

On top of the bookcase was a sculpture, in patinated bronze, of a naked, buxom woman holding a violin. It caught Mrs Fiddle's attention.

'I say,' said Celia, studying the bronze closely, 'where did you get this, Susan?'

'Cape Town. It's an early piece by Jean Doyle… probably the most famous sculptor in South Africa. The fuller figure is her international trademark.'

'I don't know what Dr Fiddle would say if I put this on his bookcase,' said Celia. 'What is it suppose to represent?'

'Jean presents the female as capable and confident, resilient and strong; the violin represents her tenderness and warmth,' said Susan. 'Jean's work is quite different from this semi-abstract carving from one piece of rosewood.' She pointed to the simple, smooth and highly polished sculpture depicting a man and woman – the loving couple – facing one another and representing affection and family co-operation.

'Where did you get that, Susan,' asked Louise.

'Zambia. That's from Zambia. My husband gave it to me.'

In Susan's opinion what they all needed was a cold drink, not a cup of tea; so she gave everybody a long-stemmed wine glass and fetched the four bottles she had chilled in the fridge. When Louise asked if they were drinking champagne, Susan told them it was *Appletiser*, a sparkling soft drink originating in Johannesburg and now being made in the UK by Coca-Cola. 'Delicious,' said Mary. They were sipping their drink and enjoying a slice of traditional South African almond cake when Mary suddenly said, 'Oh, Louise, you never did tell us why Mr Matthews is known as 'mad' Arthur.'

'Let me begin by stating that Arthur Matthews is far from being mad,' said Louise, 'A little wild looking and somewhat eccentric but certainly not mad...' She took another sip of *Appletiser* and continued. 'He became 'mad' Arthur a few years ago when Toby Barnikel... a young geographer in his first year of teaching was having trouble with one particular class... and especially with a group of five boys at the back of the geology lab.'

'I didn't know Beaumont had a geology laboratory,' said Susan.

'We don't,' said Mary. 'Reggie de Vere timetables the geology practicals in one of Dr Carratt's chemistry laboratories in the Cavendish.'

'Anyway,' said Louise, 'the story, as far as I could piece it together, was this. Arthur made Toby put on a garish tie... one Arthur hated and never wore... before going into the lab to start his lesson.'

'I remember young Barnikel. Tall, thin and always quietly dressed.' said Celia. 'Gosh! Arthur fed him to the wolves wearing that horrible tie?'

'Yes,' said Louise. 'Anyway, the class thought the tie looked absurd on Toby and became noisier than usual and, probably as Arthur expected, the five boys at the back were the noisiest, shouting out rude remarks. When the din was at its height, Arthur burst through the prep room door, into the front of the lab and alongside Toby, demanding to know what all the racket was about. As the class went silent, Arthur turned to Toby shouting angrily that he would not tolerate such noise and that he would deal personally with the ringleader. Then Arthur picked up a large pair of scissors and cut the garish tie off at the knot, saying he would not tolerate loud ties either. Then he stormed out tie and scissors in hand. You could have heard the proverbially pin drop.'

'What happened next?' said Susan.

'Two things,' said Louise. 'When the class went to their next lesson, they told their history teacher, Quentin Waite, that Arthur had gone mad.'

'So that's how he became 'mad' Arthur,' said Mary.

'That's right,' said Louise. 'Then the next day Montague Perkins... he was the ringleader of those five boys at the back of Toby's class, was interviewed by Arthur. I don't know what went on at that interview but Toby never had any trouble afterwards.'

'I know what happened,' said Mary. 'Reggie told me all about it.'

'Apparently,' said Mary, 'Arthur discovered the boy Perkins was expecting to leave Beaumont at Easter to join the Navy. So, at the start of the interview, Arthur was all friendly and sympathetic, saying what a good idea it was for Perkins to join the Navy... and how his service in the CCF would stand him in good stead... and what a good naval officer Perkins would make... that sort of thing. Arthur was really kind and encouraging.'

'Did he mean it?' said Celia. 'Did he really think the Navy would suit Perkins?'

'Oh, yes, he really did. Arthur's not one to tell fibs,' said Mary. 'Then... when everything was all friendly and relaxed, Arthur casually asked Perkins if he realised he could not leave Beaumont at Easter without the High Master's permission. When Perkins shook his head,

Arthur leaned across his study desk and whispered that if there was any more trouble in Mr Barnikel's lessons, he – Perkins - would leave school at Easter over his – Arthur's – dead body.'

'That did the trick, did it?' said Susan.

'Oh, yes,' said Mary. 'According to Reggie, Toby Barnikel had no trouble with any of his classes after that.'

* * * * *

The Rt Hon Lord Crispin Bartholomew, Chairman of the Board of Directors, was flanked on his right by Prof Sir George Frampton and Earnest Hardcastle and on his left by Henry Trevanion and Stanley Garnet. Three candidates for the post of Bursar had been short-listed. The first two had already been scrutinised by the interviewing panel and deemed equally suitable. Both were men. The third candidate was a woman.

She wore a crisp cotton shirt. The top button was undone and the starched white collar contrasted with the plain grey of her jacket and matching skirt. Around her neck was a dark metallic brown scarf of a delicate sheer silk; it was held in place by a small, antique bronze ring. She wore a pair of dark brown leather shoes with a French heel. When she sat down and crossed her legs at the ankles, her skirt hid her knees but she wore no stockings to hide her sun-tanned skin. She used little or no make-up and her fair hair, cut in a bob, was held back from her tanned, freckled face by two dark amber clips.

'Good afternoon Mrs Taylor... Oh, I do beg your pardon... Miss Wellborn,' bumbled Lord Bartholomew when Sir George nudged him in the ribs. 'Good afternoon. May I thank you for applying for the post of Bursar and for coming here this afternoon. Let me begin by asking your reasons for wanting this position?'

Susan dealt satisfactorily with that question and with the questions asked by the other members of the panel. To judge from her qualifications and from the experience she had already gained at Beaumont, she was clearly far more suitable than the two previous candidates but they, like all previous bursars, were men. Susan Wellborn was a woman and, as more than one member of the panel observed, a very attractive woman to boot.

When Lord Bartholomew, to signal the interview was coming to a close, asked if she had any questions to put to the panel, she closed her eyes and cast her mind back to the previous week.

'Mrs Taylor,' said Abigail, 'I have Mr de Groot on the telephone. It's long distance from Cape Town.'

'Hello. Susan Taylor.'

'Ja, good day, Mrs Taylor. You are speaking with Gerrit de Groot. I am head of Albers, de Groot and Klein. We are the firm of advocates here in Cape Town.'

'What can I do for you, Mr de Groot?'

'Would you first please answer some questions to confirm your identity?' He continued without pausing to take a breath. 'Would you tell me the full name of your husband, the date of your marriage and the names of the witnesses to your marriage.' When she had confirmed her identity, de Groot thanked her and said, 'I regret to inform you that your husband was involved in an accident on the Killarney race track.'

'Was he badly hurt?'

'I regret to tell you that he died in the ambulance on the way to hospital,' said de Groot. 'Are you still there, Mrs Taylor?'

'Yes, I'm still here,' Mr de Groot. 'Your news has come as a shock but not a surprise.'

'There was one other thing,' said de Groot.

'I'm listening,' said Susan.

'Documents are in the post to you already but as executors of your husband's will, we wanted you to know that you are the sole beneficiary of his estate.'

'Thank you, Mr de Groot. It was kind and considerate of you to…'

'May I offer you my condolences, Mrs Taylor,' de Groot interjected to avoid what might be an awkward moment. 'And please... feel free to contact me if I can be of any service to you.'

Susan, eyes still closed, was disturbed to recall that her sorrow at Rod's passing had been fleeting and quickly eased by the thought of the large insurance policy she carried on his life. She opened her eyes and looked across the table at Lord Bartholomew.

'I'd like to ask two questions,' said Susan. 'The first is about the new sports hall.'

'The new sports hall?' said Lord Bartholomew. 'The one we haven't built yet?'

'Exactly!' said Susan. 'I'd like to ask why you haven't built it.'

'It's a question of funding. Beaumont is short of funds,' said Stanley Garnet. 'It's as simple as that.'

'And your second question, Miss Wellborn?' said Lord Bartholomew.

'Would there be any conflict of interest if the new Bursar were to assist with funding for the new sports hall?'

'That is a most interesting legal question,' said Henry Trevanion, Beaumont's lawyer.

* * * * *

Like any good executive, Dr Llywelyn Pugh-Jones, the High Master, delegated freely. Reginald de Vere, the Second Master, was his principal delegate. He in his turn delegated whatever and wherever possible but always remained stuck with the timetable and with organising events such as the annual speech weekend. Llywelyn worried about everything. Reginald worried about nothing.

'Do you think Mrs Taylor will cope?' said Llywelyn.

'I'm sure *Miss Wellborn* is more than up to the task of interviewing the applicants for our means-tested bursaries,' said Reg. 'And before you ask... yes, she fully understands your wish to elevate Beaumont to a school that's hard to get into.'

'Good. That's good,' said Llywelyn, fiddling with the Mats Jonasson seal pup, a glass paperweight Mary Cranborne brought back as a present from Målerås in Sweden.

'Speech weekend!' said Reg.

'Sorry?'

'You wanted a word about Speech weekend,' said Reg.

'Ah, yes. Not long now,' said Llywelyn. 'Everything under control?'

'Under as much control as this annual summer event ever can be.'

'I told you Randolph Jardine has agreed to give the Warrington Prescott speech, did I?'

'Yes, High Master, you did. He and I have corresponded. He's also accepted the invitation for him and his wife to lodge with you over the speech weekend.'

'Excellent,' said Llywelyn, allowing the glass seal pup to return safely to the task of weighing down a pile of documents relating to the building of the new sports hall. 'What about the marquee for my lawn?'

'Ordered long ago from Dobson and Phipps as usual. I spoke to Fred Dobson yesterday to confirm arrangements. He knows when we want it erected and how many trestle tables we'll need,' said Reg.

'You told him we want something stronger than he provided last time, did you?'

'Definitely! Proof against water, walking sticks and cows,' said Reg, with a faint smile as he recalled what happened last year. According to Quentin Waite, it was a fiasco.

Following the High Master's strict instructions, Mary Cranborne had telephoned the local weather bureau every day of the two weeks leading up to summer speech weekend. And every day she had reported that no rain was forecast. On the Saturday morning, the sun in a clear blue sky had smiled brightly down upon the assembled throng until lunchtime.

At lunchtime, the VIP guests had gathered in the marquee unaware that dark clouds had gathered in the sky. Jean-Pierre Escoffier, the Beaumont Chef, had presented himself and with a *bon appétit* had initiated generous helpings of lunch and rain; the former caused bulges in the midriffs of guests; the latter caused bulges in the sections of canvas roof. The sun had gone into hiding and plunged the marquee into semi-darkness.

Cows ought not to wander through an open gate and bursars ought not to prod a swollen canvas roof. The 58 inch tall, 1100 pound black and white Holstein cow, unimaginatively called Daisy by its owner, habitually plodded through any open gate; but the open flap of a marquee was a new experience for her and an opportunity to get out of the downpour, albeit briefly. She wandered in amongst the guests just as Parker-Smythe pushed upwards with his walking stick in an attempt to dislodge the accumulated water. When the canvas ripped, Daisy and guests were, according to Quentin Waite, severely moistened.

'Are you still with me, Reg?' said Llywelyn. 'You seemed to be somewhere else.'

'Sorry, High Master. I was just thinking about the marquee,' said Reg still smiling.

'One more thing,' said Llywelyn, 'I have asked Mrs Jardine to present the prizes.'

'Ah,' said Reg.

'Is that a problem?' said Llywelyn.

'Probably not,' said Reg, thinking of a newspaper's revelation of the lady's habit that her husband wanted to keep secret. 'Lord Bartholomew's not going to…'

'Time for a change, I think,' said Llywelyn. 'I think Vanessa Jardine will bring a breath of fresh air to the occasion. With a famous actress giving away the prizes and her wealthy husband then giving the Warrington Prescott speech, what could possibly go wrong?'

* * * * *

CHAPTER 23

"The only thing that will redeem mankind is co-operation." Bertrand Russell

* * * * *

This year Reg and his colleagues adjusted the borderline mark of the scholarship entrance examination to allow seventy-two candidates to pass and go forward to interview. The parents of fifteen boys applied for means-tested bursaries. Susan Wellborn proposed to reject three applications out of hand without interview. The High Master asked why.

'Bursaries should help parents who put their children's education first,' said Susan. 'We should not be supporting parents whose lifestyle is their first priority.'

'Quite right,' said Llywelyn, nervously straightening his already straight tie.

'I'm glad you agree, High Master.' said Susan.

'Ah, now… What about scholarships?' said Llywelyn, talking out loud to himself. He glanced down the list. 'No!.. No!.. No!.. Those three boys would not be in the running.'

'Not high fliers then?' said Susan.

'Afraid not. Quite the opposite,' said Llywelyn.

'May I ask who is likely to be offered a scholarship?' said Susan.

'Yes, Yes of course,' said Llywelyn, handing her a list. She quickly compared the names with the twelve on her list and looked up.

'The mathematics and science scholars are applicants for a bursary,' said Susan. 'Since a scholarship covers fifty percent of fees and costs, I could only award those two scholars a bursary to cover the other fifty percent, High Master.'

Abigail scrutinised the twelve applications and documents as proof of income and wealth – assets, pay slips, mortgage statements, audited accounts, tax returns, etc. – and ranked the applicants from most to least deserving of help. Susan scrutinised the scholarship entrance examination results and ranked the applicants for a bursary from most to least likely to benefit academically from a place at Beaumont.

During the interviews conducted over a period of three days, Abigail asked the parents all the embarrassing financial questions. Susan played the friendly role and asked each boy seemingly innocent questions about his home, his parents' cars, his holidays, etc. Abigail asked the parents her questions then Susan had her little chat with the boy. Abigail ended the interviews by informing the parents a Beaumont official may come to visit them. Out of the twelve, only one father blustered and made the fatal mistake of claiming the visit would be inconvenient because he was away on business most of the time.

Susan awarded bursaries to eleven applicants. The mathematics and science scholars received a bursary covering the fifty percent not covered by their scholarships. She also awarded six full bursaries and three covering seventy-five percent. The eleven bursaries and five scholarships meant Beaumont would disburse approximately fifteen percent of its income, the figure she knew the High Master had wanted all along. Not surprisingly, Llywelyn readily accepted Susan's suggestion regarding the Speech Weekend.

* * * * *

Since the beginning of term when Mary T. Cranborne BA had transformed his report to the Governing Board of Directors, the High Master had come to rely upon his secretary more and more. He had also come to value her suggestions. He was scanning Mary's Speech Weekend programme on his desk when he carelessly picked up the seal pup from its safe haven on top of the new sports hall blueprints. It was Mary's idea to produce and print a programme. No doubt its reference to cricket touched Llywelyn's subconscious and started his recklessly tossing the Mats Jonasson frosted glass paperweight from Sweden like a cricket ball from one unsafe hand to the other.

BEAUMONT ABBEY SPEECH WEEKEND
PROGRAMME OF EVENTS
FRIDAY
First XI versus Old Beaumontians Cricket Match –
11 a.m. to 5 p.m.
Open Classrooms and Laboratories – 2 to 5 p.m.
Old Beaumontians Annual Dinner in the Great
Dinning Hall – 7.30 for 8 p.m.
SATURDAY
Open Classrooms and Lavatories – 9 a.m. to noon
First XI versus Old Beaumontians Cricket Match –
11 a.m. to 5 p.m.
VIP Guests and Beaumont Staff – 12.30 for 1 p.m.
lunch in the marquess
Parents and Guests – 5 to 6 p.m. Tea with
Housemasters and Staff
SUNDAY
Chapel – 9.30 to 10.15 a.m.
Parents and Guests – 10.30 to 11.30 a.m. Coffee
with Housemasters and Staff
Prize Giving in the Ambassador Rex Theatre –
2.30 to 4.30 p.m.

'Ah, Reg! Come in. Come in. Sit yourself down,' said Llywelyn. 'Just wanted to run over the Speech Weekend programme with you. Mary gave you a copy?' The Second Master nodded. 'What d'you think? Good idea?'

'Yes, it is, High Master,' Reg said in all honesty because he was sure it was Mary's idea.

'Wonder we didn't think of printing a programme before now,' said Llywelyn.

'Two points,' said Reg, tactfully keeping the three printing errors to himself and trying hard not to be hypnotised by the precarious to and fro of the glass paperweight. 'When are you going to distribute the programme and to whom?'

'Ah! Good points,' said Llywelyn, returning the seal pup to its safe haven, much to Reg's relief. 'Any ideas?'

'Starting with the staff,' said Reg, 'I suggest one on the Common Room notice board, one copy to each head of department and two copies to each housemaster...'

'Two to housemasters?'

'One for their House notice board,' said Reg.

'Good point,' said Llywelyn.

'Post one copy to each governor... Give a batch to Susan Wellborn to distribute to non-teaching staff as she thinks fit... And give the rest to Mary for distribution to guests, Old Beaumontians and parents as she thinks fit.'

'What about yourself? Do you want any?' said Llywelyn.

'I'll see Mary if I need any,' said Reg. 'Now if you'll excuse me, I need to speak to staff that will be organising the...' he glanced at his copy of the programme, '*open classrooms and laboratories.*' He left the High Master's study by the door leading into Mary's office.

'Everything alright?' said Mary, as Reg carefully closed the door behind him.

'Has the programme been printed?' asked Reg,

'Yes,' said Mary. 'Why do you ask?'

'How many copies?'

'Two thousand,' said Mary.

'Oh dear,' said Reg, showing Mary his copy with the three errors underlined in red.

'Oh no!' exclaimed Mary, her ears turning a deep red.

'I take it the printers never sent you a proof to check,' said Reg.

'No... At least I never saw one,' said Mary, picking up the phone. After a brief conversation, she said, 'They never sent one to Susan either. What are we going to do?'

'Nothing we can do, Mary,' said Reg. 'Not to worry... We usually read what we *expect* to see and rarely what is *actually* written.'

261

'Susan was furious. She won't pay the printers one penny,' said Mary.

'That I can believe,' said Reg. 'Our new bursar seems to have settled in rather well.'

'Oh, yes,' said Mary. 'We're very fortunate to have Susan looking after our money.'

'You may well be right,' said Reg, recalling rumours about Parker-Smythe and previous bursars, all of whom seem to have left under a variety of black clouds.

* * * * *

When they were boys at Beaumont, they stuck together and looked to their ringleader for ideas and suggestions. Now they had left school, they led separate lives and left it to Monty to keep them in touch with one another, mainly by an exchange of Christmas cards. This year Montague Perkins had sent emails to persuade his former mischief makers to attend Beaumont Speech Weekend. With varying degrees of reluctance, Nibs, Pongo, Scrapper and Stinky agreed, unaware of Monty's own programme of events.

Monty had booked their rooms for three nights in the Crown and Anchor. They arrived in town at various times during the Thursday and met together in the private room at the back of the pub that evening. They shook hands and weighed one another up.

Nibs was decidedly thin and underfed as might be expected of a relatively unsuccessful out of work writer driven to earning a crust doing odd jobs. Edward "Nibs" Trelawney had agreed to come because his old school chum was coming. Nibs knew studios hired writers and expected ZipFliks Studios to be no different. Nibs held *it's not what you know but whom you know that counts.* Nibs had come to renew his friendship with Pongo.

Pongo was decidedly fat and overfed as might be expected of a relatively successful film producer and director. Radulph "Pongo" Palfreyman ran a small television studio with moderate success using money

262

from the Palfreyman family and his well-to-do wife. Pongo thought he had come to make a serious documentary about Speech Weekend.

Stinkey had retained his schoolboy looks, physique and virginity owing in no small measure to his devotion to the chemistry laboratory and the squash court. The game kept Dr Nathaniel 'Stinkey" Fitzorme in shape and the odour of chemicals, not always faint, kept females at a distance. He had just spent a post-doctoral semester at the University of Southern California in Los Angeles and returned to England still virgo intacto and slightly malodorous. Stinkey had come to discuss some research with Dr Carratt.

Scrapper had the healthy outdoor look befitting a gentleman farmer. Gorran "Scrapper" Venton took a First in Veterinary Science at the University of Bristol and a Masters in Animal Breeding Management at the University of Sydney before returning to the family farm near Porthcothan Bay and Bedruthan Steps on the west coast of Cornwall. The farm was about a half mile from St Eval churchyard where his Venton ancestors were buried. Scrapper had come to take a professional look at the Beaumont farm.

Monty feigned the look of the naval officer he had hoped to become. If only he had not left school at Easter but had stayed on to take his GCSE and A-level exams, he might have been accepted by Dartmouth Royal Naval College for officer training. As it was, Montague "Monty" Perkins took evening classes to gain entry into Fleetwood Nautical College on a four-year degree course hopefully to qualify as a maritime officer in the Merchant Navy. Monty had his own reasons for coming back to Beaumont.

When they had eaten their food and finished their third round of drinks, Monty produced *his* programme of events and revealed to his old classmates their would-be roles as co-conspirators or, more accurately, saboteurs.

'Here's the official programme,' said Monty.

'Looks set to be three pretty dull days,' said Pongo. 'We'll have a job on making a decent film of Speech Weekend.'

'Who said anything about the film being *decent*?' said Monty.

'What are you getting at?' said a puzzled Pongo.

'When is your film crew arriving?' Monty asked, ignoring Pongo's concern.

'They'll be here tomorrow morning. I told them to meet me at Beaumont at 10 o'clock.'

'And they know why they're coming?' said Monty.

'Of course! To make a documentary for Beaumont Abbey,' said Pongo.

'You'd no problem persuading the Beak?' said Monty.

'None at all. High Master was dead keen on the idea,' said Pongo. 'The crew can go anywhere it likes and film anything it likes... even the chapel on Sunday morning.'

'Good,' said Monty. 'So as far as the Beak knows, you and your crew will be doing just that... making a *decent* documentary film.'

'Have you spoken to Nibs about the commentary?' said Monty.

'What commentary?' asked Nibs.

'Monty wants *you* to write and narrate a commentary for the documentary,' said Pongo.

'And I want you, Pongo my friend,' said Monty, 'to make sure your crew gets plenty of footage of the *informalities* as well as the formalities of Beaumont Speech Weekend.

'What devilry, may I ask,' said Scrapper, 'are you planning now, Monty?'

'More to the point,' said Stinky, 'where do we come into it?'

'Before I answer that question,' said Monty, 'another round of drinks is called for. Your shout, Scrapper, if I'm not mistaken.'

* * * * *

The Second Master's office would not accommodate fourteen people, so Reg met the heads of department in the Common Room. They all knew the drill. Reg had, as always, produced a separate timetable for the Friday afternoon and the Saturday morning. These activities and lessons were *specials* to be a showcase for the Beaumont Abbey School.

'This shouldn't take long,' said Reg. 'I just want to be sure my time-table meets with your approval and not cause unnecessary problems.'

'Everything seems to be *in ordnung*,' growled Dr Klaus Heilbronn. 'I shall be teaching probability. My boys will play games of chance...'

'You're turning out a group of card dealing, dice rolling gamblers, Klaus,' said Arthur.

'*Nein!* That is not so,' said Klaus. 'When they understand the probability of losing their money, they will not become gamblers.'

'Right!' said Arthur. 'They'll work in a casino and end up owning one... *probably.*'

'Ach! I see you joke,' said Klaus. 'Always you make jokes.'

'Remind us again,' said Arthur. 'What games will your chaps be playing?'

'Poker and Vingt-et-un for the cards,' said Klaus. 'For the board games with dice, we have the snakes and ladders and the backgammon.'

'They don't have snakes and ladders in casinos,' said Arthur. 'And it's called Blackjack not Vingt-et-un.'

'Actually,' said Geoffrey Rusbridge, interrupting. 'Some of my economics chaps have asked me if they can play Monopoly. Perhaps we should get together on that Klaus.'

The Second Master nipped further chit-chat in the bud and instructed his colleagues to co-ordinate their efforts *after* the meeting. He reminded each department head he called this meeting to be apprised of their planned activities *in broad outline.*

Dr Philip Carratt confirmed he and James Jackson would mount a display and perform a series of exciting demonstrations in the chemistry labs. Dr Herbert Newbold, not to be outdone, confirmed he and his colleagues would be doing the same in the physics labs.

Dr Hubert Millstream, Head of Biology, confirmed the visitors would *not* see frogs being dissected this year and that he would take extra precautions against the escape of...

'One thing I ought to mention, gentlemen,' said Reg, interrupting Hubert. 'A film crew is coming to make a documentary about Speech Weekend. So absolutely no nonsense... Everybody on their best behaviour... No nonsense whatsoever.'

'When you say a *film crew*,' said Carroll Ffynch, Head of Art, 'do you know...'

'All I know,' said Reg, 'is that an Old Boy has offered to shoot a film and the High Master has given the project his blessing.'

'I trust they'll only be shooting with cameras,' said Arthur, trying to look serious.

'This Old Boy wouldn't happen to be Pongo Palfreyman by any chance?' said Carroll.

'Yes, as a matter of fact it is,' said Reg.

'Let's hope our High Master won't be disappointed with the film,' said Carroll, recalling Pongo's pathetic attempts at painting. 'He hadn't the foggiest idea about composition.'

'Sorry to interrupt, Hubert' said Reg. 'Please continue.'

'As I was about to say,' said Hubert, 'We'll make sure no locusts escape this year.'

Walter Barnes confirmed his PE lessons would be held outdoors, weather permitting, and that Gregory Watson had organised an exhibition about the new sports hall - blueprints, architects impressions and the like – in the gymnasium.

Oliver Chiselhurst confirmed that he had instructed his staff – meaning his junior, Keith Bradley, and his

266

technical support, Bill Tapp - to put on some sort of show of work they do in Design and Technology.

Arthur Matthews confirmed that they had booked time in the computer room for Physical Geography lessons. Alan Radford and Quentin Waite confirmed the English and History lessons would be no different from usual. Reg expected as much and had time-tabled just one lesson each for Alan and Quentin and a double period for Arthur.

'I hear you're planning something different this year, Carroll,' said Reg.

'Yes. We're going to do our bit for the new sports hall.'

'Doing what?' asked Reg.

'My young artists will sketch portraits of the visitors and charge an exorbitant fee.'

'What about the duffers that don't know one end of a paintbrush from the other?' said Arthur.

'Ah, we'll cheat,' said Carroll. 'The *duffers*, as you call them, will use a digital camera and then produce their work of art on a computer using *Paintbrush* software. Colin Harper has agreed to help.'

'The male-voice choir up to scratch, Peter?' said Reg to the Director of Music

'No!' said Peter Morrison. 'But I thank God the poor acoustics at the Ambassador Rex will soften the blow to your ears.'

'What will they perform this year?' asked Reg.

'A piece to meet with the full approval of the High Master.'

'Cheer him up, will it?' said Reg.

'Bring a tear to his eye, more likely' said Peter.

'The choir going to be that bad?' quipped Arthur, unable to recall the choir being anything but good under Peter's direction.

'No choir of mine is ever *bad*,' said Peter. 'No, it's the song they're going to sing. It always brings a lump to my throat and I'm not Welsh like our good Doctor Pugh-Jones.'

'I look forward to hearing it,' said Reg. 'To be honest, your choir is the highlight in an otherwise pretty dull Sunday afternoon.'

'Nice of you to say that, Reg,' said Peter. 'Still, let's look on the bright side, perhaps this year's prize giving will different.'

'I doubt it,' chuckled Arthur. 'But then... you never know what the future has in store.'

Back in his office, Reg wondered if he should have told his colleagues the High Master, at Susan Wellborn's suggestion, had invited the new intake and their parents to the Speech Weekend. It seemed a good idea. A few extra people ought not to affect the arrangements. And they should after all being seeing Beaumont in the best possible light.

* * * * *

CHAPTER 24

"There is nothing like returning to a place that remains unchanged to find the ways in which you yourself have altered." Nelson Mandela

* * * * *

Speech Weekend - Friday

The favourite pastime in Britain is not the weather so much as grumbling about it. Even though at least forty-eight countries, including Germany, Holland, Italy, Luxembourg and the Netherlands, have a higher annual rainfall, Britain is still regarded as *the* country where it is always raining and the British are always grumbling about the rain or, as was the case this Friday, the first day of Speech Weekend at Beaumont, the lack of rain.

'Heads!' the captain of the Old Beaumontians called. 'We'll bat,' he said as the coin landed heads uppermost on the bone dry wicket.'

'You can start with three slips, Rupert,' said Hammond, 'but I shouldn't be surprised if we'll have to drop one to the deep third man boundary.'

The opening batsmen for the Old Beaumontians were both Cambridge *Blues*. Rupert's first ball, a fast outswinger just slightly short of a length, was cut between second and third slip for four runs. The second ball, a fast inswinger also just short of a length, was flicked between fine leg and short leg for four runs. The third ball, another outswinger but exactly on a length, cut back viciously and lifted. To Rupert's consternation, the batsman casually hooked the ball to the leg-side for his third successive boundary.

'Jardine's in for a hard a lesson this morning,' said Greg. 'The sun's baked that wicket,'

'Dieter should have watered it yesterday,' said Walter Barnes, referring to their groundsman, formerly Leutnant Dieter Strauss of the Wehrmacht.

'My fault,' aid Greg. 'I forgot to tell him.'

'Any chance of rain, Arthur?' said Walter.

'Quentin Waite told me as an historical fact that in 1892 the British Army brought the game of cricket to what we now call the United Arab Emirates,' said Arthur Matthews, talking to himself. 'And it's a geographical fact that the UAE is one of the driest parts of the world with an average rainfall of less 100 mm per year… which reminds me…'

'Sorry Mr Matthews,' said Greg. 'You've lost me.' Arthur continued his monologue.

'A sheikh visited Britain in June and returned to Dubai with two cricket bats, a ball, six stumps, four bails and two white coats. He sat under a canopy out of the blazing sun and watched. Two tribesmen, wearing the white coats, pushed the stumps into the ground and put on the bails. Eleven more tribesmen formed a circle and threw the ball to one another. Two tribesmen appeared carrying the bats and stood in front of the stumps. One man in a white coat raised his hand and shouted *play*… The sheikh never quite understood why it did *not* start raining.'

'Pay no attention,' said Walter to Greg, as Arthur left them and headed towards the Cavendish. 'Just one of his silly little jokes.'

'I'd better be getting back to the gym,' said Greg, unaware that Monty had been listening.

* * * * *

The helicopter flew low enough over Beaumont farm to ruffle their fleece and scatter the flock to the four corners of the field wherein normally sheep may safely graze or, in the words of Johann Sebastian Bach, *Schafe können sicher weiden*. Gorran Venton, Esq., cursed the idiot pilot for flying so low over a farm, risking injury to the animals and to his houndstooth check cap which he hurried to pick up before another sheep trod on it.

SMI Batters and Monty instinctively ducked as the helicopter flew low over their heads. The roar of its twin engines and its whirling rotors deafened the men and momentarily put paid to any further conversation

270

concerning rifles and ammunition. The noise brought PSI Morton running out of the armoury and sent SMI Batters marching off to confirm that the aircraft was landing on Beaumont territory and to investigate why.

As the helicopter landed beyond the boundary at deep square leg, it raised a dust cloud sufficient in density and magnitude to halt play, to bring handkerchiefs over faces and to send dutiful husbands running after their wives' hats.

While Randolph Jardine supervised the unloading of their baggage and dismissed the pilot, pressing into his hand a fifty pound banknote bearing a portrait of Sir Christopher Wren, Rupert Jardine tried to hide behind the square leg umpire and out of sight of his mother waving her large white hat and blowing him kisses in the best theatrical tradition.

Having disgorged its two passengers and their suitcases, the helicopter took off and disappeared over the trees, scattering the Beaumont flock and raising a curse from Gorran Venton, Esq., for the second time that morning.

Mrs Jardine obeyed her husband. She stopped waving to her son and re-installed her large white hat on her delicate little head just before SMI Stanley Batters arrived to reconnoitre the strength of the invasion force air-lifted in by the helicopter.

'My name's Jardine... Randolph Jardine. This is my wife hiding under the hat.'

'Sir!' barked Stanley, snapping to attention. 'Sergeant Major Stanley Batters, Sir!'

'That's just great, Sergeant,' said Randolph. 'Could you and your men haul our bags?'

'Sir!' barked Stanley, delivering a perfect British Army salute before marching off without any explanation.

'Any idea where that guy's going?' said Randolph.

'He's probably going to fetch his men,' said Elspeth. 'Be patient, Randy. We're in England now... not America.'

SMI Batters returned shortly with PSI Morton and former Cadet Able Seaman Montague Perkins. The three men picked up two suitcases each and, with Randolph and Elspeth in tow, SMI Batters led the way to the High Master's house. En route, Monty learned that Mrs Jardine would be presenting the prizes and Randolph Jardine would be giving the Warrington Prescott speech.

Louise was in the garden when she caught sight of Sergeant Stanley Batters and his contingent approaching.

'Mr Jardine. Mrs Jardine. Welcome to Beaumont. I'm Louise.'

'I guess you're the Principal's wife, right?' said Randolph.

'Yes. I'm Louise Pugh-Jones. Please come in. The *High Master* should be here shortly.'

'May I call you Louise?' said Elspeth.

'Please do,' said Louise.

'Then you must call me…'

'Oh, here's my husband now,' interrupted Louise. 'Llew! We're in the sun room.'

'Mrs Jardine. Mr Jardine. How good of you to come,' said Llywelyn, shaking hands. 'I'm sorry I wasn't here when you arrived… All a bit hectic today, d'you see.'

'That's OK,' said Randolph. 'Louise has been taking good care of us.' Just then Batters and his men appeared, having delivered the suitcases to the guest bedroom. 'Thanks guys. Great job!' said Randolph, pressing a five pound note into the hand of SMI Batters. SMI Batters saluted, pocketed the note and led his two-man contingent out of the house.

'So sorry, Mrs Jardine,' said Louise. 'You were saying?'

'If I'm to call you Louise… well, you must call me Elspeth or perhaps, High Master, you would prefer Myfanwy.'

'That's very Welsh,' said Llywelyn. 'I suppose you know it's the title of a Welsh love song and means *my fine one*?'

'Pa ham mae dicter, O Myfanwy, Yn llenwi'th lygaid duon ddi?' Myfanwy sang softly.

'That's great, Honey,' said Randolph, 'but what does it mean?'

'Why is it anger, O Myfanwy, that fills your eyes so dark and clear?' said Llywelyn.

'We have a recording of the song by the Treorchy Male Voice Choir,' said Louise.

'I'd love to hear it,' said Myfanwy. 'It's a long time since I...'

'Why were you suggesting I call you Elspeth?' interrupted Louise, sensing sadness.

'My stage name was Elspeth Baker. Randolph prefers Elspeth to Myfanwy... Elspeth is easier to pronounce.' She glanced at Randolph then said, 'I was actually christened Myfanwy Rhys Thomas. I grew up in the Rhondda.'

* * * * *

Unlike the philosophers John Locke and Gottfried Wilhelm Leibniz, Dr Philip Carratt and Dr Nathaniel Fitzorme gave no thought to the problem of personal continuity or to the conditions ensuring a person *at one time* would be the *same* person *at another time*. Their faces had changed little since they were boys in short trousers; and they would probably be just as recognisable when they finally exchanged their long trousers for a shroud. This is not to say the men had not aged.

Dr Carratt had more furrows on his brow and fewer hairs on his head than formerly but his mind and his eyes were as sharp as ever. Dr Fitzorme was now as tall as Dr Carratt. He was clean-shaven and his somewhat leathery skin was slightly pit-marked but now free of acne and acne vulgaris.

Nathaniel still had the schoolboy look that brought to Philip's mind an Arthur Matthews truism: *Once you have seen a boy in short trousers he is always in short trousers*. Today, Dr Fitzorme and Dr Carratt were in suit and tie.

'Good morning, Dr Carratt,' said Nathaniel.

'Don't tell me. Let me see now. Front bench… In the middle… Fitzorme, if I'm not mistaken,' said Phil, holding out his hand. 'And *Doctor* Fitzorme, of course.' Nathaniel smiled and the two men shook hands.

'Yes, thanks to you, sir,' said Nathaniel, holding out a brown paper parcel.

'What's this?' said Phil.

'A present, sir. I hope you'll like it,' said Nathaniel, his words almost lost in the noise of the helicopter skimming the Cavendish rooftop.

'Your doctoral thesis and your first paper,' said Phil, after carefully removing the wrapping paper. 'Splendid. Thank you very much.'

'My pleasure entirely, sir,' said Nathaniel.

'Do you remember this little demonstration,' said Phil.

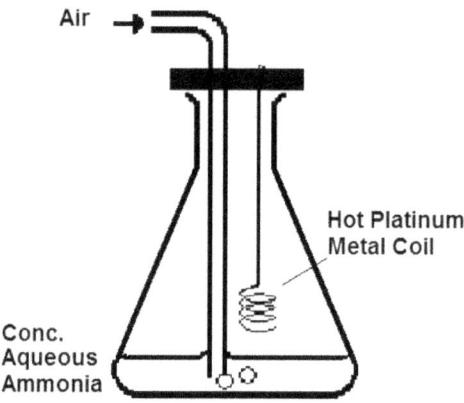

'I certainly do,' said Nathaniel. Both men watched the platinum coil become white hot, heard the whoop-whoop of the air-ammonia mixture explode and saw the coil, now a dull red, start again on its way to becoming white hot. 'I have suggestion to make, Dr Carratt.'

Nathaniel knew that this was a popular exhibit during Speech Weekend but he also knew that somebody had to keep an eye on it; the solution in the bottom of the conical flask gradually ran out of ammonia. When Nathaniel was in the Upper Sixth, Dr Carratt had put him in charge of the demonstration. That meant he had to stand by the exhibit all the time and regularly stop the demonstration to replenish the concentrated aqueous ammonia from a Winchester quart bottle.

'I think I have a way of making the demonstration run unattended for several hours,' said Nathaniel.

'How would you do that?' said Phil.

'Saturate the incoming air with ammonia,' said Nathaniel, 'by passing it through…'

'the conc. ammonia in the Winchester quart,' said Phil.

'Exactly,' said Nathaniel. 'Here, let me draw a diagram.'

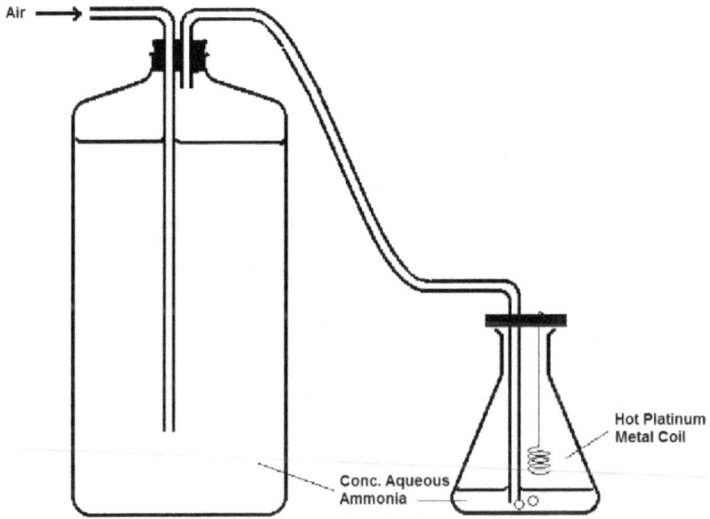

'Excellent idea,' said Phil. 'We'll have that up and running by the time we throw open the labs.'

Dr Carratt was as good as his word. When he opened the lab doors on the dot of 2 p.m. the unmanned demonstration was whoop-whooping away and continued throughout the afternoon, fascinating a constant stream of visitors including new parents with new boys, old parents with current pupils, Old Beaumontians with wives or girl friends and Pongo with his film crew who captured not only all the demonstrations but also Monty doing what looked like an Irish clog dance around the lab and in between the benches.

'What's happening?' Pongo hissed. 'Something wrong?'

'Nothing. Nothing's happening. That's what's wrong, ' snapped Monty, as he continued his curious tap dancing. 'Just wait till I see Stinkey…'

Monty waited for Dr Carratt to visit James Jackson in the other laboratory before doing what Nathaniel had not had the heart to do. When Dr Carratt returned to switch everything off and lock his laboratory at 5 o'clock, he failed to notice the damp patches on the floor by the fume cupboards and between the benches.

* * * * *

Gorran was impressed with the way Tom Mitchell was running Beaumont farm. The sheep were a flock of white-faced Exmoor Horn, a breed on the decline even though their wool is good and their ewes are good mothers and prolific, producing good quality lamb.

'Good looking flock, Tom,' said Gorran. 'Tried any cross-breeding?'

'Thought about it but never got round to it,' said Tom.

'Cross an Exmoor Horn White-faced ewe with a Leicester Blue-faced ram and you'll have the best mule in Britain.'

'Get away!' exclaimed Tom. 'I never knew that.'

'Ever had any trouble with that ram over there?'

'Looks pretty fierce, don't 'e with horns like that?' said Tom. 'Thing is… he's a right old softie. I say that but 'e acts like a goat sometimes.'

'Butted you, has he?' said Gorran.

'Never... though I've caught him chewing on that there rope keeping their gate shut.'

'What I like about these chaps,' said Gorran 'is their docility. I remember having to fit some Exmoors with a rumen cannula...'

'What's that when it's at home?' asked Tom.

'Basically it's a plastic tube... with a screw cap... You fix it into the side of the sheep so you can take samples of its stomach contents whenever you want.'

'Is that what you do on your farm in Cornwall?'

'No. It's what I did when I was at Bristol... part of the research at Langford House,' said Gorran. 'Dashed funny sight... all those sheep running around fitted with screw caps.'

* * * * *

Louise showed Randolph and Elspeth the guest bedroom and left them to 'freshen up' before the light salad lunch Edna, the house keeper, had laid out in the dining room. Louise sat across from Randolph and encouraged him to talk about his business ventures. As President of the BALI club, Louise listened with particular interest when he talked about the companies he planned to acquire in the near future.

Elspeth sat across from Llywelyn and encouraged him to talk about his plans for the future of Beaumont. She listened with particular interest to the details of the new sports hall and the intention to make provision for its use by women as well as men. With her fourteen year old daughter in mind, Elspeth asked if he thought Beaumont might become co-educational in the near future.

After lunch and a further freshening up, Randolph and Elspeth were taken on the grand tour by Llywelyn and Louise. First stop was the cricket match. The Old Beaumontians had put three-figures on the scoreboard without loss. Hammond had replaced his opening fast bowlers and Rupert was fielding on the boundary on the far side of the field. For the first time that day, one of the batsmen mistimed his hook shot and was out, caught Jardine, just inside the boundary. Rupert, surrounded by his team mates slapping him on the back, failed to notice his mother excitedly waving her large white hat.

'Jolly good catch,' said Llywelyn. 'We badly needed that wicket.'

'Do you like cricket, Randolph?' said Louise.

'No, Louise, can't say I do. I don't understand the game. Give me baseball any day.'

'Rugby football was my game,' said Llywelyn. 'Very popular in Wales.'

'Now you're talking,' said Randolph. 'Same as American football, right?'

'Not really,' said Elspeth. 'Rugby players don't wear helmets and all that armour…'

'What about tennis, Randolph,' interrupted Louise, sensing an argument brewing. 'Do you play tennis?'

'Sure do. Elspeth and I make a great mixed doubles team.'

Next stop was the gymnasium. Gregory Watson, with help from one or two members of the Lower Sixth, had produced a very professional exhibit of the new sports hall. The party of four arrived at the gymnasium at the same time as Susan Wellborn, bearing a bundle of Speech Weekend programmes.

'I don't believe you met our new bursar,' said Llywelyn to Randolph. 'Allow me to introduce Susan Wellborn.'

'Hi! I'm Randolph Jardine,' he said. 'This is my wife, Elspeth.'

'Pleased to meet you,' said Susan, shaking hands. 'Your son has told me so much about you.'

'Rupert?' said Elspeth.

'Who else, Honey?' said Randolph. 'We only got the one son… Rupert's his name and he's here at Beaumont.'

'A strikingly handsome young man, if I may say so,' said Susan. 'Takes after his…' She paused and gave

Randolph a wry smile, 'mother, wouldn't you say, Mr Jardine?'

'Randolph. You can call me Randolph.'

'How did you get to know my son?' said Elspeth, frowning.

'He's been helping me with my computers,' said Susan. 'I don't know where I'd be without his help.'

'He's been messing with computers even before he could walk,' said Randolph. 'Now he sure gets *that* from me.'

'Oh, I'm sure he's inherited lots more from you,' said Susan, exchanging admiring looks with Randolph. 'Now if you'll excuse me, I have work to do.'

They took their time studying the exhibit. Elspeth sounded Louise on the prospect of the school becoming co-educational. Llywelyn sounded Randolph on the prospect of some financial backing for the new sports hall. Randolph wanted to know who Roderick Taylor was. Llywelyn explained he was the South African racing driver and their bursar's late husband. Susan's donation in her husband's memory enabled Beaumont to launch the project. A suitable plaque would be prominently displayed in the entrance to the new hall.

'I'll tell you what,' said Randolph, 'Build a hall to work for concerts *and* sports, put my wife's name on that plaque and I'm good for whatever extra that'll cost.'

'That is exceedingly generous, Randolph,' said Llywelyn. 'Exceedingly generous.'

'OK. Then it's a deal,' said Randolph. 'Now how about some classes.'

* * * * *

When Monty eventually tracked Arthur Matthews to the computer room, his quarry was enthusiastically demonstrating the benefits of physical geography software to a group of parents and new boys who would join the Lower Thirds in September. Arthur released his captive audience when he noticed Monty.

'Mr Perkins! Fancy seeing you here,' said Arthur, extending a hand. 'Shore leave?'

'I suppose you could call it that,' said Monty.

'Royal Navy suiting you?'

'Never got in,' Monty said acidly.

'Really? I don't understand,' said Arthur.

'The interview board told me I should have gone to university,' said Monty. 'They told me the school should have advised me to stay on and take A-levels.'

'So what are you doing now,' Arthur said, genuinely concerned.

'I've finished night school. Now I'm trying to get in a four-year degree course at Fleetwood Nautical College to qualify as a maritime officer in the Merchant Navy.'

'Good for you,' said Arthur. 'Nothing wrong with the Merchant Navy. What are you going for? Deck, Engineering or Electro-Technical Officer?'

'Deck Officer,' said Monty.

'That makes sense,' said Arthur. 'You're confident, decisive, enthusiastic, self-reliant and unflappable. A born leader, I'd say.'

'You think so?' said Monty, taken aback.

'Of course,' said Arthur. 'I don't doubt it for one moment. You sound surprised.'

'I never expected to hear you say that,' said Monty with a frown. 'You see... I...'

'Will you excuse me, Mr Perkins? I really must have a word with these visitors. More parents and new boys starting in September... Let's meet and talk again later, alright?'

His meeting with the Head of Geography had not gone as Monty had expected. Arthur had been pleasant and seemed genuinely interested in him. He was not the same man he remembered who had threatened him: *any more trouble from you and your cronies in Mr Barnikel's lessons my lad and you will leave school at Easter over my dead body.* Monty now realised Arthur's threat had been a clever but idle one. Arthur had conned Monty.

As Monty wandered around the school, he realised nothing quite fitted his recollections. The classrooms seemed smaller. The Sixth Formers and Prefects looked younger. The teachers seemed older, shorter and less intimidating. Well, perhaps not all the teachers had changed. Oliver Chiselhurst had aged but Keith Bradley and Bill Tapp looked much the same as ever.

'Hello Monty,' said Keith, extending a greasy hand. 'Your first time at Speech Weekend?'

'Yes,' said Monty. 'I've been meaning to come but you know how it is.'

'I only went back to my old school once,' said Keith. 'Big mistake. Everything looked different...'

'Classrooms looked smaller...' said Monty.

'Yes... that's right,' said Keith. 'How did I ever manage to get my legs under the desk?'

'Teachers looked older...'

'And shorter... They were all shorter than I remembered,' said Keith.

'You haven't changed,' said Monty. 'You're still... Oh, what's this?'

'It's my rifle,' said Keith proudly.

'*Your* rifle?'

'I made it here in the workshops,' said Keith.

'Does it work? Could you shoot somebody with it?'

'No, sorry,' said Keith. 'Gunning for some of your old teachers, are you?'

'Why did you make it?' asked Monty.

'Dr Carratt and Peter Morrison are putting on Gilbert and Sullivan's Iolanthe next term. Act 2 opens with Private Willis on sentry duty,' said Keith. 'PSI Morton won't let them have a real rifle from the armoury, so I've made them this replica.'

'Amazing! It's looks... May I?' Keith nodded.

Monty went through the drill he learnt in the CCF then put the rifle in its place among the exhibits. Arthur Matthews should have included adaptability as an essential quality of a good officer because Monty understood the importance of being able to modify ones plans in the light of changing circumstances and opportunities. He headed for the pavilion where Dolly Brown was putting the finishing touches to the teas in the nearby marquee.

* * * * *

Louise guided Myfanwy into the pavilion enclosure where the two of them could watch the cricket in relative comfort. A tactful word from Louise persuaded Myfanwy to keep her hat on, not to wave to Rupert and to talk about him *sotto voce* only. When the players came in for tea, Rupert exchanged a few words and suffered a hug from his mother before joining his team mates. The ladies were well on their way back to the High Master's house before the cricketers entered the marquee and encountered new parents and their sons tucking into the players' teas. Reginald de Vere, the Second Master, restored order and minimised any embarrassment but was unable to explain to the haughty mother of a new boy the notice on the side of the marquee:

REFRESHMENTS
5 o'clock
PARENTS AND NEW BOYS

Llywelyn guided Randolph to the Cavendish where they met Colin Harper and Arthur Matthews in the computer room. While Colin and Randolph discussed technicalities in a language totally foreign to most people's ears, Arthur spoke to Llywelyn about Montague Perkins and Llywelyn spoke to Arthur about Radulph Palfreyman.

'According to Perkins, we should never have let him leave at Easter,' said Arthur, trying to get the High Master's attention.

'I don't much care for the name ZipFliks Studios but Mr Palfreyman convinced me that nothing but good could come of a TV documentary about Speech Weekend,' said Llywelyn.

'According to Perkins, the Royal Navy Interview Board told him Beaumont should have kept him at school and sent him on to the university to read for a degree,' said Arthur.

'I've given Palfreyman and his film crew *carte blanche* to go where they like and... shoot... yes that's the expression... shoot what they like,' said Llywelyn.

'You must excuse me, High Master,' said Arthur, seeing more new parents coming in.

'What? Oh, yes. Of course. Carry on,' said Llywelyn. 'I must rescue Mr Jardine.'

As they left the Cavendish, Llywelyn made sure that Randolph noticed the plaque, on the wall just inside the main entrance, acknowledging Beaumont's indebtedness to Jardine International Corporation for sponsoring the computer room and the language laboratory. Inside the main block, Llywelyn guided Randolph to Dr Heilbronn's classroom where the lesson on probability was in full swing.

'Geez!' exclaimed Randolph. 'The only thing missing is a roulette wheel.'

'Let me introduce our Head of Mathematics,' said Llywelyn. 'Mr Jardine... This is Dr Heilbronn... Dr Heilbronn... This is Mr Jardine...' Dr Heilbronn stood stiffly to attention and gave a slight bow with his head as the two men shook hands.

'Ach. You are the father of Rupert Jardine, is that not so?' said Klaus.

'You got that right,' said Randolph. 'Not been razzing you, has he?'

'Razzing! What is that?' said Klaus, scratching the scar on his left cheek.

'Causing trouble... Having a bit of fun at your expense I guess you'd say.'

'Never! We have no time for... for this razzing, Mr Jardine.'

'OK!' said Randolph. 'So tell me... what's going on here this afternoon?'

'The boys learn some probability theory,' said Klaus. 'Please! Why don't you take a look… Perhaps you wish to take part, yes?'

The High Master drifted to the table where two boys were playing Snakes & Ladders. His mind drifted back to his childhood and the year when this game, produced by J W Spears & Sons, was his Christmas present. He remembered playing it with his father, mother and sister. The winner was the first to get his token from the bottom left hand square to the top right hand square. If he landed on a square at the bottom of a ladder, he could move his token up to the square at top of the ladder. If he landed on a square with a snake's head, he had to move his token down to the square with the snake's tail.

Llywelyn had not played Snakes & Ladders since his childhood but he now knew it is an ancient board game whose origins can be traced to India and the 2nd century BC. Progress from the bottom to the top square represented life's journey on a path helped by virtues – the ladders – and hindered by vices – the snakes. His mind was brought sharply back to the present by the voice of Randolph Jardine, 'Cute game. It's Chutes & Ladders where I come from.'

Dr Heilbronn joined them and asked Randolph if he had knowledge of Andrei Markov. When Randolph shook his head, Klaus explained he was a brilliant Russian who died in 1922 and who is remembered for the mathematics of random chainlike transitions from one state to another where the next state depends only on the present state.

'We can treat Snakes & Ladders as a Markov chain,' said Klaus.

'No kidding,' said Randolph.

'This mathematics has many applications,' said Klaus. 'Economics, finance, the sciences, computing and so forth.'

'Is this what you teach these guys?' said Randolph.

'No. It is too difficult for them although…' Klaus paused then said, 'But I think not too hard for your son… We shall see.'

'Nice talking to you,' said Randolph. 'Maybe I'll look in tomorrow morning to shoot some craps.' Bewildered by those words, Llywelyn led Randolph away from an equally bewildered Klaus.

'I think we deserve a spot of tea, don't you?' said Llywelyn.

* * * * *

The Old Beaumontians Dinner traditionally began decorously inside the Great Dining Hall with the ante cibum Grace - *Benedic nobis, Domine, et omnibus tuis donis* – as a small gesture of thanks for an exquisite four-course meal and selection of wines provided by Jean-Pierre Escoffier, the renowned chef of Beaumont Abbey, and paid for by the members of the Old Beaumontians Association. This year was no exception.

The place cards showed Nathaniel Fitzorme, Radulph Palfreyman, and Gorran Venton on the same table as Montague Perkins and guest – the impecunious Edward Trelawney. This was their *first* OBA dinner so by tradition there was prominently displayed on their table a sixth card:

JOKERS TABLE

'Who's going first, Monty?'

'How about alphabetical order, Nibs?' said Monty.

'First name, last name or nickname?' said Nibs.

'Surname! Definitely,' said Scrapper Venton.

'I vote for first name,' said Pongo Palfreyman.

'We'll toss for it,' Monty said decisively. They did. Moments after they had settled the batting order, the assembly rose for the post cibum Grace: *Benedictus sit Deus in donis suis. Sit nomen Dei benedictum.*

'I now call upon the Jokers Table,' said the President of the Old Beaumontians. Dr Fitzorme stood up as slowly as possible and raised what was his fourth glass of red wine.

285

'Mr President…' he said, taking a drink. 'Honoured guests…' he said, taking another drink. 'Fellow Old Beaumontians…' he said, draining his glass and turning towards the source of the raucous *Get on with it, Stinkey* that came from the other side of the hall. 'And those who should neither be seen nor heard… It has fallen upon me to provide the first joke.'

A chemist in his air balloon had lost his way. He called down to a man on the ground, 'Hello there. Can you tell me where I am?'

'You're up in an air balloon,' said the man.

'Ah ha! You're a physicist,' said the chemist.

'How did you know?' asked the man.

'The information you have given me is absolutely correct but totally useless.'

'Mr President… Honoured guests… Worthy Old Beaumontians…' said Gorran Venton, raising his glass and looking towards the high table. 'And all you unworthy members of the association,' he said, turning his back on the high table to face the majority of tables. 'It is my duty to bring to your notice an incident I was told took place quite recently.'

Dr Fiddle was taking a stroll near Beaumont Farm when he encountered Jack, Tom Mitchell's son, frantically shovelling manure back onto a cart. It was a hot day and Jack was sweating like a pig. Dr Fiddle offered to help and suggested Jack should have a rest.

'Sorry,' said Jack. 'I mustn't stop. Dad won't like it.'

'Nonsense,' said Dr Fiddle. 'Your father's not a slave driver. Take a break and fetch yourself a glass of water.'

'I can't stop,' said Jack. 'Dad will be mad at me.'

'Come now,' said Dr Fiddle. 'Your father's a reasonable man. I'll have a word with him. Where is he?'

'Under the manure.'

'Mr President… Honoured guests… Old Beaumontians… I know you're going to find this difficult to believe…' ' said Edward Trelawney, pausing to fortify himself with a drop of white wine, 'but the incident I am about to relate took place when I was working part-time in my local public library.

One morning a fat hen strutted into the library, flew onto the counter and spoke to me. 'Book! Book-book!' Luckily Hugh Lofting's first book entitled *The Story of Doctor Dolittle: Being the History of His Peculiar Life at Home and Astonishing Adventures in Foreign Parts Never Before Printed* had just been returned. The hen flew out of the door with that book in its beak.

The next day the hen brought the book back, dropped it on the counter and spoke to me again. 'Book! Book-book!' As luck would have it, I had on the counter the sequel to Lofting's first book. The hen flew away with *The Voyages of Doctor Dolittle* in its beak.

The hen brought that book back the next day and said, 'Book! Book-book!' I put Hugh Lofting's third book - Doctor Dolittle's Post Office - in the hen's beak but this time I followed the bird out of the library, across the road, into the park and down to the edge of the lake. I saw the hen throw the book onto a lily pad and the frog sitting there said, 'Read it! Read it!'

'Mr President… Honoured guests… Old Beaumontians… With your permission I shall follow suit and tell you of an incident, concerning Cecil B. DeMille, the famous epic film maker, as it was told to me by his nephew, author and journalist, Richard DeMille.

Cecil B. DeMille built an entire city on a square mile of flat land bordered by hills on two adjacent sides. In his film, based very loosely on the deuterocanonical book of Judith, the Judean city of Bethulia was to be burnt to the ground. DeMille himself struck the match and started the fire. In the intense heat, the toupee of one star was singed and several extras were injured but it was in the director's own words a *spectacular spectacle.*

When there was nothing left but a heap of ashes and a few chard embers, the director turned to face his number one cameraman. 'Wow! Fantastic! I... Oh no! I'm so sorry, Mr DeMille,' said the cameraman, 'I've never done that before. I left the lens cap on. I didn't get a single frame.'

DeMille climbed angrily into his jeep and drove the one mile to camera two on the second corner of the lot. 'Wow! Absolutely fantastic, Mr DeMille... Oh no! I'm so sorry. I've never done that before,' said the cameraman. 'I forgot to put film in the camera. I didn't get a single frame.'

Now in a rage and very worried, DeMille drove the mile to foot of the hills and looked up to his third and last camera. He took off his hat, waved to the cameraman and shouted, 'OK Camera three?' The cameraman waved back. *'Ready when you are, Mr DeMille.'*

The Old Beaumontians Dinner ended indecorously outside the Great Dining Hall with men, who should have known better, being as much under the influence of alcohol as Monty was when he had informed the President, Honoured Guests and *all the other overgrown schoolboys* he had no intention of telling a half-baked joke or story.

'Do you want a proper joke?' Monty had said, swaying on his feet like a deck officer on the bridge of a ship in a severe storm. 'Do you want a proper story?' he had shouted. 'Then you'd better be in the courtyard by the school clock tower at nineteen hundred hours tomorrow. That's seven o'clock post meridiem to you landlubbers.' Nobody had the faintest idea what Monty was up to, not even Nibs, Pongo, Scrapper and Stinkey who had been taken by surprise and were completely in the dark.

* * * * *

CHAPTER 25

"I owe a lot to my teachers and mean to pay them back some day" Stephen Leacock

* * * * *

Had the first day of Speech Weekend been a success? Dr Llywelyn Pugh-Jones thought so, especially since Randolph Jardine would sponsor the new Concert & Sports Hall. Arthur Matthews thought so, especially since he had been able to speak to so many new parents and boys and to become re-acquainted with Montague Perkins. Dr Philip Carratt thought so, especially since his former pupil had given him a copy of his doctoral thesis and proposed a modification of the catalytic oxidation of ammonia demonstration.

Dolly Brown thought not. She prided herself on her teas and would have given Monty what for if she had known he was responsible for the notice on the side of the small marquee. Reginald de Vere thought the day had gone quite well especially since he had averted what might have been a major embarrassment over the cricketers' teas. He would like to have known who was responsible for that notice *and* for the TV crew turning up in time to film the incident.

Dieter Strauss, the groundsman, thought he had prepared a first-class wicket; until Greg told him, on Friday morning, he should have watered it the day before; and until Monty told him, on Friday evening, not only to water the wicket thoroughly but also to poke his fork into the ground, particularly just in front of the crease, to help the water soak in.

Even though he had brought off a magnificent catch on the boundary, Rupert Jardine thought Friday had been a disaster; he bought his one wicket for 135 runs and had been no-balled seven times. Leonard Hammond, Captain of the School First Eleven, thought the day had gone quite well considering the perfect batting wicket; the Old Beaumontians could have ended the day with far more than 450 runs for three wickets.

Radulph Palfreyman thought the first day had been a success. By a combination of luck, judgement and instructions from Monty, Pongo's film crew had been in the right place at the right time, most of the time, to shoot enough footage to produce a decent, first-class documentary. They also had enough footage to produce a special film to assuage Monty. Pongo had some hilarious shots of *informalities* including people trying to pick up coins someone had glued firmly to the floor. In a few instances where the would-be coin collectors were young ladies in mini skirts, the footage bordered on the *indecent*.

Michael Liú FRCS had arrived just in time for the Old Beaumontians dinner. He thought the meal prepared by Jean-Pierre Escoffier had been up to its usual excellent standard and he quite enjoyed the jokes. He was, however, upset by the usual drunken behaviour outside the Great Dining Hall and perturbed by Monty's ranting and raving. Michael resolved to be at the tower at seven o'clock on Saturday evening and wondered whether or not to inform his fellow directors on the governing board.

Speech Weekend - Saturday

At 5 o'clock on the Friday afternoon, Dr Philip Carratt locked the chemistry laboratories and reminded Ron Beech, the chief caretaker, to tell the cleaners that the Cavendish was out of bounds until Saturday evening. At a quarter to nine on Saturday morning, Phil unlocked James Jackson's lab and had just unlocked his own laboratory door when he heard a shout from the nearby physics lab. He dashed along to investigate.

Not to be outdone by the chemists, the physicists had gone overboard with their demonstrations and displays. In addition to the old favourites like the van de Graaf machine to make people's hair stand on end, Dr Herbert Newbold had decided to try something new. He put combustible material in a porcelain dish surrounded by a metal gauze cylinder sitting on a turntable. When he applied a lighted match, the material burst into a yellow flame. When he switched on the turntable, the flame became a spectacular helical shape but remorselessly grew taller and taller.

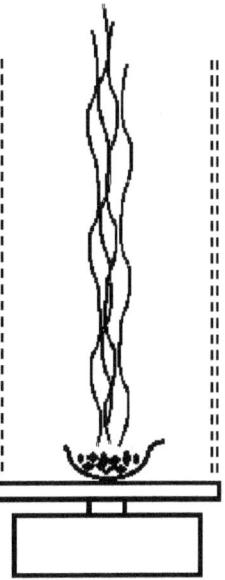

When Dr Carratt arrived on the scene, the flame was licking the ceiling. Phil snatched a carbon dioxide fire extinguisher from the wall and sprang into action. Pongo's camera crew filmed Dr Newbold and his experiment disappearing behind a dense white cloud.

By the time the cloud had dispersed, to reveal the fire out, the ceiling scorched and the Head of Physics covered in white frost like icing on a cake, Dr Carratt was dashing back along the corridor to investigate the strange noises coming from his laboratory.

Sensing another incident, Pongo and his crew were not very far behind. Well dressed parents and new boys were hopping about in what seemed a poor attempt at line dancing, accompanied by explosions under feet rapidly disappearing beneath a deepening layer of purple smoke. Pongo's crew captured it all on film. Dr Carratt brought order to the chaos by leading the visitors to the safety of the corridor just as the Second Master appeared with Randolph and Elspeth Jardine.

'What's going on?' asked the Reg.

'Nitrogen tri-iodide!' said Phil. 'Somebody's spread it all over the lab floor.'

'Dangerous stuff, is it?' said Reg.

'Can be,' said Phil. 'Fortunately whoever's responsible seemed to know what they were doing.'

'Easily made... this nitrogen tri... whatever you called it?' said Reg.

'Very easy and even easier to detonate,' said Phil. 'A feather can set it off.

'The work of a schoolboy, d'you think?' interrupted Reg.

'More likely of an old schoolboy,' said Phil.

'Got anybody in mind?'

'Well,' said Phil, wondering about Stinkey, 'I...'

'Oh, dear,' Reg said suddenly. 'I think my two VIPs have gone into your laboratory.'

The two men hurried into the lab to see Pongo's crew filming the prancing Jardines.

'Stand perfectly still,' commanded Phil.

'What kind of a show are you guys running here?' complained Randolph who, for the first time in years, obeyed an order instead of giving one.

'My shoes!' said Elspeth. 'My feet! They've all turned brown.'

'Nothing to worry about, Mrs Jardine, I assure you. The iodine will quickly evaporate and leave no permanent stain.'

'May I suggest we postpone your visit to the Cavendish, Mr Jardine,' said Reg. 'I believe you wanted to have another word with Dr Heilbronn. Dr Carratt! Please be kind enough to lead us out of this minefield.'

* * * * *

Dr Pugh-Jones was the epitome of the aloof High Master with his head often but not always in the clouds and his feet sometimes but not always on the ground. He was everything one might expect from an Oxford philosophy doctorate whose dissertation for his DPhil was *The Moral Foundations of Crime and Punishment*. In the opinion of Sir Leslie Matthews, pork pie maker and school governor, Dr Pugh-Jones was lucky having Reginald de Vere, Mary Cranborne and Susan Wellborn to save his bacon, keep his fat out of the fire and stop his goose from being cooked. Reg and the Jardines came out of the Cavendish as the High Master and Mary Cranborne were coming into the building.

'Good morning, High Master,' said Reg. 'Doing your rounds?'

'My rounds? Oh, yes... Yes, of course,' said Llywelyn. 'Show the flag...'

'May I suggest you start your tour of inspection with the biology laboratories on the ground floor?' said Reg, giving Mary a wry look. 'I'm taking Mr and Mrs Jardine to the main block for a first visit to Geoffrey Rusbridge and a second visit to Dr Heilbronn.'

'Good! Very good,' said Llywelyn. 'We'll... see you all for lunch in the main marquee.'

The Computing Science and Language laboratories may have shared the ground floor with Biology but, in Dr Hubert Millstream's eye, computing was not a science and tape recorders did not turn a classroom into a laboratory. The Head of Biology would never admit the chemistry and physics laboratories were in any sense superior to his biology laboratories other than their actually being above his on the first floor. And he never acknowledged that any reference to the three sciences invariably listed them in the order of chemistry, physics and biology; any other order, including the alphabetical order of biology, chemistry and physics, failed to trip lightly off the tongue.

When the High Master and his secretary entered Dr Millstream's laboratory, they were almost bowled over by Hubert's effusiveness and the smell of formaldehyde preserving the variety of specimens in glass jars filling shelf after shelf. Llywelyn contented himself with a broad view of the exhibits while Mary dutifully paid attention to Hubert enthusiastically explaining the details of his worm vivarium.

New parents and boys, whispering in the hushed tones normally reserved for libraries and chapels of rest, drifted quietly in and out of Dr Millstream's laboratory where nocturnal animals, sensitive to noise, were hiding from view and sleeping peacefully. Hubert was leading Mary across to the apiary, built into the outside wall of the laboratory and fitted with a glass panel enabling pupils to study the bees at work, when the respectful quiescence was suddenly broken by a shrill scream. It came from a mother, skirt above her knees, attempting to clamber onto a stool. Last year the great escape had been by locusts. This year the white mice had effected a prison break.

Hubert closed the door so neither the mice nor the visitors could escape into the corridor. Llywelyn himself was not particularly fond of rodents and might well have hopped onto a stool had he not been High Master of Beaumont Abbey with a position to maintain and an example to set. Fortunately, Mary, three new boys and their fathers helped Hubert chase the mice around the lab and return the prisoners to their cells. By another extraordinary stroke of good fortune, Pongo's crew were there to capture the episode on film.

With the cages closed and the lab door open, the mice were once more imprisoned and their visitors free to leave. Out in the corridor, Llywelyn and Mary encountered Susan Wellborn in the company of Major MacKay and another lady.

'Good morning High Master. Good morning Mary,' said Susan. 'You know Major MacKay of course but I don't think you have met his wife.'

'Ah yes. Major MacKay. How are you?' said Llywelyn. 'Mrs MacKay. How do you do?'

'Mary,' said Susan. 'We thought we heard a scream? Anything wrong?'

'Oh, it was nothing,' said Mary. 'Some mice escaped and frightened one of the visitors.'

'Is it safe to go in now?' said Fiona MacKay.

'Oh yes. They're back in their cages and all accounted for,' said Mary.

'I can't imagine you being afraid of mice, Mrs MacKay,' said Susan.

'Och, no,' said Angus. 'My wife's no afraid *of* mice. She's afraid *for* the wee sleekit timorous beasties when I'm around.'

'If you will excuse me, Mrs MacKay... Major...' said Llywelyn. 'You'll be joining us for lunch in the marquee, I trust...' Angus nodded. 'Good. Good. See you both then.'

* * * * *

As they were about to enter the classroom, Elspeth decided she would prefer to watch the cricket match. So, when he had introduced Randolph to the Head of Economics, Reg escorted Elspeth to the visitors enclosure in front of the pavilion.

Geoffrey Rusbridge was in his summer uniform: white blazer, white shirt, red and white striped tie and light grey flannels. If his white straw hat had been on his head and not on his desk, Geoffrey might have been mistaken for one of the cricket umpires.

'What's cooking?' said Randolph.

'My chaps are playing games to discover some principles of business, commerce, economics and finance,' said Geoffrey.

'I've been playing those games since like... forever,' said Randolph.

'I'm sorry,' said Geoffrey. 'I'm not sure I... What games...'

'Business!' said Randolph. 'That's the game I play, for sure.'

'Oh, I see,' said Geoffrey, not really seeing and quite unsure.

'Yes, sir. I reckon life is just a... Well I'll be... I know that guy,' said Randolph, referring to Joseph Zháng Ming, father of Stephen Zháng, Geoffrey's star pupil.

In his shiny black shoes, dark socks, three-piece pin-striped charcoal grey suit, pale blue shirt with white collar and dark blue silk tie with lion design, Joseph Zháng looked every inch the stockbroker and alumnus of Hong Kong University. His neatly brushed hair was still its natural jet black colour. His skin was smooth and his eyes were a penetrating dark brown. At five feet five inches, he stood two inches below the average height of urban Chinese males and five inches below the average height of white American males.

'Well I'll be darned,' said Randolph. 'What brings you here, Joe?'

'Same reason you come to Beaumont Abbey, Mr Jardine,' Joseph replied, looking up into the eyes of Randolph who stood six feet one inch in his socks. Allow me to introduce my son, Stephen.'

'I am pleased to meet you, sir,' said Stephen, shaking Randolph firmly by the hand then returning to his seat.

'Like your son, my son is in Wedgewood House and in Dr Heilbronn's Lower Sixth set for mathematics,' said Joseph. 'Unlike your son, Stephen studies Economics and does not play cricket.'

'Well I'll be darned,' Randolph said again. 'It sure is a small world.'

Geoffrey Rusbridge seized the lull in their conversation to ask the two men their opinion of the games his chaps were playing. Neither thought much of *Supply and Demand* or of *Monopoly*. Neither had come across *Offer and Counteroffer*, so Geoffrey explained.

Two people, X and Y, play. X starts with £1000 in Monopoly money and offers to give Y a share. If Y refuses the offer from X, £50 is taken away. Y must now offer X a share of the £950. If X refuses the offer from Y, another £50 is lost. The game ends when they agree on their shares. X and Y play the game several times and then discuss the results.

'This £1000... It sounds like the proceeds from a bank robbery... with X and Y crooks arguing about splitting the haul...' said Randolph. 'Who planned the heist? X?' Before Geoffrey could reply, Randolph continued, 'The guy who plans the heist gets the lion's share, right?'

'What do the students learn from this game?' Joseph asked the befuddled Rusbridge.

'If they continue to make and reject unfair offers, both players end up losing money,' said Geoffrey.

'So the best result would be each player having £500, yes?' said Joseph.

'Ain't never going to happen,' said Randolph. 'In the real world...'

'The most popular game,' said Geoffrey, tactfully interrupting, 'Is *Stock Market*.'

'Ah, yes!' said Joseph. 'Stephen has spoken to me of this. Just like the real world in every way, Mr Jardine, except they do not use real money.'

'Where's the fun in that, Joe?' Before Randolph could say more, the lesson ended and Reg appeared to usher the two men along to Dr Heilbronn's classroom.

* * * * *

Nobody except Monty knew who scarred the surface in front of each crease just where a good length ball should land or why the cricket pitch had been watered contrary to the rules of the game. Jeremy Davies, the Old Beaumontians captain agreed with Leonard Hammond, the School captain, to have the wicket swept and rolled before the start of play. A search party tracked the groundsman to the armoury where SMI Batters, PSI Morton and Monty were sharing a beer and Dieter's dislike for Adolf Hitler, the man who the former Leutenant Strauss claimed had brought dishonour to the Wehrmacht.

Sweeping and the heavy roller had helped but the wicket was still lively, unpredictable and in the bowlers favour. Rupert was scowling at Friday's scorecard when his mother set the Second Master free at the gate and gushed into the enclosure.

'Rupert... Darling... Why the miserable face?'

'Hello Mother,' said Rupert, trying but failing to avoid her kiss on his cheek.

'What's the problem?' said Elspeth. 'Tell mummy all about it.'

'The Old Boys batted on an easy wicket and scored four hundred and fifty for three.'

'That's a really good score, isn't it?' said Elspeth.

'Good for them. Bad for us,' said Rupert. 'Now some idiot has watered the wicket and poked holes in it…'

'That was a bad thing to do?'

'It's against the rules and… yes, of course it's bad. We've already lost three wickets…' A shout of *how's that* went up and the umpire raised his finger in the air. 'Four… that's four wickets now. This match is going to be an absolute fiasco.'

'When do you bat, Rupert dear?'

'I'm number eleven, Mother… By rights I shouldn't have to bat.'

'I thought you liked batting,' said Elspeth.

'That's not the point, Mother. I'm picked for my bowling, not my… Oh never mind.'

'Well I'd like to see you bat,' said Elspeth.

'You won't have long to wait at this rate,' said Rupert, as Raj Singh, the number six batsman made his way to the wicket.

'I shall wait here all day if I have to,' said Elspeth.

'Where's Dad?'

'I think he's gone to shoot craps.'

* * * * *

The Lower Sixth top set in mathematics had just assembled when the three men entered the classroom. Reg re-introduced Randolph and Joseph, thereby tactfully reminding Dr Heilbronn of their names. Before Reg could escape, Randolph proposed a game of craps.

'I'm not a gambling man, I'm afraid, Mr Jardine. I do recall,' said Reg, remembering a homily by Quentin Waite on the evils of dice, 'craps derives its name from *crapaud* and is a simplified version of *hazard*, an Old English game dating back to the Crusades.'

'Why *crapaud*?' asked Joseph Zháng.

'It's French for toad,' said Reg. 'I suppose it's because players crouched on the ground.' Reg kept to himself Quentin's further revelation that Bernard Xavier Philippe de Marigny de Mandeville, a politician, gambler and descendant of wealthy Louisiana landowners, had been the first to corrupt New Orleans society with the game.

'Alright! So who wants to play craps?' said Randolph, taking off his jacket.

Surrounded by a group of very bright young men, one anxious teacher and one inquiring stockbroker, Randolph explained the rules.

'The *shooter* places his bet, the other players place their bets to cover the shooter's bet before the shooter throws a *come-out* with two dice from one hand. The bet is *pass* or *don't pass*.'

'Excuse me, sir,' said Stephen Zháng. 'You lost me already. Come-out? Pass? Don't pass?'

'OK. How about *win* or *lose*?' said Randolph.

'I'm still lost. Sorry, sir,' said Stephen.

'OK. If I'm the shooter... I roll the dice... for the *first* time... that's the come-out. If I throw 2, 3 or 12, that's a don't pass or lose... we call that *craps*. If I'd bet don't pass – or lose – then I win. Got it?'

'So if a player bets pass – or win – then he'd lose,' said Stephen.

'You got it,' said Randolph. 'OK! Now if I throw a 7 or 11 on a come-out roll, that's a pass or a win.'

'And if I'd bet pass or win, I'd have won the bet,' said Stephen.

'You sure would,' said Randolph. 'You got a bright boy here, Joe, for sure.'

'What if you threw a six?' asked Stephen.

'If I throw a 4, 5, 6, 8, 9 or 10, that number is now the *point*. You can place a win or lose bet that I'll throw the point again *before* I throw a seven.'

'So, if you throw a seven *before* you throw the point number for a second time, it's a lose,' said Stephen.

299

'You got it. And somebody else becomes the shooter,' said Randolph. 'So, what are we going to use for money?'

Dr Heilbronn hurriedly produced the *Monopoly* money then drew a chart on the board to show the chances of throwing a particular number.

1 for 2 1-1
2 for 3 1-2 2-1
3 for 4 1-3 2-2 3-1
4 for 5 1-4 2-3 3-2 4-1
5 for 6 1-5 2-4 3-3 4-2 5-1
6 for 7 1-6 2-5 3-4 4-3 5-2 6-1
5 for 8 2-6 3-5 4-4 5-3 6-2
4 for 9 3-6 4-5 5-4 6-3
3 for 10 4-6 5-5 6-4
2 for 11 5-6 6-5
1 for 12 6-6

Joseph joined in the fun but did not take off his coat. Reg slipped away to check on preparations for lunch in the large marquee.

* * * * *

Major MacKay, just ahead of his wife and Susan Wellborn, was halfway up the stairs when the sound of the explosion from overhead brought back memories, long buried and best forgotten, of his two years as a civilian when his Black Watch battalion was attempting to keep the peace in Northern Ireland. Angus quickly left the women behind.

When he pushed open the heavy fire-door, Angus saw men, women and young boys coughing, spluttering and staggering into the corridor. At the open doorway, the fumes of ammonia coming from the laboratory began to make his eyes water. Angus ran in to help Dr Carratt usher the visitors into the corridor and open the windows.

The Head of Chemistry was passionate about dangerous experiments but equally passionate about safety precautions. The unexpected explosion had occurred inside a fume cupboard with the extractor fans running. Dr Carratt neutralised the ammonia solution on the lab floor and the surface inside the fume cupboard and, with Angus's help, was mopping up when Dr Nathaniel 'Stinkey" Fitzorme hurried into the laboratory.

'Everything alright, Dr Carratt?' said Nathaniel. 'I was on the other side of the courtyard when I heard the noise. Sounded like your hydrogen oxygen demo.'

'I'm afraid not,' said Phil. 'The oxidation of ammonia demo backfired.'

'Sorry tae intrude,' said Angus. 'but could you tell me what just happened?'

'I'm sorry,' said Phil. 'My name's Carratt. This is Dr Fitzorme, a former pupil. You are?'

'This is Major MacKay and this is Mrs MacKay,' said Susan. 'They're guests of the High Master. I think we'd all like to know what just happened, Dr Carratt.'

Phil and Nathaniel examined the remains of the apparatus and after a short discussion explained what caused the explosion. The platinum coil had heated the glass tube. Cold ammonia solution splashed onto the hot glass and broke the tube.

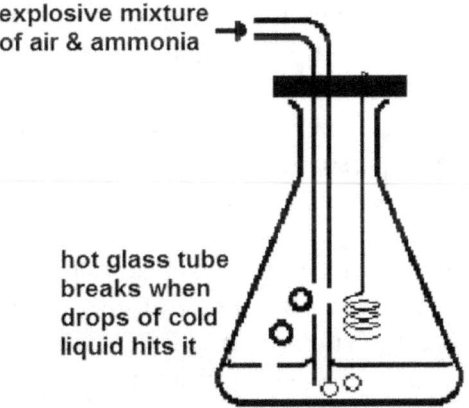

explosive mixture of air & ammonia

hot glass tube breaks when drops of cold liquid hits it

The air ammonia mixture caught fire and the flame flashed back to ignite the explosive mixture in the Winchester quart bottle.

'We were very lucky,' said Phil. 'The blast blew the top off the Winchester and the rest of the bottle just fell apart, letting ammonia solution run under the fume cupboard door onto the lab floor. Nobody was cut by flying glass… that sort of thing.'

'What about the fumes?' said Angus. 'People were gasping for breath.'

'Nothing more serious than a heavy dose of smelling salts,' Phil said lightly. 'If they came from Herbert's biology lab, they might have needed that to wake them up.'

Susan and the MacKays left the laboratory, fortunately without stepping on any nitrogen tri-iodide, and Nathaniel helped Phil restore the laboratory to normality ready for Monday's lessons when Speech Weekend would be over but not forgotten. When Nathaniel jumped at an explosion under his foot, he gave Phil the opportunity he had been waiting for.

'I'm sure you know what that was,' said Phil.

'Nitrogen tri-iodide,' said Nathaniel. 'The classic schoolboy prank.'

'Any idea how it came to be on my lab floor?'

'I didn't put it there, sir. Honest, sir,' said Nathaniel.

'Ah, the classic schoolboy reply,' said Phil.

'On this occasion, Dr Carratt, it happens to be true.'

'Any idea who might have done it?'

'If I had, I could not snitch on him, sir,' said Nathaniel.

'Another classic schoolboy reply,' said Phil. 'Might we have the same person in mind?'

* * * * *

In the small marquee, the Old Beaumontians were in jubilant mood and ready for chef Jean-Pierre's luncheon which, thanks to the vigilance of the Second Master, was not being devoured by new parents, their off-spring or any other intruders. When the umpires had removed the bails to signal the lunch interval, Leonard Hammond was still at the crease but the school had lost 4 wickets for 53 runs. Len did his best to cheer up his team. 'The game's

302

not over yet, chaps. Plenty of batting still to come. Enjoy your lunch.'

In the large marquee on the High Master's lawn, Jean-Pierre had laid out, on trestle tables covered with white double damask linen cloths, a sumptuous buffet luncheon and some pork pies Reg had persuaded him tactfully to include. There were no chairs, so the herd of guests was obliged to graze *à pied* and mingle.

Pongo had strategically stationed a cameraman in each of the two corners furthest from the entrance and arranged for a third cameraman to move discretely amongst the guests. He had impressed upon all three the need to *be prepared*, recalling the scout's motto and Tom Lehrer's parodical song. The recorded snippets of conversations and the close-ups of the conversationalists would form the basis of a collage or, as Pongo preferred to call it, *un pastiche dans le film verité*.

'I've enjoyed being a governor of Beaumont... a right privilege serving under Lord Bartholomew.'

'What sort of guy is he, Sir Leslie?'

Sharp! Sharp as a razor. Keeps a firm grip. Never wastes time.'

'Who's this Warren Cooper?'

'Cultural attaché at your Embassy, Randolph. Here... try one of my pies.'

'Do you know Mr Jardine... our new governor?' said Susan.

'Our paths have crossed from time to time,' said Joseph Zháng.

'What is your professional opinion of him and his company?'

'Their take-overs have been most shrewd,' replied Joseph tactfully.

'Would I be right in thinking of Mr Jardine as a *Black Knight*?'

'The take-overs by Jardine International have often been hostile, Miss Wellborn, and I doubt Mr Jardine has been the *White Knight*.'

'What brings you here, old buddy? Not business I hope,' said Warren.

'I don't think you've met my wife. Fiona... meet Warren Cooper,' said Angus.

'Pleased to meet you, ma'am. I never knew Stewart had such a beautiful wife.'

'Is your wife not here, Mr Cooper?' said Fiona.

'Not married, ma'am. Women always wanted me to settle down... raise kids...'

'And you didn't want that?' said Fiona.

'Wouldn't fit in with my line of work, ma'am,' said Warren.

'When did your rifle go missing?' said Reg.

'No idea,' said Keith. 'I noticed it was gone when I closed the workshop.'

'You're quite sure it's gone?'

'Quite sure! Bill Tapp helped me do a thorough search.'

'Any idea who might have taken the rifle?'

'Not a clue. Who'd want it? It's just a replica. It doesn't work,' said Keith.

'I gather you had a spot of bother this morning, sir,' said Gorran.

'Yes. Some white mice escaped. Put the wind up the mother of a new boy.'

'Any idea how...'

'Last year it was locusts... my fault then... this year...' rambled Dr Millstream.

'Perhaps one of the new boys...' suggested Gorran.

'Somebody must have opened the cages but I have no idea who and why?'

'It's a small world, High Master,' said Elspeth.

'Yes. Indeed it is, Mrs Jardine.

'Please call me Myfanwy. It's my real name and Welsh like yours.'

'Have you been back to the Rhondda.... Myfanwy?'

'Not since my mother died, Llywelyn... May I call you Llywelyn?'

'Oh, I'm sorry. When did she die?'

'Just over three years ago,' said Myfanwy. 'Now that she's gone…'

In the small marquee, lunch ended with the ante cibum Grace and the players repaired to the pavilion leaving Dolly and her helpers to clear away. In the meadow, the old Exmoor Horned White-faced ram had severed the rope, butted open the gate and started to lead his ewes to pastures new. In the large marquee, tongues were being loosened by the free-flowing wine, film footage was being shot and everything in the High Master's garden was relatively rosy.

Abstracted from the cloying Myfanwy, the High Master of Beaumont Abbey wandered, lonely as a cloud over hills and dales, to the marquee entrance whence he saw not a host of golden daffodils but a small flock of sheep led by a fierce-looking ram. True to form, Llywelyn delegated the approaching problem to the Second Master. By the time Reg had responded to his leader's signal and made his way to the entrance, the leader of the flock had ambled into the marquee. 'Beaumont's getting quite a reputation,' quipped Llywelyn. 'Even the sheep are queuing up to get in.' By the time Reg had grasped the nature of the problem and decided to call upon Gorran Venton for assistance, several Horned Exmouth ewes had joined the ram in the marquee to mingle and graze à pied with the guests.

'What the… Well if this don't beat all,' said Randolph Jardine. 'Where did these critters come from?'

'Excuse me, Mr Jardine,' said Joseph Zhǎng, pointing to the ram. 'What is this… critter?'

'A sheep would be my guess,' said Randolph, 'but it sure looks like a goat. What d'you reckon?'

'In my language it is a *yáng*.'

'What's a *yáng* when it's on the ranch?' said Randolph

'A ruminant with horns,' said Joseph. 'I do not think this is a *língyáng* so it is either a *shānyáng* or a *miányáng*.'

'You've lost me, buddy.'

'A língyáng is a gazelle. A shānyáng is a mountain yáng… a goat. A miányáng is a cotton yáng… a sheep.'

'Excuse me, gentleman,' said Gorran, taking the ram by its horns and leading it out of the marquee, 'I need to get this fellow out of here.'

'By heck!' said Sir Leslie, 'That was a turn up for the book, were that. Reminds me of the time a cow joined us for lunch…'

Randolph and Joseph listened politely while Sir Leslie reminisced. When he finished, they shared his hearty laughter at the thought of Parker-Smythe ripping the rain-soaked canvas roof with his walking stick. As Gorran passed by with the last of the ewes, Joseph elicited from him that the animal was a sheep from the Beaumont farm.

'Never cared much for lamb or mutton,' said Sir Leslie. 'No… pork for me any day.'

'Ever been to Hong Kong or China, Sir Leslie?' asked Randolph.

'No, can't say I have… but Mrs Matthews is determined on a world cruise so…'

'Well here's a tip. Don't order lamb or pig,' said Randolph, 'unless you like goat or dog!'

'I'll bear that in mind. I might even become a vegetarian like my Edna.'

'If you'll pardon me, gentlemen,' said Randolph. 'My wife wants me to go watch the cricket. Adios.'

* * * * *

While Elspeth was rounding up her husband and leading him to the enclosure in front of the pavilion, Gorran was helping Tom Mitchell and his dog round up the sheep and lead them to the meadow. While Bill Tapp and a few boys were searching for the missing replica rifle, Keith Bradley was searching his mind trying to remember who had visited the workshops and wondering who might have taken it and why. While SMI Stanley Batters and PSI Edward Morton were enjoying their Matthews pork pies, courtesy of Dolly Brown, Ted poured Stan another beer and decided to get something off his chest.

'What did you make of that bloke this morning, Stan?'

'Perkins? Monty Perkins, d'you mean?' said SMI Batters.

'Monty. Yes, that's him,' said Ted.

'He's alright. Bit of a mischief maker by all accounts. Dead keen on the Navy.'

'It's like this see. When you went off to recky that helicopter landing, Monty bet me I couldn't tell his replica from the real .22 calibre training rifles in the armoury.'

'Course you could. His wouldn't fire, would it,' said Stan.

'That's what I said. Anyway, the thing is, I let him put his rifle in the armoury and I said I'd find it,' said Ted.

'You didn't, did you?'

'Yes I did... but before I could go and find it, you came back and marched us off to carry that yank's suitcases to the High Master's House,' said Ted. 'When we got back here, you and me started arguing about splitting that fiver tip and I forgot all about the rifle.'

'Where's it now?'

'I suppose Monty took it away with him,' said Ted. 'The thing is... I'm missing a box of cartridges.'

While parents and boys were returning from lunch in the town and settling down to watch the cricket from chairs around the boundary, Monty was scanning the field with his binoculars from the top of the clock tower

At lunch, the School had scored 53 for the loss of 4 wickets. When play recommenced at a quarter to two, anyone with any knowledge of cricket knew that Leonard Hammond and Rajendra Singh would be playing for a draw. The school was 397 runs behind and had no hope of winning. The players who had batted or were waiting to bat were seated on the pavilion veranda. The knowledgeable spectators were enjoying the sunshine and resigned to witnessing the dull game. SMI Batters and PSI Morton decided to forego the pleasure of a glass of beer in the sunshine in a discrete location to watch the cricket; they began a hunt in the armoury for a replica amongst forty rifles.

The seats in the enclosure in front of the pavilion were filled by the VIP guests. All the directors of the Board were present except Cyril Phillpott, the DES representative, who sent apologies for absence, and Lord Bartholomew, chairman of the Governors, who arrived as the fifth wicket fell. The High Master sat between Randolph Jardine and Elspeth. Louise sat next to Randolph. Behind them was Mary Cranborne, Reginald de Vere, Susan Wellborn and Joseph Zháng. Warren Cooper and Michael Liú joined Angus MacKay and Fiona for a stroll around the boundary.

'We're going to see some action, right?' said Randolph.

'Good Lord, no!' said Llywelyn. 'That's the last thing we want.'

'Why not?' said Randolph. 'I don't get it.'

'We're 382 runs behind…' said Llywelyn.

'So?'

'Stumps will be drawn at 5 o'clock which means they have about 46 overs to go.'

'So?' said Randolph again.

'Well the school would have to score 382 runs off 46 overs… um…'

'How many pitches in an over?' said Randolph. 'Six, right?'

'Yes, yes. Six balls in an over.'

'Hell, that's only… 1.38 runs per pitch, right?' said Randolph.

'I expect so… I'm not a mathematician, Mr Jardine.'

'What do you get for a home run?' asked Randolph.

'A home run?' queried Llywelyn.

'I think,' said Reg, 'Mr Jardine is thinking of a boundary, High Master.

'Right. A boundary,' said Randolph. 'What's a boundary fetch?'

'Four runs... or six if the ball goes over the boundary without touching the ground.'

'There you go,' said Randolph. 'Two home runs an over ought to do it.'

A lively discussion on the relative merits of cricket and baseball ensued and proved more interesting than the proceedings on the field. It came to an end with Randolph quoting Robin Williams, the American actor and comedian, *Cricket is basically baseball on valium*, Mary quoting George Bernard Shaw *Baseball has the great advantage over cricket of being sooner ended* and Elspeth dramatically reciting the words of the French actress Sarah Bernhardt *I do love cricket - it's so very English*.

* * * * *

'Good afternoon, sir,' said Monty. 'Enjoying the sunshine?'

'Ah, Mr Perkins,' said Arthur Matthews, shielding his eyes.

'Is this seat taken?' said Monty.

'No. No it isn't. Won't you join me?'

'Thank you, sir,' said Monty, lowering himself into the deckchair.

'If I remember rightly,' said Arthur, 'rowing and sailing were your sports at school.'

'And shooting,' said Monty.

'That's right. Rowing, sailing and shooting... in the Navy section of the CCF.'

'Are you a cricket fan, sir?'

'No. I quite enjoy watching but mountaineering and tennis are my pastimes,' said Arthur.

'Is it true that you and Dr Carratt once abseiled down the clock tower?'

'Yes, there is some truth in that rumour,' confessed Arthur. 'Why do you ask?'

'It's actually something I'd like to have done,' said Monty.

'Oh dear. We're in trouble now,' said Arthur.

'I beg your pardon, sir,' said Monty.

'The School... They've just lost another wicket. That's 93 for 6...'

'What's one wicket in a game compared to the loss of a career?' said Monty.

'Sorry... what was that you said?'

'Nothing,' said Monty. 'Just thinking out loud.'

'Right,' said Arthur. 'Dashed stupid... Hastings running himself out like that. What was he thinking?'

'Probably wasn't thinking at all,' said Monty. 'People do stupid things without thinking.'

When that sixth wicket fell, Michael Liú and Warren Cooper, standing behind Arthur and Monty's deckchairs, caught a snatch of the conversation. Michael recognised Monty and wondered what stupid things he might be planning for 7 o'clock that evening. Warren interrupted his thoughts by asking what *running himself out* meant. Michael failed to explain. Before they caught up with Angus and Fiona, Michael told Warren what Monty had said after the annual dinner. 'Seven this evening at the clock tower?' said Warren. 'Intriguing! O.K. if I tag along?'

Millbank, batting at number eight, held his ground and helped Hammond bring the total to 106 before he was out caught Kells, bowled Chance for 17. Lester, batting at number nine, managed to score 21 before he was out leg before wicket to Chance. Percy, like Jardine, was picked for his bowling but, unlike Jardine, was inclined to overestimate his skill with the bat.

It has to be said that Payton Ulysses Greatorex Percy, known as Pug for short, had all the outward and visible signs of the class batsman money could buy. His whites – he had several pairs of flannels, shirts, socks and boots - were immaculate. His caps – he had three – were in the Beaumont colours of red and black. His batting pads and gloves – he owned two pairs of each –

were as white as his shirts. His bat was new and unmarked.

When Pug eventually arrived at the crease – he had paused on the way to commiserate with the outgoing batsman – he commanded the umpire to give him *two legs*, carefully marked the ground then shielded his eyes as he scanned the horizon. Two more minutes were consumed as Pug commanded the bowler to stand at the crease holding the ball above his head while several Old Beaumontians rolled the heavy sight screen six inches to one side. Pug then adopted a textbook stance, the umpire called *play* and Chance ran to the wicket to deliver a medium-paced in-swinger that landed on a perfect length to reveal the lack in Percy of any inward and spiritual grace required of a batsman. The scoreboard moved from 143 for eight to 143 for nine. Pug was out first ball.

Rupert Jardine, batting at number eleven, walked silently to the square in the centre of the ground and only spoke when Leonard Hammond, the school captain, approached him.

'Bit of shambles, I'm afraid,' said Leonard.

'You can say that again,' said Rupert.

'Question is... do we play it safe or...'

'Is their bowling that good?' said Rupert, 'or are they conning us?'

'What do you mean?' said Leonard.

'What I mean is... the wicket must have dried out by now and shouldn't be much worse than the one they batted on yesterday when they scored 450.'

'You're saying...'

'I say we go for some runs,' said Rupert.

It was not an elegant textbook shot but Rupert couldn't care less. Chance's last ball of the over landed on the pavilion roof and the school was 149 for nine. Rupert smiled. Chance scowled. Elspeth clapped her delicate hands to her face. Randolph punched his right fist in the air and his left elbow in the High Master's ribs.

Johns had pinned the batsmen down with good length off-breaks bowled to tight field setting. Leonard took a leaf out of Rupert's book. Johns' first ball only touched the ground when it landed just inside the leg-side boundary and bounced over for four runs. The scoreboard registered 153 for nine. The spectators applauded the School passing the 150 mark and sat up. When stumps were drawn just after 5 p.m. the match was drawn with the School at 259 for 9, Leonard Hammond scoring 127 and Rupert Jardine 54.

Parents and boys hurried away to the boarding houses for tea with the housemasters and staff. At Wedgewood, E. Gordon Hamilton, an ardent fan of cricket, shook hands with Randolph and Elspeth and greeted Rupert unusually warmly.

'Fine performance this afternoon. You and Hammond set the school record for a last wicket stand, if I'm not mistaken,' said the Housemaster. 'Where did you learn to bat like that? Bit unorthodox but effective without a doubt.'

'I put a baseball bat in his hands as soon as he could walk,' said Randolph.

'Ah, that would explain it,' said the Housemaster.

'Ever play any baseball?'

'No. Cricket was my game. Have you tried your hand at cricket, Mr Jardine?'

'No. Baseball was my game all the way through college.'

'I wonder,' said Elspeth, 'if Sarah Bernhardt would have said *I do hate baseball - it's so very American.*'

* * * * *

SMI Batters and PSI Morton found the replica. They checked all the rifles in the armoury and by Murphy's Law – Stan and Ted called it Sod's Law – the replica was the last rifle they examined. Stan held the replica while Ted counted the rifles in the racks. 'Thirty-seven... thirty eight... thirty-nine. That's it Stan,' said

Ted. 'We're one short.' At Stan's insistence Ted counted again. As he did so, he had a thought.

'Stan! I think we ought to make sure that's a replica your holding.'

'How are *we* going to do that?' said Stan.

'Follow me,' said Ted, leading the way to the rifle range.

Arthur Matthews arrived at the clock tower just after half past six. Montague Perkins was there ready and waiting. Arthur led the way up the stone staircase and then the iron ladder, attached to the wall, to the doorway onto the roof of the tower. The arrow loops in the west wall let in shafts of sunlight, illuminating a few steps but casting the alcoves in dark shadow. Arthur pushed open the door and clambered out onto the flat roof carrying a coil of rope he had picked up from an alcove. Monty followed with a second abseil rope.

The bottom of the flagpole in the centre of the tower was bolted to a metal plate fixed to the roof. Four steel hawsers were attached to the pole at a point about eight feet from its base. The other end of the hawsers were hooked onto cast iron guys firmly bolted to the roof. Arthur attached one end of his rope to a guy and threw the other end of the rope over the edge of the tower. Monty used the same knot - a figure of eight on a bight - to attach his rope to another guy and threw the other end over the edge of the parapet.

Facing the end attached to the guy, Arthur stood astride his rope and grasped it in his left hand. Then with his right hand, he pulled the rope up from behind, around his right hip, across his chest, over his left shoulder, behind his back and once around his right arm. Monty did the same with his rope. Arthur then showed Monty how to play out the rope with his left hand and control his descent by his grip on the rope with his right hand.

'Well I'm blowed!' said Ted as they entered the rifle range. 'What's this box of ammo doing here?'

'Now what,' said Stan.

313

'You know I said I was missing a box of cartridges…'

'Found 'em then, have we?' said Stan.

'Looks like it,' said Ted opening the box. 'Hey up! There's two bullets missing.'

'Never mind that now,' said Stan. 'Let's see if this 'ere rifle will shoot.'

SMI Batters lifted the lever, slide the bolt back as far as possible and checked the breech. It was empty. Ted handed him a bullet. In what seemed one smooth action, Stan slid the .22 rimfire bullet into the breech, pushed home the bolt, dropped the lever, aimed at the target at the end of the gallery and squeezed the trigger.

Arthur went down first. Monty watched carefully then followed him to the bottom. When Monty had freed himself from the rope, he turned to face the teacher who had once scared him.

'Was that your first abseil?' said Arthur.

'First time,' lied Monty.

'Another go?'

'Definitely,' said Monty.

'How are your hands?' asked Arthur. 'I should have brought some gloves.'

'My hands are fine thanks.'

Permanent Staff Instructor Edward Morton was only too happy for Sergeant Major Instructor Stanley Batters to take charge of the situation. The two men marched back to the armoury where Ted, under the orders and eagle eye of Stan, locked the box of cartridges in the safe, placed the rifle into the end of the rack with the other thirty-nine and finally locked the armoury outer door. Then at the double, SMI Batters and PSI Morton marched to Wedgewood House in search of the Second Master.

They had just completed their third descent when Monty spotted Pongo and his film crew in the distance. Michael Liú, Warren Cooper, Angus MacKay and his wife Fiona were close behind. Coming from the opposite direction was the Second Master, Reginald de Vere, flanked by Stanley Batters and Edward Morton.

Monty dashed out of sight to follow Arthur up the stone steps to the top of the tower. This time on his way up, Monty stopped to pick up what he had hidden in the shadow of an alcove. Arthur was looking over the parapet when he heard Monty's footsteps on the roof. 'Looks like we've got some spectators down below,' said Arthur. 'Oh... there's that film crew again.' As he spoke, he turned to look at Monty. 'I wonder what... I say, what have you got there?'

Pongo's roving cameraman captured snatches of conversation on film.

'Who's up there?' said Warren.

'The man you can see is Mr Matthews, Head of Geography,' said Michael.

'Any idea what he's up to?'

'I think a former pupil is going to challenge him to an abseil race.'

'How did he get up there?' Warren asked.

'Under the archway... There's a door to some stone steps and a ladder...'

'You're quite sure?' said Reg.

'I'm afraid so,' said Stan. 'No doubt about it, sir.'

'D'you think he knows?' said Reg.

'Couldn't say, sir,' said Stan. 'Not for me to say, sir.'

'This is Angus MacKay, Second Master,' said Warren. 'Everything OK?'

Monty, standing feet apart with his back to the parapet on the east side of the tower, was holding the rifle diagonally across his chest. His left hand cradled the end of the stock and his right hand was wrapped around the grip. Arthur noticed Monty's fingers were outside the trigger guard.

'Is that thing loaded?'

'No, sir. Not yet,' said Monty.

'I take it you intend to load it,' said Arthur.

'That all depends, sir,' said Monty.

315

'On what?'

'On you, sir,' said Monty.

'On me?'

'Oh yes,' said Monty.

'How exactly?'

Arthur stood quite still while Monty reminded him of the time that Arthur had threatened to prevent him from leaving school at Easter.

'You really scared me, you know,' said Monty. 'I really believed you would have stopped me leaving school if we hadn't stopped playing up Barnacle Bill. You were bluffing, weren't you?'

'In a way, I suppose I was,' said Arthur. 'Anyway, it worked. You stopped making Toby Barnikel's life miserable. You probably worked harder and got a good exam…'

'Thanks to you, I left school at Easter… Before the exams. I should have stayed… Got O-levels and A-levels… I didn't so I didn't get into Dartmouth.'

'That was my fault, was it?' said Arthur.

'Of course it was. If you hadn't scared me and I had gone on playing up…'

'Now what?' said Arthur. 'Going to shoot me? Is that the plan?'

'What do you think I'm going to do?' said Monty, taking a bullet out of his pocket and loading the rifle.'

'If you're intending to put the fear of God in me, Mr Perkins, you'll be pleased to know you're succeeding. Now before anybody gets hurt, why don't you…'

'I'm not sure, Mr Cooper?' said Reg. 'I'm not sure everything is OK.'

'Mr Liú thinks Montague Perkins is up there with Mr Matthews,' said Warren. 'Does he know why?' said Reg.

'Something about an abseil race down the tower,' said Warren.

'That would explain those two ropes,' said Angus.

'Sir!' barked SMI Batters. 'Something you should know, sir.'

'What's that, sergeant,' said Warren.

'Mr Perkins may have a rifle and live ammunition up there, sir.'

The sound of the shot startled everyone including Monty. A replica rifle is not supposed to work. In the stunned silence that followed, the tower clock began to strike. Warren reached the iron ladder and was almost deafened by the noise of the bronze bell striking for the fifth time. The clock had finished striking by the time Angus had made his way up one of the ropes and was peeping over the parapet.

What happened next took less time than the tower clock had taken to strike seven. Angus dropped Arthur to the leaded roof of the tower and shielded him with his own body. Warren twisted the rifle from Monty's grasp but unfortunately sent him reeling over the parapet to fall six feet onto the archway roof below.

* * * * *

CHAPTER 26

"We must learn which ceremonies may be breached occasionally at our convenience and which ones may never be if we are to live pleasantly with our fellow man." Amy Vanderbilt

Speech Weekend - Sunday

The third and last day of Speech Weekend was to be one of pomp and circumstance. For all but a few, it began appropriately with morning service at 9:30 a.m. in the Chapel. The boys wore their Sunday best. Academic hoods added a dash of colour to the black gowns and dark suits of the staff. The colourful dresses and hats of the boys' mothers more than compensated for the sober attire of their fathers. If there had been awards for hats, the judge would have pinned a red rosette on the filly Elspeth Jardine for first place. The magnificent creation on her head put two mothers, seated in the row behind her, literally and metaphorically in the shade and did not go unnoticed by Pongo and his film crew.

Mary Cranborne BA was, as usual, in the niche furthest from the organ and nearest to the chancel. She was accompanied. for the first but not last time, by Susan Wellborn BA and Abigail Rusbridge LLB. And for the first but not last time, each woman was wearing the academic black gown and colourful hood to which she was entitled. Their academicals went unnoticed by the High Master and the Reverend Dr Fiddle but not by the Second Master, the rest of the staff or by Radulph Palfreyman and his film crew.

With the voices of the choir and the sound of the Harrison and Harrison pipe organ still ringing in his ears, Dr Fiddle placed his polished reading spectacles on his nose and, from the vantage point of the pulpit, cast his unfocussed eyes over the blur of the congregation. 'In the name of the Father, the Son and the Holy Ghost. Amen,' the chaplain intoned. 'Today we celebrate the

Nativity of St. John the Baptist.' He paused as his brain tried to make sense of a large fuzzy disc of bright yellow light hovering over the heads of some of his flock. When he lifted his spectacles onto his forehead, the top of Elspeth's hat focussed in his eyes but not his brain. Dr Fiddle shook his head, dropped his spectacles back onto his nose and turned to his text from Isaiah chapter 49 verse 4. 'I have laboured in vain; I have spent my strength for nothing at all. Yet what is due me is in the Lord's hand, and my reward is with my God.'

Daydreaming is an acquired skill. Reginald de Vere had honed it to perfection in his youth during school physics lessons; so to the casual observer, Reg was wide awake and attending to the sermon. His eyes were wide open but unseeing and his ears were closed and deaf to the world. His mind drifted. Why were Mary, Susan and Abigail wearing academic gowns and hoods? Were they entitled? Mary certainly was. What about Susan? Ah yes. A Cape Town University graduate. Abigail? Where did she graduate? What was her degree? 'I have spent my strength,' Dr Fiddle said quietly, then boomed, '*for nothing at all!*' Reg blinked, closed his ears and turned to his reverie of the Saturday evening.

When he saw Angus MacKay disappear behind the parapet, he had followed SMI Batters and PSI Morton up the staircase and ladder onto the roof where Warren Cooper, holding the missing rifle, was looking over the parapet, on the east side of the tower, at a body sprawled face down on the sloping roof over the archway.

He had called over the parapet on the west side of the tower to Michael Liú for help while Ted relieved Warren of the rifle and Stan helped Angus with the ropes. He had seen Michael examine the body on the sloping roof. He had watched Angus and Stan rig a harness and lower the body to the ground. He had seen Michael depart with the body in a private ambulance to a private cottage hospital.

When the ambulance had departed, he had ushered everyone back to his cottage for medicinal brandies and a debriefing. He had heard Warren agree that Monty seemed genuinely surprised when the rifle went off. He had persuaded Stan and Ted that Monty had picked up the real rifle by accident, thinking it was the replica. He had heard Angus support Warren's account that the fall over the east parapet was an accident. '...*and my reward is with my God*,' boomed Dr Fiddle. Reg ended his reverie and returned to the present. 'In the name of the Father, the Son and the Holy Ghost, Amen.'

* * * * *

The parapet on the west face of the clock tower is forty-five feet up above the paved courtyard. It is a matter of statistical record that a human being falling thirty or more feet onto a hard, flat surface will most probably die. There have been exceptions to the rule; people have fallen much farther and survived; people have slipped on a banana skin and expired. Montague Perkins had fallen six feet onto a sloping roof.

'Good morning,' said Michael Liú, addressing Gorran and Nathaniel. 'I'm Dr Liú.'

'Good morning, doctor,' said Gorran. 'I'm Gorran Venton and this is Dr...'

'Fitzorme,' said Nathaniel. 'We were at school with Monty.'

'Ah, yes. I recognise you now. I saw you at the Old Beaumontians dinner,' said Michael.

'Were you a guest?' asked Nathaniel.

'No,' said Michael. 'I'm an Old Beaumontian...'

'Of course! Sorry! You're our representative director on the Board of Governors,' said Gorran. 'Do you practice here?'

'I'm one of the consultants,' said Michael. 'What about you Dr Fitzorme?'

'Oh, I'm not a medic,' said Nathaniel. 'I'm a PhD chemist... you might say a proper doctor instead of a real one like yourself, Dr Liú.'

'Actually, I'm a surgeon,' said Michael. 'So strictly speaking I'm Mr Liú.'

'Do you know what happened to Monty?' said Gorran.

'He fell off the clock tower onto the roof over the archway,' said Michael. 'The fall caused a minor head trauma, a nasal fracture and periorbital haematoma, an undisplaced, stable, transverse fracture of the scaphoid and an undisplaced fracture of the mandible that hopefully might not require maxillomandibular fixation.'

'In layman's terms…?' said Gorran.

'Mild concussion, broken nose, black eyes, broken wrist and a broken jaw that we may not have to wire shut,' said Michael. 'He was lucky to fall on his side and hit his face. If he had landed on his back…'

'May we see him?' said Gorran.

'He's sleeping now but if you follow me, you can take a look at him through the nurse's observation window.'

Meanwhile, SMI Batters borrowed a key from Ron Beech, the chief caretaker, and put the replica rifle back on a workbench in the Technical Department for Bill Tapp and Keith Watson to discover and puzzle over. When Stan returned the key, he thanked Ron but never told him why he had wanted it. PSI Morton reconciled his inventory and accounted for the ammunition missing from the box of cartridges; he recorded SMI Batters as having carried out a demonstration on the rifle range for visitors. Thereafter, on the insistence of the Second Master, as far as Stan and Ted were concerned the circumstance involving a rifle, the clock tower and an Old Beaumontian never occurred.

* * * * *

The pomp of the third day of Speech Weekend carried over from the Chapel to the four Houses where parents mingled with staff to imbibe coffee, nibble biscuits and discuss the future of their boys who were, by mutual agreement, *in absentia*. Pongo and his crew distributed the hour evenly between Armstrong, Burdett,

Gower and Wedgwood to garner more conversational tit-bits and close-ups.

'Your son has flair, Mr Singh,' said David Peters, Housemaster of Armstrong.'

'Oh my goodness, what is it he has been doing now?'

'He wrote to universities for their prospectus…'

'Was he not to be doing this?' said Mr Singh.

'No, no. That is what he was told to do. However…'

'He did something wrong? He was not getting prospectuses?'

'Not at all. He got his prospectuses long before anybody else in the school.'

'How was he doing this?' asked Mr Singh.

'Your son signed himself *His Royal Highness Prince* Rajendra Singh.'

'I'm not sure I follow, Mrs Shum-Williams,' said the Housemaster of Gower.

'You probably think it's too early to be fussing over Dylan's future.'

'Not at all. Your concern is commendable… most commendable.'

'I'm sure you've noticed that my son has very slender fingers,' she said.

'Ah, yes… Slender fingers,' said Alan Radford.

'When he is at home he does the most delicate needle-point with silks.'

'Ah, yes… Point lace with silks,' mumbled Alan.

'So you see, I want to be sure he is taking all the right subjects…'

'All the right subjects…' repeated Alan. 'Mrs Shum-Williams, The Lower Thirds take a broad range of subjects including craft but alas not needle point...'

'You're missing the point, Mr Radford,' snapped the little Welsh dragon from beneath her large Cossack hat. 'With his delicate fingers Dylan will be a brain surgeon, mark my words. So we must be quite sure he gets into Oxford with the top grades of course…'

'With the top grades,' said Alan. 'Ah, well... you see Mrs Shum-Williams... It is rather early days... Dylan is only in his third term with us.'

Louise, the High Master's wife, could not resist inviting the three members of the BALI club back to her sunroom for coffee. She knew they were fully qualified and entitled but she was curious to know why they decided to wear an academic gown and hood to Chapel. She herself took a First in PPE at Oxford but it had never occurred to her to wear her academicals to the morning service.

'I think it was Susan's idea,' said Mary.

'Yes,' said Abigail. 'Susan suggested it.'

'Guilty as charged,' said Susan. 'Although *guilty* doesn't sound quite right.'

'So what gave you the idea, Susan?' said Louise.

'Well, I just thought... We *are* graduates. We *are* members of staff. Why not?'

'Why not!' said Louise. 'Perhaps I'll join you at the next service out of respect for Sarah Emily Davies.'

'Sorry!' said Susan. 'Who's that?'

'She founded Girton College in 1869... The first college in Britain for women.'

'The amazing thing is,' said Abigail, 'before 1940, Girton College was not allowed to award full Cambridge University degrees to women.'

'She was a most remarkable woman... Oh, that sounds like my husband... Excuse me a moment... Please help yourself to more coffee and biscuits.'

The High Master closed the outer door and dropped his furled umbrella into the hollow elephant's foot presented to his predecessor by a Maharaja with an unpronounceable name from some Indian Province with a easily forgettable name. Even though the sun was shining in a fairly cloudless sky and the weather forecast was good, Llywelyn always carried his umbrella to the Chapel on Speech Weekend to be on the safe side. Though he disliked the umbrella stand, Llywelyn kept it in the hope of preventing the demise of another elephant by a bullet from a trigger-happy Maharaja wishing to send his son to Beaumont Abbey bearing the gift of another foot or some other segment of a pachyderm.

'Did you notice your secretary, bursar and assistant bursar at the service this morning?'

'No my dear, I can't say that I did,' replied Llywelyn.

'I thought not,' said Louise. 'They're in the sunroom now… Come and say hello.'

'I'll just take off…'

'No, leave your gown and hood on for now,' said Louise.

'Ah there you are. Good morning ladies,' said Llywelyn. 'Lovely morning.'

'Good morning, High Master,' chorused Mary, Susan and Abigail.

'We were just discussing academic gowns and hoods,' said Louise. 'Any thoughts?'

'Apropos of what?' said Llywelyn.

'I suppose,' said Susan, 'with regard to who should wear them and when?'

'The *who* is straightforward,' said Llywelyn. 'Bona fide graduates.'

'What about *when*?' said Mary.

'The *when* is not so straightforward,' said Llywelyn. 'There was a time when everybody wore a gown… schoolteachers, university lecturers and professors…'

'If they were graduates,' interrupted Susan.

'Yes. Yes, they had to be graduates. When I was at school all my teachers wore gowns.'

'What about *now*?' said Abigail. 'Do all the staff at Beaumont wear gowns to class?'

'They ought to,' said Llywelyn warily.

'I believe, High Master, you allow the science staff to wear laboratory coats,' said Mary.

'Oh yes. Of course. I'd forgotten that.'

'So the staff wear gowns when they are teaching and don hoods for formal occasions like Sunday chapel, prize giving, etc.?' said Susan.

'Yes. Quite right,' said Llywelyn.

'Why?' asked Susan bluntly.

'Why? Tradition, Miss Wellborn,' said Llywelyn slightly taken aback.

'Is *tradition* the reason only men at Beaumont wear academicals?' asked Susan.

'Well, I suppose so... yes,' said Llywelyn reluctantly.

'And *tradition* prevents Beaumont opening its gates to girls as well as boys?'

'Tradition and...' hesitated Llywelyn, 'possibly a condition of our charter.'

'If I may be so bold, High Master,' said Abigail. 'It's simply tradition. There are no legalities preventing Beaumont taking in girls as well as boys.'

'Oh dear, look at the time,' said Louise. 'You must excuse us, ladies. Perhaps we may continue this discussion some other day.'

Mary gathered the cups and saucers onto a tray then joined the others in the hallway. Susan was looking at the umbrella stand and listening to Louise explain why it was there. When Abigail asked, Louise confessed she would have preferred something inorganic. Mary shuddered, saying she would not give such a thing houseroom, but then asked Susan what she thought of it.

'I notice it has five toes, so it was the front foot of an Indian elephant. If it had four toes, it could be the back foot of an Indian Elephant or the front foot of an African elephant.'

'Don't you think it's cruel... killing animals?' said Mary.

'I wouldn't kill for sport,' said Susan. 'And I probably wouldn't eat chicken if I had to wring the bird's neck myself...'

'But shooting an elephant... to make an umbrella stand... It's horrible,' said Mary.

'Perhaps they didn't shoot this elephant for his foot. There might be a three-legged pachyderm wandering around India,' said Susan with a wicked smile on her face.

'What a horrid thought,' said Mary. 'I must go. Thank you for the coffee Louise.'

'Susan,' said Louise when Mary and Abigail had left, 'Do you think Beaumont should become co-educational?'

'Yes I do. It would be very good for business.'

'We'd need to build a house for the girls. That would take time and money.'

'I think Mrs Jardine would help with the money,' said Susan. 'As for time... We could begin this September with day girls.'

'Isn't it a bit late in the term to...'

'We could take local girls who have passed Common Entrance but not gained places in an independent school,' said Susan.

'That's an idea,' said Louise. 'I'll work on my husband so this becomes *his* idea. Oh, by the way, he wondered who invited Major and Mrs MacKay to Speech Weekend. I told him they were your guests. Was I right?' Susan nodded.

* * * * *

Prize Giving ought to be the climax of Speech Weekend. In the not too distant future the High Master would hope to hold the event in the new Jardine-sponsored Concert & Sports Hall. This year, as in past years, prizes would be given in the Ambassador Rex Cinema and Theatre. Pomp in such a circumstance is always difficult but not impossible.

Reginald de Vere never wasted time on things he could do nothing about. He could not alter the seats in the Ambassador but he could decide who sat in them. The pupils would sit in the stalls or arena. The prize winners would occupy the parterre, the stalls immediately in front of the orchestra pit, to give them easy access to the stage. The VIP guests and visitors not required on stage would be in the state boxes. Staff would occupy the sections of the dress circle nearest the stage to have a clear view of the pupils in the arena. Parents and other visitors would be ushered into the rear dress circle and the upper balconies. This year the film crew would disrupt the routine seating plan but only slightly.

Although Reg could do nothing about the seats themselves he could always do something about the apron and the stage behind the proscenium arch with the help of Beaumont ancillary staff and Ambassador technicians. They placed large floral displays on either side of the apron to hide much of the arch and a large floral display in front of the lectern, stage left, to hide the legs of any speaker standing behind it. They hung curtains to hide the wings and rear of the stage and, unfortunately, to muffle Peter Morrison's choir.

At the front of the stage, a baize cloth covered the legs of three trestle tables and those of the dignitaries seated behind on high back chairs. On the table in front of the Second Master's chair was the auctioneer's walnut gavel and block of Reg's great-grandfather. Also on the table were silver trays bearing glasses and jugs ready for iced water. A tiered platform behind the table accommodated Peter Morrison's unaccompanied choir. A cloth-covered table, stage right, bore the weight of a stack of books, silver cups and statuettes.

During his quick sandwich lunch, Reg thought over his arrangements and wondered if he had been wise to let Carroll Ffynch, Head of Art, strategically place a video camera to project a close up of each prize-winner and Elspeth Jardine onto screens to the left and right of the proscenium arch. Reg also wondered if he should have allowed Radulph Palfreyman to place cameramen in the wings and balconies and let one loose in the arena.

* * * * *

'How are you feeling, Monty?' said Gorran.

'I've felt better,' croaked Monty.

'What were you playing at?' said Nathaniel. 'You could have been killed.'

'Could have been worse,' said Monty.

'How?' said Gorran.

'I could have shot Arthur Matthews.'

'Shot 'Mad' Arthur?' said Nathaniel. 'What with?'

'A .22 rifle.'

Propped up in the hospital bed, Monty looked and felt a wreck. His face was black and blue. His left arm was in a plaster from just below the elbow all the way up to and including his thumb. He was having difficulty talking because inside his mouth the teeth in his lower left jaw were wired to keep the hairline fracture stable. The bruising down his left side and leg was hidden from view under his hospital gown and bedclothes.

'I thought the rifle was a replica that wouldn't fire,' said Monty. 'I just wanted to frighten Matthews the way he'd frightened me.'

'You're an absolute ass, Monty,' said Gorran.

'What about all that other stuff you wanted us to do?' said Nathaniel.

'I just wanted to have a bit of fun… No, I suppose I wanted to get back at them.'

'Now look at you, you twit,' said Gorran. 'Soft foods for at least three months.'

'And that hand is going to be in a plaster for three months as well,' said Nathaniel.

'Lucky I'm right handed then,' said Monty. 'Anyway, chaps, thanks for coming to see me and for all you did.'

'What do you mean?' said Nathaniel.

'Well that explosion for a start, Stinkey,' said Monty. 'Brilliant!'

'But Monty, I…'

'Then those sheep getting into the marquee, Scrapper. First class job,' said Monty.

'Look here, Monty,' said Gorran. 'About those sheep…'

'If Pongo and Nibs do half as good a job at Prize Giving this afternoon…'

'Look… We'd better go, Monty. You need rest. We'll see you later,' said Nathaniel.

* * * * *

The serious suits and tasteful dresses eyed one another from their state boxes. The academic gowns and hoods in the side dress circle and the sober suits and colourful dresses in the rear dress circle and lower balcony eyed the Sunday bests in the arena. The assorted attire of the Old Beaumontians in the upper balcony eyed everyone below.

At twenty-six minutes past two, the Dolby surround sound at the Ambassador drowned any conversations with the Academic March (Promootsiomarssi), composed by Jean Sibelius and performed by the Helsinki Philharmonic Orchestra. The procession, led by the Second Master, entered through a door at the rear of the theatre and made its way slowly and solemnly down the left aisle, up the steps and onto the stage. Reg led the way and was followed by Elspeth Jardine, Sir Leslie Matthews, Lord Crispin Bartholomew, Randolph Jardine, the High Master and Mary Cranborne in that order.

As soon as the final chord had died away, the dignitaries took their seats. Ten seconds later, at exactly two-thirty, Reg struck the walnut block three times with his walnut gavel. Moments later there was a rumbling sound from above. Elspeth knew that sound. Randolph did not, so he looked up in surprise. Slowly but surely the heavy safety curtain unfurled and after what seemed

329

an age, finally divided the stage from the house. When the curtain touched down, a group of Old Beaumontians in the upper balcony cheered before chanting *Why are we waiting* to the tune of *O Come All Ye Faithful*. When the curtain began its ascent, their chanting gave way to a round of applause.

'What the…'

'No need for panic, Randolph,' said Lord Bartholomew. 'They are probably following the Occupational Safety and Health regulations to check the iron can fully descend in thirty seconds.'

'The iron?' said Randolph.

'That's the British theatrical name for the fire safety curtain.'

'A fire curtain?' said Randolph. 'For whose safety… or shouldn't I ask?'

'Since a fire is most likely to break out back stage, I imagine it's to protect the audience.'

'Let me get this straight,' said Randolph. 'If a fire breaks out… we'll be toast, right?'

'I fear as much,' said Lord Bartholomew. 'The management strive to protect the paying customers and avoid a law suit. If any actors are, as you put it, toasted… I suppose theatre management might see that as a saving in wages.'

'You cannot be serious,' said Randolph.

'No. Just my little whimsy, dear boy. The relatives of any toasted actor are the more likely people to sue… Ah, I believe we are ready to start.'

Lord Bartholomew opened the proceedings by welcoming everyone. He paid special attention to the guests of honour and took care to express, on behalf of himself and Beaumont Abbey, his gratitude to Sir Leslie Matthews for his long service as a member of the governing board of directors. Then he called upon the High Master to deliver his customary address.

Dr Llywelyn Pugh-Jones echoed the Chairman's welcome and re-iterated his thanks to Sir Leslie. Then he reported the departure of Mr Billington from the History

Department, Mr Osgood from Biology and two assistants from the Language Department. Then he read the names of those pupils awarded Oxford and Cambridge scholarships, pausing after each one for the applause, led by the proud parents, to die down. Then he touched at length upon various aspects of the past year before focussing upon the immediate future.

'I am delighted to report not only that Mr Randolph Jardine will be joining the governing board of directors but also that Jardine International will be sponsoring the new concert and sports hall. Dr Michael Liú has agreed to take charge of fund raising for the project. He will look to the Old Beaumontians for their support and he will welcome any contribution however small from any quarter. Without further ado, I call upon Mrs Jardine who has kindly agreed to distribute the prizes.'

It was during Lord Bartholomew's opening remarks that Reg noticed the jugs contained orange juice and not water as usual. During the High Master's lengthy address Sir Leslie Matthews, Randolph Jardine and his wife, Elspeth, imbibed freely of that elixir. When Llywelyn sat down, Reg stood up and turned his attention to Elspeth. As she began to stand up, he offered her his left arm while with his right hand he started to pull back her chair. She stumbled and grabbed his arm with both hands. She would have dragged a weaker man onto the floor. Never before had Reg been so grateful for the fitness bestowed upon him by his games of tennis. Elspeth Baker, the consummate actress, quickly regained her poise; she released her two-fisted grip on Reg's arm, placed her left hand delicately on his right arm and walked gracefully to the table laden with the prizes.

When the last prize had been handed out, Reg was relieved to escort Elspeth safely back to her seat. He sat beside her and, to assuage his dry mouth, poured himself a drink, one sip of which showed it to be gin and orange with the gin heavily outweighing the orange.

The choir, wearing long-sleeved white shirts and Beaumont ties, dark trousers, socks and black shoes, responsive to polish, entered from both wings. Peter Morrison, regal in his academicals, proceeded alone from the wings onto the apron as though he were leading a procession; he bowed to the audience, turned about face and surveyed his choir. Then he produced a baton from the folds of his gown like a stage magician producing a bunch of artificial flowers from his sleeve. According to James Jackson, the staff wit, Peter should also have popped up onto the stage through a trap door.

The house lights dimmed and as the choir began to sing, photographs and paintings of the two Rhondda Valleys appeared on the screen above their heads.

There's a valley called the Rhondda… where I was born so many years ago,

Though the world be there to wander… still I am proud to call it home.

In this valley called the Rhondda… I grew amid the laughter and the tears,

See the shadow growing longer… now is the autumn of my years.

When the house lights came back up, the roving camera captured tear-stained faces of Myfanwy Thomas, Llywelyn Pugh-Jones, Mrs Shum-Williams and many other Welsh parents in the audience. Sir Leslie Matthews was not from Wales, so his tears had more to do with the amount of orange juice he had consumed. Lord Bartholomew later claimed the red rims around his eyes were caused by pollen from the floral displays.

In response to a glowing introduction from Lord Bartholomew, Randolph rose somewhat unsteadily but quite dry-eyed from his seat to make his way carefully to the lectern which he then gripped in his large hands.

'Lord Bartholomew, Sir Matthews, Dr Pugh-Jones, ladies and gentlemen, students of Beaumont Abbey… It is an honour and a privilege to stand here…' he paused and tightened his grip on the lectern, 'before you today to… to give the…' He looked at a card he retrieved from his inside pocket, 'To give the Warrington Prescott lecture.'

He peered more closely at the card. 'I didn't know this but you all probably knew Warrington Prescott was a *Lunartick*... L-U-N-A-R-T-I-C-K... a member of the Lunar Society of Birmingham... same as Josiah Wedgwood... the guy you've named one of your houses after. These lunarticks used to meet... over two hundred years ago... on the night of the full moon... that's why they called themselves the Lunar Society. No street lights in those days so they went home by the light of the silvery moon... Pardon me,' hiccuped Randolph, putting his fist to his mouth then grabbing the edge of the lectern again. 'Getting home was easier and safer by moonlight, right? I guess they cancelled the meeting if it was a cloudy night.' He beamed at the dignitaries.

'Anyway, Prescott got friendly with old Josiah who wanted someone to build canals so he could ship his pottery by boat... too much stuff got broke by road haulage, I guess. So... old Warrington made it big time... supplying picks and shovels and the guys to dig those canals. Yes sir, Mister Prescott sure knew how to use people. So... I've called my lecture *Never give a sucker an even break*... Any of you see the movie with W. C. Fields?' He turned and beamed at the roving cameraman.

The Dolby system surrounded everybody with the London Philharmonic's rendering of Sir Edward Elgar's Pomp and Circumstance March Number 1 as the dignitaries followed the Second Master off the platform stage right, up the aisle and out into the foyer.

* * * * *

Arthur Matthews drove straight from the Ambassador to the private hospital. He was so focussed on his mission that he had forgotten to take off his gown and hood. On hearing the word *Perkins*, the nurse behind the reception desk looked up. On seeing the tousled mop of brown hair, the high furrowed forehead, the dense line of entangled eyebrows above those blue eyes staring at her from a face covered in hair, the nurse put her hand to her mouth and felt her heart miss a beat.

'Montague Perkins! Which room?' said Arthur, unaware of his effect upon the nurse.

'Oh! Mr Perkins. Yes. Sorry. You startled me. Um… Room 1E… Down the corridor… First door on your left… Sorry… You…' Arthur took off before she could ask his name.

Monty was dozing. His bed had been adjusted to elevate his feet nine inches above the base of his spine and to elevate the upper part of his body at an angle of 135 degrees with his legs. His plastered left arm was supported in a cradle suspended from the framework above the bed. Arthur was looking at Monty through the observation window when Michael Liú appeared at his side.

'Good afternoon Mr Matthews,' said Michael. 'How are you today?'

'In rather better shape than Perkins, I'd say.'

'He'll live,' said Michael. 'Couple of months… three at the outside, and he'll be as right as rain. How about you?'

'Fine. Just fine. Bruised a bit when that Scotsman landed on me. Gave me a shock.'

'The rifle going off?'

'What? Ah yes, that rifle,' said Arthur. 'I don't know who was scared most when it went off… me or Perkins… Then this Scotsman came out of nowhere…'

'We heard the shot,' said Michael, 'next thing… the American had disappeared and the Scot was shinning up the rope to the tower roof. I only started moving when the Second Master's head appeared over the parapet and called for me to help.'

'Is Perkins allowed visitors?'

'Certainly. Venton and Fitzorme were here earlier. Would you like to see him?'

'If that's alright,' said Arthur.

'I'm sure it is,' said Michael. 'He's awake and I think he saw you through the window.'

Arthur departed when supper arrived. Pongo and Nibs turned up when the soft food had slipped down and Monty had napped for an hour. Scrapper and Stinkey had warned them that they were in for a shock. When they saw the state Monty was in, they offered to come back some other time but Monty insisted they stay. He wanted to hear all about the prize giving and to see Pongo's film.

'Before we begin, let me give you a bit of background,' said Pongo.

'Is this going to take very long?' asked Monty.

'No. I'll keep it short and sweet,' said Pongo.

'KISS!' said Nibs.

'Precisely!' said Pongo.

'You two have lost me already,' said Monty.

'K-I-S-S,' said Nibs. 'Keep it simple stupid.'

'Do you mind?' said Pongo. 'Just shut up and listen.

Pongo explained at tedious length how he had been influenced by the Soviet cinema and Eisenstein's theory of *montage* being dialectical and originating in the collision of shots seen not one after the other but one on top of the other. 'Using *overtonal* or *associational montage*, a synthesis of the *metric*, *rhythmic* and *tonal*, this *mockumentary* provides an abstract and complex effect upon the audience,' said Pongo. 'What I am going to show you now, is a first *découpage*. If necessary, I'll add a sound track and commentary later.'

'*Mockumentary?*' said Monty.

'A mock documentary,' said Pongo. 'It's what we in the trade call the genre for parody and satire. Anyway, as I was saying…'

'What's this film called?' interrupted Monty.

'*Beaumont Abbey Bloopers*,' said Nibs. 'That's my suggestion.'

'I might have guessed,' said Monty, stifling a yawn. 'Can we get on with it.'

'You understand it's a first cut,' said Pongo. 'There's no sound track…'

'Yes. Yes. Let's see it.'

As Pongo watched, he played over in his mind possible music and sound effects. As Nibs watched, he outlined in his mind various voice-over possibilities. As Monty watched, he began to regret ever asking his former classmates to do what he thought they did for him; and he wondered what he would ever do with this mockumentary Pongo was making. When the scenes of the prize giving appeared, Nibs couldn't resist telling Monty how he had arranged for the safety screen to be lowered and how he had spiked the orange juice.

'You should've heard the Warrington Prescott speech, Monty,' said Nibs.

'Good was it?' said Monty.

'Offbeat, to put it mildly,' said Nibs. 'He as good as called Carnegie, Rockefeller and Vanderbilt unscrupulous crooks who exploited their workforce and built monopolies that drove competitors out of business, flaunted government regulations and had corrupt officials in their pockets. He…'

'Didn't have much time for the robber barons then?'

'On the contrary,' said Nibs, 'he said they were role models for the entrepreneur.'

'I'll bet he upset old Pugh-Jones,' said Monty.

'No doubt about that. He looked like he was having a heart attack.'

* * * * *

CHAPTER 27

"Be absolutely ruthless with paperwork and be prepared to throw quite a bit away. Be selective about what you keep as current action." Sir Allen John George Sheppard

* * * * *

When the London Philharmonic played, *sforzando*, the D-major chord, Peter Morrison muted the sound before anyone in the Ambassador Rex could hear the familiar but, in his opinion, highly overrated next section. That chord and the exit of the dignitaries signified the solemn end of Speech Weekend formalities. With guests, parents, staff and boys still making their way out of the auditorium, the fastidious Director of Music did not want the solemnity of the occasion disturbed by Old Beaumontians in the upper balcony singing *Land of Hope and Glory* in a reprise of the last night of the proms at the Albert Hall.

For some people like Reg, that D-major chord signified the start of the informalities. He had to take charge of the few uncollected prizes and collect his great-grandfather's block and gavel; he also had to dispose of the gin and orange before it could do any more harm. The Beaumont ancillary staff had to deal with the floral displays, the lectern, the baize cloth, trestle tables and chairs. Pongo's film crew had to take away their cameras, lighting and other paraphernalia. The Ambassador technicians had to deal with their microphones and sundry equipment. Carroll Ffynch had to collect his slides from the projectionist and Peter Morrison his records from the sound engineer.

'May we be of any assistance, Reg?' said Peter.

'No, thanks all the same. We'll cope.'

'How d'you think it went?' said Carroll.

'Pretty much as planned,' said Reg, ignoring the safety curtain or the gin and orange.

'What did you think of the images of the Rhondda Valleys?'

'Sorry, Carroll… I had my back to the screen,' said Reg. 'Peter…?'

'Sorry, old boy. My mind was focussed on the choir struggling against those confounded curtains… Better be off… Want a lift back to Beaumont, Carroll?'

'Yes thanks… See you later, Reg.'

* * * * *

In one corner of the sunroom there was a two-seater settee and two single easy chairs. The wicker furniture was well padded with fitted cushions whose floral designs had been spared the bleaching effect of the sunshine, thanks to the Venetian blinds that Louise lowered whenever necessary.

Randolph and Elspeth sat side-by-side and hand-in-hand on the settee. Both had that dreamy look often resulting from one glass of wine too many. Llywelyn sat in one of the single chairs. He had the grey look of someone with a heart condition dissolving a nitro-glycerine capsule under his tongue and wishing he had placed it there sooner. Louise sat in the other single chair. She had the look of a healthy trainee nurse worrying about three patients rashly placed in her care. 'Well… I expect you're all glad that's over,' she said.

No effect. Or to be more precise, Louise failed to elicit a verbal response from anyone. Randolph and Elspeth simply gave each other an inebriate's silly smile. Llywelyn simply scowled at his watch while checking his pulse. She remembered the words of Jean de la Bruyère, the 17th century French moralist and satirist: *The great gift of conversation lies less in displaying it ourselves than in drawing it out of others.* Louise tried again.

'What's your daughter's name, Elspeth?'

'Daphne,' said Elspeth.

'Lovely,' said Louise.

'Daphne… Sister of Artemis... chased by Apollo and transformed into the sacred laurel whose leaves were used to crown the victors of games,' said Llywelyn.

'I didn't know that,' said Elspeth. 'We chose Daphne... because that was his wife's name... A. A. Milne... You know... Wrote Winnie-the-Pooh stories.'

'Oh! Yes. Yes of course,' said Louise. 'And what about your son, Rupert... Does his name have anything to do with the bear the English artist, Mary Tourtel, created?'

'Goodness me, no!' giggled Elspeth. 'Rupert was Randolph's father's name.'

'Daily Express... 1920... November I think,' said Llywelyn.

'What's that, Llew?' said Louise.

'Rupert Bear... Comic strip... Started in the Daily Express about seventy years ago. Best friend was Bill Badger... had a Rupert Bear Annual for Christmas when I was six.'

'What's this about Daphne?' said Randolph.

'Your daughter... name comes from a Greek word meaning laurel,' said Llywelyn.

'Well I'll be... Did you know that, honey?'

'You'll find laurel wreaths on lots of coins and medals,' said Llywelyn.

Louise remembered more words of Jean de la Bruyère: *He who leaves your company pleased with himself and his own cleverness is perfectly well pleased with you.*

'Daphne is a lovely name,' said Louise. 'How old is Daphne?'

'She'll be fifteen next month,' said Elspeth.

'Do you think she would like to come to school here at Beaumont?' asked Louise.

'I'm not sure,' said Elspeth, 'but *we'd* like her to come here, *wouldn't we*, Randolph?'

'She'd go wild,' said Randolph. 'Just one girl and all those boys.'

'Did I ask you before?' said Elspeth. 'Will Beaumont ever take girls?'

'Speaker at this year's Head Masters' Conference claimed it's what parents want. A serious demand apparently. Death knoll of single-sex education,' mumbled Llywelyn.

'Actually,' said Louise, 'my husband was talking about that the other day… weren't you Llew?'

'Was I?'

'Yes. Remember… you talked about the cost of building a boarding house for girls.'

'Did I?'

'Yes. You said it would cost a lot of money so you would need sponsors.'

'How much money?' said Elspeth.

'I've no idea. I haven't much of a head for figures,' lied Louise who had graduated in PPE - politics, philosophy and economics. 'Perhaps you'd have some idea, Randolph.'

'What are we talking about?' Randolph asked himself out loud. 'Ninety girls, same as the boys in Wedgwood, right. 4 girls to a bedroom in two bunk beds.'

'Those would be for main school,' said Llywelyn. 'Sixth form boarders would be two to a study-bedroom.'

'OK! How many sixth formers and how many main school?' said Randolph still talking to himself out loud. 'Let's say forty-six to forty-four. OK! So that's twenty-three study bedrooms and eleven bunk bedrooms, right? That's thirty-four rooms, OK?'

'You'd want at least one room as the sick bay,' said Louise.

'Right! Thirty-five rooms. How many closets?'

'Wardrobes. They call them wardrobes here, Randolph,' said Elspeth.

Randolph continued in the same vein, occasionally interrupting himself to quiz Llywelyn and Louise on furnishings, bathrooms and on the number of dayrooms where main school girls would have desks and do prep. Elspeth listened to her husband with admiration. Louise divided her attention between Randolph and Llywelyn who, to her relief, was beginning to regain his normal colour. At some point Randolph began using a pocket calculator. After a few more questions and calculations, he was ready.

'A million five ought to do it,' said Randolph, 'so I'd say Two million to be safe.'

'Is that two million dollars, honey?' said Elspeth.

'Pounds. British pounds, honey,' said Randolph.

'What's that in dollars?'

'Around three million five,' said Randolph.

'Three and a half million dollars,' said Elspeth.

'Tops!' said Randolph. 'I reckon we'd do it for two and a half million.'

'Wonderful!' said Elspeth. 'When can we start?'

'Excuse me, Myfanwy,' said Llywelyn, 'Am I to understand you're going to sponsor…'

'I'm going to pay for it,' said Elspeth. 'The whole thing.'

'And we're going to call it *Baker House*, right?' said Randolph.

It was Dr Samuel Johnson who said *the happiest conversation is that of which nothing is distinctly remembered but a general effect of pleasing impression.* That was true of their conversation over a supper. Llywelyn and Myfanwy told each other how much they enjoyed Peter Morrison's choir. Louise listened while Randolph enthused over the way Carnegie built an empire by taking over all the coal, iron ore and other companies supplying the materials his Pennsylvania plant needed to make steel. 'Yes sir. Andy knew how to cut costs by eliminating the middlemen.' Louise recalled her professor referring to Andrew Carnegie's business tactic as *vertical integration.*

* * * * *

What does Reginald de Vere have in common with Professor Sir George Sayers Bain, former Vice-Chancellor of Queen's University Belfast and Principal of the London Business School? He tries to handle a piece of paper only once. Reg threw his Speech Weekend file into the waste basket and placed the file

341

for next year into the metal cabinet. One minute later he entered Mary's office. What does Dr Llywelyn Pugh-Jones have in common with Reg, Mary and Susan? He tries to keep his desk free of clutter. To be more accurate, Mary tries to keep the High Master's desk free of clutter simply by feeding him just one problem at a time.

'Good morning, Mary,' said Reg. 'Did you enjoy Speech Weekend?'

'Yes I did.'

'Anything in particular?' said Reg.

'Oh, yes. The choir. I found the song very moving,' said Mary, tactfully not mentioning the tears running down the High Master's cheeks.

'Indeed,' said Reg, tactfully not mentioning the tears running down Elspeth Jardine's cheeks.

'Ah, here's Susan,' said Mary. 'Let's go in.'

Llywelyn referred to the paper Mary and Susan had prepared and announced *his* plans for Beaumont to become co-educational. Reg was the only one taken completely by surprise.

Contact potential day-girls - passed Common Entrance not accepted as boarders at other independent schools.

Start with day-girls - this September.

Inform parents overseas - possible opportunity for their daughters.

Board sixth form girls with staff this September.

Contact British parents of boys at Beaumont and inform them of opportunity to board daughters in one year's time.

Build new boarding house to be ready in one year's time.

Reg watched Llywelyn place the sheet of paper back underneath the glass paperweight on his desk. In the ensuing silence, the Second Master stared back at the Swedish glass seal pup and tried to marshal his thoughts. Had he been a fan of the Marx brothers, Reg might have recalled Groucho saying *behind every successful man is*

342

a woman; behind her is his wife. Had he been a fly on the wall, Reg would have known for certain that Elspeth, Louise, Mary and Susan were the forces behind Llywelyn's plans.

'When will you put your proposal before the Board of Directors, High Master?'

'I've already spoken to Lord Bartholomew... Very supportive,' said Llywelyn. *'Move with the times...* those were his words.'

'Would there be any legal obstacles to...'

'I telephoned Henry Trevanion after I'd spoken to Lord Bartholomew,' interrupted Llywelyn. 'He raised one or two points... but foresaw no legal problems.'

'Where's the money coming from?' asked Reg.

'Mrs Jardine,' said Llywelyn. 'She wants to pay for the new boarding house... *Baker House*, by the way. We'll call it *Baker House*. Elspeth Baker was her... um... her stage name. Charming lady. Welsh by birth you know... Charming lady.'

'Mr Jardine is behind you, of course, High Master,' said Reg. 'Anyone else?'

'Dr Liú, representing the Old Beaumontians on the Board, and Dr Drisdale, representing the parents. They are most enthusiastic,' said Llywelyn. 'for their daughters, d'you see.'

'Mr Trevanion?'

'I told you... I've just spoken to Henry. He's in favour.'

'Mr Cooper, Mr Hardcastle, Prof Frampton and Mr Phillpott?' queried Reg.

'As the DES representative,' said Llywelyn, 'Phillpott has always been beating the co-educational drum and trying to persuade me to march to his tune. He'll support. Hardcastle? Earnest will go along with my plan... good for his bank.'

'The other two directors?'

'Strictly speaking they shouldn't matter... they'd be out-voted... but the Cultural Attaché will probably vote yes. They're keen on co-education in America I believe.'

'That leaves Professor Sir George Frampton…'

'Ah, yes. Hard to say… but Lord Bartholomew is going to have a word with him.'

'Ah, is he,' said Reg. 'In which case the Governing Board of Directors should be unanimously in favour. What about the staff? Any of them know of your plans?'

* * * * *

Reginald de Vere revealed his inquiring mind at a tender age; he studied ants. That is to say, he poked sticks into ant hills and gleefully watch the insects' feverish activity. When he was older he came to admire the insect society with no hierarchical organisation – no leader, president, chief executive, management, central authority or control. The colony's collective intelligence is just the sum of individual ants making simple decisions and, by random interactions with other ants, solving problems beyond the capability of any individual. Colin Harper could have told Reg that computer scientists had modelled complex problem solving software on the behaviour of ant colonies.

Reg also came to admire the ability of a worker ant to bear a burden many times its own weight. In many ways Beaumont Abbey operated like a colony of ants, especially in the days following Speech Weekend and preceding the Summer Holidays. The calm routine of the Michaelmas and Lent terms, and the weeks of Trinity leading to the examinations, was replaced by a frenzy of disparate activities leading to the long holiday.

There were reports to be written and, in a few cases, rewritten at the insistence of the Second Master. 'I cannot accept the comment you have written about young Braines,' said Reg to Keith Bradley. 'Writing that a boy is an incorrigible liar is unacceptable on two counts. You imply he *never* tells the truth and that we cannot correct him.'

There were books, teaching materials and supplies to be ordered for the new academic year. Dr Carratt often dined off the eccentricities of his suppliers.

'You're not going to believe this,' said Phil to his dinner guests. 'Two weeks ago I ordered eight tiny, fragile glass spirit burners. Last week they arrived *by courier*... each individually wrapped in tissue paper and buried in straw in the centre of a cardboard carton *the size of a tea chest*. Two were broken! Yesterday the replacements arrived *by post*... shoved *in an ordinary letter envelope* that had been through the franking machine. *Not a scratch on them!*'

There were sampler Sixth Form lessons to be given to occupy the idle hands and minds of Upper Fifths waiting for the examination results. Rather than allow these lessons to be persuasive showcases for under-subscribed subjects, Reg arranged for the boys to taste the compulsory lessons: Dr Humphrey Fiddle on Monotheistic Religions, Alan Radford on English Grammar and Quentin Waite on British History, beginning as always with the words of Edmund Burke - *Those who do not know history are destined to repeat it.*

There was next year's timetable to be finalised; a major task Reg undertook with Colin Harper's help on a computer. There were also many minor but time-consuming tasks to be performed, so the last thing Reg wanted was the added burden of preparing for co-education. He feared Henry Trevanion's *one or two points* would *not* be *in*significant.

'Ah, Reg,' said Phil Carratt, seeing the Second Master about to enter the Common Room. 'May I have a word?'

'Hello Phil...'

'In your office would be best I think,' said Phil, crossing the corridor to the door of Reg's office.

'What's on your mind?' said Reg, sitting down behind his desk.

'The Common Room for a start,' said Phil, pulling up a chair. 'I need your advice.'

'Somebody not signing the chits for their drinks?' said Reg.

'No. Nothing to do with drinks. It's about membership?'

'The last time membership cropped up,' said Reg, 'it was over Bertie Cockle covering for Peter Morrison away for a term with Hepatitis A.'

'That's right. Bertie wasn't a graduate so we had to have a staff meeting to let him into the Common Room,' said Phil. 'Well… this is a bit different … delicate, actually…'

'Delicate?' said Reg, raising an eyebrow.

'Yes. You see… It's about Mary Cranborne, Susan Wellborn and Abigail Rusbridge.'

'What about them?' said Reg.

'They're all graduates aren't they?' Phil said, nervously fiddling with his tie.

'Yes they are,' said Reg. 'What of it?'

'Are they permitted in the Common Room?'

'Why do you ask?' said Reg.

'They're in there now,' said Phil. 'One of them is sitting in Quentin's chair.'

'Ah!' said Reg. 'You're Common Room Chairman. What do you think?'

'Well… they're not *academic* staff…'

'But they are *staff*,' said Reg. 'They're on the Beaumont payroll.'

'So we should make them welcome, is that what you're saying?' said Phil.

'*Move with the times*… I think that's what the High Master is saying these days.'

'Let them in then… Is that it?'

'Unless you're going to tell them to stay out,' said Reg.

'Right!' said Phil. 'What about Quentin's chair?'

'Let's leave the barrister to plead his own case,' said Reg. 'Anything else?'

'I've heard a rumour Beaumont might take girls next term. Any truth in it?'

'If there is,' said Reg, 'you'll be the first to know.'

As Reg followed Phil into the Common Room, Falstaff's words in Henry IV Part One came to mind: *The better part of valour is discretion, in the which better part I have saved my life.* Mary, seated with her back to the door, did not see Reg sink into a chair in a far corner inconspicuously to observe the goings-on. And she was unaware of Phil's presence until he spoke.

'Ah... Ladies. Glad I've caught you together,' said Phil. 'It's my duty... as er... Common Room Chairman, to... er... to raise the matter of your subscriptions.'

'Subscriptions?' said Mary, turning her head and looking up at Phil.

'Yes. Common Room subscriptions. Each year each member puts thirty pounds into the Common Room fund,' said Phil.

'What for?' said Abigail.

'What for? Ah, yes... What for?' said Phil, racking his brains. 'Well... Ah, yes... Incidental expenses... Get well cards, flowers and fruit for... in the event of... illness,' he said, thinking of Peter Morrison and Hepatitis A.

'Does the High Master subscribe?' asked Abigail.

'No. No. Dr Pugh-Jones is not a member of the Common Room.

'I see,' said Abigail. 'So how many Common Room members are there now?'

'How many members? That would be... um... fifty-five male members,' said Phil.

'With all due respect, Dr Carratt,' said Abigail, 'but one thousand, six hundred and fifty pounds per year seems an inordinate sum for *incidental expenses.*'

'Sorry! Sorry, Mrs Rusbridge,' said Phil. 'I was forgetting newspapers and magazines.'

'What newspapers?' said Mary.

'The Guardian and the Telegraph,' said Phil. 'Oh, yes... the Times and the Educational Supplement.'

'And the magazines?' said Abigail. 'Which...'

'Oh yes, Which, Punch, National Geographic and New Scientist,' continued Phil. 'If you like, we could subscribe to Woman's Weekly… or perhaps not… I… er… that is…'

'So, Dr Carratt,' said Susan. 'How much do you want from each of us?'

'Oh, no… I'm not the Common Room Treasurer,' said Phil. 'No. No. Dear me no. I don't collect the subs.'

'Who does?' said Susan.

'That'll be…' said Phil looking at Abigail. 'Your husband, Mrs Rusbridge.'

'Geoffrey? Well, well! I'll have a word with him this evening,' said Abigail grimly.

As he hurried out of the room, Phil passed Quentin Waite MA (Oxon) LLM coming in to look for the Times crossword and his favourite armchair. Reg watched Quentin stop in the middle of the room and struggle to pull the left side of his academic gown back onto his shoulder. During this manoeuvre, Quentin appeared to be totally unaware that *his* armchair was already occupied and that the crossword, already partially completed, was in Mary's hands. As soon as the gown was hanging properly, Quentin turned on his heel and joined Reg in the far corner of the room.

'I see the Rubicon has been crossed, old boy,' whispered Quentin sitting down.

'The die has been cast,' said Reg. 'or *alea iacta est* as Suetonius remarked when Julius Caesar led his legion across the river into Northern Italy to begin his civil war against the Optimates and Gnaeus Pompeius Magnus – his former ally, Pompey the Great.'

'Next thing,' said Quentin, 'you'll be telling me to teach girls.'

'You saw the ladies sitting in our chairs?' said Reg.

'Even a blind man couldn't miss them,' said Quentin.

'A blind man?'

'Their perfume, Reg. Entirely different from your cologne.'

'Ah!' said Reg. 'So we've lost our favourite armchairs in cynics' corner.'

'Temporarily,' said Quentin.

'Isn't possession nine-tenths of the law?' asked Reg.

'Actually,' said Quentin, 'this old chestnut alludes to the notion that a person actually in possession of a property is presumed to be the rightful owner unless there is testimonial or documentary proof to the contrary.'

'So we make sure we're in our chairs first?' said Reg.

'Precisely! Bums on seats!'

* * * * *

Louise called the ninth meeting of the BALI club to order. Item 1 - no apologies for absence. Item 2 - minutes of eighth meeting unanimously approved without discussion. Item 3 - secretary had nothing to report. Item 4 - treasurer summarised the club's trading and finances.

Credit Subscriptions	$2,200.00
Debit petty cash	$200.00
Debit 1000 SGEM @ $0.95	$975.00
Credit 500 SGEM @ $2.10	$1,025.00
Cash Balance	$2,050.00

'I converted our initial one thousand one hundred pounds into two thousand two hundred dollars to keep it simple,' said Susan.

'It makes sense,' said Abigail, 'if we are going to trade in the American market.'

'It sounds a lot more as well,' giggled Celia. 'Like driving in France.'

'What are you talking about?' said Maureen.

'Kilometres instead of miles,' said Celia. 'Humphrey thinks eight kilometres abroad goes by a lot quicker than five miles in England.'

'Celia!' said Rosemary, wife of the Head of Physics, 'Eight kilometres and five miles are the same. It can only seem quicker if you drive faster in France.'

'I know,' said Celia, 'but I agree with my Humphrey...'

'Ladies. Do you mind,' said Louise. 'Susan. Please continue.'

'You'll notice that it cost us twenty-five dollars when we bought the shares *and* when we sold them. Actually we paid in pounds sterling but I've shown the fee in dollars.'

Item 5 - no unfinished business. Item 6 - education.

Maureen Carratt handed out a set of notes about *options*. 'These are contracts giving us the right but *not* the obligation to buy or sell shares. It's cheaper than buying or selling the shares themselves. For example, we could buy contracts for a *call* option on a share with a *strike price* of $20. If the option price is $0.05, a contract... for 100 shares... would cost $5.00 plus $25 trading fee. Ten contracts would cost $50.00 plus the trading fee. If the share price rose to $30, we could exercise our option and buy 1000 shares at $20 per share...'

'Excuse me, Maureen,' said Rosemary. 'That's twenty thousand dollars! We haven't...'

'Let me finish,' said Maureen. 'We sell them immediately at the market price of $30...'

'Before we bought them?' said Rosemary.

'Yes. Our broker would carry out the two transactions within minutes of each other so our account balance at the close of trading would show a profit of ten thousand dollars.'

'Actually,' said Susan, 'We wouldn't have to do that. The option price would have risen from $0.05 to about $10.00 so we'd sell our ten contracts and make the same sort of profit... ten thousand dollars.'

'What if the share price goes down?' said Rosemary.

'Options have an expiry date,' said Abigail. 'If the share price doesn't go up above our strike price and the option expires, we've lost our seventy-five dollars.'

The education item took up more time than usual in spite of Louise's efforts to keep the discussion under control. Not so slowly but quite surely, the members became saturated and confused by the difference between *calls* and *puts*, *American* and *European options, Exchange-traded (Listed)* and *Over-the-counter (OTC) options, strike price, expiration date*, etc. There was a general sigh of relief when Louise called the meeting to order, thanked Maureen for her presentation and moved on to item 7 - economic report from Abigail; this was as usual short, sharp and to the point - nothing unusual happening in the markets. Louise opened the discussion on item 8 - investments.

'I believe the policy of Jardine International is vertical integration.'

'What does that mean, Louise?' asked Gladys Dawson.

'Taking over all the companies it depends on for its raw materials,' said Louise.

'Ah,' said Abigail, ' that makes sense now.'

'What makes sense?' said Celia.

'This year's Warrington Prescott speech,' said Abigail. 'Our new director admiring Andrew Carnegie taking over the companies supplying his Pennsylvania steel plant.'

'SIGEM supplied Jardine International with silicon and germanium chips. Thanks to Janet, we bought shares in that company before it was taken over,' said Susan.

'My point is,' said Louise, 'we should be able to find other companies supplying Jardine International and…'

'Buy shares before they're taken over,' whooped Celia, clasping her hands together.

'The question is,' said Abigail, 'which ones?'

Susan told the meeting about her conversations with Joseph Zháng Ming. He thought the same as Louise; Jardine International was bent on vertical integration. Louise told the group Randolph Jardine had mentioned several companies and Susan said Mr Zháng had picked two of these: DCGeldisk Inc (DCG) and Optiklasemir Corporation (OKLM). Susan had asked Rosemary, a physics graduate, to explain what these two companies did. DCG made dichromate-gelatine hologram disks and OKLM made lasers, lenses and mirrors, all of which are essential components of bar-code scanners, DVD players, etc.

'Let's buy options on both,' said Celia cheerfully.

'That's not possible,' said Susan, 'Only OKLM is listed on the options exchange.'

'Could we buy those options?' said Celia.

'Yes we could,' Susan said hesitantly.

'I think,' said Louise, 'you'd better help us, Susan.'

'Alright then,' said Susan, taking a deep breath. 'We could buy contracts for a call option, expiring in October, on OKLM for a strike price of $25.'

'What was the share price at close today?' said Abigail.

'$15,' said Susan.

'What was the option price?'

'Fifteen cents,' said Susan.

'So ten contracts would cost us...' Abigail tapped the keys on her calculator, '$150 plus the transaction fee... say $25... one hundred and seventy five dollars.'

'Is that what we could lose?' said Gladys.

'Yes,' said Abigail.

'What do we stand to gain?' said Gladys.

'Let's keep it simple,' said Susan. 'If the share price went up by ten dollars to $25, the option price would go up by a similar amount... say $10. If we sold our contracts, we'd get back $1000 for each contract. Ten contracts would give us $10,000...'

'Less the transaction fee,' said Maureen.

'Yes but I don't think we'd worry about $25,' said Susan.

'So,' said Gladys, 'if we bought *twenty* contracts for... what? Three hundred and fifty...'

'Three hundred and twenty-five dollars,' said Abigail. 'One transaction fee of $25.'

'Alright... $325,' said Gladys. 'We could make...'

'Twenty thousand dollars,' chirped Celia. 'I could go to California.'

When Louise closed the meeting, the club had agreed to buy one thousand DCGeldisk Inc shares and forty call option contracts on Optiklasemir Corporation for a strike price of $25 with an expiration date of the 19th October. All the ladies wrote the details on their summary sheets:

Credit Subscriptions	$2,200.00
Debit petty cash	$200.00
Debit 1000 SGEM @ $0.95	$975.00
Credit 500 SGEM @ $2.10	$1,025.00
Cash Balance	$2,050.00
Debit 1000 DCG @ $0.85	$875.00
Debit 40 OKLM call @ $0.15	$625.00
Cash Balance	$550.00

* * * * *

'Abigail! Ah, there you are,' said Geoffrey, peering around the door into the dining room. 'Have you seen my Financial... Oh!'

'What is it, Geoffrey? Lost something, have we?' said Abigail lowering the newspaper and looking at her husband over the top of her reading glasses.

'Today's Financial Times,' said Geoffrey. 'By the by, I couldn't find it yesterday either.'

'That's because I had *our* paper yesterday and, as you can see, I am now reading *our* paper this morning.'

'Since when have you taken to reading my... er... our Financial Times?' he asked.

'Since yesterday,' said Abigail. 'D'you have any objection?'

'Objection? I... er... No, no objection... It's just that...'

'It's your custom to read it at the breakfast table, is that it?' said Abigail. 'A tradition, perhaps?' Geoffrey sat down and poured himself a glass of orange juice.'

Abigail disappeared behind the newspaper. Geoffrey pondered this change of routine as he poured milk into his bowl of cereal. Had he been rude at the breakfast table all these past years? Was his wife upset? Was this her way of showing it? He had to admit she had seemed a different woman ever since she became the bursar's assistant. She had stopped eating buttered toast and marmalade. She no longer put cream and sugar in her coffee. She no longer ate her way through boxes of Belgian chocolates.

'How was your book club meeting yesterday evening, my dear?'

'It's not a book club,' said Abigail, lowering the newspaper. 'It's an investment club.'

'An investment club?'

'Yes, Geoffrey. The BALI Club. B-A-L-I... Beaumont Abbey Ladies Investment Club.'

'I say. An investment club. Stocks and shares... that sort of thing?' said Geoffrey.

'Yes, Geoffrey. The sort of thing I thought you've been doing these past years.'

'Ah. Playing on the Stock Market, you mean?' said Geoffrey.

'Not at all,' snapped Abigail. 'We do *not play*, Geoffrey. We *trade seriously*.'

'With real money?' said Geoffrey.

'Of course with real money,' said Abigail.

'Whose money, if you don't mind my asking?'

'*Mine*, as a matter of fact,' said Abigail. 'Whose money do you use? The £1, 650 annual subscriptions to the Common Room Fund? Or do you just *play* with Monopoly money?'

'How could you ever think I'd use the Common Room money to... Hold on,' said Geoffrey, 'How do you know about the Common Room Fund?'

'Yesterday, Dr Carratt asked us to pay you our £30 annual subscription. Here,' said Abigail, putting ninety pounds on the table, 'this is for Mary Cranborne, Susan Wellborn and me... our subscription for the current academic year. I assume you will record these payments in your Common Room ledger?'

'Ledger? Oh, yes, my Common Room ledger. Of course,' stuttered Geoffrey.

354

'Perhaps you'd show it to me.'

'Show the ledger to you?' stammered Geoffrey.

'At your earliest convenience,' said Abigail matter-of-factly. 'I have been reading about book-keeping and accounts... I should like to see how it's done professionally.'

'Done professionally. Yes, of course.'

'Now... whose money have you been investing and how much profit have you made?'

'Well, dear... to tell the truth... I never actually dared risk our money... or anybody else's money for that matter.'

'So why do you need the Financial Times?'

'Sixth Form work... particularly for *Stock Market...* the game the boys play.'

'I see,' said Abigail with a grim smile. 'So you won't object if I read the paper over breakfast, will you?'

'No, of course not, Abigail. Whatever you say, my dear,' said Geoffrey, beginning to wonder what his colleagues would think of Mary Cranborne, Susan Wellborn and his wife using the Common Room. 'No,' he said to himself, 'not *using* the Common Room; being *members* of the Common Room. Heavens above! Before we know it, Beaumont will have girls... women teachers... women Heads of Department! Good Heavens.'

* * * * *

The first thing Susan did was to telephone Daniel Baker at NatWest. She placed the investment club order for one thousand DCM shares and forty call option contracts for OKLM shares and her own order for ten thousand DCM shares and fifty OKLM options. Then she turned her attention to the mound of paperwork spread across her desk.

It was tedious work. It took time. It had to be done. She sifted, sorted and placed each piece either into one of three piles or into the shredder. In her mind, Susan had labelled one pile *financial*, a second pile *legal* and a third pile *Smith – personal*. She had completed this part of the exercise just before lunchtime when she telephoned the chief caretaker's office. 'Good morning Mr Beech,' said Susan. 'I thought I should warn you that there'll be rather a lot of shredded paper in my office this afternoon. Can I leave it to you to have it incinerated?' When Ron suggested the alternative, she said, 'Yes. That's fine by me Mr Beech. I hadn't thought of composting it down. Good idea.' After lunch, Susan transferred the third pile to cardboard boxes, labelled Anthony Parker-Smythe – Personal, then telephoned Banwell, Garnet & York, Chartered Accountants.

'Good afternoon. I should like to speak to Robert York.'

'Just a minute, please. I'll see if Mr York is available. Who shall I say is calling?'

'Susan Wellborn. The Bursar of Beaumont Abbey.'

'Just one moment.' After a delay, made longer by tuneless music Susan associated with aircraft waiting to take off, the receptionist said, 'Putting you through now.'

'Good afternoon. Sheila Woods speaking. How may I help you?'

'Good afternoon, Mrs Woods. I should like to speak to Mr York,' said Susan.

'May I ask what it's about?' said Robert York's PA.

'Please tell Mr York Susan Wellborn wants to speak to him... now.'

Stanley Garnet still held Robert York responsible for the Beaumont Abbey account. Although Angus MacKay had found no evidence of professional misconduct and nothing to connect his Robert with Parker-Smythe's wrong-doings, Stanley remembered his old comrade's words to keep an eye on the junior partner's work at Beaumont. Robert York was no fool. He knew his senior partner would be keeping a weather eye on him somehow or other. With Parker-Smythe safely out of the way, languishing in a Guernsey hospital, Robert felt he could put the past behind him and start afresh with this new incumbent. He reached for the telephone.

'She didn't say why she wanted to speak to me?'

'No she did *not*, Mr York,' said Sheila Woods huffily. 'Shall I put her through?'

'Yes. Thank you, Sheila... Ah, good afternoon Mrs Taylor... Oh, I beg your pardon... Miss Wellborn... What can I do for you?'

'You can come and see me tomorrow morning at ten o'clock, Mr York.'

'Let me see... Tomorrow morning at ten... Yes I can manage that. May I ask what it's about?' Robert said in a confident tone.

'We need to discuss the Beaumont accounts, of course,' said Susan. 'But I also need your help with another matter.' When he asked what that would be about, she said, 'The former bursar and your associate. Mr Anthony Parker-Smythe.'

* * * * *

357

CHAPTER 28

"Today knowledge has power. It controls access to opportunity and advancement." Peter Drucker

* * * * *

Strictly speaking, it was not the last Wednesday of the Summer term. There was one more Wednesday to come. Even so, for the Second Master, Reginald de Vere, today was the last day to finalise and publish the timetable for the new academic year. And for the master in charge of the CCF, Major Walter Barnes, today was the last day of the current academic year to parade his troops. But for the Bursar, Susan Wellborn, today was the first day of the new era. Reg, Walter and Susan were good organisers who planned for the unexpected but none was quite prepared for the events of this Wednesday.

'Robert York is here,' whispered Abigail, stepping into Susan's office. 'He's five minutes late,' she said tapping her wrist watch.'

'A well-worn manoeuvre I might have expected,' said Susan. 'Offer him a cup of coffee and tell him I'll see him shortly. Let's keep him waiting fifteen minutes.'

'Right you are.'

Over his cup of coffee, Robert York studied the new and formidable Assistant Bursar. Today Abigail was wearing a pair of French-heeled shoes of soft grey leather, a calf-length dark-grey skirt, a long-sleeved pale cream blouse open at the neck around which was a metallic gold silk scarf held in place by an antique enamelled brooch. Her greying hair was held back from each temple by hair grips matching the shiny black frames of her oval reading glasses. In assisting Susan these past few weeks, Abigail had become more confident and less arrogant. She was still 5 ft 3½ ins tall but having lost weight, she now seemed much taller. She picked up the telephone on its first ring.

'The Bursar will see you now, Mr York,' said Abigail, rising from behind her desk and leading the way to the interconnecting door. 'Mr York, Bursar.'

'Mr York,' said Susan. 'Do come in. Take a seat. Sorry to keep you waiting. That will be all, thank you, Mrs Rusbridge.'

'So,' said Robert, 'What did you want to see me about?'

'Let's start with my predecessor,' said Susan. 'First of all, I'd be grateful if you would take care of these documents and correspondence.' She pointed to the cardboard boxes stacked in the corner of her room.

'I'm not with you,' said Robert. 'What's in these boxes?'

'Documents and correspondence belonging to Mr Parker-Smythe.'

'Why give them to me if they belong to him?'

'Since you were associates, I'd advise you to examine the documents in these boxes very carefully before handing them over to him.'

'We were never... I wouldn't say Parker-Smythe and I were associates,' said Robert defensively. 'He was the bursar and I was... am the... your accountant.'

'Of course,' said Susan. 'Perhaps *associates* was a poor choice of word to describe your relationship, Robert. May I call you Robert? Or would you prefer Bob?'

'Perhaps we should stick to Mr York for the time being.'

'Mr York it is then,' said Susan with a cursory nod. 'Now, turning to the Beaumont accounts, I have a number of questions.'

For the next half hour, Robert squirmed in his seat while Susan plied him with questions. How did they justify investing money in Special Purpose Vehicles and off-shore accounts in Guernsey? Why did they allocate such a small proportion of the school's income to Common Investment Funds? What was the basis for the rents they charged for the farm and the use of the swimming pool, sports grounds and other facilities at Beaumont? How frequently did he and Parker-Smythe meet, where were the reports of their meetings and how much did they charge the school for their meetings?

When, at the pre-arranged time, Abigail interrupted the meeting with two cups of black coffee on a tray, Robert York was looking decidedly hot under the collar.

'May I remind you, Bursar… Your meeting with the High Master is in twenty minutes time… at quarter past eleven,' lied Abigail.

'Thank you, Mrs Rusbridge,' said Susan.

'Oh… Major MacKay telephoned,' Abigail lied again. 'I said you were in a meeting with Mr York and that you would call him back in the next fifteen minutes.'

'Good. Thank you, Mrs Rusbridge.'

'Is that Angus MacKay?' said Robert.

'Yes, it is,' said Susan. '*Major* MacKay has been very helpful… very helpful indeed. You've had dealings with him I believe.'

'I wouldn't say I…'

'Now, Mr York,' interrupted Susan brusquely, 'let's decide how *you* are going help *me*.'

* * * * *

Before personal computers arrived on the scene, Reginald de Vere was initially obliged to use a very large blackboard and lots of coloured chalks to do the timetable. He soon replaced it by two large boards of thick card with arrays of slots to hold slips of coloured paper representing a subject or a teacher. Then one day Colin Harper and Teddy arrived.

Reg ran his eye over the boards while Colin read details from the monitor's screen. They always made this final check before printing out of the full timetable, the subject timetables and the individual staff timetables.

'Let's break for lunch now, Colin,' said Reg. 'I'll meet you back here at two o'clock.'

'Whatever you say, Second Master,' said Colin.

'We should be finished by half-past two. Can everything be printed before five o'clock?'

'I'm sure Teddy and I can manage that,' said Colin, patting the bobble hat on top of the computer monitor.

'Excellent!' said Reg, trying to keep a straight face. 'I'll see you at two o'clock.'

* * * * *

Walter Barnes was fifteen when World War II ended. National service ended in 1945 but was reintroduced in 1947 for men only. So, on finishing school at age eighteen, Walter joined the army and served two years before going to Loughborough College to train and qualify as a physical education teacher. He came to Beaumont straight from his three years at college. He worked as an assistant teacher for seventeen years before taking over as Head of Physical Education. Walter was now in his twentieth year as Head of PE and looked more like a man of fifty than someone fast approaching sixty.

'Good morning, Sergeant Major.'

'Morning, sir!' barked SMI Stanley Batters, coming to attention and saluting.

'Everything under control?'

'Sir!' barked Stanley, responding immediately with his own version of *yes*.

'PSI Morton in the armoury?' asked Walter.

'Sir!' barked Stanley again. 'Giving the rifles the once over, sir.'

'Excellent! At ease, sergeant.' Stanley raised his right foot and stamped it to the floor at exactly 12 inches from his left foot. Walter looked down to see his own face reflected in each of Stanley's highly polished black boots. 'I just wanted to check with you the final arrangements for this afternoon's parade and the summer camps.'

* * * * *

When Lawrence St John Beecroft, the Head Boy, had said *Benedic nobis, Domine, et omnibus tuis donis*, the school stood in silence for the few staff on high table to be seated. Most of the teachers were on the house tables to watch over the boys and serve the food. On Wednesdays, Walter Barnes always sat at high table. Today he was sitting next to Mary Cranborne and directly opposite Susan Wellborn and Abigail Rusbridge.

'You're looking exceptionally distinguished today, if I may say so, Major Barnes.'

'Kind of you to say so, Miss Cranborne,' said Walter. 'Our final parade this afternoon.'

'Looking forward to the summer camps, Major?' said Susan.

'Yes I am and so are the lads. Lot of work of course… no picnic…'

'Where are the camps this year?' Abigail asked.

'Army section… Cultybraggan… beautiful spot near Comrie in Perthshire, in Scotland.'

'That's where you'll be going, I suppose,' said Mary.

'All being well, yes. I usually go with the Army section,' said Walter. 'Navy section goes to Dartmouth. It's the Air Force section's turn to go abroad this year.'

'Where are they going?' asked Susan.

'RAF Akrotiri… on the southernmost tip of Cyprus… south-west of Limassol Salt Lake.'

'Sounds like it might be a bit like South Africa… very hot and sunny,' said Susan.

'Do you miss the sun and the heat, Miss Wellborn?' said Walter.

'Sometimes,' said Susan, 'but I found Cape Town a little too hot for comfort.'

After the post cibum Grace: *Benedictus sit Deus in donis suis. Sit nomen Dei benedictum*, the school remained standing until everyone on high table had left the dining hall. Outside in the fresh air and away from the noises in the dining hall, Walter saluted, said *If you'll excuse me ladies… duty calls* and, shoulders back, marched briskly away.

'Such a nice man,' said Abigail.

'A gentleman,' said Mary.

'I wonder what he thinks of the three of us being members of the Common Room,' said Susan.

'Whatever he thinks,' said Mary, 'he'll keep to himself. A true gentleman.'

'Mary,' said Abigail, 'I just realised what's different about you today.'

'Different?' said Mary.

'Yes… It's your hair,' said Abigail.

'What's wrong with my hair?' said Mary.

'Nothing. Nothing at all. I think it looks… stylish.'

'I thought it was time for a change… so I did away with the bun at the back.'

'Has anybody else said anything to you about your softer look?' said Abigail.

'Who for instance?' said Mary.

'Well… the High Master for one.'

'The High Master?' laughed Susan. 'He'd never notice Mary's hair… or Louise's hair… or anybody else's hair… not even his own for that matter.'

'Dr Pugh-Jones hasn't much hair on his own head for him to notice,' chuckled Abigail.

'If I thought my new hair style…'

'Forget the High Master,' interrupted Susan. 'More to the point, has the Second Master noticed?'

'Why Mr de Vere?' said Abigail.

'Reggie's the one Mary's got her eye on.'

'If you two will excuse me,' said Mary, blushing. 'I've got work to do.'

* * * * *

In the opinion of Major Walter Barnes, Beaumont had to hold a full-dress parade each term. The first parade on Poppy Day in remembrance of the end of World War I when hostilities formally ended at the 11 a.m. on the 11th day of the 11th month in 1918. The second on Easter Sunday. The third on the last Wednesday of Trinity term. This third and last parade of the year was always the most splendid affair. For almost a year SMI Batters would have been drilling the cadets to march in step, shoulders back, head up and arms swinging properly. Major Walter Barnes always looked forward to this last parade.

By half past one, there was a large crowd of spectators. Earnest Hardcastle, Dr Michael Liú and Sir Leslie Matthews, accompanied by his second wife, Edna, were rubbing shoulders with the many parents and with the few staff, such as the Reverend Donald Meeker, not bound to the Combined Cadet Corps.

All the boys and all the staff bound to the CCF were present and correct. The only uniformed member not wearing a tie was Flying Officer Dr Humphrey Fiddle. He wore his dog collar. SMI Batters and PSI Morton wore their service medal ribbons above the left-breast pocket. The many boots, all black and responsive to polish, reflected the early afternoon sun. The distinctive badges, attached to berets or peak caps, presented Major Barnes with a gleaming array as the Army, Navy and Air Force Sections synchronously marched past the dais and the cadets responded to their officer's commands: *Left Right Left Right... Eyes Right.... Eyes Front... Left Right Left Right*.

The only component missing was a brass band with a drum major leading the way and beating time with his mace. Peter Morrison, the Director of Music, would have nothing to do with the CCF, would not countenance a military brass band and would not be persuaded by, for example, the argument that J S Bach wrote music in march time. So the spectators had to be content with the rhythmic tramp of boots and the varied voices of the officers bellowing their *Left Right Left Right*.

'I share your pacifism, Donald,' said Janet Meeker, his sister and Wedgwood's resident nurse, 'but I confess I find this parade... stirring... even without a marching band.'

'Walter Barnes is in his element,' said Donald. 'He'll miss the CCF when he retires.'

'When is he going to retire?'

'Probably in a year's time,' said Donald.

'Could he volunteer to help run the CCF?' said Janet.

'I suppose he could,' said Donald. 'I wonder if he's thought of that?'

The parade would always start promptly at thirteen thirty hours and finish on the dot of fourteen hundred hours. The cadets would then spend the rest of the afternoon preparing for their summer camps under the direction of their officers following the orders of their commanding officer, Major Barnes.

Today's parade started and finished exactly on time. Major Walter Barnes gave his final salute from the dais, gave his nod of approval to SMI Batters then gave up his ghost.

Dr Michael Liú was first onto the dais followed closely by Janet Meeker. Walter's chest was not rising and falling; he was not breathing. Michael placed two fingers on the side of Walter's throat; he could not detect a carotid pulse. 'Call an ambulance... *now*... at the double,' he said to SMI Batters. 'Help me get him onto his back,' he said to Janet, 'and we'll try Cardiopulmonary resuscitation... but I don't think it will do much good.' When Michael had started CPR, he glanced at Janet's pale face and said, 'Heart's asystolic... not much hope, I'm afraid.' His prognosis was correct. Major Walter Barnes died before the ambulance arrived. He had given his last salute at his last CCF parade.

* * * * *

The news of Walter's death spread swiftly around the school and was met with varying degrees of disbelief. Reg and Colin were checking the final page of the timetable when the telephone rang in the computer room. It was Mary Cranborne calling from her office.

'Calm down, Mary,' said Reg. 'Just tell me what happened.'

'I was only talking to him… less than an hour ago,' sobbed Mary.

'Who, Mary?' said Reg. 'Who?'

'Walter Barnes, Reggie,' said Mary. 'He's dead… died on the parade ground.'

'Are you sure?' said Reg.

'Yes, Reggie. I'm sure. Janet Meeker is here in my office. She was there when he…'

'Stay calm, Mary. I'll be right over. Does the High Master know?'

'No, I don't think so… No, not yet,' said Mary. 'No… I haven't told him.'

'Alright. Leave that to me,' said Reg. Then turning to Colin, he said, 'We can forget the timetable for the minute. Bit of sad news. Walter Barnes has just died.'

Mary, Susan, Abigail and Janet were forlornly sipping cups of Dolly Brown's tea when Reg arrived. He accepted a cup and listened to Janet tell him Dr Liú's opinion that Walter Barnes had suffered sudden cardiac death probably as a result of ventricular fibrillation.

'A fatal heart attack, is that what you're saying?' said Reg.

'I'm only a nurse, Mr de Vere, not a doctor,' said Janet, 'but if I understood Dr Liú correctly, it was not a heart attack.'

'In layman's term…'

'His heart just stopped,' said Janet.

'Would he have suffered… been in pain?' said Reg, thinking of his wife, Madeleine.

'No, I don't think so,' said Janet.

'Well that's something to be thankful for,' said Reg. 'When exactly did his heart stop?'

'Just after his last salute,' said Janet. 'Just after the Navy section marched past.'

'If you'll excuse me ladies,' said Reg. 'Duty calls.'

'It's alright,' said Susan, placing an arm around Mary who gave a loud sob.

'Sorry!' said Reg, 'Did I say…'

'I'm sorry, Reggie,' said Mary. 'It's just… those were Walter's last words to us.'

Reg left Mary's office and knocked on the High Master's door from the main corridor. Dr Llywelyn Pugh-Jones was thinking about the *one or two points* lawyer Henry Trevanion had raised when the unexpected knock on his outer door almost brought to an end the precarious existence of the glass seal pup paperweight he was tossing from hand to hand.

'Ah, Reg. Glad you dropped by. I wanted to have a word,' said Llywelyn. 'Who do you think should supervise the building of our new concert and sports hall and… who should we appoint to take charge of Baker House?'

'Excuse me, High Master,' said Reg. 'Before we get into that… some rather sad news, I'm afraid.'

'Sad news?' said Llywelyn. 'By the look on your face…'

'It's Walter Barnes… He died this afternoon… on the parade ground.'

'Oh, dear,' said Llywelyn. 'How awful!'

'Bit of a shock,' said Reg.

'Walter Barnes?' said Llywelyn. 'Our Head of PE?'

'The very same.'

'I can hardly believe it,' said Llywelyn. 'I mean… he was so fit. An accident was it?'

'I don't know all the details,' said Reg. 'Dr Liú was there at the time but he's gone with the… he's taken Walter in an ambulance to the hospital.'

'Walter Barnes… dead?'

'According to Janet Meeker, Walter's heart just stopped beating… just like that,' said Reg. He snapped his fingers and immediately regretted the action. The seal pup fell to the floor but was saved from sudden extinction by the carpet's thick pile.

The seal pup paperweight rolled under the desk and stopped against the Second Master's foot. Reg picked up

367

the glass object, placed it safely on the desk top and waited for the High Master to say something.

'Did Walter have any living relatives?'

'No, High Master, not to my knowledge.'

'He's definitely dead?'

'As far as I know,' said Reg.

'No living relatives?'

'None,' said Reg. 'Would you like me to…'

'What? Oh, sorry, Reg,' said Llywelyn. 'I was thinking… funeral arrangements… memorial service… that sort of thing.'

'Leave that to me and Dr Fiddle,' said Reg. 'You'll deliver the eulogy?'

'Ah yes. The eulogy,' said Llywelyn. 'Yes, of course.'

'Thank you,' said Reg. After a pause, 'You wanted to discuss the new concert and sports hall and the new boarding house for girls… Baker House?'

'Did I?' said Llywelyn.

'Another time perhaps?' said Reg. 'When you've not quite so much on your mind.'

Reg took the connecting door into the secretary's office. Janet and Abigail had left but Susan was still with Mary who had recovered her composure.

'How did the High Master take the news?' asked Mary.

'Pretty well under the circumstances I think,' said Reg.

'What circumstances?' said Susan.

'Walter being so fit and the High Master… Well, let's just say when somebody you know of a similar age drops dead… well it's an unwelcome reminder of your own mortality.'

'How will this affect you and the school?' asked Mary.

'We'll have to rewrite the timetable,' said Reg.

'Will that be a lot of work?' said Mary.

'It may not be too bad,' said Reg, turning his mind to the problem. 'Gregory Watson will take Walter's place.'

'As Head of the PE Department?' said Susan.

'Yes. He'll be sorry to get the post this way,' said Reg. 'Still... with Watson full time on PE, we'll need someone to teach his PE and geography

'And you'll need somebody to run the CCF?' said Susan.

'What about Mr Watson?' said Mary.

'No, I don't think we could ask him to take charge of the Corps,' said Reg.

'May I make a suggestion, Mr de Vere?' said Susan.

'Go ahead.'

'I understand Mrs Watson is a geography graduate with teaching experience. Perhaps she could cover her husband's geography classes,' said Susan.

'Mrs Watson...' said Reg. 'Interesting idea. Our first lady teacher...'

'Not the first,' said Mary. 'Ladies taught at Beaumont during the two World Wars.'

'You're right, of course,' said Reg, as the words *move with the times* came to mind.

'That would still leave the PE?' said Reg.

'I don't think Kathy Watson could teach boys physical education,' said Mary.

'Maybe not boys,' said Susan. 'But what about the girls coming to Beaumont...'

'Would you like me to talk to Mrs Watson?' said Mary. 'Sound out the ground.'

'Thank you, Mary. That would be helpful,' said Reg.

'I have another suggestion?' said Susan. 'I know a man who might be persuaded to take charge of the CCF and cover Mr Watson's PE.'

'Do I know him?' said Reg.

'I'm not sure but the High Master knows him,' said Susan.

'What's his name?' said Reg.

'Let me ask him first. If he's interested, then I'll tell you who he is.'

* * * * *

The demise of Walter Barnes that Wednesday afternoon cast a pall over the school. Reg was in his office when SMI Batters, wearing a black armband, stood to attention in front of the desk. Refusing Reg's offer of a seat, Stanley came straight to the point.

'Sir! Permission to speak?' he barked.

'What's the problem, Stanley?'

'Officer in charge,' said SMI Batters. 'Who takes over from Major Barnes, sir?'

'Good question,' said Reg. 'Why ask me? Isn't there a chain of command?'

'Sir!'

'So,' said Reg, taking Stanley's bark to mean yes, 'who's next in line?'

'Flying Officer Fiddle, sir.'

'Ah! Our chaplain! I see,' said Reg. 'Can you and PSI Morton cope for a day or two?'

'Sir!' barked Stanley.

'Good. Leave this with me,' said Reg.

Mary and Susan set about their tasks with their usual efficiency as soon as Reg had left. Mary made a brief telephone call then made her way to see Kathy Watson.

The two women sat on white plastic chairs at a white plastic table on the small tiled patio at the rear of the Watson cottage. Mark and Tracy were in an inflatable plastic paddling pool noisily splashing one another with water and enjoying the afternoon sun.

'Are you sure I can't get you something to drink?'

'No, thank you,' said Mary. 'It's not long since I had a cup of tea.'

'Terribly sad about Mr Barnes,' said Kathy. 'He was such a nice man. Greg said all the boys liked him… and respected him… he was hard on them but fair… very fair.'

'He was a true gentleman,' said Mary. 'We'll miss him.'

'It was good of you to come and see me,' said Kathy. 'You could have given me the news over the telephone.'

'I didn't come just to give you the news, Mrs Watson...'

'Kathy! Please call me Kathy.'

'Very well,' said Mary. 'I didn't come just to tell you about Mr Barnes... I'm here... to sound you out.'

'What about?'

'I came to ask you...'

'Mark! Tracy! That's enough. Out you come,' said Kathy reaching for two large towels. 'Here... dry yourself off Mark... Tracy! Come here.'

'How old are your children, Kathy,?'

'I'm five,' Mark said brightly

'I'm three,' Tracy said coyly.

'Actually,' said Kathy, 'Tracy's three years eight months... OK. Go indoors and get dressed. Sorry about that Miss Cranborne.'

'Mary. Please call me Mary.'

Before Susan flipped open the organiser on her desk, she tried to decide on the best approach. She actually knew very little about the man she was about to call but her instincts told her he would be an asset to Beaumont and perhaps a benefit to herself. He might not, of course, be free to accept the post. And there was a chance he might not be remotely interested in helping the school or her. But then again, she remembered the favourite cliché of her late, racing driver husband, *nothing ventured, nothing gained*. 'Good afternoon, Mrs MacKay. Is your husband at home.'

* * * * *

'Good morning, Mary. How are you today?' said Reg. 'Feeling better?'

'Much better, thanks. How are things with you?'

371

'Fine. I'm fine, thanks,' said Reg. 'By the way... I like the way you've done your hair. It... um... suits you.'

'I'm glad you...' said Mary blushing.

'If you don't mind my saying so...' interrupted Reg awkwardly.

'Oh, no. Not at all. It was nice of you to notice.'

'Yes... well... right,' stumbled Reg. 'High Master ready, is he?'

'Yes. He's expecting you now. Mrs Watson will be along at ten o'clock and Major MacKay at ten thirty.'

'Right. I'd better go in,' said Reg.

'Ah, good morning, Reg,' said Llywelyn. 'I thought it best to keep these two meetings as informal as possible, agreed?'

'Agreed,' said Reg. 'Let them ask us the questions.'

'Don't frighten them off, that's the idea?' he said, his fingers hovering over the seal pup.

'Kid gloves in the case of Mrs Watson,' said Reg. 'But from what I've heard, Major MacKay is not easily intimidated.'

'I'll leave you to do most of the talking,' said Llywelyn, picking up the paperweight.

'As you wish, High Master,' said Reg. There was a knock on the door and Mary entered.

'Mrs Watson is here.'

'Thank you, Mary,' said Llywelyn. 'Please show her in.' Kathy Watson, dressed in a cream and brown striped blouse under a dark green trouser suit, walked in and shook hands. 'Mrs Watson. Good of you to come. Please... Take a seat.'

Kathy wanted to return to teaching but she was concerned about her daughter, Tracy. It was with this in mind that she asked Reg if she could teach mornings only. Fortunately, Greg usually taught geography in the morning and PE and games in the afternoon so Reg was able to assure her this could be arranged. When she tentatively raised the question of salary, Reg said he would meet with her and the Bursar to iron out the details. Having asked all her questions, Kathy turned to the High Master and said, 'Mr Barnes was our children's godfather... A very kind man, High Master. We shall miss him very much.'

'That went well, wouldn't you say?' said Llywelyn.

'Yes, High Master, I think it did,' said Reg. 'Watson's a very lucky fellow.'

'Major MacKay is here, High Master. Shall I show him in?'

'If you would please, Mary' said Llywelyn. 'Won't do to keep him waiting.'

Mary noticed Angus MacKay was dressed much as he had been on his first visit to the school at the beginning of term - green/oatmeal mix Harris Tweed jacket with leather buttons, beige Cavalry twill trousers, polished dark brown shoes, cream shirt and the Black Watch regimental striped tie. The way he was dressed and the way he walked reminded her of Major Barnes. She wondered if he'd be the gentleman Walter had been.

'Ah, good morning, Major,' said Llywelyn. 'Good of you to come.'

'Excuse me, High Master... Would you like your tea now?' said Mary.

'Yes please, Mary... And coffee for...' Reg nodded. 'the Second Master,' said Llywelyn.

'Coffee for you, Major?' said Mary. 'Black, no sugar, I believe.' Angus nodded and smiled.

'This is the Second Master... Mr de Vere,' said Llywelyn. Reg and Angus shook hands and mentally approved each other's firm grip. 'Please... take a seat, Major MacKay.'

Mary re-entered to serve a cup of Earl Grey to Llywelyn, a café-au-lait to Reg and a black coffee to Angus who smiled and noted she'd remembered how he took his coffee. Angus also noted and approved of her new hair style - it had been tied in a bun the last time he had seen her; he wondered what made her let it down. He also wondered why he agreed to come to Beaumont. 'Look on it as just another of your temporary assignments, old boy, until they find someone better qualified' Stanley Garnet had said with a chuckle. 'Enjoy yourself *and* the extra cash Beaumont will pay you in addition to our retainer for keeping an eye on *our* Robert York and *your* Susan Wellborn.'

'Do you have any questions?' said Reg.

'Och, no,' said Angus, comparing Reg's composure with Llywelyn's nervous fiddling with the glass paperweight.

'May I ask you a question?' said Reg. Angus nodded. 'Do you speak Scottish Gaelic?'

'Aye. We spoke it at home,' said Angus. 'Why d'you ask?'

'I read French at Cambridge,' said Reg. 'During my year in France I studied Breton... I understand it's closely related to Scottish Gaelic. I'd like to hear how it sounds.'

'If it's anything like Ulster Irish, Breton will sound a bit like Scottish Gaelic,' Angus said in his native tongue. After a pause he repeated in English what he had said in Gaelic.

'So...' said Reg. 'Do you speak Irish Gaelic as well, Major?'

'Why would I want to speak Irish Gaelic, begorra?' said Angus with a faint smile.

On his way to becoming a commissioned officer and eventually a major in the Black Watch, Angus gained a degree in Chinese, Japanese and Korean. The three year course at the University of London School of Oriental Studies had been hard but his knowledge of Korean helped him survive and return from Korea with a Victoria Cross.

Twelve months before his Black Watch battalion began its first two-year peace-keeping tour of Northern Ireland, and before he signed off and officially left the army, Angus became proficient in the Ulster Irish, the Gaelic spoken in Donegal and in the Falls Road district of West Belfast.

Not long ago, Fiona suggested a holiday in Ireland, thinking of the famous Hills of Donegal - the Derryveagh Mountains in the north and the Bluestack Mountains in the south - and of her husband's fondness for mountains. Angus was not interested. And after the way he expressed his lack of interest, she never again suggested a holiday in Ireland.

'How do you think that went?' said Llywelyn.

'Well enough I think,' said Reg.

'What did you make of Major MacKay? said Llywelyn.

'Hidden depths,' said Reg. 'Not a man to be trifled with... as I'm sure the boys will quickly discover.'

'What about the staff? D'you think he'll fit in?'

'In Major MacKay's case,' said Reg. 'it's more likely a question will *they* fit in?'

That evening, Kathy and Greg discussed the arrangements they would have to make for the children in September. Mark was no problem; he would be at the local first school. Tracy might have been a problem but Mary Cranborne had recommended a local play group attended by children of other Beaumont staff.

That same evening, Fiona and Angus discussed his special assignment.

'Yon Robert York is the main target, Colonel,' said Angus.

'Going to keep an eye on the delectable Susan as well though, are we?' said Fiona.

'Och, aye,' said Angus. 'I cannae watch the one without the other, ye ken.'

'And what about PE? Aren't we getting a little old for gymnastics, Major?'

'Maybe. Maybe not,' said Angus. 'It's the boys who'll be jumping through the hoops.'

'And those cadets? Going to knock them into shape?'

'Maybe. Maybe not,' said Angus. 'It's the PSI needs knocking into shape.'

'Really?' said Fiona. 'What makes you say that?'

'Let's just say it dinnae do to let civilians get their hands on rifles and ammunition,' said Angus, remembering not only the incident on the clock tower but also what happened to his battalion on their first tour of duty in Ireland.

* * * * *

The days leading up to the final Wednesday of term passed almost without incident. Reg, with the help of Colin and Teddy, adjusted, printed and distributed the timetable. Kathy Watson introduced Tracy to the play group. Angus MacKay introduced himself to PSI Morton and had him chain the forty rifles to the wall of the armoury. Arthur Matthews introduced Kathy to the other members of his department and to Colin Harper who showed her how to use the physical geography programmes in the computer room. Greg Watson introduced himself to Angus and gave him a copy of his timetable, the syllabus and a tour of the gym and sports fields.

The first incident occurred on the cricket field. A unsupervised practice was in progress. Jardine was fielding perilously close to the bat at silly mid on. Hammond was fielding at leg slip. Washbrook was batting. Singh was bowling off-breaks, on a good length just outside the off stump. The batsman saw the loose ball the moment it left the bowler's hand. It pitched short and just outside leg stump. The ball fired off the bat like a rocket. Rupert instinctively ducked, turned away then fell to the ground in agony.

Hammond's father was a highly respected medical doctor in general practice. Leonard was in the Upper Sixth and staying on at Beaumont for the Michaelmas term to take the open scholarship exams to Oxford; he hoped to study medicine at his father's old college. When Len saw how hard the ball hit Rupert's flank and saw Rupert writhing in agony on the floor, he feared a blunt kidney injury which, if not treated promptly, could lead to serious complications. He sent Singh for an ambulance and Crawnshaw for Janet Meeker.

At the beginning of term Hammond and Jardine had been bitter rivals. When Rupert had helped Hammond to reach his century and to draw the match with the Old Beaumontians, their rivalry had been replaced by a mutual respect. When Hammond's prompt action saved Rupert from serious kidney failure, they became friends.

'That's quite a bruise you've got there,' said Hammond.

'Thanks to you, buddy boy,' said Rupert, 'that's all I've gotten. I owe you one.'

'Gave me a chance to play doctor,' said Hammond. 'Anyway... Singh and Washbrook are pretty upset, you know... Couple of twerps...'

'I don't blame tap washer,' said Rupert. 'I'd have hit that loose ball even harder.'

'I reckon you probably would have, at that,' said Hammond. 'I don't know what Singh was thinking...'

'He probably wasn't... thinking,' said Rupert.

'By the way,' said Hammond, 'how d'you feel about Washbrook as captain next year?'

'He'd be OK... but not as good as you,' said Rupert, laughing then wincing with the pain from his side.

'Who d'you fancy for vice-captain?' said Hammond. 'What about Pug?'

'Payton Ulysses Greatorex Percy?' said Rupert. 'You've got to be joking!'

'Who then?'

'No idea. It's your recommendation, remember.'

'I've already made it,' said Hammond.

'Who?' said Rupert. 'Who've you recommended for vice-captain?'

'Actually...' said Hammond. 'You.'

The second incident was barely an incident at all. That Thursday afternoon when Rupert was being rushed off to hospital, Susan Wellborn was meeting with the High Master in his study. The main topic of discussion was the builders for the new concert and sports hall and for the new boarding house for girls. When Llywelyn tentatively asked who she thought should be in overall charge, Susan quoted from her contract: the bursar should "*Manage facilities including use of premises and associated income, general building works and projects. Manage appropriate service contracts, level agreements and school licences and insurance.*"

'Ah, yes… I see,' bumbled Llywelyn. 'And you… you feel… that is to say…'

'Have no fear, High Master,' said Susan. 'You may leave this to my assistant and me.'

'Right! Excellent!' said Llywelyn. 'You will keep me…'

'Rest assured,' said Susan, 'I shall keep you and the governing board of directors fully informed of progress every step of the way.'

'Ah, yes… the governors… of course.'

'There is one other matter I feel I should bring to your attention,' said Susan.

She placed a sheet of paper down on the desk in front of Llywelyn, saying she'd come across the document in her predecessor's filing cabinet. Llywelyn put down the glass seal pup, picked up the paper and started to read.

'What's this all about?' Llywelyn said out loud as he scanned the page. 'Oh! What…?'

'It would appear to be a note Mr Parker-Smythe made at a meeting he had with you.'

'Yes, you're right,' said Llywelyn. 'Something about adding fictitious names of non-existent pupils to the…'

'*to the register if the number of new pupils were to fall below sixty,*' said Susan.

'Oh, dear,' said Llywelyn as Serge Prokovief's sleigh ride tune, Troika, started going around in his head.

'Are you alright, High Master? May I get you a glass of water?'

'No thank you,' said Llywelyn, slipping a nitro-glycerine capsule under his tongue.

378

'Funny,' said Susan. 'When I read that note it reminded me of lieutenant Kijé, the imaginary officer. Still... with girls joining the school in September, there'd be no need for anyone to conjure up imaginary pupils now, would there, High Master?'

'No, absolutely not,' said Llywelyn, mopping his brow and loosening his collar.

'You may rely on me,' said Susan, taking the sheet from Llywelyn's hand, 'to take care of this and all the other little indiscretions of my predecessor.'

* * * * *

On this last Wednesday of term, there were no lessons and there was little of the usual joy at the prospect of the long summer holiday. Today was the funeral of Walter Barnes.

Beaumont Chapel was packed to capacity. Radulph Palfreyman's technicians had set up cameras in the Chapel and large monitor screens in the nearby Grand Hall to relay the service to the many Old Beaumontians and the many parents of pupils, past and present, paying their last respects.

At the first of eleven strokes of the clock tower bell, SMI Batters and PSI Morton opened, for the first time in years, the two halves of the large oak door set in the west wall beneath the organ loft. The reverend Dr Fiddle stood up in the pulpit and, with the words of the poet, W H Auden, signalled the congregation to stand.

Stop all the clocks, cut off the telephone,
Prevent the dog from barking with a juicy bone,
Silence the pianos and with muffled drum,
Bring out the coffin, let the mourners come.

The High Master, standing on the chancel step, nodded and Peter Morrison began to play his transcription of the Canon in D by Johann Pachelbel. SMI Batters and PSI Morton slowly and solemnly made their way up the aisle ahead of the coffin borne by six officers, two from each section of the Combined Cadet Corps; all eight were in full dress uniform.

When the pall bearers had placed the coffin in front of the chancel step, on trestles hidden beneath a green cloth, the Chaplain read from 1 Timothy 6 verse 7, King James version: *For we brought nothing into this world, and it is certain we can carry nothing out.* After a short pause, Dr Fiddle announced, 'Hymn number five seven nine.' By way of an introduction, Peter Morrison played the first eight bars of the hymn then the congregation began to sing the words of Sabine Baring-Gould to the music of Sir Arthur S. Sullivan:

Onward, Christian soldiers, marching as to war,
With the cross of Jesus going on before.
Christ, the royal Master, leads against the foe;
Forward into battle see his banners go!

The building seemed to shake as, at the refrain, the Harrison and Harrison organ swelled and tried unsuccessfully to drown out the lusty voices of the congregation:

Onward, Christian soldiers, marching as to war,
With the cross of Jesus going on before.

At the end of the hymn, everyone took their seats except Dr Fiddle who intoned from the pulpit. 'We have come here today to remember before God our colleague and friend, Walter Barnes… to give thanks for his life… to commend him to our merciful redeemer… and to commit his body to be buried… Let us pray.'

Throughout the service, Louise kept a watchful eye upon her husband. Being the High Master of Beaumont was stressful enough at the best of times but the death of Walter Barnes, and other incidents Llywelyn had not mentioned to her, had put him and his wife on edge. For the sake of his health, Louise would try to make sure he made the most of the coming summer holiday. She just hoped their visit to his home town in the Rhondda would really be just what the doctor would have ordered.

The kneeling congregation echoed Dr Fiddle's *Amen* then rose to take their seats and turn their faces towards Dr Llywelyn Pugh-Jones standing on the chancel step.

'It is not unusual at the end of Trinity to bid farewell to colleagues leaving Beaumont for pastures new. Today Mr Billington and Mr Osgood leave to become heads of History and Biology elsewhere. We wish them well. We know where they are going and what they are going to do. But today sadly we must say a final farewell to Walter Barnes. We know not where he is going or what he is going to do but each of us, in our own way, will know what he has done for us and for Beaumont Abbey in his thirty-seven years here. We shall remember the master who set himself the same high standards he set his pupils. He once even chided me with his favourite dictum: *Your best today will be good enough today, High Master, but you will be expected to do better tomorrow.* We shall remember the major who, with shoulders back and head up, led the Beaumont Combined Cadet Corps with immense pride. We shall remember the gentleman who was an example to us all. But above all, we shall remember Walter not only as our colleague but also as our friend.'

Dr Fiddle announced, 'Hymn number two one eight.' Peter Morrison played two bars of introduction and the congregation began to sing Reginald Heber's words to the music of John B Dykes:

Holy, holy, holy! Lord God Almighty!
Early in the morning our song shall rise to Thee;
Holy, holy, holy, merciful and mighty!
God in three Persons, blessed Trinity!

At the end of the hymn, Dr Fiddle led the congregation in the Lord's Prayer. After a period of quiet contemplation, the High Master nodded and Peter Morrison began to play the Chaconne in F Minor by Johann Pachelbel. SMI Stanley Batters and PSI Edward Morton stood to attention while the six senior officers raised the coffin onto their shoulders. Slowly and solemnly Dr Fiddle, Dr Pugh-Jones and his wife Louise, Gregory Watson and his wife Kathy, Reginald de Vere and Mary Cranborne followed the eight men and the coffin back down the aisle, under the organ loft and out through the open doorway into the fresh air where the sun was playing hide and seek behind clouds drifting in the light westerly breeze.

The cortège made its way around the chapel and beyond the east wall to a small cemetery consecrated in 1587 when Beaumont Abbey was founded. As the coffin was lowered into the ground, the sun ceased its game and shone down upon the mourners who, with heads bowed, listened to Dr Fiddle say in a clear voice: *We now commit his body to the ground… earth to earth… ashes to ashes… dust to dust… in the sure and certain hope… of the resurrection to eternal life… Amen.*

* * * * *

Lunchtime at any school separates the morning and afternoon activities, nourishing the body with food and the mind with rest. Today at Beaumont Abbey school, the lunch hour provided the much needed break between the calmness and melancholy of the morning and the animation and exuberance of the afternoon on this the last day of the Trinity term.

'I think you will find, Miss Wellborn, you will have far more difficulty with the law with regard to building on Beaumont land than we had burying Walter in it,' said Quentin.

'I don't doubt that for one moment, Mr Waite,' said Susan.

'Why do you say that, Mr Waite,' asked Abigail.

'Suppose you want to bury a relative… deceased of course… in your back garden,' said Quentin sitting in his favourite armchair in the Common Room. 'There is no law to prevent you doing so provided you fill in an authorisation form stating that the grave will be more than ten yards from standing water, fifty yards from a source of drinking water and deep enough not to be dug up by hungry wild animals.'

'That's it?' said Susan.

'Not quite,' said Quentin. 'You would have to record officially the exact whereabouts of the grave…

And of course you should bear in mind the possible adverse effect this knowledge may have on potential buyers if you later want to sell your property.'

'How does this relate to the law and building on land?' asked Susan.

'Ah,' said Quentin, 'now that's where it gets interesting. We didn't need building permits to dig the hole for Walter's coffin but we may have to wait quite a long time before the authorities allow us to erect a headstone!'

On the last afternoon of term, Beaumont was more than at any other time like a colony of ants with all the pupils and most of the staff rushing hither and thither performing the many and various tasks before leaving the ant hill.

Billington and Osgood were clearing out their lockers, emptying their pigeon holes and settling their accounts with the Common Room Treasurer, Geoffrey Rusbridge.

Under the watchful eyes of Major MacKay, SMI Batters and PSI Morton, officers and cadets were checking, packing and preparing to depart to their summer camps.

Kathy Watson was packing the suitcases and getting their two children, Mark and Tracy, ready for the journey to Guernsey where Greg would work during the summer at the Beau Sejour Leisure Centre as an instructor.

David Swann was pinching out the tiny shoots from the axils of his one hundred tomato plants at Gower House while the Honourable Penelope FitzGibbon, his fianceé and only daughter of Viscount Percival FitzGibbon, and her mother were finalising the arrangements for the wedding.

Dolly Brown was preparing tea, coffee, cake and sandwiches for the end-of-year academic staff get-together while her husband Ted and Ron Beech, the chief caretaker, were helping to load the High Master's car for his trip to Wales.

Dr Phil Carratt, chairman of the Common Room, was putting the finishing touches to his speech of farewell to Billington and Osgood while Reg was trying to pluck up the courage to ask Mary Cranborne if she would like to see the cottage which he bought the year before Madeleine, his late wife, died.

* * * * *

Whatever tasks needed to be done were left undone. All the staff with the exception of the High Master assembled in the Common Room for tea and fond farewells.

'May I have your attention please,' said Dr Carratt tapping his empty cup with a spoon. Only when everyone was quiet and paying attention did he continue. 'Gentlemen... er... *Ladies* and gentlemen,' said Phil smiling sheepishly, 'may I have your attention. It's my duty... on your behalf... to say a few words of farewell first to...' He glanced around the room. 'to our language assistants... Matthieu and Adelbrecht.' The two young men stepped forward.

Phil turned first to the Frenchman. 'Monsieur Courtemanche... please accept this Wedgwood Sterling teacup and saucer as a souvenir of your time here.' When the applause had died down, Phil continued, 'please also accept my apologies, Mathew, on behalf my colleagues who persisted in mispronouncing your name.' When the laughter had died down, Phil turned to the German.

'Herr Frankfurter... please accept this Wedgwood Sterling teacup and saucer as a souvenir of your time here.' When the applause had died down, Phil continued, 'please also accept our apologies for being unable to prevent the boys giving you the nickname... the affectionate nickname I might add... of... *Hot Dog*. When the laughter died down, Phil scanned the room to confirm the presence of the other two leavers.

'I should now ask Mr Osgood to join me here at the front,' said Phil. The young biologist stepped forward

384

nervously. 'Mr Osgood joined us three years ago... to begin what will surely be an illustrious career... as soon as... I speak from the first-hand experience of marriage... as soon as he gives up his care-free existence as bachelor! To the furtherance of those ends, Terry, please accept this gift as a souvenir of your time here.' As Phil handed the young Osgood a book, he said, 'I wasn't quite sure why you chose *The Descent of Man* by Charles Darwin until I read the rest of the title *and Selection in Relation to Sex.*' When laughter had died down, Terence Osgood thanked his colleagues and related the following incident which had taught him to guard against loose questions.

'It was my first Lent term. We were doing the life cycle of the frog. I asked the class how we can tell the difference between a male and female frog. Several hands went up. I foolishly chose Augustus Thorne... aptly named as he had been a thorn in my side the whole year. "Please, sir,' he said donning his angelic look, 'a female frog's got sore and swollen thumbs under her armpits." I've yet to learn the art of asking questions.'

Alan Billington joined Beaumont straight from Cambridge Education Department to serve his first two years of teaching under Arnold Trott, Head of History for over twenty years. When Arnold retired, he was commissioned to write a history of Beaumont Abbey. Consequently, for the next two years of his time at Beaumont, Billington and Carroll Ffynch, Head of Art, were plagued by Arnold wanting their help. Eventually a limited hardback edition of Arnold Trott's book appeared in the local bookshop. It was to this book that Phil referred in his remarks to the departing history teacher.

'May I on behalf of my colleagues and myself wish you well in your new post, Alan, and ask you to accept this book as a souvenir of your four years with us.' Then turning to face his assembled colleagues, Phil said, 'Ladies and gentlemen... you may be pleased to know that the *History of Beaumont Abbey* by Arnold Trott is quite valuable on account of its rarity…' There were a few chuckles at his words. 'Indeed, it really is quite rare… This copy has *not* been signed by the author.'

Phil tapped the spoon against his cup to restore order and said, 'Before we disperse, may I take this opportunity officially to welcome two newcomers into our midst… Mrs Katherine Watson and Major Angus MacKay. Mrs Watson will be teaching geography and Major MacKay will teach PE and take charge of the Corps. On behalf of all of us, may I wish them well and trust they will enjoy their time with us. See you all next term.'

* * * * *

CHAPTER 29

"Now this is not the end. It is not even the beginning of the end. But it is, perhaps, the end of the beginning." Sir Winston Churchill (Speech in November 1942)

* * * * *

Dr Llywelyn Pugh-Jones and his wife Louise faced one another across the kitchen table. He did *not* turn on his radio and she did *not* open her Daily Telegraph. They talked. Actually they reminisced. Their motoring holiday to Wales and their visit to Llywelyn's home town in the Rhondda had been a success. They both felt refreshed and ready for the Michaelmas term. Llywelyn had acquired a light sun tan and felt the fittest he had been in the past twelve months. He was quite surprised to find himself looking forward to the year that would see the introduction of co-education. Louise was looking forward to the next meeting of the Beaumont Abbey Ladies Investment Club.

Reginald Thomas De Vere, MA (Cantab) had acquired a taste for the cereal of fruit, nuts and raw oats that Maximilian Bircher-Benner, a Swiss doctor, originally devised at the beginning of the twentieth century. Although he knew Mary Cranborne disapproved, Reg poured full cream milk over his müesli and finished breakfast with a fresh croissant and a café-au-lait. During the summer holiday, he and Mary had motored to the Dorset coast where, apart from a couple of walks to Lulworth Castle and Durdle Door, they had spent most of the week giving the two-bedroom cottage a much-needed spring-cleaning. Reggie, as his late wife had called him, was beginning to let go of the past and to look forward to knowing Mary better.

Susan Wellborn scrambled an egg on brown toast, poured herself a glass of unsweetened orange juice and finished with a cup of instant coffee. Unlike her predecessor, Anthony Parker-Smythe, she always jogged five kilometres before breakfast and left the table a little hungry. Having a great deal to accomplish, neither Susan nor her assistant bursar, Abigail Rusbridge, had taken a holiday. With the help of the lawyer, Henry Trevanion, and the bank manager, Earnest Hardcastle, they had acquired most of the building permits, had hired the principal contractors and had seen the ground broken for the foundations of both the sports hall and the boarding house. Abigail was looking forward to the next meeting of the BALI club; and she hoped to surprise her husband, Geoffrey. Susan was hoping to get to know better a certain new member of staff.

Major Angus MacKay put milk on his porridge while his wife, Fiona, poured him a cup of black coffee and performed what her husband called her battle dress inspection. No *special assignment* clothes this morning; no Harris Tweed, no Cavalry twill trousers, no polished brown shoes and no cream shirt. She approved his dark grey two-piece suit, black shoes and pale blue shirt. He might have been dressed for an *undercover operation* were it not for his Black Watch regimental tie. Angus had enjoyed the CCF Army camp and had come to like Lieutenant 'Mad' Arthur Matthews who shared his love of the hills and glens. In his own way Angus was quite looking forward to his time at Beaumont but he did not welcome having to keep a close eye on certain members of staff.

Randolph and Elspeth stayed behind in Hong Kong as guests of Joseph and Annie while Rupert and Daphne Jardine flew back to England on the same aeroplane as Stephen and Phoebe Zháng. The two seventeen year-old boys were not yet friends but they had put aside their differences and lost whatever chips they may have had on their shoulders. During the summer, Rupert had gained his pilot's licence and Stephen had reached Third Dan in judo. The two girls had become good friends and were looking forward to starting school at Beaumont. Daphne would be lodging with Mary Cranborne and Phoebe would be lodging with Susan Wellborn.

* * * * *

It was Saturday morning. The Michaelmas term was about to begin with the staff meeting in the Long Room. Ronald Beech, the head caretaker, was there when Reg arrived.

'Good morning Mr de Vere.'

'Good morning Ron,' said Reg. 'How was your holiday? Weymouth this year wasn't it?'

'That's right,' said Ron. 'We were lucky with the weather. Only rained the once.'

'I see Dolly and Tom have been busy,' said Reg.

'What with her feather duster and his Fluomatic floor polisher… they're a right pair.'

When Reg put his great-grandfather's walnut gavel and block on the green baize cloth covering the table and checked that there were two glasses and a jug of iced water on the silver tray, he recalled Speech Weekend Prize Giving and wondered still who had laced the orange juice with gin. Reg as usual had been the first to arrive. He glanced at his watch then strolled outside to await the arrival of the staff.

'Good morning, Second Master,' said Greg. 'Are we the first?'

'Yes, Greg, as usual… you're first,' said Reg. 'Good morning, Mrs Watson…'

'Kathy, Second Master. Please call me Kathy.'

'Come on,' said Greg, gently taking his wife by the arm. 'Let's go in and find our seats.'

'Ah, good morning, Major,' said Reg. 'Ready for the fray?'

'Aye,' said Angus. 'As much as I can be.'

'Please go on in. Feel free to sit anywhere except on the four high-backed chairs at the head of the long tables,' said Reg. 'That's where the Housemasters sit.'

'I ken,' said Angus. 'Must nae get off on the wrong foot.'

Inside the Long Room, Kathy sat by the high-backed chair nearest to the door. Greg sat between Kathy and Angus who cast a discrete eye over the other staff as they arrived. He nodded and smiled to Arthur Matthews who came and sat beside him. Angus recognised and could name all those he had met in the last week of the Trinity term.

One of the four new members of staff caught his attention. Angus had encountered him when his hair was black and he was clean-shaven; now this man was thin on top and he had a grey beard. He had grown older and more distinguished in appearance over the past twenty years but there was no mistake; Angus knew him.

Outside the Long Room, Reg glanced at his watch. It was almost ten o'clock. Colin Harper, last as usual, stammered his apologies. It seemed the High Master was going to be late for once but then he appeared on the path leading from the walled garden.

'Good morning, Reg. Yes... for early September... definitely a *good* morning.'

'All present, ready and waiting, High Master.'

'Excellent! Lead the way. Reg,' said Llywelyn.

When the Second Master appeared in the doorway, everyone stood up; that included Kathy, Angus and the Head of Economics, Geoffrey Rusbridge, who no longer had his Financial Times to hide behind and lose himself in. When the Second Master had taken his seat alongside the High Master, the staff sat down. Reg struck the walnut block three times with his walnut gavel and made the ice tinkle against the sides of the glasses of water. It was exactly ten o'clock. The High Master cleared his throat.

'Good morning to you all. Welcome back to Beaumont Abbey. I trust you enjoyed your summer holiday and are ready for Michaelmas term.'

'First I should like to welcome our new members of staff: Mrs Watson to teach geography, Major MacKay to teach physical education and take charge of the Combined Cadet Corps, Mr Francis Harpenden to teach History, Dr Eamonn O'Dwyer to teach Biology and...' Llywelyn paused, glanced at the note Reg had slipped in front of him then continued, 'and Monsieur André

Rousseau and Herr Axel Hartmann who will be our language assistants for this year.'

'As some of you may have already noticed, work has begun on the new combined concert and sports hall and on the new boarding house for girls. With the approval of the governing board of directors, I have asked Dr Philip Carratt to serve as Housemaster of Baker and Mr Gregory Watson to serve as head of physical education and games.'

'The results of the summer examinations were excellent thanks in very large part to your skill in persuading your pupils to give of their best. I have every confidence Beaumont will... in your capable hands... continue to build its reputation for academic excellence.

I share... with your pupils... a trust that the future of Beaumont Abbey is in very safe hands... your hands. Thank you.'

All the staff, including Geoffrey Rusbridge, stood up and stayed standing until the High Master had left the room and the Second Master sat down again. Reg struck the block with his gavel and David Peters, housemaster of Armstrong stood up to report that flights from Hong Kong and Singapore were on time. Younger members of staff at the back of the Long Room chuckled when James Jackson whispered audibly *that's a first for Chin, Chin, Kung, Fu and Woo*. Ralph Abrahams of Burdett, Alan Radford of Gower and E. Gordon Hamilton of Wedgewood all reported no late arrivals and no injuries. Reg was reaching for his gavel when Dr Phil Carratt stood up.

'Yes, Dr Carratt?' Reg said, raising an eyebrow and the pitch of his voice on the last syllable of Phil's surname.

'Baker House, Second Master,' said Phil.

'Of course,' said Reg. 'My apologies, Dr Carratt.'

'Twelve girls join us this term. Ten live relatively locally and will enter the Lower Sixth. Two will enter Upper Fifth and will board... one with the High Master's secretary and one with the Bursar. All twelve will arrive uninjured and on time,' said Phil.

'Thank you, Dr Carratt.' Reg struck the block with his great-grandfather's gavel to close the meeting.

* * * * *

'They're coming out of the Long Room,' said Tom to his wife Dolly busy in the small kitchen across the corridor from the Common Room. 'Want a hand?'

'Yes. You can push this tea trolley into the staff room.'

'Right,' said Tom. 'Anything else?'

'Yes. You can get that floor polisher of yours out of the corridor,' said Dolly.

Reg was always the last to leave the Long Room. When he stepped outside and closed the door, Dr Carratt was waiting to have a word.

'Hello, Phil,' said Reg. 'Something on your mind?'

'Baker House.'

'What about it?' said Reg.

'Did you recommend me as Housemaster?'

'Not exactly,' said Reg.

'What's that supposed to mean?'

'When the High Master sought my advice, I didn't recommend you as the Housemaster,' said Reg with a chuckle. 'I recommended your wife Maureen as the mistress and...'

'That's why he made me the Housemaster,' said Phil. 'Wise choice.'

'Was that it?'

'No,' said Phil. 'One other thing. What are my twelve girls going to do for a day room?'

'Good question,' said Reg. 'I've no idea. You'd better ask Susan Wellborn. She seems to be full of ideas these days.'

The two men took the side entrance into the main building and ambled down the corridor following the aroma of freshly brewed coffee. As they approached the Common Room, the voices of the staff, interspersed with cheering and clapping, grew louder. Just as they reached the door, a loud cheer went up. When Reg opened the door, the room fell silent.

The silence had nothing to do with the Second Master's arrival that had gone unnoticed. All eyes were on the walls. A lone voice broke the silence with *come on Arthur, he's catching up*. Arthur Matthews was edging on the dado rail with the toes of his shoes and hanging from the picture rail by his fingertips. Close behind him was Angus MacKay.

'What were you about to say?' said Phil.

'Plus ça change, plus c'est la même chose,' said Reg.

'Ah. The more it changes, the more it's the same thing,' said Phil.

'Not bad for a Chemist,' said Reg. 'But I wonder if this year *will* be more of the same.'

* * * * *

www.ingramcontent.com/pod-product-compliance
Lightning Source LLC
Chambersburg PA
CBHW070356260626
47161CB00001B/166